THE THINGS
THAT STAY
TRUE

THE THINGS THAT STAY TRUE

A VIC LENOSKI MYSTERY

PETER W.J. HAYES

LEVEL
BEST BOOKS

First published by Level Best Books 2023

This novel is entirely a work of fiction. The names, characters and incidents portrayed in it are the work of the author's imagination. Any resemblance to actual persons, living or dead, events or localities is entirely coincidental.

Peter W. J. Hayes asserts the moral right to be identified as the author of this work.

First edition

ISBN: 978-1-68512-381-9

Cover art by Level Best Designs

This book was professionally typeset on Reedsy.
Find out more at reedsy.com

To my granddaughters, Brette and Mari. Perhaps one day, many years from now, you will read this dedication—and knowing that one of your grandfathers wrote these words—realize something else: that all of the adults around you, including your thoroughly ancient parents, once (and still do) harbored dreams, passions and aspirations, made mistakes, took chances, travelled long distances from the worlds they knew, and from all of it, created long and full lives. I encourage you to ask them about it. Because many of the best stories are not written down, they are meant to be told. They are just waiting to be told. And those are the stories you will always remember.

Nobody owes anybody a living, but everybody is entitled to a chance.
—Jack "The Manassas Mauler" Dempsey,
World Heavyweight Champion, 1919-1926

I have to believe that when things are bad I can change them.
—James J. "Cinderella Man" Braddock,
World Heavyweight Champion, 1935-1937

Praise for The Things That Stay True

"*In The Things That Stay True*, Hayes—and his Vic Lenoski series—hits full stride, weaving several complex and seemingly unrelated plots into a masterful tapestry, with each storyline merging and driving towards a surprisingly and immensely satisfying conclusion. A superbly crafted police procedural with a lot of heart."—Kerry Cox, award-winning author of the Nic Tanner Eco-Thriller Series

"Another solid installment in Hayes' saga, anchored by a tenacious and savvy shamus."—*Kirkus Reviews*

"Uniquely conceived and deftly executed, devoted followers and new readers alike will become instantly engrossed and subsequently addicted to all things Vic Lenoski. Very highly recommended."—Readers' Favorite Reviews

"With writing as lyrical as the symphony orchestra that centers the book, Peter W.J. Hayes' intriguing story is international in scope, yet deeply personal. From the mysterious Chinese stranger to the unnerving investigation into a past Allegheny County Detective Vic Lenoski can't afford to reveal, this suspenseful tale will tug at your heart as you keep turning pages."—Annette Dashofy, *USA Today* Bestselling Author of the Zoe Chambers Mystery Series

Chapter One

Chen Yun wasn't sure if it was the relentless Singapore sun and the dank air of Marina Bay that saddened him, or what he'd just learned about himself. He shifted his feet under the restaurant table and stared at the three connected towers of the Marina Bay Hotel. To their left, the fingers of the ArtScience Museum reached upward, like the hands of a supplicant. He knew the building was designed as the petals of an open flower, but his own interpretation better fit his mood.

The wind rose briefly from the bay, hot and sticky. He'd picked an outdoor table, hoping the connection to the outdoors might raise his spirits. For a moment, the broad sky did remind him of Wuhan summers, of being a boy, until he remembered how little sun reached Wuhan now. Sacrifices had to be made for the future, the Chinese Communist Party claimed. Apparently, gagging smog was the cost of progress.

He pushed his criticism aside, automatically gauging its level of subversiveness. To disagree with or satirize the Party was revisionist thinking, and the Party had a preternatural way of reading everyone's thoughts. In the same breath, he heard his grandmother's words, whispered close to his ear.

"Party principles versus revisionist thinking. The Party calls it struggle. It is not. It is a method of control. A way to reach inside your mind, to make you distrust your own thoughts. The Party knows if you argue with yourself long enough, you will choose their path. Because it is the least tiring. The safest. And when you do, my grandson, you are lost."

Chen couldn't breathe.

"You are deep in thought, Detective Yun."

Chen forced stale air into his lungs. Detective-Commander Feng Wang stood directly in front of him, blocking Chen's view of the hotel, the museum, and the sun. Feng's shadow was clammy on his skin.

"Simply tired," Chen replied. "It was a long morning."

Feng pulled out a chair and took a few moments to settle himself. Feng was from Beijing and—true to type—more than six feet tall, lanky, and convinced he was the royalty of China.

Commander Wang gave Chen a humorless smile. "Yet you delivered your man to the Changi airport. Right now, he is on a flight to Shanghai. Once again, you have done well."

Had he done well? Chen didn't think so. For almost two months, he'd watched the seventy-four-year-old Bingwen Zhu walk his Pekinese to a park each morning. He'd documented Bingwen's afternoons behind the garden wall of his house, puttering with his flowers, reading, or napping in the shade. After Bingwen's forty years in the Shanghai municipal government—including ten as deputy mayor—it seemed the perfect retirement.

Yet, charges brought by the Party six months earlier named Bingwen as corrupt and a master criminal. A stunning reversal. Throughout his dynamic career, Bingwen was never once suspected of corruption.

Today, just after daybreak, Chen had knocked on Bingwen's front door. Seated in that shaded back yard and sipping green tea, Chen had told Bingwen he must return to Shanghai and submit to the charges. If he didn't, his only son would face them.

In that moment, Chen saw something break in the man's eyes. When Chen drove him to the airport an hour later, Bingwen was exhausted and shriveled, a damp-eyed old man who needed frequent visits to the restroom.

Sitting at this table, waiting for Commander Wang, Chen had worked out the truth. Bingwen's son was a rising star in Shanghai politics, renowned as a corruption fighter. It was the type of career that attracted enemies. And now, with Bingwen found guilty of corruption—as he certainly would be—his son's career would tailspin.

Bingwen was never the prey. The son was.

And he, Chen, had sprung the trap.

"Always so modest." Commander Wang made a clucking sound and smoothed his slicked-back hair. "You should enjoy your victories from time to time." Wang smiled again, reminding Chen of a rat.

"This is my job," Chen said carefully, trying not to let his mood cloud his words. "I should not celebrate for simply doing my job." He couldn't look Feng in the eye. If he did, he was scared at what Feng might see. The disgust Chen felt toward himself. The new, insolent anger that slithered inside him.

"Well, our section leader believes you should be recognized. He talked to the Global Times. There will be an article about you tomorrow."

Now Chen did meet his eyes. "It is not necessary."

"But it is. This is the sixth time you have returned a criminal to China to face charges. You are the most successful member of our Fox Hunt team. And Bingwen is remembered throughout China, making this your greatest act of loyalty so far."

A proverb slid through Chen's mind. *Xiao li cang dao.* A smile can conceal a dagger. If there was ever a proverb to describe Chinese Communist Party rule, that was it.

Chen understood the section leader's goal. The article might celebrate Chen, but by extension, would demonstrate the section leader's commitment to a program launched directly by the party chairman. And later, if abuses caused the program to be reined back, the article would prove Chen's overzealousness. He would become the sacrificial lamb. In this way, the section leader garnered praise now while protecting himself in the long run.

Yi shi er niao. One stone, two birds. Another proverb.

Chen knew not to argue. The calls to the journalists were finished. The article written. There was nothing he could do. He decided to raise a more important point.

"I am looking forward to returning to Wuhan," Chen said carefully. "To seeing my wife and son. As we discussed before I came here."

Wang was saved from answering by the arrival of the waitress. Wang took his time ordering, openly flirting with her despite a twenty-five-year age difference. He made a show of deciding what to order and finally settled on Kopi C Kosong, coffee with evaporated milk and no sugar. Chen hadn't known Wang was aware of the national coffee drink of Singapore, and was almost impressed by Wang's knowledge of its variations. Chen corrected himself. Wang was someone who slid easily from restaurant to restaurant, always certain of his choices and sure the business existed solely to please him. Of course he would know how to order.

Wang waited until the waitress departed and settled his gaze on Chen. "I know we discussed your return," he said in a diffident tone, very much the commander talking to his underling. "But there is someone else we need to reclaim."

"Aren't there others who could go?" Chen wanted to add that he hadn't been home in almost two years, but he didn't want to sound like he was begging. His question was already dangerously close to insubordinate.

"Ah, Chen, we need your particular strengths for this. I'm afraid you are the only one. And you always produce such good results."

Chen knew immediately he was being sent to an English-speaking country. There were others in his division who spoke English, but none with his fluency. Something else descended from his grandmother.

"And perhaps, afterwards, a return to my family?" Chen tried to keep the desperation out of his voice.

"I think that is a tremendous idea." Wang replied with a bureaucrat's evasion, committing himself to nothing. Wang glanced at his watch, which Chen noted was larger and more ostentatious than his new one the year before. "Your flight is this evening at seven. Tanming is loading the details on your laptop as we speak."

"Where am I going?"

Wang smiled at the waitress as she placed his Kopi on the table. She didn't smile back. Chen sensed her tightness, as if she was ready to swat away a wandering hand. If that was true, her instincts were good.

She pivoted away. Wang watched her go, his eyes dreamily considering her backside. He turned to Chen. "Your ticket is to the beating heart of corrupt capitalism. America. To a city of failed industry and dirt. It is called Pittsburgh."

Chapter Two

Vic Lenoski stood on the running path next to the Allegheny River, so close he could almost touch it. The cool, flat smell of the water centered him. Nearby, crime scene technicians tugged on Tyvek bunny suits. They called jokes to one another, none of which Vic would repeat to his wife. Forty feet down the trail, yellow crime scene tape strung between leafy green shrubs and low trees shimmered in a light wind.

Vic couldn't inspect the scene until the forensics team completed their preliminary walk-through. Irritated at the wait, he turned and stared downstream toward Pittsburgh's Point, where the Allegheny and Monongahela rivers met.

The late-afternoon sky was broad and blue. Sunlight glanced off the water, flickering among the stunted tree branches and shrubs between the river and trail. Downriver, the bridges spanning the Allegheny were painted yellow, although the city's political hotshots called the color gold. To his left was the city of Pittsburgh, to the right the looming red brick buildings of the original H. J. Heinz factory and offices.

His mind wandered.

When he was a child, the people who worked in those red brick buildings produced, bottled, and marketed ketchup, baby foods, mustards, pickles, and an endless variety of sauces, as they had done for more than one hundred and fifty years. It was all finished now, the company bought and merged, the headquarters moved to a glass skyscraper downtown. The manufacturing relocated to Ohio, Michigan, Iow, Massachusetts, and perhaps ten other places in America alone. Today, the refurbished factory buildings housed high-end apartments and offices for high-tech companies.

He and his wife, Anne, had attended an open house for the apartments when they first opened. They had stared at the narrow and angular rooms, stunned at the prices and chilled by the ghosts of the company's past.

He kicked at the asphalt at his feet, the sun hot on his head. This trail, he knew, was once a railway bed for the trains delivering tomatoes and vegetables to the factories and warehouses. How many generations of families, he wondered, worked in those buildings, along these train tracks? And beyond that, how many millions of people across the country—around the world—ate the baby food made here, globbed Pittsburgh-made ketchup onto their hamburgers, crunched on pickles soaked in vinegar and brine made from the water of the Allegheny River?

He took a slow breath. Gone. All of it. The founding family a historical curiosity, the line broken, the company dispersed.

"I do not miss dressing like that every day," Craig Luntz said, walking up to him and nodding toward the forensics team.

Vic glanced at Craig. Several months earlier, he'd convinced Craig to leave the forensics squad and join his Allegheny County detective team, with a promise to help him prepare for the detective's exam. Vic was sure Craig would scoot through the first time he sat the test. Sharp and detailed-oriented, Craig looked at crime scenes differently than Vic and their other team member, Liz Timmons. Craig's years in forensics and the Bureau of Police Tech department saw to that. Plus, Craig's father had trained Vic during his first years as a patrol cop. There was something to be said for keeping things in the family, for things that stayed true over time.

"They do set the tempo at the scene," Vic said.

Craig pushed square glasses up his nose. "Couple of them know that, and take their time." He flashed Vic a grin. "Must have been easier when the detectives just walked in and ran the scene, then called the CSIs."

"Easier, but not as effective." Vic liked seeing Craig's grin. Craig tended to be formal around him, to equate Vic to his father's generation. He hoped time would break down that wall.

Vic glanced in the direction of the crime scene, and his irritation returned.

He couldn't just wait. He motioned to Craig and led him onto River Avenue, the road parallel to much of the running trail. "Where is the reporting person who called this in? Female RP found the body, right? Maybe we can take a statement."

As he talked, Vic spotted the white hair of Sergeant Wroblewski farther up River Avenue. Wroblewski, a Bureau of Police sergeant about as old as the Heinz factory buildings, usually managed crime scenes. Vic knew him well. He started for him, and Craig fell in behind.

"Sergeant Wroblewski," Vic called as they approached. "Since you're still alive, I need to talk to whoever found the body."

Wroblewski looked him up and down from the end of his nose. His gaze settled on the county police badge hanging from Vic's neck. "I heard you're at County now. There goes the close rate."

"Nah. I got Timmons on the team."

"And Luntz." Wroblewski gave Craig a warm look. "How's your Dad doing?"

"Fishing, mostly."

Wroblewski grinned. "Good, that means plenty left for me. Now what are you whining about, Lenoski?"

"RP who found the body. I want to interview her."

"Well yeah. And my job is making you happy, is it?"

"Just looking for a little help." Vic didn't mind the banter. Wroblewski had forgotten more about policing than half the force could claim in experience, and he was a leader of the police union. Among rank-and-file officers, he was respected more than most of the commanders and chiefs.

Wroblewski let Vic's statement sit for a second or two, then pointed to an ambulance farther down the road. "Paramedics are giving her a once over. I thought she was handling it well, under the circumstances."

"What's her name?"

Wroblewski leveled watery-blue eyes on him. "What am I, your address book? I had some boys take her to the meat wagon. Told them to make sure she stays there until the big heads arrive." He pointed a gnarled finger at Vic. "And here you are. She was out running. Got those leggings and some kind of fancy jacket. Ponytail. Leggings are black, jacket is yellow." He waved an arm at the bridges downriver. "She's trying to fit in. Anything else?"

"That'll do well. Thanks." Vic gestured for Craig to follow and started down River Avenue to the ambulance. He wondered when Wroblewski decided to call detectives 'big heads.' The phrase cut a couple of ways, one good, suggesting they were thinkers, and one bad, that they had big egos. Just like Wroblewski, Vic reflected.

And honestly, it wasn't inaccurate.

He and Craig circled behind the ambulance to find the doors open and a young woman in her twenties sitting on the ambulance floor, her sneaker-clad feet on the bumper and knees drawn under her chin. A water bottle sat beside her. He thought that Wroblewski's description was only partially right. The black leggings, yellow runner's jacket, and ponytail of light brown hair was correct. He hadn't mentioned that her face was as white as Styrofoam.

Vic nodded to the paramedic inside the ambulance and the city policeman standing nearby.

"Ma'am?" Vic asked. "I'm Detective Vic Lenoski of the Allegheny County Police, this is one of my team, Craig Luntz. You're the person who found the body and called it in?"

The young woman blinked. It took a second before her hazel eyes focused. She looked at Vic. "Yes, I, I was out running. I did. Call 911."

Vic took his time removing a small notebook and pen from the pocket of his sport coat so she could gather herself.

"Thanks for calling it in. It must have been scary, finding a body," Craig said gently.

She looked at Craig for the first time and smiled, just a little, as if she wasn't sure if that was the right thing to do under the circumstances. "It was," she answered.

Her voice sounded a little too bright to Vic, as if she was overcompensating. She moved her feet off the bumper and straightened her posture, then seemed to decide that her feet dangling over the back of the ambulance wasn't right either. She hooked her heels on the bumper again, but tried to stay more upright. Vic thought it looked uncomfortable. She swiped at her hair with one hand. Vic glanced at Craig just in time to see him push his glasses up his nose, his eyes bright.

It dawned on Vic what was actually going on.

"Actually," Vic said quickly, deciding to accept the inevitability of it all, "Craig, could you take a statement from, ah, excuse me, what is your name?"

"Kasey Wells," The woman responded, not even glancing at Vic.

"Ms. Wells," Vic said carefully. He turned to Craig. "Craig?"

"Got it," Craig answered, his gaze not wavering from Kasey's face.

Vic stood for a second, unsure if he was doing the right thing. He split the difference and moved to the side, but within earshot. Craig had done preliminary interviews before, but this was his first murder case.

"So tell me about it," Craig said to Kasey. "Just what happened. Your own words." Vic was about to tell Craig to get a notebook out when Craig held up his phone to Kasey with an app open and pointed at it. He cocked his head in a question.

"Oh, sure," she answered emphatically. "Go ahead."

Vic kept his mouth shut. Of course. Craig wouldn't use a notebook. Vic clicked his pen pointedly to make sure the nib was in position.

Craig shuffled a step closer to Kasey, and her smile broadened.

"So anyway," Kasey said, her head bobbing. "I was out for a run, you know; I usually run about this time, and I'd been down to the end of the trail and was on my way back."

"That's pretty far," Craig broke in.

"Oh yeah. I played lacrosse in high school and college. So I stay in really good shape." She paused for a moment, and Vic knew she wanted Craig to conjure up a vision of what her figure might look like, in very good shape. "And anyway, when I came around a bend, I saw this body lying on the path. So I just ran up to it."

"Wow," Craig said.

"I thought she might have tripped or something. Hurt her leg, maybe. And then," the bright quickness of her account cut out. She looked down. "She had this big bash, or smash on her head. It was caved in. I knew right away it was bad. So I got down next to her and asked if she was okay, which was stupid, I knew she wasn't, but I didn't know what else to say. And I kind of touched her shoulder, but she didn't move. And then I kind of realized she wasn't breathing."

Kasey huffed out a breath, still looking down. Craig didn't make a sound or move, and Vic liked that. He'd told Craig several times to let the interviewee talk at their own pace. Kasey wiped at her eyes with the back of her hand and looked at Craig. "Sorry."

"No, take your time. You're doing great. What did you do next?"

"I got my phone out and called 911. Told them she was lying on the trail."

"Good. And then you waited for the first responders?"

Vic jotted down a reminder in his notebook to tell Craig not to lead witnesses.

"Yeah. I, I felt bad. I kept worrying she might be cold, which, again, is super stupid. I know."

"I think it's kind," Craig said gently. "And tell me, did you see anyone around while you were doing that?"

Kasey shook her head. "No, it was just us. That was kind of creepy. And she's old, right? I mean, she looked like she was in her forties or fifties. So I don't even know why she'd be out here running."

This seemed to confuse Craig. He angled his head. "Why do you say that?"

"Oh, I mean, she was wearing running stuff, but like I said, she has to be fifty. Women that age don't run. Not like us." She snuck Craig a glance as if she wanted to confirm he saw her as a much younger woman. "I mean, women that old usually do yoga or Pilates, those kinds of things. Suburban Mom stuff. They don't run."

"Good point." Craig nodded emphatically.

"I mean, look at me. I'm out here four days a week. On weekdays I always run at this time. Four or five o'clock. Saturday and Sunday, it depends on the weather." She stared at Craig as if she wanted him to commit those times and days to memory.

"Got it. And just to go back, you said no one else was around when you found her, but did you see anyone else on the trail while you were running?"

"Oh, sure." She launched into a list of bicyclists and runners, with Craig nodding encouragement and sometimes asking for clarification about where or when she saw the person and what they were wearing. Vic started to frame their conversational back and forth, thinking about how to recount the interview to Liz. She would find the flirting hilarious. So would Anne.

Kasey finished talking, and Craig asked her for her address and telephone number. Vic copied them down in his notebook and was about to walk over and thank Kasey for her help when someone called his name.

Vic turned to see Forrest King, the leader of the forensics team, standing by the ambulance. His bunny suit was half unzipped, and the hood pulled back. Vic stepped over to him.

"Lenoski," Forrest repeated. "We're just finishing the preliminary. You ready to take a look?"

"Sounds good." Vic saw the subdued look on Forrest's face. "Find something?"

"Yeah. We ID'd the victim. She had her driver's license on her." The frown on his forehead deepened. "It's Melanie Beck." He almost whispered the name as if he was worried about profaning it.

Vic stared at him. The name meant nothing to him.

Forrest read Vic's lack of reaction. "You know, the Pittsburgh Symphony? I mean, she *is* the Symphony."

Chapter Three

Vic knew three things for certain, now that he almost exclusively worked murder cases. Every single one was different, and each a double-edged blade. It was just as easy to slice off a finger as grasp how the facts of a case strung together. But most of all, they got under his skin.

He followed Forrest to the taped-off area and the body, Craig silent behind him.

"Melanie Beck," Forrest said over his shoulder, twisting his head back and forth to talk and stay on the pathway. "Big time Symphony-goer, always a big donor. Maybe four or five years ago, she made a huge cash donation. They put her on the board. She's kept the Symphony afloat. Huge wheel in the place."

Vic wondered how Forrest knew all this. He seemed the least likely person to be a classical music fan, but he knew that thought was simplistic. It didn't matter the collection of people, there was always a percentage who liked it. He glanced at Craig, who usually listened to music on his phone or computer at work. "Craig, do you like classical music?"

Craig looked preoccupied, and it took him a second to react. Vic wondered if Kasey Wells had anything to do with that.

"It's okay," he said finally. "When I was in elementary school, we had class trips to the symphony. I'd rather listen to something else now. I guess symphonies are too long. It's not like a four-minute song. And I like lyrics. Classical has no lyrics."

Vic thought Craig was working out his opinion as he spoke. He also thought it was significant that Craig found it easier to articulate what he disliked, not what he liked.

Immediately ahead, the crime-scene tape circumscribed a large square abutting a large bush on the left. Inside the tape, a woman's body lay to the right, partially off the trail. Near the victim, two crime scene technicians on hands and knees worked their fingers through the long grass.

Vic stared at the body. Melanie Beck was on her back, the top of her head pointed downriver, her face turned left toward the Heinz buildings. Her right arm was thrown out to her side. Vic ducked under the tape and approached, spotting a long and perhaps two-inch wide depression on her right temple. He didn't need a medical examiner to tell him the skull was crushed. It looked as if Melanie was walking along the trail when she was struck from the front and fell backwards.

"Wait," Craig called.

Vic stopped and turned to him. Craig pointed near the victim's feet. "See that skid mark in the grass? Don't mess it up. I bet she did that as she fell."

Vic followed the direction of Craig's outstretched finger and spotted the scarred grass. He retreated a step and took in the scene.

He imagined Melanie just before the attack, moving down the trail. Kasey said she was surprised Melanie was running, but Vic knew Kasey likely assumed Melanie was running because she was jogging herself. Witnesses often projected their own activities and mannerisms onto victims. It was one of the first witness biases he'd learned about.

He tried to visualize the attack. Melanie, walking or running, the strike to the right temple, the body sprawling back onto the ground. He looked again at the large rhododendron bush edging the trail.

"Forrest," he called.

Forrest was standing near the two kneeling techs. He pivoted slowly and stared at Vic. His bunny suit was zipped up, his hood back in place. He turned the palms of his gloved hands to Vic in the universal sign of 'what?'

Vic pointed at the bush. "Include that bush in the crime scene. Wrap the tape behind it and search the back of the bush."

Forrest studied the bush, looked at the position of the body, and rechecked the bush. He nodded. "Sorry, should have seen that."

"Seen what?" Craig asked.

Vic turned to him. "Visualize the attack. It looks like Melanie Beck was walking or running in that direction." He pointed east down the trail. "We know the skull depression is the right front temple area. In one scenario, someone hit her from the front with a weapon. If you're the killer, you want surprise. That shrub is large enough to hide behind and reaches the edge of the trail. Makes it perfect."

"But how do we know that's how it happened? Maybe she was walking with someone. They had an argument, he or she hits her."

Vic pointed at the bush. "That's why we include the bush in the crime scene. If there's evidence behind it, then the hide-and-hit scenario works. If there's none, then the possibility is better she was walking with someone. We'll call that the walk-and-hit scenario. Interviewing witnesses, we ask people if they saw her alone or with someone."

Craig nodded, his eyes locked on the bush. Vic could see him working out scenarios in his head.

"The hit was to the right side of her head?"

Vic double-checked the body. "Yep."

"So, if she's walking east and someone hiding steps out and hits her on the right side of the head, then we know something else."

"What's that?" Vic thought he knew where Craig was going.

"Well, if I'm going to hit someone, I want to nail them right on the head, full swing. Have them walk right into it, right?"

"Sure."

"Think baseball."

"Okay," Vic tried to imagine a batter at home plate, waiting for a pitch.

"So, if they step out from the left and hit the victim full swing on the right side of the head as the person approaches, a left-handed swing would be best, wouldn't it?"

As Craig's theory sank in, Vic heard a chuckle from Forrest.

"Kids got a point, Vic," Forrest called to him.

Vic studied Craig. "Agree. If they're right-handed, to connect on the right side of her head, they'd have to counter-swing from their left to hit her. It's an unnatural swing, and you don't get much power. Plus, the wind-up takes time. It's more likely a righty would wait for the person to pass, step out, and hit them from behind."

"Then the wound would be on the back of the head," agreed Forrest.

Vic found himself smiling. Yeah, he thought. I don't think Craig is going to have much trouble with the detective's exam.

Chapter Four

When Chen Yun pushed through the doors to flight departures at Singapore's Chiangi airport, Tanming, the junior detective on his team, was waiting for him. Chen Yun stood up his roller bag and held out his knapsack to him. Tanming took it and handed him an identical one.

"Everything you need is inside," Tanming said breathlessly. "The files for your assignment are on the laptop."

Tanming is still floating on the excitement of his first trip outside China, Chen thought. He decided to have some fun and gestured at the knapsack he'd given to Tanming. "My laundry."

Tanming glanced at the bag, shocked. Chen wondered if Tanming had any sense of humor at all. He hadn't seen one so far. He gave a chummy laugh. "I understand you return to China tomorrow. Just deliver it to my wife. There are some delicacies from Singapore for her and a dress. And a toy for my son. Nothing more. There is no laundry."

Tanming was visibly relieved. "I will give it to her the day I return."

"The next day is fine. You will be tired."

They hesitated, neither speaking. Chen knew he needed to find a way to trust Tanming, but so far, the young man hadn't given him a reason. From birth, Chen's grandmother warned him never to trust anyone completely, but he'd found that if he trusted the moments when people showed they were human, a rapport was possible. Perhaps it was a crime a colleague solved and liked to mention from time to time—a sure sign of pride. Or the occasional hangover or grousing exasperation with a spouse. Sometimes it was a shared glance when the team was given an order that was, without doubt, designed only to shed positive light on a commander. Those moments of human emotion allowed Chen to feel comfortable with someone. But Tanming had yet to display anything like that—beyond a vague excitement at being outside China for the first time.

Tanming's military service and four years in the Ministry of State Security made Chen doubly wary. Chen knew how seven or eight years in those organizations, with their incessant political training, cauterized people's emotions. Transformed them into unswerving Party loyalists.

"Singapore was a great victory, Detective Yun," Tanming said.

"Yes," Chen Yun replied. He thought, but didn't say, 'But for who?' Instead, he hefted the new knapsack and tilted his roller bag, ready to leave. He considered Tanming. "If you return to Wuhan tomorrow, what is your plan for tonight?"

Tanming straightened, almost to attention. "To complete the report of our work here. I will email it to you." He smiled, but it looked forced.

Chen Yun studied him for a moment, searching for a hint of sarcasm, for some indication Tanming might really want to slip out of the hotel after dark. Tanming was barely a year past thirty and unmarried. Surely he would see this as an opportunity to steal along the Marina Bay boardwalk, to flirt with the young women seated with their drinks at the outside tables under the hanging lights. Perhaps visit one of the nightclubs the American and European women preferred to ogle their full figures, skimpy clothing, and uninhibited dancing.

He saw none of it in the young man's face. He was sure the first draft of the report would be waiting in his inbox when he landed in Los Angeles.

That fact disappointed him.

With a sinking feeling that Tanming could never be trusted, Chen said goodbye and turned for the departures desk.

Later, as his airplane leveled out for the long haul to Los Angeles, Chen folded down his tray table and waited as his laptop booted up. He watched the servers farther up the aisle deliver drinks from a cart. His laptop screen flickered and presented his desktop. Three files waited for him, all placed there by Tanming. The first was the Mission Order, which he knew would contain a summary of the case against his new target and a bullet point list of what he was expected to do. The second was background research to help him find ways to approach his target and convince the person to return to China. The third was a summary written by Tanming, a simple outline of an approach that Chen could take. Chen wasn't about to admit it, but in Singapore, he'd found Tanming's suggestions helpful. He decided to read that document last.

The server reached him, and he ordered a double scotch on the rocks. He wanted to sleep during the overnight trip, and the liquor would help. He ignored the files on his desktop and opened his email account.

Slowly, as the whisky warmed his stomach, he composed an email to his wife, apologizing for not returning home after Singapore. He explained that he had another mission and with luck, would return afterwards. He asked after their son, and let her know that Tanming would stop by with the knapsack.

He sipped the whiskey again, enjoying the taste. His countrymen might have invented the compass, gunpowder, paper, and the printing press, to name a few things, but they'd never come up with anything approaching a good whiskey or scotch. He considered mentioning it in his email but caught himself. Of course, his emails were read, especially the ones from overseas. Admitting a preference for something Western would be seen as defeatism. That it was a type of alcohol was even worse. He would be making a stated preference for something Western that labeled him as weak and corrupt.

He sipped the last of the drink, letting the flavor sit on his tongue. He finished his email and parked it in his outbox, so it would automatically send the next time he connected to the internet.

He rubbed his eyes, glanced around to be sure no other passengers could see his laptop screen, and opened the background file. Tanming had outdone himself. Chen counted at least thirty scanned or downloaded documents. He skimmed the titles, a collection of newspaper articles, court documents, and glossy brochures for a steel company. He recognized the company name.

His father once worked for the same Wuhan steel mill following his forceful removal from his mathematics classroom during the Cultural Revolution of the 1960s. He'd been put to work lugging iron ore from rail cars to the furnaces, his only tool a basket and sling.

The memory unsettled the whiskey in his stomach. He looked up and saw the servers near his seat row, handing out dinner trays. He rubbed his eyes, shut the lid to his laptop, and stuffed the computer into his knapsack. He would read the articles after dinner. A few seats ahead, the server tore foil from the top of a bowl and plonked the dish on a tray. Chen smelled the sour and slightly revolting tang of a cheese sauce.

The west might have whisky, he thought, but give me Chinese food every time.

Chapter Five

Vic's left leg was beginning to bother him. He and Craig had worked their way through the crime scene a step at a time and found nothing. They had even waited for Forrest to restring the crime scene tape to include the rhododendron bush and the area behind it. A dead end. Apart from their early theorizing about the perpetrator being left-handed, they had found nothing else. When his phone rang, and Vic saw it was Liz, he knew she would have something to say about their lack of progress.

He answered, and Liz immediately asked, "What do you have?"

"Not much. Nothing physical at the site. Looks like the victim was hit in the head with a bat or something. ME should be here any time."

"Huh. You guys having dinner? Is that it?"

"Pretty sure the crime scene is having us for dinner."

"The perp took the bat with them, then?"

Vic pivoted slowly, staring across the Allegheny toward downtown Pittsburgh. "If it was a bat, I bet they tossed it in the river."

"No witnesses? People run that trail all the time."

"Not so far. Somehow, we managed to hit a fifteen-minute window when no one was around."

"Huh. And how is our greenhorn doing?"

Vic smiled to himself. At least he had something to report about that. "He's doing fine. Although I do have something to tell you about that. We can do it later." He glanced at Craig, and knew from the tilt of Craig's head he'd guessed Vic and Liz were talking about him.

"If we don't have forensics we need witnesses," Liz said. "Anything I can do from here?"

"Yes. We ID'd the victim. Melanie Beck. I guess she's a big deal with the Symphony. Can you start looking into her? If she's on the board and a big supporter, there will be newspaper articles on her. Anything you can find. Where she lives would be a good starting place. Might explain why we found her here."

Liz was silent, and Vic knew Liz was taking notes. Along the path came a heavyset man in a white bunny suit, lugging what looked like a tackle box designed to transport fishing lures large enough for whales. He kept stopping to rub at his glasses, which were fogged from the medical mask he wore over his mouth and nose.

"Got it," Liz said

"And our ME is here." Vic watched as the man set the box next to the body, and with some difficulty, kneeled down.

"Who we got?"

"Doc Martin."

"Dammit. He always makes me think of boots. But he's good. Let me know what he says."

"You got it." Vic ended the call and slipped his phone into his jacket pocket. For a few moments, he watched Doc Martin examine and adjust Melanie Beck's head. Vic's fear that he had missed something transformed into a dread, and he tamped it down. He knew himself well enough to know the reason. When a crime scene gave him little to go on, that feeling always appeared. Still, he needed to pay attention to it. He glanced at Craig, who was standing near the eastern perimeter of the crime scene, watching Doc Martin. Forrest had moved over to speak to the Doc. Vic joined them.

"Hey Doc," Vic said when he reached them. "Anything you can give me?"

Doc Martin held up a gloved finger instructing him to wait. Forrest was explaining something about the photographs the forensics team had taken. When he finished, Doc Martin glanced at Vic, and with some effort, rose from his knees.

"I've been here less than two minutes." The Doctor's voice was raspy. "I guess you want TOD and the results of a full panel workup on her blood?"

Vic heard the sarcasm and the note of annoyance underneath it. "Just whatever you have. The scene hasn't given us anything we can really use."

"You kidding?" The doctor wiped at his glasses again. "You learned the victim is Melanie Beck. How much more do you need?" He glanced at the body. "This is a damn crying shame."

Beside the doctor, Forrest nodded his head in agreement.

"Right," Vic said slowly. "The symphony."

"Right. The symphony," the doctor echoed Vic's words, his sarcasm sticky as peanut butter. "Pittsburgh probably wouldn't have an orchestra without her. You're going to have the mayor, the county exec, and every rich jerk in town up your ass on this one."

"Exactly," Vic shot back, suddenly tired of the sparring. "Which is why I need to know what killed her."

The doctor leveled his brown-eyed gaze on Vic. "Pretty obvious. Single blow to the head. Unless I find something else when I get her on the table. But nothing is final until I do that."

"Any idea about the weapon?"

"Heavy enough to kill her." Doc Martin didn't blink, his eyes disappearing behind a wall of steam on his glasses.

Vic held up his hands in surrender. "Okay. Let me know as soon as you can. But like you said. She's well known. Pressure will be on us to solve this. We need all the parts of our investigation cranking...." Vic let the end of the sentence hang in the air. He hoped Doc Martin would get the implication that he would point fingers if the autopsy report was slow or late. Vic would never actually do that, but he didn't think it hurt to make the threat.

Doc Martin compressed his lips. "You clearing the scene? I need to get an ambulance down here."

Vic knew Doc Martin was calling his bluff, but clearing the scene was a major decision. Once the tape came down, the scene would be lost forever, and Vic couldn't shake the feeling he had missed something. He glanced at Forrest, who nodded to tell him the forensics team was finished.

Vic took a slow breath and looked at Craig. "You good?"

Craig nodded, looking surprised Vic would ask him. Vic noted his expression. He guessed Craig understood he was just stalling.

Vic turned to Forrest. "If you guys are good, then I'm calling it. Clear the scene. I appreciate your help."

Forrest nodded. "Least I can do." He nodded at Melanie's body.

"It is a crying shame," Doc Martin added.

"How do you know her?" Vic asked.

Doc shrugged. "Wife and I have season tickets. At least I know what the dinner conversation will be tonight."

Vic made a note never to accept a dinner invitation to Doc Martin's house. He thanked Doc and Forrest again and crossed to Craig.

"Good to go," he said to Craig. He let his gaze wander around the crime scene. *Was* he missing something? He stared at the rhododendron bush, wishing it had given them something more, and realized with a start that a gap existed in the thin lines of shrubs and trees that hid the trail from River Road and the Heinz factory buildings. He'd seen the gap and not registered its importance. Vic stared into the space, all five feet of it, spanned by a single strand of yellow crime scene tape. He turned and looked at the body and then back at the gap.

"Dammit," he said slowly. He reached for the walkie-talkie on his belt and dropped his hand. Crossed to Forrest. "Did Sergeant Wroblewski give you a radio?"

Forrest tapped his hip. "Yeah. When I walked in."

That was a weakness 9/11 uncovered. Before then, first responder units —fire, police, and medical—all used different communication equipment and frequencies. They couldn't talk to one another. Some cities and municipalities had standardized their communications, but Pittsburgh had yet to do so. Knowing this, the first responders lent each other comms to stay in touch.

"Okay," Vic said quickly. "Dial him up and tell him I'm on my way out and need to talk to him. His guys handled the original canvass of the area, right?"

"They did."

"Good. Thanks." He turned to Doc Martin and pointed at the gap in the shrub line. "You might want to pull your ambulance up there rather than run it down the trail. Easier."

Doc Martin nodded.

Vic looked back at Forrest. "Why didn't you just come through that gap rather than walk everyone down the trail?"

Forrest shrugged. "First responders put up the tape. I think they were directed to the scene by the RP. They came in down the trail, and everyone followed their lead."

Vic shook his head at how rote people could be. He gestured to Craig and walked him over to the gap.

"What's going on?" Craig asked.

Vic arranged his thoughts. "Keep this in mind. When you get to a crime scene, first thing you do is search the scene, right?"

"Right."

"Second thing you do, and remember this, is search *around* the scene. And if you scanned what's around the scene, what do you see?" He gestured at the gap.

"A gap."

"And beyond that?"

Understanding bloomed on Craig's face. "You'd see the Heinz factory and its apartments."

Vic pointed at the building. "And there, at the corner on the second and third floors, are four large windows. Two apartments, I bet."

Craig swiveled his head to look at the crime scene. "They overlook the scene."

"Exactly, and if we can see the windows from here, whoever is inside that apartment can see this area."

"Making them witnesses."

Vic didn't answer for a moment. "Well, *if* someone was inside, and *if* they happened to be looking out of the widow, yes. But it's worth knowing who lives there and talking to them. And Wroblewski should be able to say if anyone was home."

Chapter Six

Chen Yun stared at his laptop screen, reading the last of the articles from Tanming's background file. The dinner trays were gone, the cabin lights low. All around him was the high-pitched hum of the airplane and shadows. Many passengers were asleep. The few still awake watched movies on the seatback screens in front of them, their faces aglow from the light. They looked like ghosts, Chen thought, searching their faces. And perhaps we are. Moving in this tube through a black sky, miles above the ocean, an eternity from anyone who might care for us. How was it possible?

His grandmother, of course. And China.

She had shaped the trajectory of his life, as the airplane shaped the trajectory of his passage to America. She was the one who taught him English. The one who taught him to keep his thoughts to himself. To never trust. To be always on guard.

Yet he knew so little about her life. She'd grown up in the household of American missionaries, his great-grandmother the family's housekeeper. His grandmother was the same age as the missionaries' middle child, and she played, took classes, and even Sunday School alongside them all. The English language was as natural to her as breathing. How long had that lasted? Twelve years, perhaps, until the Japanese invasion in 1937?

His grandmother did tell him that story. How, ahead of the approaching Japanese army, the missionary family returned to the protection of the Western concessions in Shanghai, and her father led the family west from Wuhan into the arms of Chiang Kai-Shek's army in Chong Ching. Once there, his great-grandparents used their bare-bones English to obtain jobs at a joint Chinese-American military base nicknamed Happy Valley.

But it was his grandmother, barely eighteen, who became the favorite of Milton Miles, the base's American commander. As his grandmother later told him—with a tinge of pride—Miles liked the precision of her translations, her quick grasp of subtext, and her ability to explain how cultural influences shaded people's words.

His grandmother translated all of Miles' meetings with his Chinese counterparts. She met Chiang Kai-shek, his generals, and too many American commanders to count. But when the war ended, and the base was decommissioned, she returned to Wuhan with her family.

As Chen and every middle-school child in China knew, Wuhan fell to the Communists in 1950. That led to what Chen's grandmother called simply 'the darkness.'

The Communists assumed that anyone associated with Chiang Kai-Shek's army, and worse, Americans or missionaries, was suspect and likely a traitor. His grandmother's older brother, Chen's great-uncle, was arrested and disappeared. No one would employ her mother and father. And yet, two years later, the marriage of his grandmother ended the darkness.

She was twenty-six, her husband forty. Chen thought he understood that marriage. The man who became his grandfather was a Communist Party member. He'd joined the Party as a teenager, rising to a position in the propaganda department in Bao'an during the Japanese occupation. When the American journalist Edgar Snow visited, he'd attended Snow's interviews of Party leaders Mao Tse-tung and Chou En-lai and realized the necessity of translators. It was, Chen thought, what attracted him to his grandmother.

Within a year of their marriage, at his urging, his grandmother was teaching English to a small group of Party officials.

Two years later, again with the blessing of the Party, she founded an English language department at Wuhan University and gave birth to Chen's mother.

Chen's mother always spoke happily of her childhood in the 1950s, despite the horrendous failures of the Great Leap Forward and the debilitating famines that killed millions. As the wife and daughter of a Party official, his grandmother and mother were protected more than most.

Yet even Chen's grandfather couldn't save them from the student-led Cultural Revolution of the 1960s. Chen was aware of the pitched street battles between student Red Guards and the police. But what remained with him was the story of his grandmother being dragged from her classroom by her own students and condemned as an intellectual and capitalist roader. Her English books, with the exception of several she managed to hide, were presented as proof of her crimes and burned in the street outside her house. Chen's grandfather, who had protected her for so many years, was dragged onto a stage at the university, stripped of his party status for being married to Chen's grandmother, and forced to undergo struggle sessions. He refused to admit guilt and died of a heart attack in front of three hundred chanting, red-book-waving Red Guards.

His collapse was considered proof of his guilt. His body remained on stage for three days through other struggle sessions and wasn't removed until the smell became oppressive. To this day, Chen didn't know where his grandfather was buried.

His grandmother was sent to a rural commune to work the fields. She didn't return for twelve years.

Chen only learned these facts much later. What he first remembered was his grandmother holding him as a child in the late 1970s, after her return. Rocking him slowly in her arms and singing to him in English. Lullabies, he learned later. The face gazing down at him was gaunt, eyes ablaze, the skin tight across her cheekbones and crisscrossed with creases at the neck. Even as a child, he instinctively understood the wiry strength of her arms from those years of hard labor.

His mother supported them, working in a local factory. His father, for a time, was a mathematics teacher at a local high school, but due to a disagreement with a Party official at the school, was forced to labor in a steel mill, the same one named in the brochure among his background materials. Chen's father was rarely home. His grandmother cared for Chen during the day, speaking only English to him.

When he began school, his grandmother's fierce words were clear. Never tell anyone you speak English. Never speak English outside. There is inside the house, and outside the house. Learn the two ways of living. Inside the house, there is kindness, acceptance, and English. Outside there is the Party, constant scrutiny, and betrayal. Chinese language and Chinese ways. She would tap her index finger hard in the center of his forehead.

"Remember this difference," she would hiss. "Trust only this difference. Inside your head, outside your head. Inside this house, outside this house."

She dedicated her life, Chen knew now, to his survival. But more recently, he had come to realize something else. English was her religion, her way of proving to herself that she could survive whatever the Party took from her. It was her private rebellion.

He learned his grandmother's lessons well. All of them. He never spoke English and pretended not to understand when someone used an English phrase. Not in high school or early in college. Even now, outside his job, he was cautious.

He glanced around the airplane. We truly are ghosts, he thought. All of us. And yet we are also the survivors, the ones who somehow made it here, just here, through the machinations of genealogy, health, politics, ambition, love, and hate. He closed the lid of his laptop and settled into his seat. Closed his eyes. You never know, he thought, which livelihoods, which people, will somehow continue, somehow survive.

When he was promoted to his current job, he'd received training from country experts on the places he was likely to travel. By then, at a teacher's urging, he'd stopped hiding his language skills at work and was recognized by everyone as skilled in English. That led to a requirement that he take additional classes on American history and culture.

He remembered that instructor discussing the idea of happiness, tracing its corrupting influence from America's founding documents to the actions of individual Americans, how it made America a country doomed to failure. Chen opened his eyes and glanced about the airplane. Certainly, that was his instructor's opinion, as approved by the Party. He understood that, but it made him wonder. Do ghosts feel happiness? Chen smiled to himself. He slid his tongue over his teeth, searching for a last flickering taste of whisky.

He found nothing. And that was the real problem with happiness, he decided. It was fleeting, as impossible to grasp as smoke.

No different than a ghost.

Chapter Seven

As Vic and Craig reached the apartment parking lot, Vic's cell phone rang. He glanced at the caller ID and put the phone on speaker. "Liz?"

"Yeah. Lucky one of us is still working. I looked up where our victim lives. Two residences. One is an apartment in the Heinz Lofts. The old Heinz factory?"

"Explains why she was exercising here. The other?" Vic made the universal sign of writing in the air with his free hand and watched as Craig took out his phone to take notes.

"Sewickley Heights, near the country club. I checked online. Nice place. Big house. Very white."

Vic caught the double meaning in Liz's last sentence and ignored it. "Okay, do you have the number of the apartment here? Maybe we can get inside."

Liz reeled off the address, and Vic relayed it to Craig. Vic squinted at the position of the sun in the sky. "Her house will have to wait until tomorrow. It's too late in the day. We'll check the apartment and come back. I'll see you then."

"Yeah. I figured, and I asked for warrants for both places. I should have the one for the apartment any time now. I'll email it to you." Liz hesitated. "Your turn to pick up Lettie tonight, right?"

Liz's tone was thoughtful, and Vic noted it, wondering why. "It is," he answered, a vision of his granddaughter flitting through his mind. It was Lettie that morning, giving a squeal and giggle as she darted away from Anne, his wife, who was about to take her to daycare. The thought was uplifting, but a weight settled on his shoulders. The memory of his daughter, Dannie, buried in Allegheny Cemetery, had returned. Somehow, more and more frequently, a memory of Dannie followed any thought of Lettie, like a counterweight.

"Yep. My turn to pick her up." Vic knew he sounded distracted. He was aware of Craig looking at him side-eyed, and he turned off the speaker and put the phone to his ear. "Is there something you want to ask?"

"No," Liz said after a moment. She fell silent in the way of people working through a problem. He was sure she had something to say. He waited, staring across the parking lot at the police cars and ambulance. His eyes drifted back to the two apartments that overlooked the crime scene. The sun reflected off their windows, harsh and baleful.

Vic gave up, guessing that Liz thought the phone might be on speaker and didn't want to be overheard. "Okay. We can catch up when I get back." He wondered why whatever she wanted to say was associated with Lettie.

"Yeah." Liz recovered herself. "And you need to be ready. This victim? Melanie Beck? She's connected. I bet the mayor is on the phone to the DA right now, and that means your buddy Hana is going to park her DA butt on our desks until we figure this out. Especially since she's still interviewing people to be our commander. She's got no one to yell at but us."

"Good point." Vic knew Liz was right. He hadn't had time to think through the ramifications of a high-profile death. He also knew that wasn't what Liz wanted to talk to him about. She was covering for her silence.

"We'll talk," he said and hung up. He turned to Craig. "Let's find Wroblewski. Maybe we can get inside Beck's apartment and find out who lives in the two overlooking the scene."

They found Sergeant Wroblewski in the center of a square created by the parked police cars and the rear of the ambulance, surrounded by patrol officers and paramedics. A lean man in civilian clothes Vic hadn't seen before stood on the edge of the group. From the way everyone leaned toward Wroblewski, Vic guessed the sergeant was telling a story. Vic looked around and spotted Kasey Wells still sitting in the ambulance door. He watched her direct a shy smile in Craig's direction.

As Vic approached, the group erupted into laughter. Wroblewski, who stood a few inches taller than most of the group, spotted Vic. "You need something else, Lenoski?" He called.

Vic crossed to the group. "I do." He felt everyone's attention settle on him. "We need to get into one of the apartments. Do you have a lead on the super or anyone who can get us inside?"

Wroblewski nodded toward the lean man in civilian clothes. "You get what you ask for. Building management had a number posted in the lobby. I called to say we'd taken over the parking lot, and this guy showed up."

"Ted Garrett," the man called to Vic. "I work for Rivercross Management. We run the apartments. What do you need?"

Vic led him out of earshot of the group as Craig sidled up next to them. Vic stuck out his hand and introduced both himself and Craig.

"Ted Garrett," the man repeated, shaking hands with both of them.

"What did Sergeant Wroblewski tell you?" Vic asked.

"He just said he had a crime nearby, and the police and paramedics were using the Lofts parking lot. He asked for someone to come over in case it involved more of our property."

"Good." Vic studied the man. Ted was tall and lean, his thin black hair long and swept back over his skull in fruitless denial of his hair loss. His eyes were deep brown, and he hadn't shaved in easily a week. The stubby black hairs of his beard were scattered across his face and neck like ants.

"You got here fast," Vic said, watching him.

"Yeah. We have another building across the river in the Strip District. There's three others I manage. I was there and just had to cross the bridge to get here."

"Okay." Vic glanced at the red brick walls of the old Heinz plant. "Can you get us inside one of the apartments? The owner was found dead on the running trail there, and it looks suspicious. I'd like to look inside her place."

Ted frowned slightly. "Don't you need a warrant or something for that?"

Vic dug out his phone and opened his emails. Right at the top was an email from Liz with the phrase Heinz Lofts Warrant in the subject line. Vic opened the attachment and showed it to Ted. "We have one."

Ted squinted at the phone and gave up after a moment. "I believe you. I have a master key. Which apartment is it?"

Vic gave him the number and turned to Craig. "Before we head up, I want you to do something."

Craig pushed his glasses up his nose. "Sure."

"We can talk about your interview with Kasey Wells later, but you missed one critical thing. Ask her what time she started her run, from where, and what time she got to the end of the trail and turned around. If she really runs three days a week, she'll know her intervals. We have the time when she made the 911 call. We put all that together, and we have a pretty good time window when the attack happened. Do that, and then tell Wroblewski to cut her loose."

Craig flushed. "Got it."

"Then meet me at the apartment, okay?" Vic softened the last word to let Craig know he wasn't too angry with him.

"On it." Craig pivoted and started for the ambulance, eager to correct his mistake.

Or talk to Kasey, Vic thought. He called to Wroblewski. "Can you lend me someone?"

Wroblewski tapped a nearby uniformed officer on his broad chest and pointed at Vic. Vic nodded his thanks and turned to Ted. "Lead the way."

Chapter Eight

As he crossed to Kasey, Craig's cheeks burned. He'd made a stupid mistake, and he knew it. He'd read the best practices guide to witness interviewing three times. He knew the takeaways needed. He could recite them. And then Kasey had smiled at him, and the guide had gone right out of his head. Worse—and he forced himself to admit this to himself as he walked—he'd wanted to impress her.

He saw Kasey spot him approaching, her hand a flash as she smoothed her hair. He knew he had to set some kind of boundary, but he didn't know how or what it should be. He'd never needed one before.

He skirted a patrol car. The officers and paramedics were still in the center of the square, the tall white-haired sergeant again telling a story. Craig saw the sergeant spot him and register what he was doing without losing the patter of his storytelling.

The truth was, Craig had to admit to himself he wanted a girlfriend. The urge annoyed him because his parents were pushing him to get married. The real pressure came from his mother, but lately, he'd notice his father falling into line as well. When he was at the University of Pittsburgh, and his mother began her series of questions about whether he had any "special friends" or "young ladies" who might want to join them for Christmas or Thanksgiving, his father would hide a smile and roll his eyes. Craig knew he had an ally. But recently, now that he was six years out of college and on his third job, he'd noticed that his father kept his peace whenever his mother talked about Craig finding someone "lively" and "bright." Someone with "spark in their eyes."

On one level, as the only child, he understood his mother's frustration. She wanted grandchildren. On another, he didn't understand his mother's choice of adjectives and her preferences and priorities in a girlfriend. He knew enough, from his short-lived relationships in college and afterwards, that "lively" and "bright" didn't interest him. In college, he'd discovered a fascination with how things worked, with the details and the mechanics of things. It was why he shifted majors to computer science. He appreciated substance. Depth. And that led him toward women who knew what they wanted to do with their lives, who'd made their own choices. His mother was supposed to know him best, yet she seemed to think he was most compatible with someone glittery, whose primary purpose was to light up a room. Which—of course—suggested she thought that was all *he* was good for.

That irked him.

He stopped and blinked himself back into the moment. Kasey was staring up at him from the back of the ambulance, a bright smile on her face.

"You look serious." She laughed lightly and flashed her amber eyes at him.

He didn't know what tone to take with her, or how to present himself. Instead, he just said, "Sorry, I have a couple more questions."

"Fire away." She leaned back and arched the small of her back.

Craig knew she was presenting herself to him. He focused on her eyes. "Tell me where you started your run."

"Oh." She jerked her thumb at the back of the ambulance. "Back there."

It took Craig a split second to understand she meant the trailhead on the other side of the parking lot, next to the river. "And you said you ran to the end of the trail near Millvale, right? What time did you start, and what time did you reach the end of the trail?"

"I started just before four, it takes me twenty-two minutes to reach the end of the trail. I like to go fast."

He ignored the suggestion implicit in her sentence. "And about as long to come back?" He was doing his own math. The murder scene was about two hundred yards from the trailhead. Detective Lenoski was right. This would give them a very specific time window when the crime occurred.

"Maybe a couple of minutes longer. I slow down on the way back. Try to enjoy the run. Ride the endorphins, you know? Nothing like an endorphin high." Her voice dropped lower, huskier.

Craig realized she was changing tactics, giving him a bedroom voice. He looked directly at her and pushed his glasses up his nose. He was annoyed suddenly by Kasey's relentless flirting and his incessant need to reset his glasses. "You realize this is serious, right? Someone died. It's up to us to figure out who killed her. We're the only ones who can do that. Who can make it right."

Kasey pulled back. "Sheesh. Okay. You can't have some fun along the way?"

Craig found himself preoccupied with his own statement. He'd heard those same words but never spoken them, and the syllables clung to his insides. Gripped him with the responsibility of what he had to do. They drew his breath away.

"Thank you," he said, hearing a new tone in his voice. It was level. Sober. He turned off the recording app on his phone and focused on her again. "We'll need you to sign a formal statement. We'll let you know when it's time to do that, or if we have any further questions."

He pivoted away from her. A little brusquely, he knew, but he didn't care. He needed to find Vic. To get to work. To do his job the right way.

As he passed the gaggle of people surrounding Wroblewski, the sergeant caught his eye. Without breaking stride, Craig called, "You can cut her loose."

Wroblewski didn't react for a second, then nodded. To Craig, it was as if Wroblewski recognized what he'd just gone through, sensed Craig's new understanding of the importance of his job.

Craig imagined that perhaps Wroblewski wasn't nodding in agreement, but in approval.

He kept walking toward the apartment buildings and pushed his glasses back up his nose. And that was something else. It was time for the glasses to go. He wanted contacts. He wasn't going to hide behind his glasses any longer.

Chapter Nine

Vic and the uniformed officer followed Ted across a modern lobby with a carpet so thin it felt like concrete under Vic's feet. Ted led them past an empty receptionist's desk to the elevators, up to the third floor and most of the way down a hall to a gray door. He stopped, as if unsure what to do next.

Ted waved at the door. "This is it."

"Thanks. Do you mind waiting in the lobby until I come down?"

Ted shuffled his feet but stayed where he was. Vic wondered why Ted didn't like the suggestion, but corrected himself. Ted's job was to care for these apartments, and Vic guessed he was just being protective.

Vic softened his tone. "Look, I'm just going to take a quick look around and see if anything jumps out at me. A full CSI team will be up to process the apartment. If you come in, we'll need to take a sample of your DNA and your fingerprints to rule you out. I'm just trying to save you some trouble."

Ted shifted back a step. "Okay, I get it. I'll wait downstairs."

He turned to go, and Vic called after him. "Ted, the key?"

"Oh." With an embarrassed shrug, Ted pulled a large keyring from his pocket, squinted at the lock, sifted through half the ring, and singled out a key. The door opened on the first try, and Ted propped open the door with his foot. "Doors are set to close automatically."

Vic planted his foot to keep the door open as Ted backed away. "I'll be downstairs," Ted said and started down the hall.

Vic asked the uniformed officer to stay in the hall and only allow Craig inside. He searched his pockets for latex gloves, found a pair in his inside pocket, worked them on, and stepped into the apartment.

Just inside the front door, a long hallway led past three doors to a living room with tall windows. As the front door slammed closed behind him, Vic started for the living room, checking behind each of the three doors as he went. Two bedrooms and a bathroom. A galley kitchen appeared on his left, separated from the high-ceilinged living room by a breakfast bar. The windows overlooked the Allegheny River and the Pittsburgh skyline. Vic crossed to the windows and stared down at the parking lot, River Avenue, and the line of trees that hid the running trail. He spotted the gap into the trail, near a newly parked coroner's van.

He retreated to the center of the living room and closed his eyes. He tried to feel the apartment, to smell and hear it. This was the real reason he'd sent Craig back to Kasey. He wanted a few moments alone inside the apartment to orient himself. Find his center. Lately, he needed this time when he started a new case. If Craig was with him, he was sure Craig would watch him owlishly the whole time, distracting him.

Eyes still closed, Vic listened to the rooms around him, to the walls. Silence. Even the air in the apartment was still. He opened his eyes and took a breath. Okay, he told himself. He dug out his phone, called Forrest, and told him where he was.

"Full run-through?" Forrest asked.

"Yes." Vic looked around the living room, past an open laptop on the breakfast counter, and into the kitchen. "I have to tell you," Vic added slowly, "this place feels like a motel suite, not a place someone actually lives. I think this is just a place for the night."

"We'll still give it a once-over."

Vic told Forrest where to find Ted for directions to the apartment and hung up. He walked to the computer and tapped on the space bar. A password prompt loaded. He wondered who might know the password and tried to remember if Melanie wore a wedding ring. He hadn't checked. "Start paying attention," he chastised himself out loud.

He looked about. An electric kettle stood near the sink, a mug and open box of tea bags next to it. The furniture was modern, all hard-looking surfaces and neutral colors. Even the framed print on the wall, despite its large size, was subdued in color. The place really did feel like a motel room.

Someone knocked on the door. Vic walked down the long hall and let Craig inside.

"Kasey did know her time intervals," Craig said once he was inside. Vic returned to the living room, Craig following. When Vic turned, he noticed Craig was wearing latex gloves. He was glad he didn't need to remind him.

Craig pulled out his phone to check his notes. "We have about a ten-minute widow when the attack happened. I can give you the exact times." He looked up, but Vic shook his head.

"When we get back. We'll put everything on a whiteboard."

The phone disappeared into Craig's pocket. "Sorry about that. I should have worked out the timeline in the first part of the interview. I think I got distracted."

Vic thought he saw a trace of red on Craig's face. "Next time, you'll know." He waved his hand at the apartment walls. "What do you think of this place?"

Craig did a slow pivot, taking his time. His forehead scrunched into a light frown, his brown eyes thoughtful. "Not personal," he said slowly. "Feels like anyone could live here."

"Right. I thought motel room."

"Yeah. I get that." Craig walked into the kitchen and slid open several drawers, followed by a once-around with the cabinets. "No cooking stuff. Just a few basic pots and pans."

"Fits. Let's check the bedrooms before Forrest and his guys get here. I'll take the one closest to the front door. You take the other."

Vic found the bedroom had an ensuite bathroom, making it the master. He guessed that whoever used the other bedroom was expected to use the hallway bathroom.

Vic circled the bed. The top sheet and white duvet were rumpled enough to show someone had slept there the night before. A small framed photograph of two children in front of a Christmas tree sat on the nightstand. Vic picked up the photograph and studied it. The children were perhaps eight and ten, an older girl and younger boy. To the right of the tree was a window framed in dark wood, and underneath it, a cast iron radiator. An old house, perhaps a Victorian, he thought. And no husband. He replaced the frame. A chest of drawers stood against the far wall, but he didn't open it. Instead, he walked into the bathroom.

Finally, a room someone clearly used. The countertop was cluttered with cosmetics, and a large towel hung askew from the door handle into the walk-in shower. He opened a nearby jewelry box. Inside were several strings of pearls and a gold chain. No earrings or bracelets. Vic wondered if they were real and if anything was missing.

He returned to the bedroom and slid open the accordion doors of the closet. To the left were sets of matching skirts, dresses, and jackets, all with the St. John label. The other side was a selection of pants and blouses. Vic studied the clothes. They radiated sophistication and the sedate, relaxed confidence of wealth. Nothing glamorous or attention-getting. He took two photos of the clothes, returned to the bathroom, and photographed the cosmetics and jewelry. As he checked the shots on his phone, voices rose outside the apartment. He went into the hall and opened the front door.

The officer in the hallway was backed up to the door. Vic had to look around his bulk to see a thin, brown-haired woman pressed against the far wall, eyes wide in anger.

"What are you doing here? I need to get inside!" The woman repeated, her voice shrill and demanding.

Vic touched the shoulder of the uniformed officer to move him aside and stepped into the hall. He let the door close behind him. "Allegheny County Police, ma'am. We have a warrant to search the premises. Who are you?"

The woman stared at Vic, eyes flashing.

Vic noticed a door key in her right hand. Her other hand was empty. No purse or shopping bags. "My name is Detective Vic Lenoski, ma'am. I'm going to show you my ID. My associate, Craig Luntz, is inside."

The woman blinked at him.

Vic slid his hand into his jacket pocket for his ID. "Ma'am, do you have any identification?" Vic kept his voice low and calm, hoping to defuse the woman's anger. He opened his badge wallet and held it out to her.

She frowned. "So?"

Vic doubted she could read it at that distance. "We understand that Melanie Beck lives here. Are you a friend of hers?"

"This is her place." Her voice was softer, but she remained tight. "In case she wants to sleep downtown. Why are you here?"

Vic carefully returned his ID to his jacket pocket. He estimated she was five-five in height, early thirties. Stringy shoulder-length brown hair framed a pale, bony face. Her blue jeans were tight, offset by a loose-weave white cotton blouse. She wasn't wearing make-up, just a few silver bangles on her right wrist. Vic doubted she weighed more than one hundred pounds.

Behind him, the door opened. Vic nudged the uniformed officer to step aside to make room for Craig. Vic noted that Craig had the presence of mind to block the door jamb with his heel to keep the door open.

The woman stared at Craig as if he was some kind of wraith. "And who are you?"

A curl of annoyance twisted in Vic's stomach. He wanted to know who she was and why she had a key to the apartment. He leaned toward her. "I already said. Allegheny County Police. We're investigating a crime and have a warrant that allows us to search the premises."

"What crime?" She looked sharply from Craig to Vic.

Vic felt himself losing his temper, but Craig said quietly to her, "I'll tell you something. You gave us a scare. I bet we gave you one too. Sorry about that. We're wondering if you could help us."

Vic watched her process Craig's words. To his surprise, she nodded. "Okay. Okay."

He thought the second "okay" was more for herself than anything else.

"Great. I'm Craig Luntz. Like Detective Lenoski here, I work for the Allegheny County Police Department." He held out his ID. "That's who we are. Now how about you?"

Her eyes locked on Craig as if he was some kind of lifeline. "I'm Jessica Teel."

"Great. And I guess you're here to see Melanie Beck?"

The question seemed to confuse Jessica for a moment, and she glanced at the uniformed officer, now standing several feet to one side. "No. Yes. I stayed here last night. I was supposed to meet Melanie to get my stuff and a ride home."

"The stuff you need to pick up, is that the viola?"

Vic gave Craig a sidelong look. He hadn't seen a viola in the apartment. He also wanted to see Jessica's ID, but let it go. Craig was making headway.

"Yes." Jessica stared at Craig, a look of relief on her face. "I have practice tomorrow. And my overnight bag is here."

"You slept in the spare room last night?"

"Yes. right." Jessica frowned, suddenly annoyed Craig needed to ask. "Where is Melanie?"

Craig turned to Vic, silently suggesting he take over the discussion.

"Unfortunately, Melanie Beck was in an accident," Vic said gently.

"Oh." Jessica frowned. "Is she okay?"

Vic told himself to lower his voice. "I'm afraid the accident was fatal."

Jessica's mouth opened. She blinked.

"Which is why we are here," Vic supplied. "The accident is suspicious."

Jessica pressed her fingers to her mouth, her brown eyes wide. "That's terrible." She rocked back against the wall.

"It is," Craig broke in. "But that's how you can help us. Can you tell us about last night, or anything about what Melanie did today? If you saw anything unusual?"

She nodded. "Sure, I stayed here last night. So did Melanie. She sometimes lets us sleep here rather than go home. If a performance or something goes long."

Vic tried to unpack everything she said. "Okay, when you say "us," what do you mean?"

"Members of the symphony. I play the viola."

"Good, okay. And you had a performance last night?"

"No. Well yes. A party. I'm in a quartet, and we played at the party. I knew it would go late and Melanie would be there, so I asked if I could sleep here rather than go home. She gave me a key."

"There's a backpack with clothes in the guest bedroom," Craig said gently to Vic. "And a viola."

Jessica looked at Craig, and Vic thought she might complain about her property being searched, but she seemed to think better of it. She turned to Vic. "Melanie does that a lot. I mean for the musicians. She lets us stay here and at her house. I joined the symphony a few months ago, and I haven't found anywhere to live. She's letting me stay at her house until I find somewhere."

"The one in Sewickley Heights?"

She nodded emphatically.

Jessica's voice was calmer, closer to what Vic guessed was her normal speaking voice. He decided to take advantage of that. "And what did you do today?"

"I had practice this morning." Her voice rose a notch, and Vic categorized her as nervous by nature. "After that, I went to the Strip District to shop. I was supposed to meet Melanie here about now. She was going to give me a ride back to the house." She frowned. "What happened exactly?"

Vic kept his voice even. "From what we can make out, she went for a walk on the trail by the river, and someone attacked her."

"Yes, she liked to walk that trail. For exercise."

At the end of the hall, the elevator doors ground open, and three people in white Tyvek bunny suits stepped off. Vic indicated them. "That's our forensics team. They'll need to process the apartment. We'll need your fingerprints and DNA. Do you have a way to get home?"

Jessica stared at the forensics team with morbid fascination. "I can call a car, I guess."

Forrest led his team down the hall, their suits swishing in the silence.

Vic gestured to Craig to keep up the conversation with Jessica and met Forrest halfway down the hall. He lowered his voice. "We have a curveball."

Forrest stared at Jessica. "Yeah?"

"Jessica Teel. It turns out she spent last night in Melanie Beck's apartment. I guess she plays viola for the symphony."

Forrest grinned. "I recognize her. No problem. We'll process her as well."

"And then cut her loose. She said she can get a ride home." Vic thought about that as he said it. If Jessica was headed to Melanie's house, they couldn't wait. They needed to get inside the house in Sewickley Heights before she returned. "Actually, don't cut her loose, not right away. Take your time. I want to see if Liz can get out to the Beck house before Jessica does."

"Whatever floats your boat."

As Vic rejoined Craig, Jessica, and the officer, Craig handed Jessica back her driving license. She stuffed it into what looked like a small man's wallet and slid it into the front pocket of her jeans. It crossed Vic's mind that after the mistakes with the Kasey interview, Craig wasn't missing anything now.

Vic explained that Forrest would take Jessica's fingerprints and DNA and would need to document her belongings inside the apartment. She didn't look happy about it, but nodded her assent. He waved Craig into the apartment and followed him inside. He shut the door.

"If Jessica is living at the Beck house, we need to look at it before Jessica gets there."

"Absolutely."

"Okay. Liz lives in Sewickley, meaning she lives near the Beck house. The two of you can do it."

"Sure." Craig stared at him, and Vic knew he wanted to redeem himself from his earlier interviewing mistakes.

Vic called Liz. He explained about Jessica and the need to see the Beck house.

"And do forensics tomorrow?" Liz asked.

"Let me think about that. I'm not sure we need to. If there's anything to find, I feel like it'll be here in the apartment."

"No problem. I can be at the Sewickley house in about an hour. Tell Craig to meet me."

"Make sure you check in with the local police. I'll ask Jessica if we can borrow her key. Craig can bring it. When Jessica gets there, Craig can give it back to her."

"Works for me," Liz said. "I'm leaving now. Oh, and guess what? You had a call. I have to pass along a message."

"Okay, what?" Vic frowned down the hallway. Liz was just one surprise after another today.

"Our boss, the DA? Your buddy? She called. She wants updates. She wants you to call when you clear the scene."

"I already cleared the scene. And it can't be that bad, or Hana would have called me directly."

Liz laughed. "Yeah, really? Somebody like Melanie Beck, this is just the start."

Vic ended the call, thinking Liz was right. He thanked Craig for helping with Jessica and told him to get going. Alone in the apartment, he walked into the spare bedroom and found the viola case lying on the end of the bed. He unsnapped the latches, lifted the lid, and stared at the instrument. Not sure what to make of it, he closed the lid and latched it again. It seemed bothersome to lug around every day for work.

Then again, he mused, so was a gun.

Chapter Ten

Chen Yun paced the terminal at Los Angeles Airport, liking the feel of blood returning to his legs. Outside, the sun was bright and flat under blue skies. He'd landed two hours earlier and cleared customs. He'd half expected to be pulled aside at immigration, given that he'd shown his police identification along with his passport. But his police ID earned nothing more than a disinterested scan from the immigration agent before he was waved through. That was something he would never understand. Here he was, a Chinese national announcing himself as a law enforcement officer, and no one in the United States was interested in why he was visiting their country. Or what he intended to do while he was here.

The arrogance of that immigration officer, he thought. Or the stupidity. Chen had no legal jurisdiction in the United States, and the country's law enforcement personnel simply assumed he would follow international and U.S. laws. They never paused to think that perhaps the Chinese who lived in America would think differently, would see a Chinese police officer as a force to be reckoned with. As someone to be obeyed.

Or that China's Operation Fox Hunt saw all international and local laws as irrelevant.

This was the fourth time he'd entered the country this way, the fourth time his entry caused no stir. Even after his second visit, the one to Dallas, when it all went wrong. He reached the end of the hallway and turned back.

He didn't feel like he actually inhabited his body. The lack of sleep, the time zone differences, the bright, relentless sun, the confounding, slack indifference of the immigration official. He trudged the length of the hall and chose a seat that overlooked his gate. Another hour before they boarded. He took out his laptop, hoping that work would shake off his dislocation.

Once his laptop was running, instead of reviewing his downloaded files, he connected to the airport's dodgy Wi-Fi and searched on Pittsburgh. As he read the city's history, his interest grew. Feng Wang had called Pittsburgh dirty and failed, but in Chen's mind, that wasn't true at all, or more accurately, that opinion was out of date. What he read showed a city's resurgence and reinvention after the inevitable decline of its industrial base. A shift to high technology, a new environmental focus, and a healthy cultural and arts community funded by the donated wealth of the city's long-dead industrial barons. Even its sports teams were storied and successful. It was a city that remade itself. Reinvented itself. This city has strong *chi*, he decided, a life force that would inhabit the people who lived there.

He thought about that. His approach to the target would need to be angled and patient, to give himself time to understand the target's network of friends and acquaintances. To determine the strength of their influence.

He didn't want to repeat the mistake he made in Dallas.

He still believed his approach of Hu Zhao was right. He'd chosen the Dallas gym Hu frequented for the first contact. Strip a man of his home, clothes, and car, and he feels vulnerable. Hu lived in a pricey Dallas penthouse, drove a Ferrari, and wore bespoke suits from London. Hu's first name meant tiger, so he'd thought it better to corner him away from his jungle and let his shorts and t-shirt leave him feeling undressed.

But when Chen introduced himself, Hu turned stoic. That was the first sign, Chen knew now, and he missed it. Hu also threw out his trump card in that first conversation. Hu was a resident alien of the United States. Chen and China had no jurisdiction over him.

Chen reminded him that according to Chinese law, overseas Chinese are required to support and help all Chinese intelligence-gathering agencies. And then Chen made his second mistake.

He lied.

Hu's case was simple enough. The eldest son of a wealthy manufacturing family, Hu had risen quickly in the family business. He was talented and attacked his job with an energy befitting his name. He was also naïve. When he discovered several false client accounts used to channel money to a senior provincial official, he accused the official of requiring bribes to approve construction and wastewater permits. In Hu's mind, he was simply saving the family business some money. But the official was well connected in the Politburo and was quick to say he knew nothing of the accounts. Instead, the official claimed that Hu's actions were an attempt to pressure him into providing favorable permits.

Hu's father, still the chairman of the family business, had the good sense to send Hu to Dallas, purportedly to expand the company's American distribution network. Hu found an apartment in Dallas and applied for citizenship.

Chen's lie was simple enough. He said the Chinese government had decided to accuse the provincial official of corruption, and Hu needed to return to China to testify.

But in subsequent meetings, it became clear someone warned Hu of the truth. That, in fact, the official was so petty he'd decided to sue Hu for defamation in a hurried attempt to clear his own name. Which was the true reason China wanted Hu back. To face those charges.

Hu told Chen he wasn't going back to a rigged trial.

Chen's response was to drop what they called the emotional bomb. Chen told Hu that if he didn't return to China, his father would be arrested instead. He explained that a plane was leaving Dallas in three hours, and they both needed to be on it.

When Chen gave Hu that message, he was sitting across from Hu in the living room of Hu's Dallas penthouse. A determined look came over Hu's face, just as the corners of his mouth drooped in an echo of that stoic look from the gym that first day. Chen couldn't forget that look, or how Hu didn't reply for several moments, his face shadowed by the twilight outside.

Hu then rose and called out, "Jared."

Chen knew Jared. He'd watched Hu and Jared together a number of times, at bars and attending a Cowboys football game. Their size difference amused him. Jared was over six feet tall and barrel-chested, Hu no taller than five feet five, slim-waisted and narrow-shouldered. The door to the bedroom opened, and Jared stepped into the living room. He wore the jeans and one of the cowboy shirts he preferred, although his blond hair wasn't hidden by the white Stetson he liked. Hu rose and crossed to him.

When they were barely a foot apart, Hu said fiercely, "Jared, I have no choice. Just know this. I love you. You mean everything to me." Hu clutched Jared to him fiercely and after a few moments, reached up and kissed Jared deeply on the lips. Stunned, Chen watched. How had he missed that Hu was *tongzhi*?

Hu released Jared, the two of them staggering at the other's passion. Hu recovered first, turned, and slid open the patio door. He took two steps and, with a smooth vault, disappeared over the railing.

By now, Chen was standing. He couldn't move. He stared at the open patio door and the darkening sky outside. Dully, he registered they were on the thirty-sixth floor. Jared bellowed and sank to his knees like a gutted bull.

The sound freed Chen to turn, his feet heavy, and let himself into the hall.

Chen remembered that moment as if it was yesterday. He blinked himself back to the present. Stared at the departure gate. Boarding had yet to begin, or to be announced.

Chen remembered how he left Hu's apartment, drove himself to the airport, and turned in the rental car. Boarded the plane to Chicago and his connecting flight. Arrived in Wuhan twenty hours later.

He had come to the conclusion, during that long flight, that his career was over. Yet it wasn't. Instead, with Hu's death, everyone simply looked the other way. Hu's father publicly disowned his son, because suicide is an insult to the dead person's parents and ancestors. Hu's younger brother took over Hu's position in the family business. The accusations made by the official were assumed in the press to be true, with Hu's suicide the proof of his guilt. Hu's father paid a sizeable fine to the government to settle the case, and the official who brought the charges quietly gained a coastal villa in Beidaihe, the conclave on the Bohai Sea popular with Chinese politburo members. Chen guessed that was courtesy of Hu's father as well.

Chen was given a week off work. Each night he stood in his six-month-old son's bedroom in the evening, rocking him in his arms, afraid that if he placed him in his crib he somehow might disappear over the edge of the railing. That gravity would overwhelm him.

That was almost two years ago, the last time he'd seen his son in person. Touched him.

Chen closed his laptop.

He knew he couldn't let anything like that happen in Pittsburgh. Not because he was scared of losing his job. Somehow, now, he didn't care if he did.

He didn't want to lose anyone else. Especially this target. For the first time, he was being asked to repatriate a young woman.

He breathed carefully, and smiled.

When he thought of Dallas, there was one association he could never shake. His grandmother first told him about American cowboys, how they won the West. She even read him two Zane Grey novels she'd managed to hide over the years. When he played inside the house, he imagined himself on a horse, chasing criminals, a six-shooter at his hip. But now, thanks to Jared, whenever he thought of cowboys he assumed they were *tongzhi*. He couldn't help himself.

And for some odd reason, the notion pleased him.

Chapter Eleven

Craig negotiated the switchbacks and twists of the road rising from Sewickley to Sewickley Heights, his old red Jeep groaning at the effort. His GPS warned him of a left turn. He followed the instructions, the new road rising and dipping twice before reaching a golf course. He'd never visited this part of Allegheny County, but his main concern was to be on time. He wasn't sure when Liz would arrive, but she lived nearby and would know the area. Being lost meant arriving late, and he'd already made enough mistakes for one day.

He thought about the tone his voice produced with Kasey when he was desperate to find a way to keep the interview professional. It was better, he decided, but still not quite right. But it was an improvement, and he decided to trust he would find the right pitch in time.

A four-way stop loomed ahead, and the GPS indicated he should take a left. A Joe Bonamassa song blared on his stereo, Beth Hart's aching voice promising to take care of him. He knew that was a fantasy, but still found it comforting. The GPS announced his arrival, and he turned down the music. To his left were the rolling drives, sand traps, and greens of a golf course, to his right, ten feet from the road, a tall, black wrought-iron fence. Beyond that was a low-slung, sprawling white house partially hidden by hundred-year oaks and pruned shrubs.

Fifteen yards ahead, a black police cruiser sat in the entrance to the estate. The vehicle was backed up against a gate facing the golf course. Craig pulled in next to it and rolled down his window.

"I'm Craig Luntz, Allegheny County Police. You're Sewickley Heights?"

The officer in the other car didn't quite keep the surprise off his face. Craig knew he looked young, and once again wanted to remove his glasses. He watched the sergeant gather his thoughts.

"Yeah. Sergeant Coopse. We got a call you were coming. Two of you, right?"

"Right. Detective Sergeant Liz Timmons."

"That's who called. She hasn't shown up yet. She said this is a crime affecting a resident of the house?"

"Right, Melanie Beck."

Coopse pursed his lips. "I've met her. She's the owner. Nice lady."

Craig had a flash of Melanie's body lying on the running path, blood from her head wound clotted in her hair. His stomach churned, the first time he'd had a reaction to a murder victim, despite the times he'd worked similar scenes with the forensics unit.

"What happened?" The sergeant's face inclined toward him, interest in his eyes.

"She was found on a running trail on the North Side. She'd been attacked. Fatal head wound."

The sergeant pursed his lips. "No wonder it's suspicious. I get why you guys want to move fast."

"Right." Craig had the thought that he might be overstepping his position, that really Liz should be asking the officer questions, but he went ahead anyway. "Who lives here, apart from her?"

"Good question. Varies. I see a fair amount of people in and out."

"Anyone stick out?"

"Yeah. Lately, there's been a guy." Coopse craned his head around and looked through the bars of the gate toward the house. "See the pick-up? That belongs to him."

Craig followed his gaze and spotted a blue Ford F-150 pick-up. It looked new. "Anyone else?" He knew from Jessica Teel that she also lived in the house, and he was interested if Coopse knew that.

Coopse thought for a moment. "I've seen a Prius parked here lately, but I don't know who it belongs to."

"And that's it?"

"Yeah. Mrs. Beck's husband moved out a couple of years ago. Good riddance to him. Total jerk."

Craig smiled at Coopse's vehemence. "Why's that?"

"Prize asshole. I pulled him over for speeding my first year working. He gave me shit for ten minutes straight."

Craig was about to ask if he ticketed the man anyway, but a small black SUV arrived from the opposite direction Craig had driven. He pointed with his chin. "Detective Liz Timmons."

"I'll let you guys in." Coopse climbed out of the cruiser, walked around to the passenger side, and bent to a white brick column. Craig couldn't make out what he was doing, but guessed there must be a number pad. In answer to his thoughts came a clunking sound, and the twin gates moved inward. Coopse returned to the driver's side of his car. "I'll get out of the way so you can enter, then I'll follow." He pulled into the street.

Craig followed the gravel driveway to the loop in front of the house. In his mirror, he saw Coopse wave Liz inside. By the time Craig parked and slammed his door enough times so it stuck, Liz had drawn up beside him. Coopse backed in next to her, again facing the golf course. The gate was closed.

Liz joined Craig by his Jeep. He thought she looked tired, almost distracted, and it gave her an angry look. She didn't say anything. With the sun low in the sky and the shadows of the surrounding trees, the gray in her close-cropped hair was noticeable. They both watched Coopse approach.

Liz introduced herself. Craig thought Coopse was more reserved with Liz than he'd been earlier, and he wondered if that had to do with Liz's rank, the look on her face, or the color of her skin. As they turned for the front door, he thought it might be all three.

Craig decided to ease the moment. He looked at Coopse. "I asked earlier if anyone stood out. You mentioned a guy who's living here now. Drives the truck?" Craig pointed in the direction of the Ford. "What made him stick out?"

Coopse took two more steps before he spoke. "I guess I can't figure out why he's here. He's out of place."

"How's that?" Liz stopped and looked at him. Craig realized Liz didn't want to have this conversation too close to the house, where they might be overheard.

Coopse took another step before he realized Liz had halted. He stopped and turned. "Just a feeling. He started living here maybe four or five months ago. I don't know where Ms. Beck found him. Young guy, early thirties. When he first got here, he drove an old pickup, rusty. I cited him once for an out-of-date inspection sticker. He was making all these excuses, saying he plays Triple-A baseball and is too busy traveling to keep up the inspections. Gave me this whole 'we're bros' attitude. His truck had West Virginia plates, and he told me down there they don't cite anyone for a missed inspection. They just give warnings. Which is crap. Anyway, I cited him, and a week later, he's driving around in the new Ford there. Pennsylvania tags. Now how did that happen?" He glanced from Liz to Craig.

"Might be interesting to ask him," Liz said. "But let's get inside."

They trooped to the front door. Craig rang the bell, and the door opened almost immediately.

The man who answered was six feet, the muscles of his shoulders and upper arms straining his white t-shirt. His hair was coal black, and his face smudged by a five o'clock shadow. Below dark blue athletic warm-up pants, he wore snow-white sneakers. His clothes looked as new as his truck.

"What can I do for you?" The man scanned Coopse and Craig before settling on Liz, as if he'd made his choice about who was the most dangerous of the three.

Liz introduced herself and took her time pulling her ID from her jacket pocket. Craig knew she'd read the man's look and was being slow and methodical on purpose. Goading him a little.

"Okay," the man said, impatient with how slowly Liz was returning her ID to her pocket. "What do you want?"

"A couple of things. First, what is your name?"

The man's large hand flexed slightly where he held the door. "Ryan Telst."

Liz wrote the name down as if she had all the time in the world. "And you live here?"

Ryan opened his mouth and closed it, thinking about the question. It seemed to stump him. "Yeah. I guess." He said the words slowly.

Liz let them hang in the air. "And do you know Melanie Beck?"

"Sure, yeah. Her house." He sounded relieved, glad for a question he could answer.

"Could we step inside?" Liz motioned inside.

"What's this about?"

"I think it would be better if we step inside." Liz's voice was even.

Ryan frowned, but retreated from the doorway.

Liz turned to Coopse. "Can you stay out here? There's a Jessica Teel who says she lives here. She might show up. Just keep her and anyone else outside until we're finished."

"Sure."

Craig had the feeling Coopse was relieved.

Ryan shut the front door and led them along a wide hall past traditionally furnished living and dining rooms. He guided them into a family room with a television tuned to a sports channel. Two west coast baseball teams were playing, and Craig guessed it was an afternoon game or the start of a doubleheader. One set of couch cushions was crushed from someone sitting on them, and an open bottle of a sports drink sat on the coffee table in front of the indented cushions. Next to the drink, a bag of potato chips gaped open like a beached large-mouth bass. Craig had seen enough fish after his father's trips to make the comparison.

Ryan left the television on and turned to Liz. "What is all this about?"

Craig caught an undercurrent of anger from him, as if he resented being interrupted.

"One question first. Is there anyone else in the house?"

"No."

"And you live here with Mrs. Beck and Jessica Teel?"

"Yeah. And some guy Kwan. He plays for the symphony, like Jessica. Cello or some crap. Can't really speak English."

Craig thumbed the name into his phone, aware of Liz watching him. When he finished, she turned back to Ryan. "Could you explain your relationship to Melanie Beck?"

Ryan's eyes flashed. "I don't have to explain shit to you. Now what is going on?"

Liz stared at Ryan and didn't say anything. Ryan chafed at her treatment of him, and a few moments later, faced the television to salvage his pride. He said, "I take care of stuff around here for her."

"Okay." Liz remained impassive. "Well, I'm sorry to tell you, but Melanie Beck was found dead this afternoon. She's the victim of an attack."

Ryan's head snapped around, his eyes wide. "What do you mean?"

"She was on the running trail outside the apartment she rents on the North Side. A jogger found her body."

The blood drained from Ryan's face, and he swayed slightly. "No. How is that possible?"

Liz stared at him for a few seconds. "That's what we'd like to know. Maybe we could sit down and talk about it?"

"Yeah. Right." Ryan looked about as if he was seeing the room for the first time. He saw the television, picked up the remote, and the television faded to black. He pointed at a chair and settled heavily into what was clearly his favorite spot on the couch.

"She's dead?" he asked.

"That's about the only thing we can say for sure, right now."

Craig was surprised at how gentle Liz sounded and how that tone continued into her next sentence. "But I have two things I need you to clarify. First, when you say you take care of things around here. What does that mean exactly?" She pointed at the energy drink and chips. "I mean for a caretaker, you seem to feel right at home."

Ryan stared at the coffee table, as if the snacks had magically appeared. He looked at Liz. "I live here."

"Are you and Melanie Beck in a relationship?"

Ryan tapped his fingertips on his knee. "I don't think that's any of your damn business."

Liz let the silence unspool, but Ryan was willing to wait.

"Okay," Liz said finally. "Where were you this afternoon? I need a timeline from noon until now."

"When did Melanie…" Ryan looked away. "When was she attacked?"

"Just answer the question."

His fingertips beat a short tattoo on his knee. "I had lunch here. I had some stuff to do around the house. She was supposed to come home tonight for dinner, so I cleaned up. Then I went to the batting cages. Hit some balls."

Liz was slow to answer, and Craig saw an opportunity. "Which batting cages?"

Ryan seemed annoyed that Craig could speak. "North Park. Why?"

"As Detective Timmons said, we need a timeline." Craig gauged his tone of voice. He'd been steady and deep. It felt like he was getting it right. A thought came to him about Ryan's answer. "Just interested. Why North Park? Seems a long way to go."

Ryan didn't answer right away. The pause widened until he said, "I like the drive. And those machines."

Craig thought about that. He knew there were batting cages near the airport, which was a much shorter drive, and those facilities were newer. He'd seen both locations. The cages at North Park were run down.

"You go there a lot?" Liz asked.

"Yeah. I used to play Triple-A ball. I like to keep my swing in shape."

Craig started to work out the time involved in driving from the North Park batting cages to Melanie's North Side apartment. "And what time did you leave?"

"About three-thirty."

"And where did you go afterwards?"

From how quickly Liz asked the question, Craig knew she was constructing her own timeline.

"I came back here." Ryan looked from Liz to Craig. "What's up with all this?" His eyes shifted. "You think I did this?"

"Did you?" Liz shot back.

Ryan leaped out of the couch. "Hell no. I liked Melanie. I mean, yeah, she was older than me, but I liked her. We got along great. She gave me a job."

"And bought you a new truck." Liz stared at him.

Ryan's lips tightened. "If you say so. So what?"

Craig did more math. From her driver's license, he knew Melanie was forty-six years old. He guessed Ryan was in his early thirties. It was some gap.

"Okay." Liz rose as well. "Can you give Officer Luntz your driver's license? We need proof of ID. We have a search warrant for this house. I'd like to take a look in Mrs. Beck's bedroom." She emphasized the word *Mrs.* "And while you're doing that, tell me, when was the last time you saw *Mrs.* Beck?"

Craig knew Liz was sledgehammering Ryan with the word *Mrs.*, trying to upset him enough to say something he didn't mean to.

Ryan stopped in the act of removing his driver's license from his wallet. "Yesterday morning. She had meetings downtown, and then she had some party to go to last night. That's why she was staying at her apartment."

Craig remembered Jessica Teel's statements outside Melanie's apartment. "Was that the same party where Jessica Teel was playing viola?"

Ryan held out his license to him. "Yeah. And I heard it got crazy."

Craig glanced at the West Virginia license, noting that Jessica hadn't mentioned anything unusual about the party. She also hadn't identified Kwan, he realized.

Liz shifted closer to Ryan. "How did it get crazy?"

Craig glanced at Liz, knowing he should have thought to ask that question. Liz had beaten him to it.

Ryan shrugged. "I guess Mr. Beck showed up. Melanie's ex? They got into it in front of everyone. Screaming. It was so loud the band stopped playing for a while. Then Melanie left, and when Jessica goes on break, the ex hits on her. She texted me about it. She got out of there as soon as she could."

"And you guys all live together here," Liz said slowly. "You, *Mrs.* Beck, and Jessica. And this Kwan guy. All in this house. Together. Bit cozy, isn't it?"

Ryan looked at her, and for the first time, Craig saw anger in Ryan's eyes. "Yeah. We do. What of it?"

"You guys all get along?"

"Pretty much." From the upward tilt of his words, Craig knew Ryan wasn't actually answering the question

Liz stared at Ryan as if he was a dense seventh-grader stumped by an algebra question. "All right, Mr. Telst. Why don't you show me Mrs. Beck's bedroom. We'll talk about any other rooms we might want to check after that."

Chapter Twelve

Vic arrived at daycare two minutes before closing time, ignoring a scowl from the middle-aged woman who stayed for the last pick-ups. Lettie was sitting by herself on the floor, experimenting with building blocks. The woman tapped a clock on her desk that was turned toward the doorway, its large face a reminder for parents.

"Lettie, time to go," Vic called

Lettie stood, collected the blocks, and in two trips placed them in a nearby wooden chest. That earned Lettie a spoken thank you and smile from the teacher. Vic realized he needed to try harder to get the same treatment.

Twenty minutes later they were home and Vic started dinner, Lettie in front of the television watching an Anne-approved public broadcasting show.

Six months earlier, when Vic returned to work, he and Anne developed a routine to manage dinner. They planned meals a week in advance to avoid last-minute supermarket runs, and whoever picked up Lettie cooked. Tonight was boneless chicken breasts pounded flat and sauteed in butter, white wine and garlic. As Vic prepped the ingredients, he thought about Melanie Beck, and checked his phone to see if Wroblewski had responded to his question about the two apartments that overlooked the crime scene. Nothing. He tapped out a text reminding Wroblewski to contact him.

As he laid out what he needed for a side dish of egg noodles, his phone rang.

Seeing the caller ID, he answered, "Liz, how'd it go?"

"Still here," she answered, sounding resigned. "I just finished Beck's bedroom and I'm headed down to her study."

"Anything?"

"Not really. Bedroom is pretty much the same as how you described the apartment. Just more of it. We did find her hot young guy when we got here. He's called Ryan Telst. Also calls himself the caretaker, which is one way to describe his job here, I guess."

Vic smiled. A joke from Liz was a good sign, especially after the odd conversation earlier in the afternoon. Just then, Anne walked into the kitchen, lugging her briefcase. She placed it on a kitchen chair, reached up and kissed him on the cheek.

Vic showed her his phone so she would know he was talking to Liz. She nodded and pointed upstairs, and whispered she planned to change.

As Vic watched her leave, he asked Liz, "Anything interesting on this Telst guy?"

"Oh yeah." Liz gave a dry laugh. "Ex-triple A ball player. I bet he knows his way around a baseball bat. And he was at batting practice this afternoon before the attack, but something was hinky with that. Craig caught it. He went to batting cages way over by North Park, when there's one closer. We need to timeline his day hard."

Vic thought about that. "Okay, before you leave, make sure you figure out something."

"Sure."

"If Telst is left-handed, or was a switch hitter in Triple-A."

"Why's that?"

"Wound to Beck's head was on the right side. Craig caught it. Might mean someone left-handed. We need to consider it."

"Makes sense. Our boy Craig is on his game."

"Well, he needs to work on his interviewing techniques." He told Liz about Craig and his interview with Kasey Wells. "Kasey was coming on to him, and he had no idea how to switch her off. Made him miss a couple of things."

"You mean this Wells girl finds a dead body and then comes on to the cop who interviews her? There's an operator."

"My thoughts as well."

"Oh, and we have two more people in the mix. There's a guy named Kwan who lives at Beck's house with Jessica and Ryan. He also plays for the symphony. Sounds like Beck liked to take in strays."

"Who's the other one?"

"Beck's ex-husband. Telst claims he got into a shouting argument with Melanie at a party last night."

"Let's get onto him first."

"Yeah. I'll track down his name and details tonight."

Vic squeezed his eyes shut. The number of interviews they needed to do was expanding exponentially. He needed Craig to be competent at interviewing as soon as possible. He opened his eyes to find Anne staring at him, a quizzical smile on her face. "Okay, thanks, Liz. Let's catch up in the morning."

"Yeah, about that."

Vic waited, surprised. Liz seemed to be formulating what she wanted to say. Usually, she came out with it immediately.

"I might be late. Something came up."

"Okay." Vic waited for an explanation.

"See you when I get there," Liz said quickly, and hung up.

"Something going on?" Anne asked as Vic placed his phone on the counter and, bemused, looked at the chicken breasts.

Vic turned on the burner for the frying pan, his mind preoccupied with Liz's quick drop from the phone call. "We got a murder thrown at us today. It's going to get hectic."

"Not the Melanie Beck case, is it?"

Vic stopped what he was doing and turned to her. "How did you find out about that?"

"It was on the news. Radio. The receptionist at work listens while she works. She told me about it. And everyone knows Melanie Beck."

Everyone but me, Vic thought to himself. "I'm starting to get that feeling."

"You need your A game for this one."

Vic stared at her. Anne's blue eyes twinkled.

"You're having way too much fun with this," Vic said finally.

Anne came over and hugged him. When she stepped back, she said, "I tell you what. You haven't had a murder case in three or four months. Why don't I take care of Lettie for the next couple of weeks, so you can focus on it."

"Are you sure?"

"Sure, I'm sure. You'll have the DA and mayor second-guessing you on this. You need to focus. And it's off-season for the Penguins. No evening games for me to attend. We can get back on schedule later."

Relief shot through him, and just as quickly, he felt guilty. When he'd searched for his daughter in North Dakota—and brought home his granddaughter Lettie instead—he'd known the consequences and the responsibility. He'd never given it a second thought. And yet, here he was relieved to be free of the requirements of raising her.

Anne punched him lightly on the chest. "Don't overthink it. You'll owe me later. Penguins have a minicamp next month, and I need to be there. Okay?"

"Okay," he said softly. He kissed Anne on the forehead and turned back to the frying pan. He felt disjointed. Glad for the extra time and guilty about it at the same time. He tossed a nob of butter into the frying pan and watched it skid across the surface, trailed by yellow bubbles.

The heck with it, he thought. Just find whoever killed Melanie Beck.

Chapter Thirteen

Chen Yun woke and edged up the blind of the airplane window. They were descending toward Pittsburgh, the sky a fierce orange-red, which seemed fitting for a city that once forged the world's steel. He felt prepared, if not jet lagged. He'd watched a romantic comedy after leaving Los Angeles, chosen because that genre had more dialogue. He would have preferred a British comedy, with its layered irony and sarcasm, but the American film was enough to refresh his English.

He was proud of his language skills, although it hadn't always been that way. In his first English class in college, his fluency scared him. His grandmother's warnings in his ears, he'd masked the quality of his accent and purposely missed questions on exams. He almost didn't take the second-year class, but was intrigued when he learned an American would teach. He'd never met a Westerner, and was interested to see if his fluency might survive a native speaker. He realized quickly that it could, and he reverted to making silly mistakes in class and purposely missing exam questions.

Whatever happened, he had promised his grandmother he would never stand out.

Until the day he received an invitation to tea from the statistics professor Hongzhu Tai. Unsure who Tai was, Chen warily presented himself at the professor's office at the requested time. Hongzhu was friendly and warm, and offered green tea. He still remembered how they sat facing one another on large armchairs with lace doilies decorating the backrests. The light in Tai's office was washed out and dust motes hung in the air. The low wooden table between them was glass-topped, the tea served in small white porcelain cups with blue dragons on the side. The cups were wafer thin, of a quality rarely seen, given the Red Guard's focused destruction of historical artifacts and the heirlooms of wealthy families.

"You will be wondering why I asked to see you," Tai *Laoshi* said after discussing the weather and insisting Chen use the old-fashioned teacher's honorific of *Laoshi*. Tai was in his late fifties, Chen guessed, but spoke with energy and engagement.

"I am surprised," Chen offered carefully.

Tai sipped his tea. "Your American English teacher, Hansen *Laoshi*, he and I meet twice a week. I speak a little English and wish to keep it fresh in my mind. He and I set aside that time for me to practice."

Chen nodded, unsure where the conversation might be headed.

"Hansen *Laoshi* told me about you. He asked me, teacher to teacher, what he should do with you."

"I'm not sure why he would take an interest in me." Chen sipped his tea, suppressing his nervousness.

"Ah." Tai peered at him. "He believes your English is much better than your performance in class. Much better. He wanted to know if I had any suggestions on how to," Tai switched to the English phrase, "Ferret you out." He reverted to Chinese. "But I am a statistician. I prefer facts. I asked him why he believed in your abilities, and he said you instantly understood his instructions for classwork, but your comprehension doesn't translate to your exam performance. An interesting problem for me, don't you think?"

Chen still remembered the dread he felt at that moment, despite his confidence about his mediocre test performances and purposeful fumbling of the language in class.

"I proposed a solution," Tai *Laoshi* continued, "To test his instincts. I asked to review your quizzes and tests before he returned them to you. To see how you performed."

Chen saw a metaphorical door offering an escape and reached for it. "Then you are aware of my average performance. And my question remains, why would you have any reason to talk to me?"

Tai Laoshi's eyes twinkled. "As I said, I am a statistician. You must remember that. I reviewed your test answers, and I discovered something interesting."

Chen sensed the metaphorical door slam shut.

"There is a pattern to your incorrect answers," Tai continued. "Almost always, the fourth question on written tests is wrong. It is as if, as you take the test, you remember that you must camouflage your knowledge. In the multiple-choice answers, it is frequently every third answer that is incorrect, no matter how easy or hard. Now, a student truly struggling with a language would make random mistakes, not produce a repeating pattern. And the pattern certainly wouldn't recur, test after test."

Chen still remembered how the floor of the room seemed to open like a funnel, the slanted edges slick with gravity. He wanted to say the man was mistaken. He glanced at the office door, gauging the distance.

"As a result," Tai *Laoshi* continued, as if they were still discussing the weather. "Hansen *Laoshi* and I decided you might enjoy this book. And if you enjoy it, Hansen *Laoshi* would be happy to meet with you privately to discuss it. In English, of course. But this is completely up to you."

Tai *Laoshi* placed a hardback book on the table next to their tea cups. Chen didn't know where it came from, up his sleeve? Tai placed the book so the spine was toward Chen, and he read the title: *The Grapes of Wrath*, by John Steinbeck. Chen looked up to see Tai studying him.

Two forces clashed inside Chen. Was it a trap? Yet he wanted to read that book. Apart from the Zane Grey novels, it was one of five or six his grandmother hid from the Red Guards. Years earlier, she had asked him to read passages out loud to her. He wanted to know the ending. Without breaking eye contact, he picked up the book and slid it into his briefcase as if it was never between them on the table.

"I could attempt it," Chen said.

"Good," Tai *Laoshi* said gently. "And you will meet Hansen *Laoshi* here. I believe you will find it more private. Just tell him when you have finished reading. Now, I have another question."

Chen waited.

"How is your father?"

The question, after the incident with the book, was almost too much to take. Tai saw his discomfort and waved a hand.

"Your father and I, we met at college. Here. He was studying mathematics, and I was earning an advanced degree in statistics." Tai sipped his tea, giving Chen time to recover. "We spent many evenings together, he and I, discussing our futures and the future of China. Perhaps there was *biru* involved." His pronunciation of the word 'beer' ended with a checked tone, a mannerism unique to Sichuan province. "I tried to convince him that teaching mathematics in high school was a waste of his talent, but he was certain of himself. He wanted to nurture the best students. Prepare them for college. He felt the Party would need mathematicians."

Chen remembered thinking that perhaps this topic was at the bottom of Tai *Laoshi's* willingness to speak to him, to take such a risk. After all, if Tai *Laoshi* knew his father, it was likely he also knew the history of his family and the quality of his grandmother's English. Perhaps the unconscious patterns in his quiz answers only confirmed Tai's suspicion that Chen's English was stronger than he pretended.

"How is he, your father?"

Tai's question, Chen felt, was genuine. Someone asking after a friend. Wanting to know, hoping he was well.

Chen told him of his father's work at the steel mill. His job unloading iron ingots from rail cars, using nothing more than his hands and a basket. He didn't mention his father's clash with the Party Secretary at the high school where his father taught and how that led to his father being required to write self-criticisms. All because his father maintained a high standard in his classroom and expected his students to meet it, failing those who didn't. The Party Secretary had seen that standard as dividing the students, as applying old ways to new problems, instead of finding new ways to meet new problems. There was no point telling Tai *Laoshi* that story. Every Chinese person had a similar one to tell.

Instead, Chen said, "The work doesn't suit him. I believe he would be better teaching in a classroom. But the Party is wiser about these things than me."

"Indeed," Tai replied.

Chen heard just the whisper of sarcasm in the word.

"The next time you see him," Tai continued, "Tell him I said hello. Tell him I would like to meet him, if he believes the moment might be right. That I miss our nights of discussion and *biru*."

Chen noted how delicately Tai chose his words. This was a curse on all of them. Party policy constantly changed the fortunes of people and their families. Those vacillating circumstances damaged long-term friendships, as people once friends, once equals, found themselves subordinate or superior to one another. In and out of favor. Tai was empathizing with his father's position and sending the message that, in respect of their old friendship, he was open to meeting his father, if Chen's father felt up to it.

Chen never did deliver that message. A month later, his father collapsed under a loaded basket of iron ore. The factory sent his body home with a small sum to cover the cost of his burial. His father's death was Chen's first brutal lesson in how the Party sapped people's strength. Took their vitality. How they drained away the will to fight. Made people surrender.

It reminded him of what he'd seen in Bingwen's eyes, in that moment when he told Bingwen he must return to Shanghai.

And now he had arrived in Pittsburgh, where his goal was to produce that look in the eyes of yet someone else.

The airplane bumped as it landed on the runway.

Chen felt a warmth of excitement, tinged by disgust. He needed to resolve the contradictions inside himself. The thrill of a new city and a new case. His revulsion toward the actual task.

He knew he couldn't do this job much longer. He didn't have it in him. He thought of his son, of the advantages his family would lose if he quit. He couldn't stand that thought. He chastised himself to be patient. Perhaps a solution would present itself.

The airplane trundled across the runway. Outside, the burning sky of dawn gave way to flat, hard, steel-gray clouds. A clutch of raindrops slapped the window and streamed away.

First, find the hotel, then a shower.

Afterwards, visit a restaurant run by a man whose uncle was jailed in Guangdong, an uncle nabbed by Guangdong police for smuggling Western brand-name merchandise from Hong Kong.

He would give the jailed man's nephew a choice. Help Chen, and perhaps his uncle's sentence would be shortened. Don't help, and the sentence would lengthen.

A knife edge of a choice.

Chen stared at the hard, steel-gray clouds, believing it was the type of choice his country was founded upon.

Chapter Fourteen

Vic slid into his desk chair at seven the next morning. He reviewed his emails, and read Liz's preliminary report from her interviews the night before. Her search of Melanie Beck's house had found little, but she did have some choice things to say about Ryan Telst. Vic knew those comments would soften before she submitted her official report.

Liz's research into Holden Beck, Melanie Beck's ex-husband, was pithy and, to Vic's eyes, sadly predictable. Holden had grown up in a wealthy enclave just north of the city and attended a private school. He'd matriculated at a private liberal arts college in Ohio, not the east coast, suggesting his grades were subpar. Despite needing five years to graduate, within the following six years he'd landed a prestigious job at a company that offered private banking and investment services to people with more than one million dollars to invest. Landing that job smelled of family contacts and connections. There was nothing in Holden's background to suggest he deserved it. On the company's website, Holden's prematurely gray hair was long and swept back in a wave, a style that might suggest bravado on someone in their twenties or early thirties, but for a pink-faced and well-fed man sailing through his fifties, reeked of desperation.

Craig slung his sport coat over the back of his desk chair.

Vic nodded to him. "Just reading Liz's notes from yesterday. We need to interview this Holden Beck."

Craig grinned. "I read them last night. I might want to add a few things."

Vic sensed Craig wanted to add more than just a few things, but didn't want to criticize Liz. "We can talk on the way. With this traffic, it'll take forty minutes to reach Beck's business. They should be open by then."

"Do you want me to call and tell him we're coming?"

Vic considered it. This was always a question, but in his experience, showing up made it hard for someone to dodge them. "No. Let's just head over. When we get close, you can call and ask if he's in today. I guess there's a chance he begged off work, given what happened to Melanie. But let's get going."

Creeping along in rush hour traffic, Vic glanced at Craig. "I'd like you to run the interview. After yesterday, you know the key requirement for today. We need a timeline of Holden's day yesterday and proof he was where he says he was."

"Sure."

Vic thought Craig's voice was a bit tight. "If you're unsure about anything, just toss it back to me. Okay?"

Craig nodded.

"Anything we can pick up on his relationship with Melanie Beck is gravy. But that comes second to the timeline." Vic nudged the car forward a couple of yards. "Anything you want to add to Liz's update from last night?"

Craig was quiet for a moment. "Two things," he said finally. He pushed his glasses up his nose. "The first is from the local officer who let us in. He had nothing good to say about Holden Beck. The second is Jessica Teel. When we talked to her outside Melanie's apartment, she didn't mention the third roommate. Kwan, I think his name is. She only mentioned Ryan. I just thought that was odd."

Vic turned Craig's observation in his mind. "Running into us upset Teel. She might have just forgotten." Vic changed lanes, using a slow-moving van as a blocker. The traffic picked up speed now that they were inside a tunnel. "But don't forget that point. It might help explain something later. And give Beck's office a call. Let's see if he's in."

Holden Beck's company took up four floors in a glass-sheathed skyscraper near the Point. Vic watched Craig out of the corner of his eye as they crossed the lobby, trying to gauge how confident he was about the interview. In the elevator, he gave up. In some ways, it didn't matter. They had too many leads to follow up, and Craig needed to find his way. But Vic just couldn't shake feeling responsible for him.

The elevator opened onto the thirtieth floor, and he and Craig pushed through double glass doors to a high-fronted receptionist's desk. Vic showed his identification and asked if Holden Beck was available. The receptionist, a middle-aged woman with perfect hair, aimed a professional smile at him.

"You called a little while ago?"

"We did."

Vic liked that Craig answered her question. It was better to enter interviews in an assertive frame of mind.

The woman gestured to a small sitting area and lifted her phone. Within a minute, a young woman opened one of the doors to their right and gestured for them to follow. She held the door open for Craig and flashed him a quick smile, and once they were inside, led them along a hall. She opened another door onto a surprisingly long room with offices against each wall. Between the offices was a row of low-walled cubicles for assistants and administrators. Vic disliked the obvious status divisions. The offices on the right were large with window views of the city, while the offices on the opposite wall were cramped and windowless. As the young woman led them wordlessly toward the far end of the room, Vic thought about people dedicating years of their lives to simply moving from a cube to a windowless office and finally to an office with an outdoor view. The thought depressed him.

The young woman stopped at the far corner of the building and spoke through the doorway into what was obviously the largest office on the floor. Her face was tight and business-like. Hearing a grunted response, she waved Craig and Vic inside. Vic saw her face soften when she looked at Craig. Vic stepped aside so Craig could enter first, wondering how Craig rated this kind of attention from young women. He also considered the reasons why Holden's assistant felt the need to manufacture a stern face when she talked to Holden.

Standing behind his desk, Holden looked like his photo on the company's website. Well fed, florid, his neck spilling over the collar of his shirt, even the desperate swirl of long gray hair. But he did have presence, Vic thought. Or perhaps he just radiated arrogance. It was hard to tell.

Craig introduced himself, and Vic did the same. As they finished the introductions, Holden led them to a small conference table in the corner where the windows met. Holden, Vic noticed, was quick to take one of the chairs. He might be on his home turf, but he seemed to need the confidence that came from familiarity.

Once they were seated, Craig said, "We're very sorry for your loss, Mr. Beck."

Beck stared at Craig for a moment and glanced at Vic. He seemed surprised that Craig was taking the lead, but didn't comment on it.

"Well, we've been divorced for several years. But thank you."

Craig followed up. "We'll need to ask you a few questions, if you don't mind, given your relationship with the deceased."

Vic thought he heard a deeper timbre to Craig's voice, something more commanding and mature, but it wasn't fully formed. He slid out his notebook and was surprised to see Craig do the same. The day before, Craig had used his phone to record his interviews. Vic hadn't liked it, but avoided mentioning it so he didn't overwhelm Craig with suggestions. Craig had decided on his own to use a notebook.

Beck stared at Craig. "I doubt you know what my relationship with my wife was."

"I didn't mean it in that way," Craig replied evenly. "I meant that you and her were once married and would know each other well. Nothing more. Unless there is something about your relationship with Melanie Beck now that you'd like to tell us?"

Beck blinked. Vic fought down a smile. So far, so good.

Craig tapped his pen on the tabletop. "I think to start, Mr. Beck, we'd appreciate it if you could take us through your activities yesterday, where you were, and what you did." Craig opened his notebook, waiting.

"Yeah, uh, okay." Beck licked his lips. "Well, I was here all day. Up until about six-thirty."

"So you didn't leave your offices at any time?"

"Well, I had a lunch meeting with a client."

"We'll need the name of that client and the restaurant," Craig said easily. "And about what time did you return to these offices?"

"I don't know. About two?"

"Good, and you were here in your office until you left at six-thirty?"

"Why would I leave?"

"Perhaps…" Craig glanced through the windows, "you could tell us what you were doing during those hours?"

"Sure." Beck frowned. "After I got back from lunch, we had a staff meeting that went maybe an hour. I had another client come in at three-thirty. That was maybe another hour. After that, I caught up on emails and made some phone calls. Worked on a presentation for a possible client. Talked to a couple of people on the phone."

"Who was that?"

Beck mentioned two names and explained they were on the floor.

"To be clear, you were in your office from about four-thirty to six-thirty?"

"Like I said. A presentation for a new client and catching up on emails."

Craig nodded. Vic wondered if Craig caught the subtle way Beck didn't answer the question. Vic wasn't sure what to make of it. Innocent people often glided past direct answers as easily as guilty people just because they were confident in their innocence. They didn't feel the need to be precise. He glanced through the office door. Beck's assistant was sitting outside, her head down, and on the far side of the desk, he saw another open office door and someone hunched over their computer, working. Leaving the floor without being noticed wouldn't be easy.

"Where are you in this investigation?" Beck asked abruptly.

"It's just early stages." Craig gave him a light smile.

Again, Vic was impressed. Craig wasn't intimidated, despite the way Holden's answers grew sharper with each question.

Vic decided to push a bit more. "I was wondering if you could tell us a little about your relationship with Melanie Beck, I mean, since the divorce.

How often you see each other, how you get along."

Beck turned to him, and Vic thought he saw the man's face flush.

"I don't think that's any of your damn business."

"Your ex-wife was murdered, Mr. Beck. I would think you might want to cooperate completely with our investigation." Craig's voice remained light and even.

"I am damn cooperating," Beck shot back.

"Let's do it this way." Vic slowed his words to defuse the situation. "When was the last time you spoke to Melanie?"

At the sound of his ex-wife's first name, Holden relaxed. He looked out of the window, although it was obvious he wasn't seeing anything. "A couple of nights ago. We were at a party together. Fundraiser. I saw her there."

Vic studied Holden's face. "And how would you characterize your relationship with her at that time?"

Holden focused on him. "Oh, I get it. You heard. Yeah, we had an argument. She was being stupid. It got out of hand."

"Screaming…was how one person put it," Craig said mildly.

"It wasn't that bad." The sharpness crept back into Holden's words. Vic wasn't sure if that was to minimize how bad the fact of an argument sounded or to feel better about himself.

Craig opened his hands. "Just repeating how someone else characterized it."

"Yeah. Let me guess who. The boy-toy Ryan? Let me explain something to you." Holden glared at Craig. "Melanie wants me at all these fundraisers, not our little boy Ryan. Why? Because I can carry on a conversation. Make quips. I actually stay up-to-date on the news. Little Ryan has nothing to say beyond the best techniques to steal second base. Which is pretty funny, because I looked up his stats, and in three years in Triple-A, he stole second a total of five times. Thrown out twice. So yeah, that's the level we're dealing with. And that means every time Melanie wanted to go to a fundraiser, I got the call. And you know what? I was sick of it. I told her if she's screwing Ryan, she can damn well bring *him* to the damn things. They're already screwing in my damn house, which she got in the divorce. What am I? The rent-an-adult? I told her that, and she started on this thing that I owed her. *Owed* her? She already took my house and half my damn money. So yeah, we got into it."

"And what happened?"

"She left." Holden waved his hand in disgust. "She couldn't take it."

"And that's when you started talking to Jessica Teel?"

Vic was impressed. When Craig asked the question, his voice was mild and completely innocent.

"Who?" Holden frowned.

"The viola player." Craig was somehow deadpan. "At the same party?"

"Oh, for Christ's sake. Her? I was just bored."

Vic thought it was more than that, given that Jessica lived in Melanie's house. It smelled of a petty revenge. Vic happened to glance toward Holden's assistant, just in time to see her roll her eyes. She was looking down at her desk, and he realized she could overhear them. He wondered if the stern look she'd used when she announced their arrival to Holden was to appear unfriendly. Perhaps Holden had a reputation among the young women on the floor and interpreted their polite smiles as a come-on. Interesting, but it had little to do with Melanie's murder.

"If you were attending parties with Melanie at her request, I guess that means your divorce was friendly?"

Vic realized that Craig was following a more important line of thought.

"For her, sure. Did you miss the part where she got the house and half my money?"

Craig glanced at Vic. He knew what Craig was asking. Vic leaned forward and extended his hand. "Thanks, Mr. Beck. I think that's all we need for now."

Holden popped upright as if his bus was passing him without stopping. "Good. I've got things to do."

Craig and Vic stood as well. As Craig shook hands, Vic looked around the office. He noticed drawn blinds at the top of the windows that overlooked the office. As they shuffled out of the office, Vic looked back and said to Holden, his hand on the doorknob, "Open or closed?"

Holding was standing behind his desk, reading something. He didn't look up. "Closed." He almost barked the word.

Vic pulled the door closed and turned to Holden's assistant. "Excuse me."

The young woman looked up with a glance at Holden's door. Vic pointed to the nameplate attached to the low wall of her cube. "You're Karen Daley?" She nodded.

"Just a quick question. I noticed there are blinds on all of the interior windows in Mr. Becks' office. Does he use them?"

Karen stared at Holden's office for a moment, as if it gave her a bad taste in her mouth. Vic saw Craig drift closer to listen to the exchange.

"Sometimes. When he doesn't want to be disturbed."

"How about yesterday afternoon?"

Karen focused on him. "I don't know. I wasn't here."

"You had the day off?" Craig asked.

"No. Holden asked me to sub for an assistant to one of the other partners. I was on a different floor. Mr. Kreen. He's nice."

Vic understood why she made the last point. "Then you don't know what Mr. Beck was doing yesterday afternoon?"

She shook her head, but swiveled in her chair and pointed at the office directly across the hall. "But you could ask Jack. I'm pretty sure he was here."

"Thanks." Vic gave her a smile.

A few minutes later, as the elevator whisked them to the ground floor, Vic looked at Craig. "Nice job on the interview."

"Thanks." Craig looked lost in thought. "Did you see what was on the end wall, just past Holden's office?"

"Yes." Vic watched the floor numbers above the elevator door blink on and off. "Exit door to a stairwell. And yesterday afternoon Karen was absent and Jack was in meetings."

"That means we have no idea if Holden was actually in his office, right about when Mrs. Beck was attacked."

"Exactly." Vic watched a couple more floors slip by. "But he'd need to get from here to the North Side."

"Can't be more than fifteen minutes by car. You could probably walk it in less than half an hour."

"Doable," Vic said slowly.

Craig shuffled his feet. Vic knew the tell. Craig was excited. It wasn't a break in the case, but the idea was seductive. However, Vic knew breaking alibis was hard. "We need proof of him outside the building during the time window." Vic turned to him. "I guess it's worth taking the time to find where he parks his car and check if they have video. If his car leaves, we have an angle. That's where to start."

"On it." Craig grinned.

Vic smiled to himself. He'd been that charged up about his cases once. Perhaps he still was. It just didn't show as much.

Chapter Fifteen

hen Yun crossed a bridge high above the Monongahela River and entered a town called Homestead, just south of Pittsburgh. He followed the main road to a strip mall on the edge of town and turned into the parking lot. He'd read of steelworkers fighting private police at a nearby steel mill many years earlier, the several-day battle ending with more than a dozen dead and the local militia called in to retake the mill.

The thought reminded him of his early schooling, when he'd repeatedly heard the comparison that American capitalists enslaved their workers, while the Chinese encouraged their struggle. As proof, his teachers always pointed to the Chinese flag, explaining how the workers were proudly represented by a star, alongside three equally-sized stars, each representing the peasants, the petit bourgeoisie, and the loyal national bourgeoisie.

Even then, as a child, the comparison angered him. He knew what the Wuhan steel mill was doing to his father. His father's chronic exhaustion, wasted frame, and slumped shoulders. How his father had no way to leave that work.

When discussing those four stars on the flag, his teachers always ended the lecture by pointing to the flag's fifth star, the largest, explaining how it symbolized the leadership of the Chinese Communist Party. A leadership of equals, they always said.

His grandmother had taught him a phrase he considered apt. An English phrase with a subtle, barbed meaning. "Some are more equal than others," she liked to say, referring to the Party.

He pulled his car into a parking space.

The phrase stuck with him after he closed the car door and crossed the parking lot.

The restaurant was tiny, just two booths to his left and a counter that ran along the rear of the room. A cash register stood to the right near the kitchen entrance. The back wall was filled with backlit photographs of Chinese dishes. They spread down the wall from the ceiling to a waist-high shelf, dwarfing a small pass-through to the kitchen. The florescent lights gave the entire space a beat-down and exhausted feeling.

As Chen approached the counter, a stocky, middle-aged Chinese woman stepped from the back, eyed him up and down, and retreated into the kitchen. A few sharp phrases of Cantonese drifted through the pass-through.

A Chinese man with a belly grown of sampling his own cooking exited the kitchen. His brown eyes were set as hard as the stains on his apron. A mole, the size of a one-yuan coin, glared from above his right eyebrow. He stopped at the center of the serving counter, beefy forearms crossed, facing Chen.

Chen knew the woman had identified him as a Chinese police officer. Some people had the knack. He guessed that his leather jacket and stocky build were a giveaway, but it always had something to do with attitude. He took his time getting to the counter. He wanted Yiptou Ng's own imagination to unbalance him a bit.

"You are Yiptou Ng," Chen said after giving them both a few seconds to get used to the situation.

"Perhaps."

Chen drew a passport photograph of Yiptou from his jacket pocket, thoughtfully provided to him by Tanming. He placed it on the counter. "Of course you are." Chen smiled. From his other pocket, he produced a second photograph, this one an official police photograph of a convict. "And this is your uncle."

Yiptou's resistance drained from his eyes. He looked up from the photograph, lips compressed, and waited for Chen to speak.

Ten minutes later, Chen was back in his car, listening to a gentle Chinese voice on his phone as it guided him toward Carnegie Mellon University.

He hadn't expected much resistance and didn't get any. If Yiptou refused to help, his entire extended family in Guangdong would hear about it within a matter of hours. Yiptou would be ostracized for abandoning them. It was a risk no Chinese could accept.

Yiptou would start watching their target in an hour or so. Good. Barely in Pittsburgh for three hours, and surveillance was underway.

Carnegie Mellon University would provide him with two more people. They were graduate students and leaders of the CMU chapter of the Chinese Student and Scholar Association. Most major universities had CSSA chapters, all aligned with the Chinese embassy and by extension, the Party. While the CSSA's purpose was to support and help the Chinese studying in America, the Party used the network to track the activities of overseas Chinese students and visiting scholars. As a rule, Chen avoided CSSA contacts. He'd found that chapter leaders fell into two groups: the overzealous Party advocate or the nakedly career-minded. It was unusual to find a chapter leader who was thoughtful and deliberate and understood the need for a low profile.

This time he had no choice. Pittsburgh's once-booming Chinese Community was too well integrated into American life and culture, too many generations removed from the Mainland. One of them was even a well-known Hollywood and Broadway actress.

It didn't get much more American than that.

So the CSSA it was. That and a tight rein.

Chapter Sixteen

B y lunchtime, Craig had canvassed the four parking garages nearest Holden Beck's offices, and no one remembered a navy-blue BMW seven series that parked regularly or held a monthly lease. That meant Holden parked somewhere else, because a seven series was a car people noticed. Not because it was flamboyant, but for its controlled and muscular elegance. And people remembered someone with money who felt no need to advertise the fact.

Craig wondered if Holden owned a second vehicle they had missed during their search of the vehicle database. He broke off his search to visit an optometrist, and after an eye test and some discussion with the doctor, ordered contact lenses. They felt like an impulse purchase. Afterwards, he bought a hot dog from a downtown vendor and ate while staring at his phone, trying to identify the other parking garages near Holden's work.

There were none, so he tried a different point of view. If Holden didn't park for convenience, how would he choose a garage?

He finished his hot dog and wiped mustard from his fingers, thinking about the cost of the contact lenses. As he tossed the napkin into a garbage can, the answer came to him.

Money.

The single word was a strobe light. If Holden managed money for a living and drove a car that smelled of money, wouldn't he park somewhere connected to money? And one garage literally did. Four blocks from Holden's offices was the only garage with a connecting door to The Duquesne Club, the city's most prestigious business club. All of the city's business leaders were members. Since the late 1800s, the club had hosted two presidents and a British prince. The club would be a happy hunting ground for new clients, and four blocks was a short walk to Holden's office. After work, the club was the perfect place for drinks and dinner with a client, his car only a short walk through the club's private door into the parking garage. And if the weather was bad or the drinks too stiff, well, the club's guest rooms were perfect for an overnight stay.

Craig started for the garage before he finished his line of thought. Fifteen minutes later, a security guard led him onto the fifth floor and pointed to Holden's BMW, parked in its usual spot.

Twenty minutes later, he had a copy of security footage from the afternoon of Melanie Beck's death in his pocket, given to him by the same security guard. All it cost him was a few vague answers to questions about possible job openings at the Allegheny County Police.

The footage showed Holden's BMW smoothly—with an almost oily grace—leaving the parking garage a little after four o'clock on the day of Melanie's death. It also showed the car returning just before six.

Somehow, Holden had slipped out of his office.

They would need a warrant to obtain the specific times Holden used his lease card to log in and out of the garage, but Craig was sure the footage would be enough to obtain the warrant.

Outside, he called Vic.

"Vic, I found something," he said quickly, when Vic answered.

"The garage?" Vic's voice was distant, almost disembodied.

"Yes. It isn't near his offices. It's the one on Liberty Avenue that connects to the Duquesne Club. And guess what?"

"What?"

"Day of Melanie's death, Holden drove the car out and back right in the time window Melanie Beck was killed."

A moment of silence. "Good find."

"Thanks." Craig heard a slight crack in his own voice, and it annoyed him. He was trying to sound calm, as if breakthroughs like this were routine for him. "I'll head back now. A security guard gave me a copy of the security footage."

"No. You're outside the garage?"

"Yes."

"Liz and I will pick you up. We can time how long it takes to get from that garage to the trail where Melanie Beck was killed. We're headed over there now anyway."

"What happened?"

Vic chuckled through the phone. "Well, you found something that might break this case wide open. There's that. The other thing is, do you remember that apartment that overlooked the crime scene?"

"I remember."

"Right. Sergeant Wroblewski got back to me. He did get an answer when they canvassed those apartments. A woman. Said she didn't see anything. I thought we should go over and ask again. Stay outside the garage, and we'll pick you up. Give us twenty minutes."

Craig ended the call and had to stop himself from punching the air. He'd had breakthroughs before, but they were about finding a way to unlock a victim's phone or discovering a stray hair at a crime scene. Nothing like this. They'd caught Holden Beck in a flat lie. And he knew the distance from the parking garage to the crime scene was less than fifteen minutes. Timing it would prove Holden was a suspect in the murder of his ex-wife.

This and contact lenses, he thought, grinning.

Money talks.

Chapter Seventeen

Vic spotted Craig on the sidewalk outside the parking garage, standing at an intersection with a traffic light. Craig was shuffling from foot to foot, too excited to keep still. Vic had to smile as he pulled the car up to the curb. Craig had the right to be elated, he thought. He'd done well.

Craig piled into the back seat of the car. Once the door was shut, he leaned forward. "Want me to time the distance?"

"Go for it." In the rearview mirror, Vic watched Craig slide out his phone, his fingers dancing on the screen. He glanced at the traffic lights and saw they were red.

Liz twisted around in her seat. "Good find, Craig. I mean the parking garage."

Craig looked up from his phone. "Yeah. I thought about money and remembered this garage is attached to the Duquesne Club. My Dad was on the local protection detail when Bush visited the Club. He told me about the door to the garage. Made sense for a guy like Beck to be a Club member."

"We'll make a detective out of you yet." Liz shifted back around in her seat.

In the rear-view mirror, Vic saw satisfaction flash through Craig's eyes.

The traffic light turned green. Vic timed his movement into traffic and took the next left toward the North Side and the Heinz Loft Apartments.

As he drove, it occurred to him that was the first time Liz had spoken since she arrived at work following her appointment that morning. He needed to ask her about that, because it was out of character. Silence didn't suit her.

Sergeant Wroblewski had identified two apartments that overlooked the crime scene, one on the third floor and another on the fourth. Wroblewski's team had canvassed both apartments, finding no one home on the third floor and a woman in the fourth-floor apartment. She was the resident who claimed not to have seen anything.

Vic, Liz, and Craig took the elevator to the third floor and knocked on the apartment door to find no one home again. After a decision to check again that evening to confirm the person worked during the day and wasn't home, they moved to the fourth floor.

Like the first apartment, this one was at the end of the hallway farthest from the elevator, tucked against the eastern corner of the building. Vic lifted his hand to knock and stopped. Through the door came the strains of a violin, the music slow, complex, and moving. It was a new sound to Vic, and he dropped his hand.

"What is that?" Vic couldn't help himself.

Liz was frowning. "A violin?"

"Wait." Craig held up his hand, his eyes burning. "Wait." He whispered the repeated word.

All three listened. To Vic, the song, or whatever it was, flowed on. He was surprised to feel himself being drawn in. It was magnetic. He leaned toward the door to catch every note.

"It's sad," Liz said softly.

"Mournful." Craig's ear was cocked to the door, his hand raised and index finger extended, as if he wanted to conduct.

"Yeah." Liz closed her eyes. "Mournful. I get the difference."

"It's the Chaconne." Craig looked from Vic to Liz. "Bach. It's the hardest violin solo to play. The longest."

Vic linked the pieces of what Craig was saying. "This is classical music?" Craig nodded, entranced.

Vic shook his head. Maybe it was. He thumped on the door, and both Liz and Craig sagged back, as if their earphones had been yanked out.

The music stopped, the silence sounding out of place. He knocked again.

The door opened on the chain, and Vic stepped forward, holding up his ID. The woman at the door looked Chinese to him, although he could never separate Chinese from Japanese or Korean.

"Detective Vic Lenoski." He held the woman's gaze, and she didn't look away. "I'm with the Allegheny County Police. We're investigating a crime near here, and we'd like to talk to you. Can we come in?"

Vic found her continued gaze unnerving, but tried not to show it.

"You may." She closed the door, the safety chain clinked, and the door reopened. The woman stepped against the wall to let them enter. She nodded down the hall. "We can talk in the living room."

Her accent was British, something he'd missed in the woman's first response. Vic swept past her, automatically thinking five-six, thin, long hair swept into a bun and held by two yellow pencils. He caught a whiff of something. Sandalwood soap, perhaps? As he entered the living room, he glanced over his shoulder. Past Liz's shoulder, he saw Craig stop in front of the woman and say something he couldn't hear. Her eyes warmed, and she looked down, a small smile on her lips. Vic blinked. Craig wasn't wearing his glasses. They'd disappeared.

"What the hell are you doing, Vic?"

Vic looked at Liz and realized he had blocked the entrance to the living room.

"Sorry." He stepped forwards and pivoted to absorb the space. The layout was similar to Melanie Beck's apartment, with large windows overlooking the Allegheny River and, directly across from the windows, a breakfast bar separating the kitchen from the living room. A long couch occupied one wall, a quilt, and pillow neatly folded at the far end. This time, however, Vic had only counted two closed doors as he walked the hallway from the door to the living room, not including the opening to the kitchen. "A one-bedroom apartment, then," he thought to himself.

Liz crossed to the windows and looked outside. "Overlooks the scene."

The young woman entered the room, followed by Craig.

Vic studied a stick-like metal stand a few feet from the window, holding sheet music. A violin stood on a separate stand next to it, the bow resting on the same ledge that held the sheet music.

"That was you playing?" Vic asked the woman, now that they all stood in the living room.

She studied him, and Vic realized the question was silly. She was the only person in the apartment.

"Of course," she said, managing not to sound as if she was making fun of him.

"And you are?" Vic asked, feeling the question was clumsy.

"I'm Liling Liang. I use the English name Eileen. Perhaps Eileen Liang to you, if that is easier."

"And you live here?"

"I do."

Vic introduced Liz and Craig and was surprised to see her hold out a hand to Craig. They shook, studying each other like gallery patrons admiring a new art piece. It took Craig some effort to drop his hand, and she was slow to look away from him and back to Vic.

"Craig." Liz said it under her breath, loud enough for Vic to hear. He almost missed it, as he was preoccupied, tracking down the source of a soft, rhythmic ticking.

"Eileen is with the symphony," Craig said to the room, then turned to her. "I saw you play last season. You lead the second violins."

She turned back to him, the small smile back. "A cultured policeman. How unexpected." Vic heard gentle teasing under the words.

"What is that?" Vic waved a hand at the room. "The ticking."

"Ah." Eileen crossed the room and lifted her phone from the windowsill. Her long fingers danced across the face, and the clicking stopped. "Electronic metronome. Tool of the trade, I'm afraid."

"Right." Vic carefully didn't glance at Liz. He felt she might be suppressing a smile and didn't want to see it. Vic turned the facts in his mind. What were the odds. Melanie Beck, president of the symphony, attacked and killed within sight of an apartment inhabited by one of the symphony's violinists. Whatever a second violinist was. "We'd like to ask you a few questions. It shouldn't take long."

Eileen moved away from the window and back into Craig's orbit. It was as if she felt safer there. "Yes?"

"As you've probably heard, Melanie Beck was the victim of a crime two days ago. It happened within view of this window. Were you home at the time?"

Eileen considered the question. "I was questioned about this before. A uniformed policeman."

"Yes, but that was right after the crime, and we were wondering if you might have remembered something else. Perhaps you could tell us what you were doing between three-thirty and six o'clock two days ago?"

Eileen glanced at Craig. "I was here. Practicing."

Liz pointed at the window. "At the same place? Beside the window?"

Eileen turned to Liz as if she was seeing her for the first time. "I believe I was closer to the kitchen counter. I move around. It depends on my mood. It is sunny today, and I wanted to practice the Chaconne. Somehow the contrast of sunlight helps me interpret the depths of that particular piece."

"It establishes a breadth, a scale, maybe, between happiness and sadness." Craig's voice was gentle, thoughtful.

"Exactly." Eileen searched Craig's face, her eyes probing. Craig didn't flinch from her gaze.

Vic stared at Craig, unsure what he meant. And where were his glasses?

"Okay, that's nice and all." Liz didn't hide the annoyance in her voice. "The question is whether you saw anything. Anything at all. I mean, these windows aren't exactly high up the wall." She stepped next to the kitchen counter. "Even from here, I can see that gap in the shrubs and the running trail." She looked at Craig. "That's the scene, right?"

Vic decided what Craig did with his glasses was his business. "That's the scene." He looked at Eileen. "Even if you were standing here, you can see the place where Mrs. Beck was attacked."

Eileen studied Vic, and once again, he had the sense that she was making a decision about the best way to respond. He also sensed a tightness about her now, but he wasn't sure if that was because she was nervous or angry at Liz's suggestion that she might be lying.

"Unfortunately, when I practice a piece I know well, like this one, I often close my eyes. I see very little, but the notes I am playing. Later, I did see the flashing lights of emergency vehicles. But that was after I finished practicing."

Vic studied her. She was wearing jeans and a loose sweatshirt. Her feet were bare. Clothes anyone might wear to practice. He didn't know what to do with her British accent. It was so incongruous. He glanced again at the window. "Miss Liang, right?" He hoped he hadn't mangled her last name too badly. "The victim of this crime was a leader of the symphony where you play. You must have known her. We're trying to find out what happened. Someone needs to pay for this crime. Please, is there anything you can tell us that might help us?"

Eileen's face shifted, and Vic thought he saw sadness shadow her features. "I wish I could, detective. I knew Mrs. Beck well. She convinced me to come here from London and audition. She personally offered me my job. But I was engrossed in playing. You have to understand, this is my job. I practice every day. It is all-consuming. The simplest failure, and I lose my position."

Vic studied her face, but couldn't see anything in her expression that told him he should press.

"Okay." Vic avoided using her last name, so he didn't insult her by mispronouncing it. He rummaged in his sport coat pocket, found a business card, and placed it on the breakfast counter. "If you think of anything, please give me a call."

Eileen inclined her head. "Of course."

Vic, Liz and Craig took the elevator down to the parking lot and climbed into the car in silence. Vic didn't start the engine.

"What do you think?" Vic glanced at Liz, his gaze drifting around the parking lot.

"Beats me." Liz fell silent for a moment. "She can see the crime scene, no question." She glanced at Craig. "Not sure you could, without your glasses. But she didn't deny being home. And I can never figure out what people with English accents are really saying."

Vic started the engine, his gaze coming to rest on a rusty blue compact sitting in the corner of the parking lot. It was backed into its space, the driver's window cracked, a man sitting low behind the wheel.

"Okay." Vic pulled out of his space, but turned in the opposite direction from the exit. In his peripheral vision, he saw Liz glance at him, frowning. He circled past the rusty blue car. The man behind the wheel was so low in his seat Vic only saw enough to know he was Asian and had a mole the size of a quarter above his right eye.

"What's with him?" Liz had caught Vic's maneuver.

"Beats me. A guy sitting in his car. A crime scene. I don't know."

"Delivery driver? Look, we got leads to run down. A guy who's good with a baseball bat and another guy who lied about where he was. And he's the angry ex-husband."

Vic glanced in the rear-view mirror. Craig was staring pensively out of the window. His glasses had returned to his face. Vic guided the car out of the parking lot and toward their office. "You good back there, Craig?"

"Yes."

"You saw Eileen play last year?" Liz's emphasis on the word *saw* had a needling tone to it. Vic knew she'd spotted how Craig and Eileen looked at each another.

"I did." Craig fell silent as the car approached a traffic light. "But you know, there was one thing about that."

Neither Vic nor Liz answered. They waited.

"When I saw her, she never closed her eyes when she played. Only briefly at the very end of a piece, as the music finished. Like she was pleased. That was the only time. So usually, she plays with her eyes open."

Chapter Eighteen

Vic, Liz, and Craig picked up coffee after leaving Eileen Liang's apartment, and back at headquarters, commandeered a conference room. As Liz and Craig sipped coffee, Vic started writing on the whiteboard.

First, he listed the core facts of the case in a column: the victim's name, estimated time of death, location, and all the facts of her life they knew. The gaps were obvious. Among other things, they didn't know her close friends and business associates or the contents of her will. Next he wrote a partial timeline of Melanie's activities on the day she died. They needed more. To the right, he headed two more columns, one with the name of Ryan Telst—Mr. Bush League, as Liz was calling him—and the other with Holden Beck.

Under Holden's column, Vic added the details of Holden's false alibi. He turned around.

"You want to move on Holden?" Liz continued reading the board as she spoke.

Vic considered her question. The simple solution was to ask Holden to stop by, show they'd cracked his alibi, and lean on him. See if he admitted to anything.

"He's the likely one." Craig rose and carried his coffee cup to the corner garbage can. They all watched him drop it into the can.

Vic made up his mind. "Not yet. He doesn't know that we've figured out he lied, so we have time. First, I want to discount Telst, if we can. Remember how Holden badmouthed Telst? My guess is that when we question Holden, he'll point the finger at Telst. But if we've discounted Telst we can tell Holden to forget it. That puts the screws to him. Guy like that, he's arrogant enough to come in for questioning without a lawyer, but once we tell him we know he sneaked out of his office, he'll lawyer up. We only get one chance at him. We need everything in place before we talk to him."

"What about this Asian girl?" Liz turned to Craig. "You pretty much said she lied to us. That she plays with her eyes open. Maybe she saw the attack and doesn't want to tell us."

"Why would she lie to us?" Craig sounded defensive.

"You tell me, lover boy."

"Okay, okay." Vic jumped in the moment Liz finished speaking. "Craig is right. Why would she lie to us? Or hide what she saw?" As Vic spoke, another thought came to him. He turned to Craig. "Tell me something. You said Eileen played with her eyes open when you saw her play for the symphony. But you didn't watch her the whole time, right?"

Craig looked away. "Well, I saw a fair amount."

"Which is it?" Liz broke in, grinning like someone who just hooked a fish.

A light flush rose on Craig's cheeks. "It's where she sits on the stage. You can see her easily. So yeah, I'd say she regularly plays with her eyes open."

Clearly, at that concert, Craig had watched Eileen, and her alone, play. He'd been interested in Eileen for some time. Vic glanced at Liz and saw her look down to avoid eye contact with him.

"Then maybe you could help us out." Vic wrote Eileen's name on the board, the final column, hoping he spelled Liang correctly. "Do you know anything about her?"

Craig lifted his pen and tapped it on the table. "Sure. Her bio is in the symphony program. She was born in China and went to a British boarding school when she was seven or eight. I think her parents divorced. She started playing violin at the British school and got into the Royal Academy of Music."

"You have her bio memorized?" Liz tried to sound serious and failed.

"No. I just remember because it's impressive. Do you know how hard it is to get into the Royal Academy of Music?" He turned to Vic. "Anyway, she played for The London Philharmonic after she graduated, in the second violins. That's one of the best symphonies in England. And then she came here as leader of the second violins."

Vic noted the passion in Craig's voice. He also thought the fact that Eileen's parents were divorced was unlikely to appear in a musician's bio. Craig had done his own research. "How long ago?"

"Two years ago. I give her another year or two, and she'll go to New York or Los Angeles. Play for them. I bet the only reason she took Pittsburgh is because they do a European tour every year. That gives her a chance to be seen in Europe."

Vic fought down a smile. It was as if they'd lifted a stone and found something Craig usually kept hidden away. It made him wonder about Craig's relation to his father, the duty sergeant who trained Vic his first few years on patrol. Music and art were foreign countries to Craig's father. His watchwords were duty and toughness, and that a man's job was to earn loyalty and respect. What had it been like for Craig, Vic wondered, when he was fifteen? Craig wearing glasses and listening to classical music? How did he and his father get along? Did they talk to one another? It brought back Vic's last memory of talking to Dannie, his daughter. The argument about the leggings she wanted to wear to school. A weight dragged on him, pulling him down, darkening the corners of the room.

"Vic?"

He blinked. Liz and Craig were staring at him.

Liz pierced him with her gaze. "You still with us?"

"Yeah." Vic turned back to the whiteboard. He tapped the second column with his knuckle, the one listing Melanie's activities on her last day. "We start here. Get this nailed down, then on to Telst. We clear him, or not. Somewhere in that, we circle back on Eileen Liang. Push her again, and then when we're ready, we drag Beck in here and see if we can crack him. Okay?"

No one answered. Vic turned around to find Craig and Liz staring thoughtfully at the tabletop. He looked up. At the far end of the room, the District Attorney, Hana Richards, stood leaning against the closed door, arms folded, a small smile on her lips.

"*District Attorney* Richards." Vic drew out her title, a reminder of the banter they'd both used when she came to his house to offer him a job six months earlier.

"*Detective* Lenoski." A glint in her eyes told Vic she remembered the reference. "I was in the building to talk to a few people. I was wondering where you are on the Beck investigation. Perhaps you could give me a quick update?"

Vic nodded, ignoring Liz's shot glance of *I told you so*. He also knew that if Hana was talking to people in this building, most likely, she was interviewing candidates for the commander of detectives. His next boss. She had no other reason to visit. He wasn't about to fool himself that she'd driven from downtown Pittsburgh to hear his update.

"Yes, ma'am." He stepped back so she could see the entire whiteboard. Summarizing quickly, he explained the four columns, their two suspects, the questions around Eileen Liang, and their plan of action. Hana absorbed his words without an outward show of opinion.

When he finished, she nodded once, slowly. "Holden Beck." She said the name as if she'd been handed someone's best china and was afraid to drop it. "I would not have thought that."

"He lied about his alibi. Craig here," Vic pointed at Craig, "figured it out."

Hana turned to Craig and walked alongside the table to him. She held out her hand. "Vic told me you'd be a good addition to his team. He's rarely wrong."

Craig stood up and shook hands with her. "Thank you. I'm glad to be here."

Vic was impressed. Hana had complimented both him and Craig in a single sentence. Somehow, when he'd first met her during her days as a public defender, he'd recognized that she was tough and honest. Now he saw her ability to work a room. Build loyalty.

Hana turned to Liz.

"You keep these guys in line, will you, Liz?" She gazed at Vic. "Holden has connections in this town. You need to be absolutely sure when you move on him. And I have to say… I've met Holden a few times. This is not something I expected. I never thought he was the type."

"Maybe that was the context of how you met him." Liz watched Hana. "What did you think of him?"

"That's a point." Hana's eyes drifted for a moment. "I met him at the Symphony a couple of times. He was always there with Melanie, even after they divorced, which surprised me. He's also active in politics, at least the fundraising part. Makes sense he was on his best behavior in both situations." She frowned as she marshaled her thoughts. "I do have to say, too, that I always thought he was kind of sharp with me. That's not the right word." Her frown deepened. "Brusque. That's a better word. And I've seen him act the same way with other women, too. Almost like he had a chip on his shoulder about women. Or blamed us for something. I never understood it." She smiled at Vic. "I guess I'm used to men being a bit more accommodating to me." She gave him an apologetic smile.

Vic thought her last sentence was misleading. Hana was good-looking and two levels more intelligent than most people, all of it wrapped in a kind of moral strength. He thought it more likely those men were actually intimidated to the point of deference. He dismissed the thought. As a general rule, Hana knew exactly the effect she had on people. Especially men.

"Thanks." Vic gestured at the whiteboard. "And you're right about Holden. Our plan is to button down the case before we chase him. No mistakes that way."

"Good." Hana made a point to look at Craig and Liz directly before turning to Vic. "Keep at it, and keep me updated." She retreated to the door and left the room.

The door had barely clicked shut before Liz spoke up. "Accommodating? Girl who looks like that with her country club hair? The city's first female DA? She scares the hell out of half the guys in this town. That's what's going on there."

Vic fought down a smile. "Something like that. Okay. Craig, you work on the timeline of Melanie's day. Get her phone records and a list of everyone she met." He turned to Liz. "You go after Telst. Check out his batting cage alibi and where he went afterwards. When he got home. I bet Melanie's house has a security system. Get their records. That'll give us exact times when the front door opened and closed. Test that against what he says. Which reminds me. What was the name of the other person staying at Melanie's house? We need to find and talk to him. Kwan, right? Liz, you track him down as well." He added the name Kwan to a corner of the whiteboard and turned to Liz and Craig. They both stared at him.

"Now, maybe?" Vic looked at them and opened his palms in a 'what is going on?' movement.

Craig hurried from the room. Liz started to follow him, but as soon as the door clicked shut, she turned back.

"You need to know something." She stared at Vic, the expression on her face fraught. It was a look he hadn't seen in years, since the days when she first arrived in Pittsburgh from New Orleans, small son in tow, her husband missing and presumed dead following Katrina. A thousand miles from home. Vic the only detective in the department willing to take her on as partner.

"What?"

"Where I was this morning." Emotion thickened her voice. "I was invited to a sit-down. Informational meeting. With the FBI."

Vic didn't understand. If the FBI was interested in her as a candidate to join them, then why the emotion?

Liz took a step toward him. "All their questions had to do with one thing. You. Why you were in North Dakota. What you did there. Who was with you."

Fear ran like quicksilver through Vic's veins. "That was five years ago. The State Police already investigated."

"Vic. They told me about a house fire with two bodies. A police chief shot in his car. I don't know about any of that. But I kept thinking it all comes down to one thing. Lettie. Where did you find her? What gave you the right to take her? Is she documented? Can you answer any of that? To them? Make it sound real? Because if they keep asking questions, they will get right there. And you can't bullshit Lettie away."

"She's my granddaughter. Absolutely." His words were raspy, his veins and throat tight.

"Vic." Liz took a short breath, as if her lungs burned. "You never told me what happened out there. Levon was with you, and he never talks about it. I don't ask, because if you guys aren't talking, I know better."

Vic grasped the edge of the conference table and steadied himself, tried to fight how his body and the room were shrinking, trapping him. "Why now?" he heard himself say.

Liz stared at him, and Vic swore he saw tears in her eyes. "Vic." Her lips moved, and she managed to take a deep breath. "You need to be ready. They could take Lettie. You need to be ready."

Chapter Nineteen

C hen Yun shifted on the classroom's hard wooden seat. Jet lag twisted behind his eyes like a corkscrew, trying to close his eyelids. The two young men sitting across from him weren't helping. The visit with Yiptou Ng was easy. A stern warning that if Yiptou didn't cooperate, his extended family in China would learn he'd ignored a chance to reduce his uncle's prison sentence. Yiptou was a realist, and that was enough. Even now, he guessed, Yiptou was sitting outside Liling Liang's apartment, monitoring her movements. Even better, Yiptou was from a family of smugglers and petty thieves. Chen didn't need to explain surveillance to him.

But these two.

Disoriented by their decision to meet in this deserted classroom, only now was Chen beginning to keep the two separate in his mind. Baihu Song was the one who talked incessantly about working for one of the Little Giants of Chinese tech and the strength of the 996 system—working nine a.m. to nine p.m. six days a week. Chen had finally connected Song's lean, sharp-boned face to the graduate student in computer engineering whose father was a Politburo official.

The other, Yulong Lin, round-faced with a smile frozen on his face, interjected regularly with a steady stream of questions about who Chen and his commander knew inside the Party. At least Chen understood the reason for his questions. Lin's father was a high-level banking executive. As one of the National Bourgeois—with their own star on the flag—the Party would always consider his family suspect. Lin needed a broad *guanxi*

100

network of contacts to protect themselves and anticipate the Party's shifting priorities. Lin's line of questioning about Chen's Party contacts was simply a well-honed survival skill and naked ambition. Chen found Lin's questions shameless and his endless smile untrustworthy.

But mostly, they just wouldn't stop talking.

It was Song with the reins now, jabbering about Alibaba and Baidu's search capabilities. Talking as if he'd founded both companies. Chen felt it was impossible for anyone who talked that much to be good at their job.

Chen raised his hand to stop him, waiting until Song finally fell silent. "If you please, Song. I have a simple question for both of you. Will you help me?"

Thankfully, they didn't glance at one another. Chen had worried they might put up a united front.

"Of course," Lin replied, much too easily, his smile never slipping.

Song sat back, his head tilted back so he was looking down his nose. His eyes were flinty. Chen suspected Song learned the mannerism from his father, a Politburo member known to undercut his enemies.

Finally, Song asked, "Perhaps you could be more specific about what you would like us to do?"

Chen wasn't surprised Song smelled a deal to be made. He had inherited his father's political instincts.

"Are you both aware of Operation Fox Hunt?" Chen looked from one to the other.

They nodded.

Chen leaned forward. "One of the men identified on Premier Xi's list is Zixin Liang."

"Steel Magnate Liang," shot back Lin. "From Wuhan."

It crossed Chen's mind that Lin's banker father might have his own dealings with Liang, but he didn't have time to check. "Exactly. And Liang is wanted on charges of corruption. Lining his own pockets. We are, however, having trouble finding him."

Both young men gazed at him, Lin's mouth slightly open. This was news. Chen took advantage of the rare, stunned silence. "However, his daughter,

Liling Liang, is much easier to find. She is quite public. She plays the violin for the symphony orchestra here and calls herself Eileen Liang. We hope to find Steel Magnate Liang through her."

"I told you that was her." Song smacked Lin on the shoulder. A thin-lipped grin creased his face, the first Chen had seen. Chen didn't know why, but he sensed cruelty behind that smile.

"Do you know her?" Chen realized this was a possibility. They were young men, and would be aware of the city's available Chinese women. It was natural. And from her photos, Eileen Liang was a good-looking young woman, and a celebrity. He wondered if Tanming—while he prepared Chen's files—considered Eileen in that light. Somehow, he felt Tanming only looked at her as a target. It saddened him.

"I went to the symphony to watch her play." Song's whisper was conspiratorial, his tone the one men use between themselves. "She would look very good in my bed." Song's eyes brightened with lust. "I will approach her for you. Half an hour with me, and she will tell me where her father is hiding."

Chen felt a jab of disgust, and his jet lag evaporated. "No. Listen to me. I simply need to learn her schedule. Who her friends are. Who she meets. That is all."

"What is the plan?" Lin looked pained by Song's comments, the smile finally gone from his face. Chen liked him a little better for it.

Chen wasn't about to explain his plan to them. He couldn't trust them farther than he could spit a sunflower seed. He saw weaknesses in each that would lead them to brag about their involvement. Song would use it as a way to impress, Lin to broaden his *guanxi* network.

"I just require you to do one simple thing." Chen looked directly at Song. "I absolutely do not want you to approach her. That is critical. If you do, I will have to report your behavior to my commander."

Now Song and Lin did exchange a glance, but Chen knew he had them on their heels. He pushed ahead. "I need one of you to watch her in the afternoon, another at night. It would be best if you switched the time of day sometimes. Again, all I want to know is where she goes, who she talks to, and what she does. That is all. Ten days should be enough. You will be compensated for your expenses. And you must tell no one about this."

Chen didn't mention Yiptou, or that Yiptou would watch Liling in the mornings. Yiptou had requested that time slot, explaining that his wife could do his morning restaurant prep, and he could return to cook for the lunch and dinner rushes. Chen had agreed. He knew Yiptou sent money back to his family in China every month, and didn't want to disrupt that. He didn't have the same respect for these two young men. As far as he was concerned, they could give up a few evenings of drinking and chasing girls to sit by themselves in Liling's parking lot.

Time with nothing but their own thoughts would be good for them, he thought. But he doubted they were the self-reflecting types.

Especially Song.

Chapter Twenty

Vic was squeezing the edge of the conference room table in his right hand. He didn't know if it was from anger or for support. Liz stood a few feet from him, the lines on her forehead hard-etched. Vic struggled to slow his rushing mind. He squinted at her, a trick he'd learned when he was boxing to help himself focus. "What exactly did they ask about?"

"Why you went out there. Who you met. Who was with you. When it happened."

"Were the questions structured, or was it fishing?"

Liz gave the slightest of nods, and Vic knew she'd considered this as well. If the questions were asked in a specific order, then the FBI already had information and were looking for lies, misrepresentations, and avoided topics. If they were fishing, they were just getting started and didn't know what was important.

"Felt like fishing to me. They started out all buddy-buddy. 'We're all on the same side here; we're just trying to clean up some loose ends.'" Liz feigned a whistly voice that must belong to one of the agents. "Bunch of crap. But I didn't feel like they were trying to trap me or confirm something. Questions were all over the lot."

"What did they ask?"

"Like I said, why you went out there. Who you were with. I told them your daughter disappeared, we suspected she was trafficked, and you went alone, looking for her. They did know that Cora Stills was your lead, and that you found her body. Then they mentioned the house that burned down.

Ewan Fleck's house, with Ewan and some other guy dead inside. Ewan's dad, the police chief, shot in the driveway. I didn't know about any of that." She stared at him. "Do I want to know any of that?"

"No."

They held each other's gaze.

"Yeah. I didn't think so either." Liz looked away from him. "They asked me if I knew about Ewan Fleck. I said no. Said I was in the hospital when you went out there. I had no idea what you were doing. Hell, I'd almost died."

Liz had lied to them. She was the one, recovering in her hospital bed, who'd found the link between Ewan Fleck and Cora Stills in a high school yearbook photograph. She was the one who teased the knotted strings of that relationship apart, laid them out flat so Vic and Levon could retie them. Knot them around Ewan's throat.

"Did they ask about anyone else?"

"They didn't ask about Levon." Liz turned back to him, her eyes burning.

This was the heart of it, for her. Vic knew it. Levon was his best friend and Liz's lover, after all those years she'd spent grieving for her lost husband.

Slowly, Vic drew air into his lungs and held it for a moment. Let it out slowly. He forced his mind to consider the possibilities. His thinking cleared, and he released the edge of the conference table. "The only people who know Levon was there are you and me and the guys who were helping us. Jimmy Pronghorn and Charlie Running Bear. Couple of other guys, but they answer to Charlie Running Bear, and all of them hate the Feds. I mean fifteen generations of hating them. FBI will get no help from them."

"Who else?"

Vic ran through the sequence of events from his week in North Dakota. It was more than five years ago, but he remembered who he'd met, who'd helped him, as if it was yesterday. "There's only three that matter. There were a couple of FBI agents, but they only knew I was looking for Cora Stills. They took over her case when I found Cora's body. Nothing there. Karl Swenson is a North Dakota state trooper, and investigator, he was the one who took my alibi for the night Ewan Fleck died." Vic fell quiet. He knew part of the reason Karl Swenson accepted his alibi was that it also absolved Karl's friend, Jimmy Pronghorn. Because of that, Karl hadn't pushed. The FBI would. Another name came to him. "And Crush."

He and Liz exchanged a glance about their previous commander with the Bureau of Police.

"What did Crush know?"

An image of Crush rose in Vic's mind. His sculpted free-weights body, skin-tight shirt, the shaved, gleaming head. "He can put me with Chief Fleck, and so can Karl Swenson. Crush talked to Chief Fleck about me. So did Swenson." Vic looked away. On the day of the house fire, he'd asked Crush to lie about him to Chief Fleck. Crush had done it. That would be raw meat to the FBI. It led to the obvious question of why Vic wanted Crush to lie. Needed him to.

Liz prompted him. "Anyone else?"

Vic nodded, more to himself than anything else. "There was a woman who ran a halfway house for battered women. I stayed in her barn a couple of days. She knows me pretty well. She was the one who gave me the alibi."

"And Susan Kim. You found her."

"I don't know where she is." Strictly that was true, but it felt like a lie. Susan was somewhere on the Fort Berthold reservation, living with Jimmy Pronghorn. And Susan knew everything. Where Lettie came from. She'd been there, in Ewan Fleck's house as it burned, holding Lettie to her chest. Vic looked at Liz. "They'll never find her."

"It's the FBI."

"Trust me on this." Vic knew Susan would disappear. Susan had more to hide than he did. Much more. The blood on her hands didn't wash off. "I don't see how they link Levon to this," Vic said slowly. "And no one will tell the FBI Levon was there. Levon saved Charlie Running Bear's life in Iraq. And like I said, Charlie hates the Feds. He won't mention Levon or cooperate with the FBI."

Liz frowned. "Levon saved Charlie's life?"

"Ask him about it." Vic didn't add that Levon also saved his own life inside Fleck's house. Had done so by shooting Fleck's lieutenant minutes before the fire started.

"So it's Crush." Liz tapped her knuckle on the table. "He'll talk faster than diarrhea. He'll figure if he tells everything to the FBI, it might lead to a job with them."

Vic heard Liz talking, but his mind circled back to Liz's original statement. Lettie. He had no way to explain Lettie. When the FBI learned about her, they would ask how he found her. How he knew for certain she was his granddaughter. They'd ask for the legal documents proving his right to take her from North Dakota.

He had none.

The horror of that thought pressed against his heart. Crush was one thing. What Crush told the FBI would raise questions, but Vic knew his answers could be couched, contextualized, ultimately passed off with a lie. He couldn't do that with Lettie. She was a walking, living, breathing, incontrovertible fact.

Vic leveled his gaze on Liz. "Thanks for telling me."

"Like I said." Liz's voice was a whisper again. "It's Lettie. It's all about her. You need to be ready."

Chapter Twenty-One

A	t his desk, Craig checked his emails for Melanie's phone records, but her mobile phone provider had yet to respond to their warrant. The night before, at Liz's suggestion, he'd copied down the name of the burglar alarm company Melanie used to protect her home. He found the company information and inserted it—along with a request for the activation history of the house's motion detectors, windows, and doors—into the electronic request form for warrants. For date parameters, he used the week prior and up to two days after Melanie's death. He knew now that a large part of a detective's job was these kinds of data requests, and one trick was to learn which organizations took the longest to respond. The companies quickest to respond were sent requests for information last.

As he hit the return key to file the warrant request, Liz appeared at her desk. Her face was drawn and distracted. He noticed she'd stayed behind to talk to Vic and wondered about that conversation.

Liz slumped into her desk chair, lost in thought. She looked so distracted, Craig called to her. "Hey, I know Vic asked you to track down this Kwan guy, but I've got a couple of minutes. Want me to try?"

Liz straightened. "Yes. Thanks." Slowly, she opened her email program.

A few mouse movements and clicks pulled up the symphony's website. Thirty seconds later, he'd identified the only Kwan in the symphony, a John Kwan, who played the cello.

From the website bio, Craig learned Kwan was born in Taiwan and was new to the symphony this season. Before Pittsburgh, he'd spent two years with the Bangor Symphony. He found no social media profile for him, and a check of the DMV database came up empty. He made a phone call, and when he was finished, turned to Liz.

"I found him, he's new to the symphony this year. Can't find a PA license for him."

Liz barely returned a glance. "Figure out a way to talk to him."

"I just talked to the symphony. There's a practice on right now. He's there. We could go over to Heinz Hall and catch him."

Liz stopped typing, her fingers poised above her keyboard. "Sure. We'll both go. Maybe half an hour?"

"Sounds good."

Vic appeared, his face drawn. Craig glanced from him to Liz and again wondered what they had talked about.

The arrival of Melanie's autopsy report delayed them almost an hour. The cause of death was massive brain trauma to the right side of Melanie's head; the coroner's office postulating the murder weapon some kind of club. Nothing about the wound indicated the type or make of the weapon.

After they all finished the report, they clustered around Liz's desk.

Liz looked at Vic. "The only thing this tells us is that Melanie was hit on the head."

To Craig, Vic seemed balled inside himself. He watched Vic raise his head and squint, clearly struggling to focus. "No defensive wounds, you mean?"

"Right. She never got a hand or arm up to ward off the blow." Liz spoke evenly, almost calmly. "You'd expect bruising on a hand or lower arm, or a cracked bone or something. I guess she didn't react, or never saw it coming."

Craig had the feeling Liz chose her careful, moderated tone to help Vic.

Vic spoke as if he'd taken a reverberation of the blow to Melanie himself. "And no bruising anywhere else. A single strike. It was someone who knew what they were doing. Maybe someone she knew."

Liz rose and turned to Craig. "Let's go see what this Kwan guy has to say."

Craig collected his sport coat. After a quick goodbye to Vic, he followed Liz into the parking lot. He was convinced that whatever conversation Liz and Vic had in the conference room, it was important. It chafed him not having the seniority to be included.

Heinz Hall, the home of the symphony, centered Pittsburgh's cultural district and the city itself, just a few blocks from the Point where the rivers converged. Liz parked in a nearby garage, and together they entered the outside doors, passed a row of ticket windows, and showed their IDs to an usher who waved them into the lobby. In the distance, music swelled.

Liz turned to him. "You know what they're playing?"

"Mozart, I think."

She studied him. "How do you know this crap? I know you listen to music all the time, but that's rock and pop. Not this old white people crap."

Craig fought down a smile. He'd seen Liz taken in when they overheard Eileen playing the Chaconne. He shrugged. "Is it just old white people's crap? I'm pretty sure Eileen is Chinese."

"Don't get smart with me."

Craig hesitated. He'd thought Liz was kidding him, but now he wasn't so sure. He decided to be honest. "It talks to you differently than music today. It's old music, but it shows us everything that makes us people."

Liz stared at him, eyes wide, waiting for him to elaborate.

Craig had the distinct impression she didn't know what to do with him, that she considered him some kind of plant or animal she couldn't categorize. He hurried his answer. "You remember when we were in the hallway listening to Eileen Liang? You said the music was sad, and I said it was mournful? That's what I mean. With classical you hear sorrow, joy, exuberance, happiness, anger, even fear. All the things we feel. Those old dead white guys, and women, figured out a way to express those feelings in music. Songs today more often need words to explain what they mean, what they want to say. That's fine; it's just different."

"And how about people killing other people? Is that in there?"

Craig smiled at her, glad she hadn't ridiculed him. "That's opera, I think."

"Yeah. I get that. But how did you get into all this? Your Dad was a cop."

Craig listened to the music swell. "It was a way to get out of school. When I was like in fifth grade, they had this program. If you signed up, once a month, they took us to a symphony matinee. I signed up to go because you got to miss class. Sometimes they took us to a play. I don't know. I got into it. Then in college, I took a music appreciation class, and that's when I started recognizing what piece an orchestra is playing."

"Okay, culture boy." Liz jerked her head toward the nearest double doors leading into the symphony hall. "Let's go figure out who's got anger or fear enough to hit Melanie Beck in the head with a bat." She turned and started for the doors.

Craig followed, scooping up a program from an open box sitting next to the doors. He guessed they were for the ushers to hand out.

Liz led him halfway down the aisle, slid sideways along a row to the center, and picked a seat. Craig sat as well, an empty seat between them. The conductor had his back to them. Craig found it disorienting. All the players were dressed casually, in everything from sweat clothes to jeans and T-shirts. He spotted four tracksuits. The conductor wore too-tight jeans and a form-fitting shirt that only highlighted the rolls of fat at his waist. Craig checked for Eileen, one seat in from the front of the stage. She and the other violinists were swaying back and forth as they played, their bow arms moving as one. Craig was suddenly conscious of his glasses and slid them off.

"How you gonna spot Kwan like that?"

A warm flush shot through him. He slid them back on and searched for Kwan. He was just to the right of the conductor, two seats from the front of the stage, hunched over his cello. He scanned for Jessica Teel, spotting her in the middle of a clutch of seven or eight musicians directly in front of the conductor, the viola tucked under her chin. Her arm moved smoothly as well, but her body was still. Craig glanced at Eileen Liang. Eileen's bow movements were fluid and graceful, her whole body moving just slightly with the music. To Craig, Jessica was playing the music, but Eileen was part of it, the music an expression of herself.

"You got him?" Liz whispered.

"Yeah. To the right of the conductor. Two chairs in from the audience. Only Asian guy among the cellos."

"Next break, we grab him."

Craig nodded, his eyes sliding back to Eileen. She wore jeans and a loose white cotton shirt. She twisted at the waist to face the theater's empty seats, then, as if she sensed him. Her brown eyes locked onto him. He saw distance and electricity in her eyes, but she was so absorbed in the music and her playing that he didn't think she recognized him.

Chapter Twenty-Two

The conductor called a break twenty minutes later. Without notes, his finger jabbing rapid-fire toward different sections and players, he broadsided the group with hoarse instructions for six full minutes before announcing a half-hour break. As the stage echoed with the shuffling feet and scraping chairs of people rising, he sneeringly asked everyone to return actually ready to play. He started offstage in an electric huff.

Liz was out of her seat, along the row, and down the aisle, calling to the conductor as he neared the wings. As Craig caught up, Liz said something to him and offered her ID. The conductor bent at the waist and studied her credentials.

He then turned, pointed his baton at Kwan, and beckoned to him. Kwan, who was writing notes on his score, rose, placed his cello on its side next to his chair, and squeezed to the edge of the stage. Craig noted several of the musicians watching them, including Jessica. He glanced in the opposite direction, but Eileen and her violin was gone.

"John," called the director in a blunt voice, "these people want you." The conductor nodded at Liz and strode from the stage, his baton extended from his right hand like a knitting needle in need of a soft belly.

Kwan was short, clad in rumpled chinos and a polo shirt, his neck and arms thin and pale. Craig thought he would look uncomfortable with a baseball bat or any sporting equipment in his hands. Kwan looked down at them from the edge of the stage, blinking.

Liz held up her ID. "We're investigating the murder of Melanie Beck. We'd like to ask you a few questions. Can you climb down?"

Kwan nodded and sat on the edge of the stage, dangling his legs into the seating area, and launched himself into the air. He landed clumsily and took a step to steady himself.

Liz confirmed Kwan's name and where he lived. Craig automatically took notes. He'd switched to a notebook after seeing how Vic and Liz worked, and was starting to appreciate the technique. Writing felt more substantial than holding his phone, as if he was more committed to the case. He wanted that commitment.

Kwan answered each of Liz's questions with one or two heavily accented words, and Craig wasn't sure if he was being cautious, or had a poor grasp of English. Then Liz asked why he lived in Melanie Beck's house. He reddened and looked down.

They waited until Kwan raised his face. "I, um, no good finding apartment when I come here. Mrs. Beck very nice. Tell me to stay her house until I find place."

"How long have you been there?"

"Six week. I want to find place soon. Is this problem?"

Liz hesitated, and Craig guessed she was thinking the same thing he was. With Melanie gone, staying at her house just might be a problem.

"I'm sure you'll find somewhere to live." Liz smiled at him.

"Tell us about your roommates." Craig kept his voice low, not wanting Jessica to overhear. She was intently studying her score, but leaning toward them, and Craig thought she was trying to overhear the conversation.

"Which ones?" Kwan seemed surprised by the question.

"Ryan Telst." Liz shifted closer to him. "What does he do at the house?"

"Many things. He works in garden, cleans kitchen. Fixes things."

"And does he spend time with Mrs. Beck?" Liz's voice dropped lower, and Craig knew she too was also worried about Jessica overhearing.

Kwan stared at Liz. The question seemed to perplex him. "Just like all of us."

Liz straightened. "When you say just like all of us, what does that mean?"

He shrugged. "We eat dinner together, sometime. Watch TV."

"Okay." Liz stared at the ceiling for a moment before leveling her gaze on Kwan. "Did Ryan Telst and Mrs. Beck have a relationship? Were they girlfriend and boyfriend?"

Kwan frowned, and his lips moved as if he was repeating one of the words.

"If I may." The voice came from behind Kwan, and Craig and Liz both looked around him. Eileen Liang stood near them, a small smile on her face. She hugged her violin loosely to her stomach. "I believe I can help, if that would be acceptable. I could translate."

Liz hesitated, and Craig guessed she didn't like the idea of including someone else, but she waved Eileen over anyway. "Eileen Liang, correct? We interviewed you yesterday?"

Eileen nodded.

"We were trying to confirm if Mrs. Beck and Ryan Telst were in a relationship."

Craig heard Eileen repeat the word 'confirm' under her breath, and knew she understood the implication of that word choice. She squatted so she was closer to Kwan and spoke rapidly in Chinese.

Craig caught a shift in Eileen as she talked and noticed Kwan stand a little straighter. It was more than the tone of Eileen's words, her whole attitude shifted. Craig thought at first it was confidence at speaking Chinese, but he wondered if he also heard a note of imperiousness. Of command. One that somehow translated to Kwan even though she was squatting.

Kwan answered rapidly.

When he finished, Eileen turned to them. "He said he doesn't understand the question." Her voice was again her fluid English, with its British accent. "He says he never saw any indication that this man and Mrs. Beck were in any kind of relationship." Eileen frowned as if she'd just thought of something else, and Craig saw two tiny vertical creases appear at the center of her forehead. He thought they were about the prettiest things he had ever seen.

Eileen spoke rapidly to Kwan, and after listening to his answer, settled her gaze on Liz. "I hope you don't mind, but I asked Mr. Kwan how he would categorize this Mr. Telst, in terms of what he did in the house. That seems to be what you want to know. He says the best term is 'handyman.'

"Yeah. That's it. I could have told you that."

Craig turned toward this new voice, Liz doing the same. Jessica Teel stood nearby, looking down on them. She must have moved closer to hear the conversation. "You could have asked me."

"Okay." Liz's voice was sharp. She pointed at Jessica. "We'll talk to you next. Can you return to your seat? We'll tell you when we're ready to talk to you."

She turned to Kwan, took him by the elbow, and half dragged him up the aisle. As she did, she called over her shoulder, "Can you join us, Ms. Liang?"

Craig knew Liz was angry she'd let the interview get away from her, but he blamed himself. As her partner, he should have spotted Jessica moving toward them. He turned to Eileen. She was standing on the stage, and for a moment, they stared at one another, Craig not quite feeling his feet on the floor. Eileen bent toward him and held out her hand.

It took him a split second to comprehend her action. He stepped closer and took her hand. Without hesitation, she hopped from the stage and landed next to him, her knees absorbing the impact. She turned to him, her face inches from his, her eyes bright and gleeful, like a child's.

"I always wondered if I could do that." Her voice was clear and unencumbered.

"Jump down here with the rest of us?" Craig felt himself smile as well.

"I knew you would catch me."

"Craig!" Liz's voice cut between them.

Craig realized he was still holding Eileen's hand. It was cool and strong in his, and he reluctantly let go. He stepped aside so they could walk up the aisle together, and she fell into step beside him, holding her violin to her again.

"You seem very studious for a police detective." Eileen let the observation hang between them.

He knew his next words would be important and chose humor.

"It's the glasses. Makes me look like a bookworm."

"So you like criminals to underestimate you."

He glanced at her and saw a tiny smile on her lips. She was kidding him. "Pretty sure that's a given at this point in my career."

They reached Liz and stopped. John Kwan was staring at them as if they were unicorns. Eileen turned to Craig. "I have a feeling you are a person it would be hard to overestimate." Before he could respond, she turned back to Liz. "Yes?"

Liz considered them both for a moment, frowning, before asking Eileen to translate more questions for John.

The earlier process repeated itself, except this time, Kwan's answers were longer. Kwan reiterated that he'd seen no signs of a relationship between Melanie and Ryan Telst, and had no idea how they first met. He'd only lived in the house for six weeks, and both Jessica and Telst were already in residence when he arrived. At the time of the murder, he'd been at the symphony hall with the other cello players, involved in a section practice. He had no car and borrowed rides to practice with Jessica and sometimes Melanie. In a pinch, Telst drove him, or he ordered a car.

"When did you get home two days ago?"

Craig could tell Liz was losing interest. Kwan's answers led him right out of suspicion. Apart from an alibi that would be easy to confirm, he had no reason to want Melanie dead. In fact, it was more to his benefit for Melanie to be alive. With Melanie gone, he might have nowhere to live.

Liz gave up. "Thank you, Mr. Kwan." She turned to Eileen. "And thanks for your help as well, Ms. Liang."

Kwan scuttled down the aisle toward the stage and darted through a side door.

Eileen smiled at Liz. "Glad to be of assistance." She turned to Craig. "Perhaps you could give me a hand back onto the stage? It would be quicker than walking around."

"I think he'd be glad to hold your hand again." Liz barely kept the sarcasm out of her voice.

Eileen turned back to Liz and cocked her head. She looked Liz straight in the eyes. "I do believe common politeness is too often ignored these days, don't you?"

Liz didn't break her gaze, her face stony. "I wouldn't know. There's never been much of that in my world."

"That's unfortunate. But barely an excuse, is it?"

To Craig's surprise, Liz stayed silent. She appraised Eileen, her expression hard to read.

After a moment, Liz turned to Craig. "Bring Jessica back with you." She stepped away from them and made a motion with her hand, telling them to go.

Craig turned to Eileen, who gave Liz another second of her gaze before turning to walk back down the aisle next to him.

Craig waited until they were out of earshot. "I'm not sure I've ever heard anyone talk to Detective Timmons that way."

Eileen didn't reply, and Craig felt let down. He was seized with an unreasonable fear that he'd misspoken. They stopped when they reached the stage, and Craig saw Eileen gauge the height from the floor.

"I can give you a leg up." Craig interlaced his fingers and bent slightly, creating a step with his hands. She understood his intent and switched her violin to her left hand, placed one foot in his hand, and hopped up as he lifted, her right hand using his shoulder for balance. Eileen pivoted in mid-air and landed on her feet at the edge of the stage.

She gave a little laugh. "I'm lucky I didn't end up in the horns section." She squatted and looked up the aisle toward Liz. "I like her. You are lucky to work with her."

Craig resisted the urge to turn and look back. He didn't want Liz to know they were talking about her. "She's a good detective. So is Detective Lenoski, our senior. I was fortunate they asked me to join them."

She studied him with warm eyes. "They asked you to join them?"

"Detective Lenoski did." He didn't mention Vic's friendship with his father and felt guilty he didn't. It was as if he'd somehow cheated to get where he was and didn't want her to know.

Eileen held out her hand, and he took it, so she could steady herself as she stood. He knew she didn't need the help. She was clearly athletic enough to stand without him. He took the touch as a good sign.

118

Standing, she gave her jeans a quick brush and looked down at him. "Do you have a business card? I feel that it would be fair. Since you already know where I live."

Craig took one from his inside jacket pocket and held it out. "If you think of anything else from the day when Mrs. Beck was attacked, give me a call."

She took the card between her long fingers. "Of course." With a flash of her eyes, she carried her violin back to her seat.

Chapter Twenty-Three

Craig pivoted to find Jessica Teel standing a few feet away, watching. He noted that she had left her viola on her chair.

He climbed out of his absorption with Eileen. "Ms. Teel, Detective Timmons and I would like to ask you a couple of questions. If you could join us?"

Jessica stepped to the edge of the stage and held out her hand with a smirk. Craig knew she was making fun of him. He considered ignoring her hand, but took it. She hopped down from the stage as easily as Eileen.

"Oh, thank you so much," she said with exaggerated formality.

"Of course." Craig decided to play along. "If you please, ma'am." He waved up the aisle where Liz was standing, watching them.

Jessica started up the aisle, and Craig followed, thinking the day had become a lot more interesting.

They'd barely reached Liz when she pinned Jessica with a look. "Ryan Telst. What the hell does he do at the Beck's?"

Jessica stopped and composed herself. "He helps out around the estate."

"So he's a handyman?" Disbelief dripped from Liz's words.

Jessica took her time responding. "Well, kind of an antiquated way to put it, but you could say that."

"And were he and Mrs. Beck in a relationship?"

Jessica's eyes hardened. "Hardly."

Liz was so disgusted she looked away across the rows of seats. From the stage came the slow notes of a piano. They rose to the ceiling and just as quickly stopped, the silence a heartthrob.

Liz leveled her gaze at Jessica. "Are you absolutely sure?"

"As sure as I can be. I would have heard them moving around at night. And he would have told me."

This last statement intrigued Craig. "Why would he tell you? Especially if they were trying to keep the relationship secret?"

Jessica gave him a look that suggested she felt sorry for him. "Because I'm the one who got him the job. We're distantly related."

A bemused expression came over Liz's face. "Perhaps you could explain that."

Jessica shrugged. "Sure. My grandfather moved from West Virginia to Ohio when he was eighteen to work in a mill. His brother stayed in West Virginia and ran the family dairy farm. My grandfather married and had kids, which meant my father grew up in Steubenville. He went to Chicago for college, stayed, and that's where I grew up. But every five years, my family goes back to West Virginia for a family reunion. We have like fifty or sixty people. Ryan is descended from my great-uncle, the one who stayed on the dairy farm. He's like a third cousin twice removed or something."

"And you got Melanie Beck to hire him?" Liz sounded skeptical and interested.

"Sure. Everybody knew Ryan growing up. He was this huge high school and college athlete and was drafted by the pros. The family sports star. I'd see him at the reunions. When I got the job here, I texted him and said we should get together, because this is much closer than Chicago. When we did, he told me he was done with baseball; he'd missed his shot. He asked if I knew someplace to work around here. His family had sold the dairy farm by then, they'd been priced out. I mentioned it to Mrs. Beck, and she wanted some work done on her estate, and Ryan is good at that kind of stuff. He grew up working the dairy farm and did construction in the off-season. He did some odd jobs for Mrs. Beck, she liked the work, and asked him to stay full-time." She shrugged. "He moved in."

Craig finished writing an abbreviated version of Jessica's story and made a note to himself to check the dates when all the people living at the Beck estate moved in. There was a congruence to their arrival times he didn't trust.

"And from that, you think he would have told you if something was going on with Melanie?" Liz's skepticism was on mute.

"For something big like that? Yes. It might have created problems for me. Ryan is thoughtful that way."

Craig couldn't help himself. "What kind of problems?"

Jessica turned to him. "Like I said. We're related. It would be weird. I might have to move out."

"I thought that was your plan?" Liz watched Jessica carefully.

"Well, yes. Of course. But it would add weirdness to the process."

Craig thought Jessica looked flustered, but was hiding it well.

Liz's eyebrow arched in skepticism. "And the day Mrs. Beck died. Where were you?"

A flicker of annoyance crossed Jessica's face. "Well, as I told the other Detective and him." She gestured at Craig. "I was in the Strip District. I had some shopping to do. It's right on the other side of the bridge from Mrs. Beck's apartment. I walked."

"Uh-huh. Where did you go?" Liz tilted her head toward Craig. "*He* can write it down."

Craig knew Liz was calling Jessica out on the way she referred to him.

Jessica shrugged. "Sure. I was at that store that sells all the cheeses. And I looked at the Steelers merchandise from the store with all the sports team's stuff."

Liz goaded Jessica with a smile. "Not a Chicago fan, then?"

"I work for the *Pittsburgh* Symphony, for God's sake. I'm a public figure representing *Pittsburgh*. Of course I wear Steelers clothing."

"Well, aren't you the fanboy."

"We're finished here." Jessica pivoted and stared at Craig. "And I don't need you helping me back onstage." She started toward the orchestra.

Craig couldn't help himself. He glanced toward Eileen's seat. She was back, a bottle of water by her chair, sitting very straight, concentrating on some sheet music.

"That girl has anger issues," Liz said slowly.

Craig turned to Liz, who nodded in Jessica's direction. "You know what? We've talked to all three people who live in Eileen's house, and you know what none of them said or did?"

Craig waited. He wasn't sure what Liz was thinking.

"Eileen Beck opened her house to them. Two symphony players and an ex-athlete down on his luck. Gave them a place to live while they got their feet under them. Then she dies, and not one of the people living in her house says they feel bad, that Eileen Beck really helped them out, is helping them out right now, or that she was a good person for helping them."

"I hadn't thought of it that way."

Liz turned to him, her dark eyes thoughtful. "What people don't say matters. And those are three ungrateful people."

Craig nodded, unsure what to add.

Liz nodded toward Eileen Liang. "And that Eileen girl. I like her. She's got spine. Don't let her get away."

Chapter Twenty-Four

Vic's heart was leaden all the way home. He couldn't get the FBI out of his mind. The questions running through his head were endless. What made them start investigating now? What did they actually know? Had they officially opened a case?

He wrenched his mind back to Melanie Beck's murder. Holden Beck lying about his alibi placed him at the top of the suspect list, but Liz and Craig had returned from the symphony with the news that Ryan Telst was likely not having an affair with Melanie Beck. That eliminated the most likely reason Holden had for killing Melanie. Granted, Holden claimed his wife was sleeping with Telst, but it was only a claim.

Worse, it was looking more like Telst might be a suspect. Craig had called the batting cages where Ryan practiced the afternoon Melanie was killed. Ryan finished practicing before four o'clock, which gave him time to drive to the North Side and attack Melanie on the Riverside trail.

It also meant Telst had a baseball bat in his truck the afternoon of the murder.

Vic negotiated the rush hour traffic, the weight in his chest swinging his mind's pendulum back to the FBI.

The feeling was of rats scurrying from a burning ship. What happened in North Dakota involved too many people. With Liz, he'd narrowed the weak link down to Crush, their former commander, but that was hopeful thinking and an attempt to make Liz feel better about Levon. In fact, too many people knew the truth, and any one of them might talk to the FBI. A tip-off from someone, perhaps Rosa, the midwife who cared for his daughter when she was pregnant and helped with Lettie's birth. Or the arrest of one of Running Bear's men. Any one of them might offer information about that night in trade for a lesser sentence. He forced down his fear. If he let his imagination run, it would eat him alive. There were at least five ways the truth of that night might come to light.

Yet how the case caught the interest of the FBI didn't really matter. Only two things did. The first was not losing Lettie. The second worried him even more.

He had lied to Anne about Lettie.

Anne had left him once. She would never forgive him for this.

He eased his car into their driveway, killed the engine, and took a deep breath. Anne would read him. She always did. She would notice something was wrong. He might be able to blame the case and get away with it tonight, but she would spot it within a day or two.

He slid out of the car and let himself in through the front door. Lettie shot out of the kitchen and clamped his leg with her entire body. He ruffled her hair, leg dragged her to the hallway table, and locked his service firearm in the drawer. When he turned, Anne was standing in the doorway to the kitchen, smiling at him.

"You look exhausted," she said.

"Well, thank you for that." Now that his hands were free, he detached Lettie from his leg and lifted her up against him. Lettie giggled and burrowed her face into his chest.

"How's it coming?" Anne asked.

"Two steps forward and one step back. But we've got one solid lead."

"Good." Anne knew enough not to ask more. "I had some days due to me, so I took them. I'm off the next couple of days."

"Nice. Relaxing."

Anne stared at Lettie, clinging to Vic's chest like a barnacle. "Is that what you think?" She winked at him and returned to the kitchen.

Vic hiked Lettie up a bit higher and looked into her face. "Can you help grandma? I want to change."

"Okay."

She loosened her arms, and Vic lowered her to the floor. Without a backward glance, she sprinted into the kitchen. Vic trod the stairs to the second floor. He needed to know what the FBI knew, if their investigation was real. Right now, it was an ax, threatening to split away Anne and Lettie, even Liz. Because if the truth came out, any number of charges might be leveled against him. And Levon would be jailed for murder.

The stairway felt long and harder to climb than he could remember.

Chapter Twenty-Five

I t was almost ten o'clock at night when Chen Yun emerged from the shrubs lining the Riverwalk Trail. He wore jeans and a jean jacket in black, with a navy-blue baseball cap pulled low on his forehead. On the other side of the parking lot loomed the Heinz Loft Apartments, the roof line lit by large lights at the upper corners of the building. He stepped next to a young oak tree and scanned the face of the apartment building, his gaze drawn to a glowing window in the upper right-hand corner.

Liling Liang, or Eileen Liang, was up there, he knew. He'd scouted the building earlier and memorized the location of the apartment.

Tanming had included the address with the background materials. Eighteen months earlier, Liling had emailed her mother to say she had taken the job in Pittsburgh and, as all filial children do, listed her new address. Of course, given that her father was a fugitive and the Party's security services routinely monitored overseas email traffic, her email was flagged, copied, and stored. Tanming had found the address in the email archives.

Chen watched the window, feeling more tired and dispirited the longer he stood. He knew this wasn't jet lag or lack of sleep, but his growing disgust with the work he was doing. He'd chosen policing for two reasons. Finishing college, one of his professors suggested he join a new government program designed to fight corruption. It was a unique team that would be appended to the provincial police, with the goal of investigating party officials and business executives. The requirements were a background in mathematics or finance and foreign language skills. His grandmother had taught him English, and he had a knack for mathematics, something inherited from his father. Only later did he learn he was attracted to the job for another reason. Like many Chinese, he harbored the need to rebel against the Party. Speaking English was one way, but he needed more. This new job, he'd instinctively understood, might use the rule of law to limit Party power.

Instead, he'd become a tool the Party used to manipulate the law for its own use.

He sighed in disgust. He didn't know what to do with himself. He needed to decide.

A shadow flitted across the apartment window.

A flame of interest and excitement rose inside him, one he couldn't suppress. He should also thank his job for this reaction. Before he took the job, he hadn't known how much he liked the hunt, how attracted he was to solving complicated problems.

Alright, he was here now, he thought. If he couldn't decide how to extricate himself from his life, he might as well find Liling.

Slowly, he scanned the cars in the parking lot. In one of these cars, assuming the two students were responsible enough to actually do as they promised, was either Yulong Lin, the banker's son, or Baihu Song. Chen watched the parking lot patiently, waiting for a sign. He had a feeling it wouldn't take long.

Within a minute, a dull glow unfolded inside a white car at the edge of the lot. Someone checking their phone.

Chen angled away from the tree to approach the car from behind. The vehicle faced the parking lot and front entrance to the apartment building. A good decision, but Chen knew that amateurs never think to regularly check their mirrors for someone behind them. That, and the phone screen still glowed, so the person's eyes were focused on the screen.

Moving swiftly on his black sneakers, Chen swung behind the car and approached the passenger side door. He ducked and looked through the back window. His face, awash with light from his phone, Chen recognized the sharp features of Baihu Song, son of the Politburo member, his face awash in light from his phone. He was playing a game. So much for his commitment to the 996 working life, Chen thought. He stepped to the passenger side door and rapped on the window.

Song's head shot up, and his phone leapt from his hand. His face strained by shock and surprise, he groped in his lap while trying to see who was outside the car.

Chen made a come-to-me motion with his hand and pointed at the door. Song blinked, and recognition dawned. He turned to the driver's side door and hit several switches until finally, the door latch clunked.

Chen opened the door and slid into the passenger seat, the dome light almost blinding him. He closed the door as quietly as he could.

"Comrade Yun, you surprised me."

Chen waited until the dome light extinguished. He turned to Song. "You were easier to spot than a pig in a bridal suite. I saw the glow of your phone, and those," he pointed at the dome light, "should always be turned off during surveillance. At night any light calls attention to you, and if you have to get out of the car, they damage your night vision. Do you understand?"

Song's eyes flashed in annoyance, but his response was contrite. "Yes, I'm sorry."

"I also approached you easily from the rear. Keep your back windows cracked a little to hear noises from behind, and regularly check your rear-view mirrors. Do you understand?"

"Yes. I will make those changes." The irritation slid into Song's voice.

"Good. You should have accounted for those possibilities before playing video games." He pointed at the phone clutched in Song's hand. "As for that, turn the screen brightness down as far as you can to still read the screen. And use it as little as possible."

"As I said. I understand." Song was terse, the anger overtaking him.

Chen let the silence widen. Song hesitated, finally interpreting the silence as an opportunity to make amends, and with a bit of fumbling, cracked the two rear windows and slid the switch controlling the dome lights to the off position.

Chen checked Song's work. "Good. On the back windows, only a tiny bit.

From the outside, you want it hard to notice they are open at all. If they are too far open, they are a signal."

"Obviously. Yes."

Chen let Song stew a few moments longer. "All right. Do you have a report?"

"Um, Lin was here this afternoon. He told me that…" he hesitated, clearly unsure if he should use the name of their target or some other word, "Liling Liang returned to her apartment at about two o'clock. She was home for about an hour and then went out again. He followed her." Song glanced at Chen, unsure if Lin had done the right thing.

"Good. What did he discover?"

"She walked to a Chinese supermarket across the river. He watched her go in and come out. And then she came home and went into her apartment. That was about forty minutes later."

Chen nodded, thinking. "How many shopping bags was she carrying?"

"I, uh, he didn't say."

"Ask him." Chen shifted in his seat and decided to take a different approach. He tried to sound like a teacher. "Every single detail matters. Do not miss anything."

Song lifted his phone and glanced at Chen, irritation glowing in the sharp lines of his face.

Xiao huang di, Chen thought. You little emperor. "Yes. Text him and ask."

This time there was almost no glow from the phone, and Chen relaxed. These young men were amateurs, nothing more. So far, they hadn't shown any real lack of intelligence, just an unwillingness to think through what they were doing.

Song's thumbs tapped out a text, and he lowered the phone.

"Anything since then?" Chen maintained his teacher's voice.

"No. I haven't seen her leave the apartment."

"And she hasn't taken her car anywhere."

"Not that I have seen." Song's words were rushed. As he spoke he seemed to realize it was possible Liling had left by another door on foot.

"That's fine." Chen decided to use the carrot as well as the stick. "You are parked in the correct location, and we can't cover every eventuality. But that means you must be very specific in your reports. For instance, it matters what time the light in her apartment window goes out and when it comes back on."

Song's phone vibrated, and he glanced at the screen. "Four bags. Lin says she returned carrying four plastic bags of groceries."

Chen waved at the phone. "Thank him. Good. Now, if you can, stay here until about two o'clock. There will be someone to cover starting at five. You don't need to know who that is. As I said, we can't cover every eventuality."

"Yes." Song nodded his head vigorously. His irritation seemed to have evaporated.

Chen smiled. "Just remember what I told you, and we'll be fine." Without another word, he slid from the car, the dome light unlit. He closed the door carefully and with as little noise as possible. He padded back to the oak tree and looked up at the brightly lit window through the branches. It has begun, he thought to himself. He waited another minute and crossed the road to the walking trail, followed it to the bridge, and started across to his parked car.

Four shopping bags, he thought to himself as he walked. A lot of food for a young single woman living by herself. Of course, it was possible she did her entire week's shopping in one trip. He would just have to wait and see if she made other trips.

But four bags was a lot.

Chapter Twenty-Six

Craig still sat at his desk. He'd decided soon after taking the job to beat Vic to work and leave after him. He knew what all the work/life balance experts would say about that, but they missed the point. He didn't have a life, and he knew it. His home was a one-bedroom in a subdivided Victorian in Pittsburgh's Shadyside neighborhood. There were cheaper places to live, but the apartment was within walking distance of the bars on Walnut Street, and he couldn't stand the identically modern apartments springing up to house the increasing number of high-tech workers in the East End. His apartment's hardwood floors creaked, and the molding was stained too dark, but he liked the high ceilings and light from the tall windows, even if the single-paned glass leaked cold air in the winter.

But sitting at home alone and listening to his collection of vinyl records on his ancient stereo system left him so empty it scared him. It wasn't boredom with the old blues albums or the simple and repeated guitar chords of his favorite sixty's songs. He just wanted to turn up the music and make a meal with someone, bumping elbows and hips in the narrow galley kitchen, laughing, slurping wine, maybe with the window propped up on a wood-framed screen so the curtains swayed and traffic noises drifted to them between song tracks.

The few times that had happened, the music felt alive to him, had framed his life and added meaning rather than just being something to listen to.

So he stayed at his desk, the darkness pressing in against the wide office windows, alone on the floor except for the overnight shift.

132

At least tonight, he had something to work on. Toward the end of the day, he'd received an email with an attached file from Melanie Beck's cell phone carrier. It listed her texts, calls, and the pings from her phone on cell phone towers, enabling him to track her movements. A second spreadsheet listed the apps on her phone and when they were accessed.

He was almost finished building a profile of Melanie's whereabouts during her final day. The cell tower pings showed her starting at her North Side apartment. Jessica had confirmed that she was there, as had Ryan Telst, so that was a safe starting point. He followed the phone's movements into Pittsburgh and to Heinz Hall, where the symphony played. Her telephone remained there for several hours before shifting close to a downtown specialty clothing store that he guessed was for women. He made a note to call the store the next day to confirm her shopping trip and to review her credit card charges. The phone had pinged again at the Heinz Loft apartments at about three forty-five in the afternoon and again near the Riverside trail a little after four o'clock.

After that, nothing.

Craig sat back, feeling low. He knew this feeling from working in forensics. Melanie's last day was so prosaic and in a painful way, hopeful. The combination unsettled him. So many of Melanie's activities were routine, yet combined with the plans she'd made for the future of the symphony. She'd bought clothes in preparation of soon-to-be-held meetings, events, and parties. A swift blow to her head ended all of that. Murder was a life taken, but it was also stolen possibilities, the dismissal of everything the victim might become and do.

He saved his work with a dull tap of keyboard keys. He would walk Vic and Liz through Melanie's day tomorrow. It didn't reveal anything that helped their investigation, at least that he could tell. He checked her texts and found only seven. The carrier had provided the phone numbers of the receivers. He knew he should find the owners and at least review the apps on her phone, but he was tired, and he couldn't shake the feeling of loss.

He typed Eileen Liang's name into a search engine, knowing as he did that he wanted to cheer himself up. Her photo appeared, a promotional shot for the symphony. She was standing, wearing a black velvet suit, the pants wide and loose, the jacket buttoned, no blouse, just a simple gold pendant in the shape of a teardrop at her chest. She held her violin against her hip, her long hair cascading over her opposite shoulder. He stared at her face, the smooth cheekbones and flawless skin. In her eyes, he saw a trace of the haughtiness he'd noticed when she spoke in Chinese to Kwan, but it was offset by the soft and flowing fabric of her suit.

He breathed through his nose. His feeling of loss evaporated, replaced by the pull of attraction. He made himself return to the search findings, skimming a series of links until he found a British newspaper. He clicked on it and read a review of a violin solo she had performed. The writer was effusive. Toward the bottom of the article he found a short biography that included Eileen's Chinese name, Liling. Out of interest, he put her Chinese name into the search engine, wondering about the right way to pronounce it. He listened to a translator program offer several options, and realized the pronunciation depended on the meaning of the Chinese characters used for her name. He had no good way to find her name correctly written in Chinese.

He returned to the search results, skimmed through to the second page, and noticed her name highlighted in an article in a Hong Kong English-language newspaper. He clicked on the link.

He sat up as he read. The story was recent, and recounted much he already knew about Liling's birth to a wealthy family and her education at a London boarding school starting from an early age. The divorce of her parents when she was barely a teenager. But the next few paragraphs tightened his stomach. The article recounted her father's career as a prominent steel executive, his retirement four years ago, and his disappearance eighteen months later when the Chinese government named him a suspect in a corruption investigation. The article listed sightings of him in Monaco and Macao. It suggested he was gambling away the millions of dollars he had stolen from the state-owned steel company he once managed.

Craig was wide awake now, all of his senses buzzing. He searched the name of the newspaper, learning quickly that it supported and was likely a mouthpiece for the Chinese Communist Party. That explained the unsubstantiated claims that he was gambling away a fortune. But one fact was undeniable.

Eileen's father was a target and a fugitive.

He thought back through his interactions with Eileen at her apartment and Heinz Hall. She'd given no indication of her father's problems. She'd been relaxed, engaged, and lighthearted. It was hard for him to reconcile the two.

He closed his eyes and concentrated on his memories of Eileen, this time reliving each meeting as slowly and carefully as he could. Nothing in her behavior indicated any concern for her father's situation.

It wasn't her behavior, he realized. He opened his eyes. He remembered standing in her apartment that first afternoon. He hadn't been wearing his glasses, but he had noticed the neatly folded sheet, comforter, and pillow sitting on the end of her couch. And how the doors to Eileen's bedroom and powder room were shut tight.

No. He was getting ahead of himself. Making assumptions. He tapped his hand on the desktop, his mind buzzing.

Still.

He closed out of the search engine and chastised himself for jumping to conclusions. When they'd been in Eileen's apartment, she'd been too relaxed, too centered on herself to be hiding her father in her bedroom. It was outlandish.

He stood to clear his head. And honestly, he told himself, this has nothing to do with Melanie Beck.

He sat down again. He was wired now, his nerves too jangly to go home. He shook his head.

For something to do and as a way to move past his thoughts about Eileen, he reopened the file of Melanie Beck's phone records. He skimmed the cell tower pings again, seeing nothing new. He then looked at the list of applications on her phone and their usage. His eyes fell on one near the bottom of the list, and he studied the series of entries beside it. He looked again at the name of the application and, with a jolt, lost any chance of sleep that night.

The entries didn't show Melanie's usage of the application. They were queries to the application from an outside source. Someone had accessed the application on Melanie's phone regularly. And it wasn't just any application.

It was a tracking app.

Someone had monitored Melanie's movements in the days before her death.

Chapter Twenty-Seven

Vic rose early, tugged on his sweats, and took the stairs to the basement. He wasn't avoiding Anne, he told himself, although, in his heart, he knew that was untrue. He'd stayed quiet through dinner, made an excuse about needing to work afterwards, and had gone to bed before her. Now he was in the basement tightening the Velcro straps on his boxing gloves well before Anne awoke.

He did some stretches in front of his heavy bag. He would have to tell her about the FBI investigation, he knew. The sooner, the better, and that meant tonight after work. He needed a day to find out what he could. He knew better than to tell Anne without at least the outline of a plan about how to deal with it.

He tapped the heavy bag with his boxing gloves, tightened his shoulders, and threw three hard gut punches, feeling the shock travel up his arms. He skipped back and was about to throw a combination when his cell phone rang.

He checked the screen. Levon Grace. As he used his teeth to unstick the Velcro on his right glove, he realized he should have expected the call.

"Levon?"

"Yeah. I figured you're awake by now."

"Just starting to work out."

Levon was silent for a few heartbeats, as if he was thinking through what Vic's workout might involve. "Lunch?" he asked, finally.

Vic knew what the topic of conversation was going to be. Liz had told him about her meeting with the FBI.

"Sure. It's been a while."

"Good. Noon. I'll text you where."

The call died. Vic stared at his phone. "Good talking to you, too." He placed the phone on his workbench and reached for his glove, only to have his phone spring to life again, the ringtone echoing in the small space.

This time it was Craig. Vic pressed the screen button to accept the call.

"Vic? Sorry to call so early, but I thought it was important."

"No problem. What's up?" He noted that Craig used his first name, not the formal Detective Lenoski. Good. Baby steps, he thought.

"I got some records for Melanie Beck's phone last night, so I went through them. I have her day pretty well mapped out, but there's one thing I thought was important."

"What?"

"Someone placed a tracking app on her phone. The only entries to it are from an outside phone. Melanie never accessed the app herself, at least not in the last month. I'm thinking the murderer accessed the app, found out she was on the trail, and attacked her."

Vic struggled to put this information into a form he could understand. "Are you sure she didn't put it on her phone herself?"

"It's not that kind of program. It's sold as a spy app so people can track someone and read their texts without them knowing."

"Huh. Can you tell who was tracking her?"

"No, the requestor is masked. But I'll ask the phone carrier, they might be able to give us some kind of identifier."

"So I guess...." Vic stopped, sorting through his thoughts. "Let me get my head around this one step at a time. To install the app, someone needed access to her phone, right?"

"Yes."

"Okay. Then they must be close to her, and they needed enough time to place the app and hide it so she wouldn't see it?"

"Right. But hiding it is easy. Spy apps are designed not to show up once they are loaded on someone's phone."

Vic thought about the implications. "Holy hell. And you said someone checked Melanie's location just before the attack happened?"

"Yep. About three-thirty."

Vic frowned at the concrete of the basement floor, his mind working. He saw a problem with the timeline. He started slowly, not wanting Craig to lose his excitement. "Does that work, though? I mean, for the killer? If I think it through, at three-thirty, I doubt Melanie was on the trail. And remember what Kasey Wells said? Wells ran to the end of the trail and back and never saw Melanie until she found the body. That means Melanie had just started her walk. But the attacker needed to know she was on the trail, then get into position. That takes time. It could tell us something else, though. The killer had to already know she would be walking the trail. More than likely, the check at 3:30 was to confirm Melanie was near the trail and hadn't changed her schedule. So the attacker was likely someone who already knew she planned to walk the trail, and they were close to being in position by 3:30. Maybe they already were. Put it all together and we need to find someone with access to Melanie's phone who knew she was going to walk the trail."

Craig was silent. Vic tacked. "Craig, this is a good find. Get after the phone company and see if you can find out who accessed the app. Chances are very good this is the killer, or is working with them. And now we know that when we interview, we need to look for access to Melanie's phone and knowledge of her schedule. And this also explains why we haven't found Melanie's phone. It's possible the killer took it, hoping to hide the fact there's spyware on it. Plus, the spyware means premeditation. Once we find who placed the app on her phone, I bet we get motive. Also, if the app lets them secretly read her texts, maybe the killer suspected Melanie of something. Otherwise why go to the trouble? Did the texts tell us anything?"

"No. They were pretty tame. 'What's up' and 'How are you' kind of stuff."

Vic thought Craig sounded mollified. "Get onto the carrier and see if we can figure out who accessed the app. We find that out and we're much closer. We'll go through the timeline of Melanie's day when we're all together."

When they hung up, Vic stared at the heavy bag. He was still wearing only one boxing glove.

"The hell with it," he said to the bag, pulled off the remaining glove, and went upstairs to take a shower.

Chapter Twenty-Eight

Craig sat on the edge of his bed, his phone lying next to him on the rumpled sheets. He'd worked until almost eleven o'clock, sure that he'd had another breakthrough in the case. He didn't like it, but Vic's thinking made sense. The timing just didn't work if someone checked the app and then set an ambush. He knew he should have spotted that fact before calling. He looked around the bedroom, at the bedside table he'd taken from his parents' house. The design was early American, and it didn't match the Ikea three-drawer wardrobe against the far wall. His closet door hung open. Like all Pittsburgh homes from the late 1800s, the bedroom closet was smaller than a phone booth. All the clothes piled on door hooks meant the door couldn't close.

Craig hated how little he had to show Vic and Liz from his work the night before. He rose and sorted through the clothes piled on the only chair in the room, found chinos and a shirt clean enough to rewear, and dressed. He'd found the old wooden chair at a yard sale. It dated to the fifties and sported the futuristic design of furniture made during the space race.

He padded down the hall to the kitchen. The oven and refrigerator were in the avocado green of the nineteen-sixties.

He ate a bowl of cereal leaning against the metal sink, staring across the living room. As he crunched through each mouthful, he thought about his last girlfriend, the administrative assistant to Vic's commander at the Pittsburgh Bureau of Police. They'd dated for almost a year, what, five years ago now?

Was it really that long ago?

At first, he'd thought there might be more between them, but when she saw his apartment, she'd joked about him living in an old building, given his job as a high-tech whiz for the detectives. It was funny at first, the old-house-modern-job trope, but the joke turned barbed when they discussed living together. She wanted modern, preferably in one of the buildings that Craig thought looked identical to all the other apartments and condominiums springing up around the city. Within a couple of weeks, they stopped talking about it, and three weeks later simply neglected to call one another. Apart from a couple of Saturday bar-night episodes, Craig hadn't brought anyone else home.

He made himself stop thinking about his sorry love life. Instead, he thought about why someone would place spyware on a phone. It was a type of behavior he couldn't understand. He guessed with the spyware, there was some fundamental insecurity involved, or some debilitating need to control. Both were extremes. He thought about the people involved in the case and saw nothing in their personalities that might lead to that kind of behavior.

But then again, he didn't know them very well. He reminded himself that people are capable of all kinds of things no one expects.

As he drove to work, he thought about interviewing. How exactly did you ask someone if they had access to Melanie's phone and not have them lie to you? The same with asking them if they knew her schedule. It seemed an easy thing to lie about and a hard thing to disprove if the person did lie. He couldn't think of anything in the training manual that explained how to circumvent that problem.

We need the phone number of whoever accessed the spyware, he decided finally. It was the only way.

Chapter Twenty-Nine

By the time Vic left to meet Levon for lunch, he, Liz, and Craig had discussed every permutation of Melanie's last day alive. They'd taken a break at ten o'clock for Liz to confirm Melanie shopped at the specialty clothing store while Craig called Melanie's cell phone carrier for the phone number that accessed the spyware on Melanie's phone. Craig also called Melanie's home security company for the security system data. Neither company delivered, although they were quick with promises.

Afterwards, the discussion shifted to the suspect pool. The idea that someone needed access to Melanie's phone to plant the spyware created a problem. Their number one suspect, Melanie's ex-husband Holden, had the least access to Melanie's phone. Telst emerged as a better suspect, given he lived with Melanie, and Liz remained convinced Telst and Melanie were lovers. But they needed to confirm the affair was real.

As a group, they decided to reinterview Melanie's house guests once they obtained the data from the security system and the phone number. Vic hoped something would emerge to corner Holden. To Vic, Holden was the most likely to plant the spyware, given how raw he was about the divorce. It also fit with his lie about his alibi.

Driving out of the parking lot, Vic's mind shifted to Levon and the FBI investigation. He jerked upright and checked his mirrors, fear sparking through him. For several seconds he skated on that fear, even as he told himself the probability of being followed was tiny. Whatever crime the FBI was investigating, it couldn't be high profile enough to commit the agents and automobiles needed to track his movements. He drew in a breath. He was getting paranoid.

But, as he pulled onto the Parkway, a second thought came to him. Levon had suggested lunch at a restaurant underneath a Mexican supermarket in the Strip District. The narrow entrance steps were hard to find, meaning the restaurant and its high-backed booths were usually half empty. It was perfect for a private conversation. Levon must have considered the same possibility they were being followed.

Then again, that might simply be his training. He wondered if Levon contracted for the CIA anymore.

As Vic negotiated the narrow, crowded sidewalks of the Strip district, it crossed his mind they were perfect for losing a tail. Something else Levon would have considered.

He ducked into the restaurant entrance, descended the steps and found Levon waiting for him, folded into a narrow booth in the far corner of the restaurant, facing the door. When Vic approached, he slid out of the booth, and they hugged. He was as muscular as Vic remembered.

They took seats opposite one another. "How's the PI business?" Vic asked once they were settled.

"Law firm keeps me busy." Levon gave him a boyish grin, which was incongruous on his weathered face. "Apparently, a lot of rich jerks try to hide their money before they divorce their wives for younger women. I think I spend half my time tracking down where they hid it. I've burned a couple of them now. I'm kind of liking it."

"God's work."

"Yes, it is."

They sat back so a waitress could place glasses of water on the table, along with menus. She disappeared without a word.

"I've got an overseas thing coming up. That'll be more interesting."

That answered the question of whether Levon still contracted for the CIA. Vic knew better than to ask about it. "Liz okay with that? Last time you came back from one of those, you needed two months to heal."

"Can't say she is, but I have to do at least one more." Levon opened the menu and studied it. "I promised someone. And the money's good."

Again, Vic let the comment pass. They fell silent as they stared at the menus and closed them at almost the same time a few moments later. Vic had noticed before that they tended to move in parallel, but didn't mention it.

"The FBI." Vic watched him for a reaction.

Levon nodded. The waitress appeared at their table as if she'd been watching for the signal of lowered menus. She took their orders and disappeared into the kitchen.

"Liz told me." Levon shifted his shoulder as if it still bothered him. "Do you have any idea why they're looking into this? I mean, apart from the obvious."

Vic smelled the bitter smoke of the burning North Dakota house, and Levon, grabbing his shoulder, pushing him toward the staircase that led to the second floor.

"Nope."

"Okay." Levon glanced about the restaurant. When he started to speak, his voice was lower. "I talked to Charlie Running Bear last night. He's going to check with Jimmy Pronghorn. See if anyone in North Dakota is taking a second look."

"I wondered," Vic said slowly, "If any of Charlie's guys were arrested. If someone is peddling information for a deal."

"I had the same thought. Charlie said no. His guys are in South Dakota now, anyway. He also told me about the woman who runs the halfway house...Kelly, right? Somehow I missed that you left her a duffel bag full of cash. Apparently, she's now your number one fan."

"Seemed like the right thing to do at the time."

"Sounds like it." Levon sat back, his eyes tracking the restaurant. "That cash is still helping people, so Charlie was sure Kelly wouldn't rat you out. I can't figure out why, but even without the money, Kelly liked you." Levon looked him right in the eyes. "That seems unlikely."

Vic heard voices behind him and guessed the waitress was leading customers to a booth. He listened. A man and a woman.

"I think," Levon said slowly, his eyes on the new patrons, "And you already know this, the real problem is Lettie. She's impossible to explain."

Vic's stomach tightened. "Exactly what I'm thinking. Jimmy sent me a birth certificate, but that's it. He kind of made it up that Lettie was born on the reservation."

"Who's to say she wasn't?" Levon focused on him. "Until we know different, I think we gut it out. Stick to the facts. The night of the fire, we were at Kelly's. That was our alibi, and clearly, she'll stick to it. We got Lettie from her. Charlie is going to talk to her and make sure she adds that part. Parents unknown."

"I doubt she said that in the original interview with the State Police."

"Probably not. But that was more than five years ago. She can say she thought she did."

Vic shook his head. "The State Police investigator, I met him. He's good. He'll have a record of what she said back then."

"He can doubt all he wants." Levon's face tightened, and he tapped his hand once on the table in a command to stop the conversation. Vic froze. Levon took an exaggerated swig of his water, which Vic realized neatly hid his face, at least for a second or two.

When he placed the glass back on the table, Vic gave him a quizzical look.

Levon didn't say anything for a few seconds. "Guy came in and asked the waitress to see a menu. Checked it slowly, looked to see who was here, returned the menu, and left."

"FBI?"

"He had the smell. Somehow he wasn't dressed right for it, though."

"What did he look like?"

Levon frowned. "Asian guy. Maybe five foot nine. Stocky."

Vic ached to turn around and look, but didn't. "He's gone?"

"Yeah." Levon sat back, and the waitress appeared next to their booth. She placed their orders in front of them, and Vic thanked her. He stared at the food. He didn't feel hungry at all.

Levon frowned at his plate. "You being followed doesn't make sense."

"I had the same thought." Vic looked at him. "No way they'd commit that many resources to me."

CHAPTER TWENTY-NINE

"Not unless they were sure of what they had."

"But why here? What do they think I'm still doing related to North Dakota that would make them follow me now?"

"Beats me." Levon studied him. "You need to get in front of this somehow."

"You think I don't know that?"

"I know you do." Levon took a slow breath. "Just showing off my keen grasp of the obvious. I guess because I don't know what else to say."

"Me neither." Vic gave him a smile to show he wasn't offended.

They both started their food, but Vic didn't taste anything as he chewed. That capability seemed to have slipped away from him, as everything else threatened to do.

Chapter Thirty

Craig received an email from the home security company late that afternoon. He'd never worked with security system data and stared at the spreadsheet's rows and columns, unsure where to start.

Liz shuffled next to him and studied his computer screen. "Good luck with that. And all we really need to know is what time Ryan Telst got back to the house on the day of the murder, right? If it's before four o'clock, he's in the clear. Why'd the company give us so much crap anyway?"

Craig wasn't sure what made him ask for so much data. "I asked for two weeks, plus the two days after the murder." Slowly, the columns and rows began to make sense. He understood he was looking at the list of security system sensors inside the Beck house, followed by a chronology of the dates and times each was activated. In looking at it, he saw a way to use it. He just needed to untangle it all.

Craig shut his laptop and stood. "I'm going to map it out in the conference room. I need the whiteboard."

Liz shifted to one side so he could pass and followed him. Inside the conference room, Craig reopened his laptop in the crook of his left arm, and, writing on the whiteboard, listed the sensor codes in a column from the most frequently activated to the least. Finished, he placed his laptop on the conference table and pointed at the sensor at the top of the list. "I bet that's the front door. Jessica and Ryan park outside, they use the front door to get to their cars. Melanie parks in the garage, the sensor for the garage door she used will be in the middle of the list somewhere."

Liz cocked her head. "Maybe. We need a floorplan that shows where each sensor is located."

"And then we get a pattern of how and when people move about the house."

Liz gave him a small smile. "Might be useful. We could see if anyone is moving about the house at two in the morning."

They stood together in silence, staring at the whiteboard before Liz turned to him. "Does that matter, though? I mean, really? As I said, we just need to know when Telst got back to the house on the day Melanie was killed. He told us about four. If that turns out to be true, then he's in the clear. We move on to the husband. And we already caught Beck in a lie."

Craig turned to his laptop and scrolled through the security firm's spreadsheet. "True. If the front door is the sensor triggered the most, then on the day of the murder, it was triggered at... one-ten in the afternoon. And the whole system was armed just after that. Then nothing is triggered until the whole system was disarmed at..." he stared at the time stamp to make sure he wasn't misreading it, "Five-thirty-two p.m. The front door sensor activates less than a minute later."

"Crap." Liz let out a sharp breath.

"So Ryan lied to us as well. He stays in the frame."

They both turned. Vic was standing just inside the door, looking haggard. "He told you guys he was home by four, right?"

Craig wondered when Vic entered the room.

"Right." Irritation shaded Liz's voice. "Jerk lied to my face. But what pisses me off is that the more we learn, the easier the case is supposed to get. Not the more complicated." She frowned. "Wait. If the sensor that gets triggered the most is the front door, why isn't the whole system armed before the door opens? That delay thing is so people can turn on the alarm and get out before the alarm goes off?"

Craig was fairly sure he knew the answer to that. "I bet Ryan arms the system through an app on his phone. He goes outside, the front door sensor captures that, then he uses his phone to arm the system."

"They both lied," Vic intoned from the door. "Ryan Telst and Holden Beck,

Melanie's ex-husband."

For a full thirty seconds, no one spoke.

"I was thinking," Craig said slowly, returning to his earlier thoughts. "It might be a good idea to go out to the house, map out the rooms and identify where each sensor is located. That way, we can be sure of what we're looking at. The most used sensor might not be the front door."

Liz eyed him. "Lots of work when we only need to know about the front door."

"Like you said, we'd see how people move about the house," Craig said quickly. "At what times."

Vic squeezed his eyes shut and pinched the bridge of his nose. He dropped his hand and gazed at Craig. "Yeah. I think we have to do it. Especially since we have two people who lied about their alibis. We need to be absolutely sure we know what we're dealing with."

"Okay." Liz didn't look upset that Vic agreed to Craig's suggestion. More bemused.

Craig glanced at the clock on his computer. "I can go out there right now. There's still time today."

Liz glanced at her wristwatch, and Craig saw her calculating. He guessed her thoughts. By the time they drove out, talked to Telst, mapped the floorplan, and located the sensors, it would be late enough for Liz to go home. And she lived a scant two miles from Melanie Beck's house.

Liz dropped her hand. "I'll go too. If Telst is there, I can give him some shit. Maybe get him to repeat what time he got home, so we got him clean on the lie."

"Sounds good," Vic said softly. "Just don't signal that we know he got back after five, in case that turns out to be true. I want to do that with at least two witnesses."

Liz picked up the eraser and cleared the whiteboard.

Craig had the odd feeling the trip might turn out to be interesting.

Craig and Liz drove their own cars, and along the way, Craig called the local police for access to the Beck estate.

When they arrived, the officer from their first visit was waiting. He plugged the numbers into the keypad and waved them inside as the gates swung open. This time he didn't follow them.

Craig and Liz parked next to Ryan's truck and Jessica's Prius. Craig was about to knock on the front door, but the barely muffled shouts of an argument inside the house made him stop. He pointed at the door. "Do you hear that?" he whispered.

Liz shuffled closer and tilted her head. "Can't make it out. One of them is Telst. Jessica has to be the other one. I don't think Kwan has shouted in his entire life."

Liz turned the doorknob and hesitated as the door opened. She made up her mind and gently pushed the door ajar.

"Why not?" The woman shouted.

Craig recognized Jessica's voice.

"Why not?" Jessica repeated, this time in a shriek.

If Ryan answered, Craig didn't hear it. Silence pulsed through the house.

Liz called out, identified herself, and stepped into the hall. Craig followed her. Liz called out again, and Ryan Telst appeared out of the den at the end of the hall.

Ryan stared at them, his slack face shocked and exhausted. Liz kept her right hand propped on the butt of her holstered Glock.

Jessica pushed past Ryan. "What are you doing here?"

"Investigating." The way Liz said the word was so dry, Craig half expected the hallway to sprout cactus and Brittlebush.

Liz looked from one to the other. "Is everything okay here? Sounds like a heck of an argument."

Jessica's face flushed. "You can't just walk in here."

Liz slid her hand inside her leather jacket and removed her phone. Held it up with a gentle wave. "Actually, we can. Our warrant is good for multiple entries."

Jessica spun on her heel and disappeared in the direction of the kitchen.

Ryan blinked and just stared at them. "What do you want?"

Liz started toward him. "Spoken like a true handyman. We need to map the house. Get a floor plan. It won't take long. By the way, how do you set the burglar alarm? Turn it on, I mean." She stopped in front of him, so close he shied back.

"I have an app on my phone."

"Don't we all." Liz looked him up and down. "Glad we could arrive in time to break up the fight. What were you guys arguing about?"

Craig joined them in time to see a flicker in Ryan's eyes. "I have no freaking idea." He turned and disappeared into the den. Craig guessed he was keeping as much distance between himself and Jessica as possible.

Liz looked at Craig, a smile on her face. She was enjoying herself, he realized. She made a motion with her hand, which Craig took to mean he was to start mapping out the alarm sensors.

He went back down the hall, found the alarm control pad near the foot of the broad stairway, and opened the front door to see which sensor appeared on the alarm system's readout. He noted it down in his notebook. He then walked around the first floor and drew an accurate floor plan. As he did, he noticed all the rooms with large windows also contained a motion detector opposite the glass. He guessed those sensors were designed to capture movement from someone breaking in through the windows. He started a second circuit, noting the location of each sensor on his floor plan. After doing so, he waved at the newly identified motion sensor or opened and closed the door before checking the main alarm panel to note down the name of the sensor he'd just triggered.

He worked through the living room and dining room, the den, study and kitchen. At the rear of the house, he found a long sun room stretching the width of the house, the outside wall a row of adjoining French windows. A wicker furniture grouping filled part of the space, the rest a jumble of music stands, straight-backed chairs, and musical instrument cases. A place to practice. Past the French doors, a broad backyard sloped uphill to the edge of a wooded area.

He spent upwards of twenty minutes in that room. He discovered that in addition to three motion detectors facing the French windows, each set of doors had a sensor in the door frame near the hinges. Belts and suspenders, he thought, wondering why the double set of sensors was needed. As he walked to and from the hallway alarm panel, he heard Liz talking to Ryan. It didn't sound as if Ryan was saying much in response to Liz's questions.

He finished in the garage, where he found a second security panel just inside the doorway leading into the house. Finished, he counted how many sensors he'd found and compared it to the number provided by the alarm company. He was two short. That didn't bother him particularly. There might be more upstairs.

Something nagged at him, and he stopped to think about what it was. While he was working, he hadn't run into Jessica. Not in the kitchen or any of the rooms. If she was upstairs, he hadn't seen her use the front staircase, despite all the times he'd visited the alarm panel near their base. He didn't know what to make of that.

Slowly, he did a second loop through the downstairs rooms, ending in the kitchen. She was nowhere to be seen. He looked about the kitchen, which was larger than his entire apartment. The center island, easily fifteen feet long and five feet wide, was designed so anyone cooking or washing the dishes could look across the kitchen, through the windows, and into the flower beds and woods at the edge of the back yard. Behind him were cabinets framing the entrance to the den. Liz and Ryan were no longer talking, the only sound from the room was the rumble of a television.

He followed the line of cabinets to the corner and along the side wall. The last cabinet door was recessed and stretched from the floor to the top of the cabinets.

Craig opened it. It led into a pantry the size of his apartment's kitchen. The shelves lining the side walls were jammed with foodstuffs. The entire back wall was a large glass-doored wine cooler. And directly to the right was a second door. He pulled it open. Steep, narrow stairs led upwards. Craig climbed them, looking for sensors. Two-thirds of the way up, the stairs took a forty-five-degree turn to the right and ended six steps later at a door. Craig turned the knob and emerged on the second-floor landing, in the back third of the house.

The stairway, he knew, was for the domestic help. His aunt had lived in a large Victorian in the East End of Pittsburgh when he was growing up, and her house contained the same partially hidden back stairway connecting the kitchen to the second floor. He'd loved playing on it, of its suggestion of secrets and hidden passageways. Yet his aunt's house, he knew, was more than one hundred years old. According to the county real estate listings, this house was barely fifty years old, built when architects no longer worried about the need to hide a phalanx of live-in servants from the homeowner's family. Whoever built the house, he realized, must have expected domestics to be in residence, was familiar with the traditional ways of keeping them out of sight, and requested the stairway from the architect.

Nice to have money passed down from generation to generation, he thought grimly.

He checked the hallway ceiling line for sensors. None. He walked down the hall to the head of the stairs, pivoted, and looked back down the hall. To his left were double doors. He knew from his previous visit they led to the master suite. Two doors were spaced apart on the right, then came the door to the back stairs, and finally, two narrow doors faced each other at the very end of the hall. Those rooms were meant for servants, he guessed.

He knocked on the double doors, and, hearing no reply, stepped inside the master suite. Finally, he spotted a motion detector. It sat on the side wall overlooking the room's front windows. On the other side of the windows was a porch roof, and he understood the security company's logic. They were worried about someone climbing onto the porch roof and using it to enter the master bedroom. He noted another security system keypad near the bedroom doors, placed there so someone going to bed could turn on the alarm before lying down.

He waved his hands at the sensor, checked the keypad screen, and noted the name of the motion detector. He then checked the bathroom and, next to it, a walk-in closet as large as his living room.

No sensor, not that he expected one. However, a thought crossed his mind. Now that he knew the layout of the bedrooms, he was aware that one of the servant's rooms shared a wall with the back wall of the closet.

He walked to that wall and separated a line of hanging blouses. A door looked back at him, locked with a deadbolt. He slid back the bolt, opened the door, and stepped into the narrow bedroom beyond.

From the sweaty, musty smell, he guessed this was Ryan's room. An open duffel bag of baseball equipment confirmed it. The narrow bed was unmade, clothes stacked on the desk chair. A tiny attached bathroom presented nothing of interest beyond shampoo bottles and a toothbrush. Craig checked both rooms for sensors, and, finding none, stepped back into the master bedroom's closet. He slid the bolt home. He suspected that Ryan's bedroom was the smallest on the second floor, but it did have one big advantage: Whenever Melanie Beck felt like it, she could slide back the bolt and invite Ryan into her suite. In a very quiet and confidential way.

The lives of the rich and famous, Craig thought, stepping back into the upstairs hall.

He knocked on the second door, and Jessica responded, anger still tinging her voice.

"Jessica, I need to check your room for a security system sensor. Can you open the door?"

It was a full minute before the doorknob rattled, and Jessica open the door. She'd changed since they arrived and was now dressed in leggings and a loose sweatshirt with Northwestern's logo on the front. Her hair flowed freely around her shoulders. From the loose movement of her sweatshirt, he knew she no longer wore at least one item of underwear.

She smiled, leaned against the door, and arched her back. "Check out whatever you want to check out."

"Thanks." He carefully ignored her and searched the ceiling line. No sensor. He glanced around the room, seeing the door to an ensuite bathroom set into the back wall. He thought about checking it, but didn't want to walk into her room. He suspected she might close the door. Instead, he bent slightly and checked the door frame for the tiny plunger used by the door sensors, trying to keep as far away from Jessica as he could. Even so, they were close enough together to feel the warmth of her breath. He straightened and maintained eye contact. "Is Kwan's room the next one? Down the hall?"

"Yep. The one after Kwan's is empty, and the one across the hall from the empty one is Ryan's."

"Got it. Thanks." He thought about saying something about the argument he'd overheard and decided against it. From their first meeting at the Heinz Loft apartments and their interaction at the symphony, he knew Jessica could run hot or cold, friendly or bitterly sarcastic with the flip of a button. It was a whiplash quality he didn't like.

"Stop by any time." She lightly touched his forearm.

Craig backed away as politely as possible, nodded to her, and headed for Kwan's room. The door to Jessica's room thumped shut.

When he emerged from Kwan's room, Liz was standing in the hallway. "You done yet?"

He pointed at the last room. "Almost. I'm one sensor short."

Liz followed him to the doorway of the last room, the one just past the entrance to the back stairway. It was as narrow as Ryan's room, with the same tiny bathroom, and contained the last sensor pointed at the window. Craig checked outside and saw an overhang for the back door a few feet below. He waved at the sensor and said to Liz, "I want to show you something."

He led Liz back to the master suite, checked the alarm panel readout, and noted down the name of the last sensor. He then opened the closet door and showed Liz the door to Ryan's room, hidden behind the hanging blouses.

"Well, isn't that convenient," Liz said slowly.

"Isn't it. Ryan's room is on the other side. I think originally, a maid slept there. I bet the door was to let them in and out of the master suite without being noticed."

"Why would you do that?"

"Help the woman who lives here dress. Pick up and put back laundry."

Liz shook her head. "I don't live right."

They walked back into the suite.

"I've identified all the sensors. Did Ryan say anything?"

"That boy forgot the English language. I don't know what's going on between him and Jessica, but it's nasty."

"Maybe Jessica thought he was sleeping with Melanie and didn't like it."

"Seems the logical reason." Liz closed her eyes for a moment. "But there's something about him I can't figure out."

"Did he change his story about what time he got home?"

"Still says it was about four, but I didn't push it. Vic's right about needing two of us there when we challenge him. And he repeated that while you were walking around checking the alarm system. You'd think he'd see what you're doing and realize his alibi might be shot."

It crossed Craig's mind that perhaps Ryan wasn't sharp enough to draw a line between those two dots. He chastised himself. When he took the job with Vic, his father had warned him never to underestimate suspects or make assumptions about them. It reminded him, with a pang of satisfaction, of Eileen Liang telling him criminals would underestimate him. He'd liked that idea. Now he told himself not to fall into the same trap with suspects. He turned to Liz. "I'm ready to go."

"Be nice to place Telst downtown at four." Liz's voice was wistful. She looked at Craig. "And we also got Holden Beck in a dead lie. This case is weird."

Craig thought of Jessica arching her back against the door and what she was and wasn't wearing. "You've got that right."

Chapter Thirty-One

Vic arrived home as Anne was putting out dinner for Lettie. He'd spent the afternoon veering between schemes to discover what the FBI was investigating and his dread of going home. He had to tell Anne. He'd decided to wait until Lettie was asleep to have the conversation. Anne set a third plate for him, but the food was as tasteless as his lunch.

Lettie's pleasure and excitement over her food made him feel worse.

"It was a nice day, and I took Lettie to the park," Anne offered, watching Lettie eat. "Must be because she was on swings and playing tag most of the day."

"It shows."

After dinner, Vic waited an hour as Lettie played, then offered to put her to bed. Anne was surprised, but didn't question it. He took Lettie upstairs, helped her bathe, and watched in amusement at the sheer determination on her face as she struggled into her pajamas. He read to her, the routine a balm.

When he came downstairs, Anne was sitting on the couch with her feet tucked underneath her legs.

"My turn?" She asked, smiling.

"I just read Green Eggs and Ham three times. Hold out for something better."

"God. She should be past that." Anne laughed lightly and climbed the stairs.

Unable to concentrate, Vic turned off the television. Anne was happy as she went upstairs, and he was about to destroy that. He breathed deeply.

There was nothing he could do about it. She had to know. They needed to be ready for what was coming.

The gentle murmur of Anne's reading voice started upstairs. Vic picked up the newspaper from the coffee table and shook it out. Slowly, he reviewed the front-page stories, reading one, then opened the pages, his eyes sliding from article to article.

He stopped on the third page. Toward the bottom, a headline proclaimed,

Ex-Staffer Sues DAs Office

Vic stared in surprise. He skimmed the story, finding it thin on facts. But he knew the actual history. The staffer bringing the suit was John Lee, one of Hanna's first hires as DA and Vic's initial commander at the Allegheny County Police. Vic had started working a few days after John. But late into their first case together, Vic discovered John leaking information about the case to the press. John's plan was to hurt Hanna politically, then run against her in the next election.

When Vic told Hanna who was leaking information to the press, Hanna fired John immediately. Vic was sitting in Hanna's office when she did.

And now John was suing the DA's office for wrongful termination. The article failed to mention John's leaks to the press, which told Vic the source of the article was John or his lawyer. John was still at it, trying to gain traction for his campaign for DA.

Vic shook his head. John angered him. He was also sure John couldn't win his case, but knew John didn't care about that. He simply wanted to throw doubt on the competence of the DA in a public, showy way.

"What's the problem?"

Vic looked up. He hadn't heard Anne come downstairs. She smiled at him. "You look like thunder, as my mother likes to say."

He held up the newspaper. "Remember my commander when I started working again? John Lee? He's suing Hana and the DA's office for wrongful termination."

"I thought he leaked details of a murder case."

"He did. He just wants a way to make Hanna look incompetent or sneaky, when she's got more integrity than any DA I've seen. He's been after her job from the start."

"It shouldn't be hard to prove he leaked confidential information."

Vic folded the paper and tossed it on the couch. "I'm not so sure. The journalist involved can refuse to say it was John. He can say he won't give up his source."

Anne frowned. "But can't Hana tell the press why John was fired?"

"Not easily. If Hana makes the claim, but the journalist doesn't corroborate her story, then John can bring a defamation suit. Hana's counsel will want to avoid that." Vic thought for a moment. "She's on a knife edge. And you know what? I bet John doesn't even care if he loses the case."

"Then why bring it?"

"He just wants the case in the courts and newspapers as long as possible. Right up to the next election, if he can do it. That way, he can use it when he runs for DA."

"I hate that kind of manipulation of the courts."

Vic avoided saying the obvious. That people did this all the time. Instead, he thought about Lettie. "Lettie went to sleep, okay?"

"Pretty quickly, actually. I read her some Paddington, and she was out within about two minutes. You did a good job getting her ready."

Vic nodded, and they fell silent.

Anne watched him. "Something on your mind? I mean, other than the article? You were quiet tonight. You hardly ate."

Vic stretched his legs in front of him. "Yes. And I'm not sure what to do about it."

"Okay. Try me."

"It has to do with Lettie." He looked at Anne in time to see her face tighten. She folded her arms on her chest. "What do you mean?"

Vic looked around the room. He wanted a drink suddenly. "Liz." He stopped and gathered his thoughts. "Liz got called into the FBI. They had a ton of questions about what happened when I was in North Dakota."

The silence widened. Anne frowned as she tried to absorb the information.

She met his gaze. "I didn't ask what happened out there. I could tell you didn't want me to. But I did ask you if we're okay. If anything can come back to hurt us. You told me we were fine." An accusatory note crept into her voice.

Vic looked away across the living room, to the seam where the ceiling and wall met. "Mostly, that's true. But there's always something you don't expect. I talked to Levon today." He couldn't meet her eyes. "He talked to the people we worked with in North Dakota. There's no obvious way the FBI could know everything that happened."

"But there must be something. Or they wouldn't be talking to your *partner*."

"Who was recovering in hospital here at the time. Which is what she told them."

Anne raised her hand for him to stop.

"We can't have this conversation without you telling me what happened. And I do not want to know. My only question is this. Does this involve Lettie in any way? Are we in danger of losing her? Our grandchild?"

Pressure squeezed Vic's heart. "I don't know. But I can't rule it out."

"And where would she go?" Anne's voice rose, a mixture of desperation and fear.

"Who would want her?"

"I don't know." But the phrasing of Anne's question threw a switch, made him think of something he hadn't considered. "I guess, I hadn't thought of this, but Lettie's father. I mean the father's family, they could make a claim." The pressure in his chest rose to his throat and made him feel lightheaded. He hadn't considered this possibility. Lettie's father and grandfather were dead, he knew that for a fact. But was there a grandmother? An aunt or uncle? The thought was like grabbing a live wire. Of course. Had someone claimed Lettie was kidnapped? It would explain the FBI's involvement. But why after five years? Why now? He blinked against the cascade of thoughts, bringing his gaze to Anne's face.

She stared at him, pale, her face taught. She tried to speak, her lips shifting, but no sound came out. Her entire body shivered once, quickly, and she found her voice. It came from a long way inside her. "I will not lose a third child."

Unable to breathe, Vic rose, crossed to her and sat next to her on the couch. Wrapped her in his arms. Dannie, their daughter. Trafficked to North Dakota. Stolen from them. Dead. But he and Anne never talked about their first child. The boy. Dannie's elder brother. Miscarried fifteen weeks into Anne's pregnancy.

In his arms, Anne was rigid.

"That won't happen." It was an impossible thing for him to say. He knew it. He had no control over events. "I'll do everything I can. Whatever I have to do."

In his arms, Anne shivered, softened. She gave in to him, spoke to his chest. "Please," she whispered. "I can't go through it again."

He held her. He had nothing to add. But, for the first time since talking to Levon, he sensed a way forward. Of course, Ewan Fleck and his father had relatives, and that was something he could find out. A fantasy rose in his mind. He envisioned Chief Fleck's wife, the mother of Lettie's father, Ewan. He saw her as rawboned and rail thin, scarred by the grief of her lost men and white-hot with vengeance. She strode toward him, aching to reclaim her grandchild, the endless sky behind her, the wind whipping her gray hair about her head.

Vic held Anne tight.

He had a place to start. He could find out if she existed, if the family was pushing the FBI.

Yet, in the same moment, he understood that was futile. If someone like her was out there, they would be living by the feud. She would never stop. She would want Lettie for herself and a knife through his heart.

She would want her revenge.

Chapter Thirty-Two

C hen Yun glanced from Song to Lin as they talked. He could tell them apart, finally. Song, arrogant and full of himself, the politician's son. Lin, smiling but sly, the banker's son. Perhaps that's the problem, Chen thought. I can only think of these two as people's sons. Not as men themselves.

Somehow they hadn't earned more than that.

The table between them was littered with smeared empty plates and water glasses beaded with condensation. Needing an update, Chen had met them at a small restaurant near the university that specialized in American breakfasts. His own plate was only half finished, a mound of potatoes barely touched. He could never get over the portion sizes in America, how the plates in restaurants arrived loaded with twice the food anyone needed. The waste, he often thought, must be tremendous. But that was America in a nutshell. The country that produced more garbage than any other in the world. He was glad China had stopped accepting America's refuse. Let them drown in it, he thought.

He realized Song and Lin were no longer speaking and focused on them. Song was smirking. "What do you think, Comrade?"

"I don't," Chen responded. "Not yet." He grabbed at the last fragment of conversation he remembered. "You said Liling went grocery shopping again yesterday afternoon. How many bags?"

"Four, again. It is the second time." Lin grinned.

Chen couldn't deny the quickening in his stomach. Liling was buying more food than she needed for herself. That was significant. It almost made

Lin's need for acceptance bearable.

"I could ask her out," Song said. "When I take her home, I will enter her apartment. See if her father is there."

Chen turned to him. This was the third time Song had offered to approach Liling. Chen didn't like it. Song talked too much about Liling's looks, her curves, what she wore. Song didn't seem able to bridle his lust. "No." Chen kept his tone sharp and clipped. "You will not approach her. You will not give her cause to approach you. Do you understand? That could jeopardize our plans."

Song shifted against the straight back of the booth's seat. He didn't like being talked to that way, or for someone to disagree with him. That was obvious. "What plans?" His voice was just as clipped as Chen's. "We wish to know what to do next."

Chen stared at him, noting how Lin turned away slightly, as if he didn't want to be included as part of Song's question. In an odd way, Chen was impressed at Song's arrogance. To speak to a superior that way. To someone older than him.

"I can see you have been away from China for a long time, Comrade Song." Chen took his time with the sentence, weighing his options. This was the problem with recruiting students. In Singapore and other cities, the people he recruited were in fear of him. Yiptou Ng fit that category. That made them compliant. But students were always so full of their own futures they believed themselves superior to him.

But he couldn't put up with Song's insolence. It was time to give him a warning.

With distaste, Chen pushed away his half-plate of uneaten food and leaned forward on his elbows, his face only a foot from Song's. "I will decide on the steps we take, and when to take them. Do you understand? Since you can't understand that, I will let you know when I need you again. You may go. Lin, please stay. There is something I wish to discuss."

Song's eyes widened, and he opened his mouth to speak, but Chen was faster.

"Thank you, Comrade Song. As I said, when I need you, I will call."

Song rocked on the bench seat like a small boy unhinged by the theft of his balloon. Anger shifted to resentment in Song's eyes. "If you would do as I say, by now, Liling would know men like me are to be obeyed. We would have the location of her father already." Song's voice cracked. "My father will hear about your impertinence." Song slid out of the booth, his face stony. He disappeared outside.

Chen sighed. Right now, he needed to separate Song and Lin. Song was acting as if Lin supported him, and that gave Song strength. Chen didn't think Lin agreed with Song, but Song had the stronger personality. If he could work with Lin for a day or two, he might be able to turn Lin into his ally. Then Lin would help to keep Song under control. Once that happened, he would call Song back to work.

"I apologize for that," Chen said, making his tone as friendly as possible. "Your reports are detailed, and I want to thank you for spotting the amount of shopping Liling is doing."

Lin nodded. For the first time that Chen could remember, Lin wasn't smiling.

But Chen meant the compliment. Lin had, automatically, counted the shopping bags and noted it. Lin seemed to have a banker's eye for detail, like his father. It was useful. "I was wondering if you could watch Liling this afternoon and evening. Is that possible, with your schedule?"

Lin looked uncomfortable. Chen guessed it wasn't convenient at all, but Lin wasn't about to admit that.

"It isn't a problem," Lin answered. "However, tomorrow?"

"Yes. I will try and find someone to relieve you. If necessary, I will do it myself. Do you prefer afternoon or evening?"

"Tomorrow afternoon would be better for me."

"Good." Chen studied him. Lin waited expectantly. "When I first told you about Liling's father, you knew about him. How was that?"

Lin's face turned slack. "He is a well-known executive. He had great responsibility before he retired."

Chen knew Lin was being cagey and decided on a frontal assault. "Does your father know him?"

"I think so. Although not well."

"You will not, of course, mention your activities with me to your father. Do you understand why?"

Lin hesitated a moment, but nodded. "I do not believe they are in touch. But I will say nothing."

Chen believed him and had a vision of what Lin would be like in fifteen years. Sly, subtle, careful, impossible to pin down, and very well connected. He was a perfect replacement for his father. Disgust soured Chen's mouth.

"Good. Be sure you are in position at the correct time. And thank you again for your help."

They slid out of the booth together, and Chen took the receipt to the cash register to pay. Afterwards, he and Lin stopped on the sidewalk as people swirled past them. Out of habit, Chen checked both up and down the street as he and Lin said their goodbyes.

Chen's rental car was parked some distance away. That was the problem with this area of tightly packed restaurants and shops. It was close to the university, and the area boasted Chinese restaurants where the food was reasonably authentic, but the parking was difficult. As he walked, he checked the large glass windows of the stores. The second or third time he did, something tingled on the back of his neck. It was enough that when he crossed the street, he gave the road careful scrutiny in both directions.

When he reached his rental, he slid behind the wheel, his heart beating faster. He wasn't absolutely sure, but twice he'd spotted a similar white pick-up truck some distance behind him.

He clasped and unclasped the steering wheel before turning the key.

It seemed unlikely, but was someone following him?

He slid the car into gear and pulled into traffic, watching his rear-view mirror. The tingle on the back of his neck started to itch like a mosquito bite.

Chapter Thirty-Three

Vic tried once more to focus on the email on his computer screen. Craig's words blurred slightly. Vic blinked and refocused on Craig's schedule for Melanie's last two days, cobbled together from her financial records, phone, and alarm system data.

His mind kept sliding back to Anne the night before and the one action he'd already taken. After they talked, Anne needed almost a full hour before she was calm enough to go to bed. After seeing her upstairs, he'd sat at the kitchen table and thought through his options. He knew that if he was being investigated, the FBI were monitoring his email and phone traffic, or would later review and catalogue them. Reaching out to people in North Dakota that way wasn't an option—it would look like he was trying to establish a cover story, a sure suggestion of guilt. Instead, he'd written a letter to Jimmy Pronghorn. He told Jimmy about the FBI and asked him to look into Ewan Fleck's family and see if Chief Fleck's wife, Ewan's mother, was still alive. Jimmy, he knew, had the good sense to read the letter and destroy it, leaving no trace of their communication.

That letter had already left with the outgoing mail from his office, but he kept worrying about how well he'd described the problem. That, and the fact it would take at least a week before he was likely to receive a response. Snail mail it was.

"What do you think?"

Vic looked at Liz, who was leaning back in her desk chair. She also had Craig's email on her computer screen.

"Let's have Craig walk us through it."

Liz studied him for a moment, then leaned toward Craig. "Hey, walk us through your email. I guess reading is too damn hard for some people."

They pulled their chairs together, and it only took Craig two minutes to review his work. Vic managed to stay focused the entire time and was impressed at how succinctly Craig explained his findings.

When he finished, Liz gave Vic a glance that said she was impressed as well and then turned to Craig. "So let me get this straight. There are three things here."

"Right." Craig looked guarded, as if worried he missed something and expected a reprimand.

"One, you confirmed that our super-stud Ryan Telst got back to the house at about five-forty-five on the day Melanie died. Which means he could easily have been nearby when Melanie started her walk."

"Right."

"Two, there's no record of Melanie telling anyone she was going for a walk, at least from her phone texts. So either the attacker didn't know her, or they knew her so well they were sure she would be on the trail."

"Right."

"And three, two days before the murder, there's activity from the sensor in Melanie's bedroom when we know she was at Heinz Hall at business meetings for the Symphony."

"Exactly."

"Did Melanie have a maid service?" Vic asked.

Liz pivoted her chair to face Vic. "According to Telst, yes, but they come on Fridays. That was a Tuesday. I asked Telst about that when I was there yesterday. I was trying to figure out who else has access to the house or might know the disarm code for the alarm."

Craig tapped his laptop screen. "But someone definitely entered. We just don't know why."

Vic drew in a deep breath. "Okay, so there's bullshit going on in the house. I think the next step is we grill Telst on why he lied about what time he got home the day of the murder. We have him cold on that. We do that, he might give up what's going on inside the house and why someone was in

Melanie's room."

"There's two other things." Craig scratched his ear. "I don't know if they mean anything, so I didn't list them as the main findings. But I noticed the motion detectors are sometimes triggered in the middle of the night. The ones in the kitchen and sunroom at the back of the house. It happens like every two or three days, at about the same time."

"Like a schedule?" Vic was intrigued. He had no idea why someone would be wandering the rooms of the house at a specific time of night. "They don't have a cat or dog that could set them off, do they?"

"No, I asked Telst about that yesterday as well," Liz broke in. "Craig checking the motion detectors made me think of it."

Vic saw Craig glance at Liz and realized she had surprised him. He guessed that Craig thought she wasn't doing much while he was collecting information on the security system. Vic tamped down a smile. Craig needed to grasp how thoroughly Liz did her job.

"What was the other thing?" Vic asked Craig.

Craig hesitated. "I don't think this means anything, I just came across it a couple of nights ago."

When Craig hesitated again, Vic made a beckoning motion with his hand. "Out with it."

"Well, it turns out that Eileen Liang, the violinist whose apartment overlooks the murder scene? Her father is a fugitive."

It took Vic a moment to grasp what Craig was saying. "Why? In this country?"

"No. I guess the Chinese want him. Something about embezzling money in China."

"You're right," Liz said slowly, a frown on her forehead. "I don't know why that matters."

"Agreed." Vic looked from Liz to Craig. "Let's stay in our lane. Get Telst in here, and let's smack him on his alibi. I mean, the fugitive thing is interesting, but it doesn't have any connection to our case."

Craig looked like he wanted to say something more, but didn't. Instead, he looked at Vic and said, "You said you want to bring Telst in here to question him?"

Vic thought about it.

"He might lawyer up if we bring him in," Liz said slowly.

Vic knew Liz was right. "Okay. Out at the house, it is. But let's catch him this afternoon." His mind slid back to his letter to Jimmy Pronghorn. Silently, he urged on the mail system. Another thought came to him. "Let's all three go to see Telst. Liz, you and I can talk to him. While we do, Craig, I want you to go through Melanie Beck's bedroom as carefully as you can. Maybe you'll find something explaining why someone was in there when they shouldn't have been."

Chapter Thirty-Four

Vic and Craig arrived at Melanie Beck's house after Liz. It was Vic's first visit to the Beck estate, and he knew that was a mistake. Understanding why a murder was committed required understanding the victim. Where they lived was the best place to start. At first glance, he liked the long, low white house nestled within several acres of lawn and established trees. Whoever built the house had felt no need to dominate their surroundings or make a statement, and somehow that gave the house an unexpected appeal and power. The sense was one of elegance, in the best sense of the word. It was logical to him that someone dedicated to the arts would live there.

Liz's car was already parked by the front door, next to an SUV from the local police force. Vic parked nearby. As he stepped onto the pea-gravel drive, a tall man with a shaved head exited the SUV and walked over to meet him. He introduced himself as the local police chief. Vic was surprised. He couldn't be older than in his mid-thirties.

"I appreciate you doing this," Vic said after they exchanged names.

"No problem. I liked Mrs. Beck. This shouldn't have happened to her." The chief looked around as a light wind lifted the branches of an oak tree high above them. "Always feels peaceful here. Kinda surprising when things like this happen."

"Keeps us in jobs." Vic glanced at the front door where Craig and Liz waited. "Have you heard what the plans for the house are? They going to sell? Who will own it now?" Vic reminded himself that he needed to see a copy of Melanie's will. It felt like he was always a step behind.

The chief nodded. "There's a daughter who got married here last summer. The reception was at the country club. Lives on the west coast. She called yesterday and asked us to keep an eye on the place."

"Does she know people are living here?"

"Yeah. I guess she and her mother were close. She said she's working with a lawyer to notify them they have thirty days to find somewhere new."

"Pretty generous."

"That seems to run on the woman's side of their family." The chief settled his light brown eyes on Vic in a steady gaze. They suggested nothing, but Vic understood what he was saying. It was yet another reminder. They really needed to take a run at Holden Beck. Pin him down on why he lied about his alibi.

"Thanks. I appreciate your guys letting us in here."

"No problem." The chief hesitated. "I'd like to find out who did this as well."

"You'll know when I know."

They shook hands, and Vic joined Liz and Craig on the front steps. "Telst is here?"

Craig pointed at a pickup truck parked near the garage.

"I called him on the way out. Told him to sit tight," Liz added.

Vic thought about that. This was the third time they were talking to Telst. "How'd he take it?"

"He sounded resigned. Like he'd known all along we'd be back."

"I thought you said he was kind of pissy the first time you talked to him."

Liz shrugged. "Maybe he's finally figured out his meal ticket just disappeared. That he needs a real job and somewhere new to live."

Craig broke in. "And Jessica was beating up on him last time we were here."

Vic turned and looked at Craig. "You guys didn't mention that."

"Neither of them would say what they were arguing about." Craig pointed at the door, a question on his face.

Vic nodded, and Craig knocked.

Telst opened the door a few moments later. To Vic, it felt like he'd been standing on the other side of the door all along and had counted to ten after Craig knocked so he didn't appear anxious about opening it.

Vic introduced himself and asked if anyone else was at home.

"No. Just me." The effort of speaking seemed to bore him.

Vic gave him a questioning look, and after taking a moment to process it, Telst waved them inside. Vic suggested they sit in the dining room, and they all headed in that direction. Craig peeled off and climbed the stairs to the second floor.

Vic had never seen a dining room table of that size except in movies. It was easily five feet across and long enough that sixteen chairs were spaced around it, seven on each side and one at each end. Six more chairs rested near the walls, and Vic gauged they would easily fit at the table. The dark wood looked like mahogany, and the two silver candelabras of eight candles spaced along the table center were reflected in the table's waxed gleam.

By unspoken agreement, they clustered at one end of the table, Telst on one side and Vic and Liz across from him.

"What do you guys want this time?" Telst asked once they sat down. He emphasized the words 'this time,' as if he wanted to communicate annoyance, but there was no force behind the words.

To Vic's ear, he just sounded petulant. It was discordant, coming from such a tall, well-muscled man.

"Well," Vic said slowly, arranging his thoughts. "You know we have to be thorough, right? Go over everything five times?"

He waited for Telst to respond, but all he did was pick at the sleeve of his warm-up suit. Vic let the silence extend until, finally, Telst shifted position and gave a brief nod.

"Okay." Vic settled into his chair. Telst was going to be one of those interviews that felt like extracting teeth. "On the day Melanie Beck was attacked, my colleagues came here and talked to you. You gave them a timeline of what you did that day, am I correct?"

Again, after a long silence, Telst nodded.

Vic turned. "Liz?"

Liz took her time shuffling through the pages of her notebook. "When my colleague and I talked to you, you said you left the house about two o'clock that day, went to batting practice at the North Park batting cages, drove around for a bit, and returned home. You told us you got home at about four o'clock. Is that correct?"

A light frown creased Telst's forehead.

Vic prodded him. "Yes or no?"

Telst shifted, as if he was moving his legs under the table. Vic knew Telst smelled a trap, but he didn't seem able to see where the interview was going. "If you say so," he said finally. "I'm not sure I remember exactly when I got home."

"Okay, then let's do it this way. "Was anyone here when you got back to the house that afternoon?"

Telst frowned, as if the shift in topic confused him. "No."

"Jessica? Kwan? Either one or anyone else?" Liz asked carefully.

"No. It was like today. They were at practice."

"And was anyone here when you left for the batting cages?" Liz smiled at Telst.

Vic thought the smile must be a new technique she was trying out. Usually, Liz smiled about as often as the appearance of seven-year cicadas. He wasn't sure the smile worked.

Telst squinted at her. "Nah. They weren't around."

"So walk us through it. You decided to get some batting practice in. What did you do after noon?"

Telst raised one shoulder in a tired shrug. It crossed Vic's mind that Telst's behavior suggested he was stoned. He didn't know what Telst might be taking, or smoking, but the exaggerated concentration and struggle to understand their questions suggested it.

Vic decided to get a bit more aggressive. "Isn't the question clear, big guy?"

Telst blinked. "Yeah. Uh, I guess I had lunch."

Vic cut him off. "You guess you had lunch? Did you or didn't you?"

"Yeah, yeah. I had lunch. Tuna fish or something. Then I hung out, then I grabbed my bats, and went out to my truck. Headed for the batting cages."

"Did you do anything when you left the house?" Liz drummed her fingers on the table. Vic knew she was getting annoyed as well.

Telst frowned, clearly trying to remember. His eyes cleared like a fourth-grader who just saw the solution to an addition problem. "Set the house alarm."

"Bingo," Vic said. "And how do you do that?"

"App on my phone."

"Good. And how long were you at the batting cages?"

"I usually do eighty minutes. Forty minutes on my right, forty minutes lefty. I'm a switch hitter." He smiled, clearly happy to have found a rhythm to the questions and answers.

Vic kept it going. "Right. So figure half an hour to get to the batting cages. An hour and twenty minutes of practice. It's three-fifty, four. Where did you go next?"

"Downtown."

"Good." Vic's heart skipped. This was new information, and put Telst in the vicinity of the murder. He tried the tactic of smiling, copying Liz's lead. He wasn't sure it worked any better. He forced himself to stay calm. "And what did you do there?"

"Oh." Telst gathered himself. "I thought you wanted to know when I got home?"

Vic dropped the smile. He didn't think it made any difference. "We do. But we're also interested in what you did downtown."

Telst licked his lips. "I met the guy I got my truck from. We hung out, then I came home."

"And who was that?" Liz flipped a page in her notebook, ready to write down the name.

Telst leaned back. They waited. Several seconds passed. Vic heard a shuffling sound from the ceiling and guessed it was Craig moving about in Melanie Beck's bedroom. Telst seemed to unwind something inside himself. "Not sure I can say."

"Let's come back to that," Vic said quickly. He wanted to keep Telst talking. "So, how long did you stay with the person you got your truck from?"

"Beats me. Maybe an hour."

Vic did the math in his head. Telst must have reached downtown around three-fifty to four. An hour with the unnamed person moved it to five o'clock, give or take. "What did you do after that?"

Telst smiled. Vic guessed it was his turn to smile. "Came back here."

Vic glanced at Liz. His timeline fit with the security system data. Vic studied Telst. "Ryan, when you got home, what did you do?"

Telst frowned. "Came in the house."

"Anything else?" Liz prompted.

It took a moment, but the frown cleared. "Turned off the security system." His eyes brightened. "You guys have the times I turned the security system on and off."

"Nailed it." Vic let Telst enjoy his discovery. He didn't mention they only had the times *someone* turned the system on and off, but Telst's timeline did match the system data. Vic glanced at Liz, who gave a slight nod that said: *go for it.*

"Okay," Vic said, slowly gazing at Telst. "So you can see our problem."

"What?"

"Melanie Beck was killed in a two-hour window between three-thirty and five-thirty. You were downtown then, and you were carrying a bunch of baseball bats. You and she were close, so you'd likely know she stayed at her northside apartment the night before. Maybe you even know she liked to walk along the Riverside Trail in the late afternoon. The only people who know that are close to her. So you knew where to find her, you were in the area, and you had a weapon of the kind that killed her. Normally, I'd handcuff you right now, read you your rights and charge you. I even have ideas why you'd want to kill her. You guys were lovers, you had an argument. Maybe she was kicking you out of the house. Beats me, but we'll find out. Kwan might know. So might Jessica. We just need to ask the right questions. You get where I'm going with this?"

Telst's mouth opened and closed. For the first time in the interview, Vic saw something like fear in his eyes. Telst stretched back, as if he wanted to be as far from Vic and Liz as possible. "You think Melanie and I were sleeping together?"

"Of course you were," Liz said sharply. "We've been told that, and your bedroom is the only one with a door directly into her bedroom. All she has to do is unbolt the door, and in you go."

Telst's eyes flicked from Vic to Liz and back. Again, his mouth opened and closed. "No," he managed to eke out.

Vic kept his gaze directly on Telst's face. "Like I said, normally, I would have handcuffs on you. But you said you were with someone downtown, from about four to five. Which means I need answers to two questions."

Telst nodded slowly.

"Where were you downtown?"

"Oakland." His voice was thick.

"Big place." Liz couldn't keep the sarcasm out of her voice. "Where, exactly? Classes at the University of Pittsburgh?"

"No." Sweat popped out on Telst's' forehead. "I'm not supposed to say."

"Your call." Vic took out his handcuffs and placed them on the table. "We can go either way on this. But if you don't answer those questions, you go downtown with us. Right now."

Telst stared at the handcuffs. "Okay. Okay." He looked at the ceiling and back down. "Screw this. I'm not the weird one here. I was at that hotel on Bigelow Boulevard. The one near the old Schenley School?"

"With who?"

Telst took a deep breath. "I got the truck to keep quiet. You have to understand that. Can you guys not tell anyone? I don't really give a shit about me. It's them."

Vic tapped the handcuffs. "Need a name." He remembered Liz and Craig had assumed that Melanie had given Telst the truck. Something shifted in him. This wasn't what he expected.

Telst looked down and to the side and spoke quickly as if he half-hoped they wouldn't hear. "Holden Beck."

Vic almost jumped out of his seat. "Holden Beck? Melanie's ex-husband?"

Telst looked up. "Yeah." He shrugged. "We got a room."

Craig walked in, staring at Telst. His eyes were wide, and Vic knew he'd heard the last part of the conversation.

"We need specifics," Liz said flatly. "What were you guys doing together?"

Telst looked at her and laughed. "Holy hell. We got a room together. It had a bed in it. What do you think we did?"

"You guys are lovers?" Vic asked, surprised at how evenly he said the words.

Telst couldn't wipe the smile off his face, as if he liked how shocked they were. He shook his head slowly. "If you can call it that. He's not out. He hates himself for being gay. Keeps telling me we're done, then calls me and wants more. That's why he gave me the truck. I'm not supposed to tell anyone. It's also why I wasn't sleeping with Melanie. But screw this. I'm not going to jail." He looked at everyone sitting around the table. "What? You guys don't know life's for living?"

Silence surged through the room. Vic stared at him, fighting back the first urge to laugh he'd felt in days. All he could think was, Hell, the damn guy actually *is* a switch hitter.

Chapter Thirty-Five

Outside Melanie Beck's house, Craig stood to one side, watching Vic and Liz. They'd stopped in a loose group by their cars, Vic looking like he was trying not to laugh. Craig couldn't understand why. When Craig heard Telst's revelation, he'd known that in one sentence, Telst had neatly provided alibies to himself and Holden Beck. Their two prime suspects. Yet Vic found it funny.

Craig wondered if he'd missed something and thought through the part of the conversation he'd overheard. After Telst's 'life's for living' statement, Vic asked Telst if he was gay or bisexual.

"Bi."

"Who else in the house knows that?" Vic had asked, the first curl of a grin appearing on his face, fingers interlaced and hands sitting on the table top.

"Don't think anyone knows. Maybe Melanie suspected it, I don't know. The Chinese kid, Kwan, he avoids me. I think he's scared of me. And Jessica, she's family. My family doesn't know. I tell her, and she tells the rest of my family. Not happening. I want to tell everyone at the next reunion." He'd grinned. "Those crappy things need a hand grenade. The reunion that goes boom."

Craig still couldn't see what Vic found so funny.

Vic kicked the pea gravel of the driveway with his toe as if he wanted to ground himself. Finally, the smile faded from his face. "Well, that screws everything."

"Yes, he does." Now it was Liz who struggled not to smile. "This job kills me sometimes. But yeah. Doesn't leave us with much."

Vic looked at Liz, and Craig thought he saw some kind of communication between them before Vic said, "Always goes this damn way, doesn't it? Okay. Back to Holden Beck. I want to see the receipt from the hotel. I want to hear him confirm everything Ryan said."

"If Beck's all up in his own underwear about sleeping with guys, that's going to be a nasty interview." Liz glanced at the sky. "But maybe it explains why Hana told us he's a pain to girls. Basically, he's so pissed at himself for liking guys that he blames them. Some guys who grew up with his kind of money never take responsibility for themselves. That fits."

Vic slid his phone out of his pocket and checked it. "It's too late to get him tonight. Tomorrow morning." He turned to Craig. "Find anything upstairs?"

"Not really." Craig pushed away the thought at how easily Vic and Liz had accepted their case crumbling around them. He needed to learn that resilience. "You know that island in the middle of the closet? The one with the granite top and drawers on both ends? There's a safe in the bottom drawer. Built-in. The top drawer is shallow and has a bunch of jewelry in it, I'm thinking that's costume jewelry, and the good stuff is in the safe."

Liz nodded. "When the daughter gets here, she needs to inventory the jewelry. All these people living here, anyone could steal shit. But Melanie wasn't killed over that."

"Proves the police chief had a point." Vic squinted across the front yard toward the golf course. "Pretty generous daughter to let people she doesn't know stay in her mother's house when no one's around."

"People grow up in a place like this, they have no idea what people are really like. What they're capable of. What you have to watch out for." Craig thought the tone of Liz's voice agreed with Vic.

The wind shifted, and the tree branches around them bowed and rustled. Craig had planned to mention his other discovery, but he let it drop. While searching the closet, he'd accidentally knocked a hanger from the rack beside the door to Ryan's room. Picking it up, he'd noticed a piece of fluff stuck to the bottom of the door. It was unusual. When he touched it, he realized a small portion of the door and its frame were sticky, which was how the fluff adhered to it. He didn't know what to make of it, but with the topic of the conversation shifting, he let it go.

Jessica's Prius pulled up and they all waited as the front gate swung open. Moments later, her car crunched along the driveway, the motor oddly quiet. Jessica parked in front of one of the garage doors and climbed out. Kwan got out of the passenger side. Together, they went around to the back of the vehicle and removed their instrument cases. Jessica stopped directly in front of them, her viola case hanging from her shoulder. Kwan aligned himself so he was partially hidden behind his cello case.

"What are you guys doing here again?" Jessica asked.

"Investigating," Liz shot back. This time the word wasn't sarcasm, but aggressive.

Jessica stared at Liz as if she was something on the bottom of her shoe. "Well, good for you." She turned to Vic. "What have you learned so far?"

Vic was slow to reply, as if he was honestly considering her question. "Not to jump to conclusions?"

Craig suppressed a smile. Jessica wouldn't know, but Vic was being honest. They'd all assumed that Ryan was sleeping with Melanie, and that Melanie had given Ryan his truck. But those assumptions led them to the wrong spouse. And Vic was right, they shouldn't have assumed Ryan was heterosexual. The phone in his pocket vibrated. He pulled it out and saw a call forwarded from his desk phone. He frowned, trying to remember who owed him a call back. He turned from the group and stepped away.

"Hello?"

"Ah. Is this Detective Luntz?"

Craig's stomach flipped. He knew the English accent, even if he felt embarrassed to be called detective. His exam was still three months away. He fought down his nervousness.

"This is Craig Luntz. Who is this?" But he already knew.

"Eileen Liang, the violinist from the symphony?" She hesitated, and Craig knew he was supposed to fill the gap.

"I remember. What can I do for you?" Craig winced at how formal he sounded. Somehow he never found the right footing when he talked to a woman he liked.

"Um, I realize this might be unusual, or perhaps incorrect?" Eileen's voice contained just a touch of nervousness in it. "I don't know the protocol. But I was wondering if we might meet for coffee? I wanted to talk to you, there was something I hoped to ask."

Craig fought down the excitement in his stomach as he considered the legality of meeting. "Is this about the Melanie Beck case?"

"No. I don't think so."

"Okay. Then I don't see why not." Craig strained to think of the right thing to say next.

"If you don't mind, I was hoping sooner rather than later? Perhaps this evening?"

Craig had a flash of his apartment, the high ceilings, the hollowness of it. The aching emptiness. Her question was a relief. "Absolutely. I'm outside Pittsburgh right now. At the Beck estate." He glanced at Jessica, who was talking to Vic. "I'm guessing the symphony finished practice not long ago?"

Eileen laughed, the sound clear and bright. "Ah. Jessica and Kwan must have arrived home. Yes, you are right. We finished forty minutes ago."

"I'll need at least ninety minutes," Craig said slowly, adding time in case Vic produced an assignment for him. He guessed Liz would go home after they finished, but he knew now that she would keep working. He'd made his own assumption that she stopped working when she was at home. He wouldn't make that mistake again.

Eileen suggested a chain coffee shop in the Strip District, just across the river from her apartment, and he gave her his cell number so she could text him. He promised to let her know if he was delayed in any way. He hung up, excited, and turned back to the group.

Jessica, he saw, was leaning toward Vic, her eyes bright. "I don't understand why you can't tell me where you are with the investigation. Are you close to catching Melanie's killer?"

"We're making progress. We announce significant breakthroughs when we have them."

In Vic's words, Craig heard the standard PR patter from their media training.

Jessica looked from Vic to Liz and back and rolled her eyes. "Well, you need to get a move on," she said finally. She hefted her viola case and marched toward the house, giving Craig a long look as she passed. Kwan followed with a gangly gate, his cello case bumping against his legs.

Ninety minutes later, Craig walked into the Strip District coffee shop. He spotted Eileen near the back, a mug in front of her, fingers flickering over the screen of her phone. After Eileen's phone call, Vic had mumbled about rebooting the investigation, starting with the interview of Holden Beck the next morning. As he climbed into his car, he'd called out they should expect to review all of the evidence after the Beck interview.

That gave Craig enough time to visit his apartment and shower. He'd done the best he could picking out what to wear, because it was easily two weeks since he last washed anything. But the surprise was in his mail. His contact lenses had arrived. He debated wearing them for the first time to meet Eileen, but was determined to stop wearing glasses. After some experimenting, he got the hard lenses onto his eyes. They felt like grit under his eyelids. He blinked repeatedly, trying to accustom himself to them. Leaving his apartment, he made sure he had the contact lens case and his glasses with him, in case something went wrong.

Driving to the Strip District, he was surprised and pleased at how much sharper the contacts made his vision. The eye doctor was right to recommend them.

Eileen looked up and smiled as he approached, and Craig lost track of the ground and the feel of his contacts in his eyes. He told Eileen he needed to order and, a few minutes later, sat across from her. He reminded himself to wipe the smile off his face and keep his eyes off her shoulders, presented to him in the wide gap of her black sweater's neckline. The edge of her left shoulder was covered by the sweater, the right naked, and on that same side, the thin deep burgundy strap of her bra showed a shiny line of what looked like silk.

"You're very punctual." Eileen's eyes were bright with humor.

"I got lucky. Sometimes the days are pretty long. I'm never sure how it will go." He caught himself just before saying they needed to reboot the investigation. He was desperate to impress her, he realized, but he couldn't talk about the investigation. "Some days it's late, some days not."

"I might like that better. My days are very disciplined. Practice. More practice, and performance." She toyed with the lip of her mug. "It gets boring."

"But look how far you've got. And so fast."

"Yes." The shadow of a frown crossed her face. "And look what I've given up."

He knew she was giving him an opening, but he didn't think it was the right time to discuss regrets. He wanted to keep the conversation light. "You mean getting drunk in bars and complaining the world won't give you a break? Are you upset you missed all that?"

She cocked her head at him, the muscles of her neck flickering under the skin. Craig breathed carefully. She smiled. "I think I did a little of that at one time."

Craig returned the smile. "But it doesn't get you very far, does it?"

She considered him, her brown eyes deep. "Are you a philosopher, Craig Luntz?"

"Just a cop. With a long apprenticeship. And a dad who was a cop. In a place called Pittsburgh."

"Perhaps being a cop teaches you a lot about life."

"I think music is more likely to do that."

Something shifted in her eyes. She studied him, and he thought it might be a recalculation, as if she was discarding an opinion about him. Formulating a new one. He hoped so.

"I'm surprised," she said slowly. "And I mean this in a good way. Most men, when I pay them a compliment, it encourages them to talk about themselves." She made a dismissive upward motion with her hand. "To go on about how successful they are." She leaned a bit closer. "They don't compliment me back."

"Then I don't think they are paying attention. And they should be."

She shifted in her seat and cupped her hands around her coffee mug. Craig noticed how precisely her nails were cut. They were polished, but lacked color. They were perfect, he thought. Exactly what he would expect from a violinist.

"You are easy to underestimate, Craig Luntz."

"I think you said that to me before." He half-smiled at her. "And I'm not sure it's a compliment."

"Then I will have to restate it so there is no confusion about what I mean."

"Good. Something for next time we meet." Heat surged at the base of his neck. He knew the statement was a risk that she might think he was pushing too hard. But then again, the whole conversation was a tightrope walk. He wasn't sure how much longer he could balance. Yet he liked it. Truly liked it. She thought about things and knew herself, he could see it, and so far, he hadn't had the luck of meeting women like that.

Eileen tapped her thumbnail against her mug, but Craig thought he saw just the smallest smile at the corners of her mouth. She met his gaze. "Well, I was the one who asked us to meet. I have something I want to talk about."

"Like what?"

"I was wondering if you are making progress finding Melanie Beck's killer?"

He was disappointed. He'd hoped it would be something he could talk about. He decided to dodge the question. "You two were friends. You said she recruited you."

"Yes. And I'm not asking because I'm concerned about my future and what might happen to me now that she's gone. I'm asking because she was a friend."

Suddenly his left eye felt like a splinter had lodged there. "I wish I could tell you more, and I'm sorry." He tried to blink away the pain. "But I can't really talk about it. We have information and leads. We're following them up."

She laughed lightly. "I feel as if your press training is immaculate."

"I wouldn't go that far, but I can't talk about the case." He tried to flatten his tone, so he didn't sound self-important. He tried to stop blinking, worried she would think him odd.

"Are you all right? Your eye."

He rubbed the skin on the side of his eye. "It's my contact lens. Bad timing. I'd better check it."

"Go. I wear them, too. It feels like someone stabbed your eye with a needle if you get something in there. It happened to me in the middle of a performance one time. It was terrible."

Relief flooded him. "Right back."

Relieved at her reaction, he found the bathroom. After several tries, he got the contact out, which started his eye watering. Unsure what to do, he slipped the contact into his mouth to moisten it, and when the pain subsided, reinserted it in his eye. It was uncomfortable, but manageable.

He sat across from her again.

"Are you alright?"

"New contacts," Craig told her, opting for honesty. My left one might need some work."

"For a moment, I thought you were winking at me."

"I'm not smooth enough to pull that off." He grinned, so she knew it was a joke.

"Anyway, what happened to Melanie Beck wasn't why I asked to meet."

Craig felt his heart skip a beat.

She leaned forward, not a lot, just in the way of someone passing along a confidence. "This may seem silly to you. And perhaps there is nothing you can do about it."

"I'll need to know what it is."

Her gaze darted around the café. "I think I'm being followed. Twice, when I went to the supermarket, I've seen the same man. A Chinese man. My age. I don't know what to do about it."

Every protective instinct Craig owned jostled to come out. "You mean stalked? You think someone is stalking you?"

"Perhaps. And I've seen someone sitting in a car in the parking area for the trail. Watching. Sometimes for hours at a time. I just don't know if they are watching me."

The need to protect her transformed into something like panic. He fought it down. "Do you have any details? Make or model of a car? Description of the person you saw?"

"Not yet. It's been glimpses. I didn't think to identify the car."

"How long has this been going on?"

"Just the last week? I feel foolish about it. It's never happened before. But I've seen that young man twice. He was acting as if he was doing something else, but I could tell he was watching me. The man in the car, I don't know, but it feels too coincidental." Her eyes flickered, and Craig realized she was angry more than scared.

"Okay." Craig sat back, thinking. "Has this happened before? In London?"

"Never."

"Tell me what you remember about the man you saw."

"As I said, he was a young Chinese. A little older than college age."

"Did he follow you here?"

"I don't think so."

Craig fought his instinct look around and check. "Okay, two things. If you see him again, try and get a photo of him with your phone. If you do, text it to me right away. If you can't get the photo without him knowing, just text me he's following you and your location. I can get uniforms there in a hurry, and we can ask him what he's doing. They might be able to ID him. The second thing is, whatever you do, if you see him, stay in a public place with other people and do not approach him, okay?"

Looking at the table, she nodded.

He was crestfallen he couldn't make her feel better. He felt like he had utterly failed. He wanted to touch her arm and tell her it was going to be okay, but he didn't think he knew her well enough.

She looked up, a small smile on her face. "If I have my violin case, I could hit him with it."

Craig grinned, glad to get the conversation on a better footing. "I have a feeling you would take him out."

She raised her right arm like a bodybuilder, flexing her bicep. "Field hockey in high school. I still have my sticks."

"There's a weapon."

She giggled, and at that moment, Craig had another thought. Carefully, he asked, "Is it possible it has something to do with your father?"

Her face turned serious. "What do you know about my father?"

"Very little." He heard a placating tone in his voice and didn't like it. Again he forced himself to speak evenly. "I don't know the whole story. Only that authorities in China want to talk to him, and he can't be found. I don't even know if that is true anymore."

Her eyes flashed. "The charges are false."

Craig gave her a moment to continue, but it was obvious that was everything she planned to say.

"I'm just considering options," he said slowly. "I'm not sure how close you are to your father or when you saw him last. Even if you know where he is, not that it's any of my business." He waved his hand. "Forget it."

She relaxed. "No. You are right." Craig was surprised at how apologetic she sounded. "And it is possible, unfortunately."

"Well, if the Chinese authorities really want him and he's in this country, they would need to make a formal request for extradition. That's the law."

Her eyes turned sharp and searched his face. "I don't think you understand the Chinese government. They would consider catching my father their own internal police activity. That would take precedence over the laws of another country."

"They can't just stick their hand into our country and pull out your Dad, assuming he's even here." Yet as Craig said the words, he knew he was being naïve, and that he didn't want to argue with her. He just didn't know enough. "Anyway, tell me. What about those things you gave up to get here? Are you sure you can't give yourself a second chance at them?"

For a moment, she didn't say anything, and he guessed she was also pulling herself away from the freighted topic of her father. Gently, she tapped her hand on the table, as if she was signaling herself to speak. "I think the worst is that I've never had time for anyone. I couldn't. I needed too much practice time. I had to be completely focused on what to do next."

Craig lost the sense of his feet again. "You just need someone who understands how committed you are to music. Someone who gets that—they won't demand your time. But they'll help you make the most of the free time you do have."

She stared at him, and Craig saw just the hint of a flush on her neck. It almost separated him from his body.

"I am starting to believe you truly are a philosopher, Craig Luntz."

He grinned at her, sinking back to earth. "If it helps."

She picked up a large leather purse from the chair next to her and dug around inside. Removed a white envelope. "I brought you a ticket for tomorrow's performance, if you would like." She held it out to him.

"Thanks. I haven't been in a while. That would be great." He took it. "Thank you."

"And if you are interested, afterwards, you could come backstage." She leaned forward, like a conspirator. "I could give you a secret tour."

He bent closer. "The secret ones are always the best." And he meant every word.

Chapter Thirty-Six

Vic knew from his years as a detective that, no matter how hands-off his commanders might be, they all unerringly asked for case updates exactly when an investigation derailed. He thought about that as he sat on a wooden bench in the hallway outside Hana Richards' office. He should have seen it coming. He'd hoped, by now, to be on his way to interview Holden Beck. But Hana's phone call the night before was unambiguous. Stop by her office first thing the next day. Alone.

Hana might be the County District Attorney, but until she hired a new commander, Vic reported directly to her. He wasn't looking forward to the meeting.

Hana's secretary stuck her head around the frosted glass of the office suite's door and beckoned with her hand. He rose and followed her.

Hana's office was the same. The circular logo of Allegheny County behind her desk, inset among floor-to-ceiling bookshelves. A Civil War cavalry saber and scabbard hung on the side wall. The only addition since his last visit was a small, silver-framed black and white photo hanging above the saber. It showed a gloriously mustachioed man in a Union uniform.

From her desk, Hana pointed Vic to the conference table that overlooked the courtyard of the City Council building. Her telephone was pressed to her ear. Vic took a chair facing the bookshelves and endless spines of law tomes.

Hana finished her call and came around her desk to the conference table. She wore a navy pants suit and a starched white blouse. When she sat down, he saw her only jewelry was a silver bracelet of turquoise stones on her left wrist.

She gazed at Vic thoughtfully, but with a tinge of humor. "Okay, Vic. Update. I got a desperate call from the Mayor yesterday afternoon about the Beck case. I told him we were turning rocks. Getting close. Don't make me throw those rocks at you."

Vic took a slow breath. "I wish I had better news." Talking carefully, he outlined their progress to date and how the day before, their two prime suspects provided alibis for each other. When he finished, she stared at him, her face blank, until a slow smile widened her mouth. "Well. Would not have expected that. Holden Beck swings both ways?"

"Switch hitter. Which is what we said about Ryan Telst. He's the baseball player. Anyway, we need to confirm all this. We'll do that today. But that's the shape of it. If everything checks out, we'll need to start over."

"I would not have expected that. But it does explain some things about Holden." She sighed and sat back. "And you really have nothing else that's even close to a lead?"

"Not yet. Like I said. We plan to review everything we have today."

"Anything that stands out? I mean, give me something."

Vic felt lost. He liked Hana and trusted her. He wanted to bring her better news than this. Worse, she had trusted him and brought him out of retirement, and right now he was failing her. The need to be better twisted in his stomach. "There's a few anomalies. A lot of odd things going on in the Beck house late at night. We picked that up from the security system. We also found an app on Melanie Beck's phone, so we know someone was tracking her. We're waiting for the carrier to provide us the number of the phone that accessed the app. But the main thing is we don't have a witness to the murder or immediately afterwards. Which is weird. It isn't a remote area. I'm planning to circle back to all the people who might have seen something and push harder."

"Sounds like grasping at straws."

"It is." Vic fell quiet, waiting. He couldn't sugar-coat it.

After several seconds, Hana asked, "Want me to tape record anything?"

Vic smiled. She was making a joke, harkening back to her help seven years earlier when they first met. Her tape recordings of two interviews had helped solve a case.

"I wish it was that easy."

"Okay." Hana straightened in her chair. "Go back through the evidence and double-check your witnesses or lack of them. That tracker app is interesting. But go fast and get back to me when you've finished. If you're still stalled at that point, I need to think about how to handle that. We'll need a strategy for the press."

"I will. Sorry about this, Hana, I thought by now we'd had Holden Beck pretty much in our gunsights. Yesterday was a surprise."

"It's how it goes, sometimes. I have faith in you, Vic." She rose.

Vic stood as well. "One other thing. I saw that Joe Lee is suing you. Is there anything to it?"

"You mean apart from trying to make me look bad? No. I fired him because he was leaking information to the press. As you know. That was a clear violation of his employment contract. I'm guessing we can get his case thrown out in a summary judgment, but that'll still take six months."

"He's going to play it for all its worth. He wants your job."

"He's made that clear enough, but he's not going to get it." Hana stared at him for a few seconds. "I also heard a rumor."

Vic chilled. "What about?"

"FBI has an interest in your North Dakota trip."

Vic was surprised, but in the same breath, knew he shouldn't be. She was in regular contact with the local FBI office. "They talked to Liz."

"I heard it from Tomlinson, your old commander."

"Crush? They talked to him as well?" Vic reflexively balled his hands into fists. The FBI was moving faster than he'd expected. And Vic knew Hana would never reach out to Crush. "He called you about it?"

"He did." She smiled, her eyes bright. "He told me he didn't tell them anything. He then asked me a bunch of questions about what I knew about your trip. What that means, I think, is that he's trying to figure out what the FBI is looking for, so he can decide what to tell them and land on the right side of things."

"That sounds like him."

"I'm not a fan of operators like that, but they are predictable, which helps." She studied him, her face serious. "Do I have anything to worry about there, Vic?"

Vic felt his feet take root. "Hana, you brought me out of retirement, gave me a whole new job and career. I will not have anything blowback on you. I would resign first."

She looked him up and down. "Not the answer I was hoping for."

"I just want you to understand my position."

"And I appreciate that. I would have expected it from you. But Vic, don't jump too fast. I won't bring you out of retirement a second time."

"The city needs you to win the next election. End of story."

"And my point is there's always more than one way to solve a problem. Sometimes you just need time to find the solution. Like you are doing right now with Melanie Beck."

"I appreciate that. But if it involves you in any way, the press will be all over it. And they use pointed sticks and throw heavy stones."

Hana turned and stared through the window, down at the courtyard. "True enough." She pivoted back to him. "Just do me a favor. If you start to think you need to resign, talk to me first. There's times it's useful for me to take a hit, believe it or not."

Vic wanted to tell her that if the truth about North Dakota came out, it wasn't going to be just a hit. It would be poison gas. "Thanks, Hana." A fleeting image of Lettie came to him, and he fought it down. He pointed at the photograph on the wall. "I hadn't seen the photograph. Impressive whiskers."

Hana followed his gaze. "My uncle asked me where the saber was, and when I told him it was hanging in my office, he said he had a photograph to go with it. Captain Adolphus Adonis Richards. They could really name people in those days. But I feel bad for his wife. She gave him six children, and childbirth was torture in those days. And facial hair like that must have been brutal for her, so she even missed the fun part at the start of the pregnancy process. I should have her photo up there, not his."

Vic laughed. He couldn't help himself. It was the first time he'd let himself enjoy something in days. "I feel like you're warming up for a fundraising speech."

"Talk about not having any fun at the start of a process." Hana returned to her side of her desk and looked at him. "Keep it in mind, Vic. There's always more than one way to solve a problem, you just have to find it."

"Thanks, Hana. I'll keep you updated. Are you any closer to hiring my boss?"

She gave a slight shrug. "Interviewing. No one has jumped out at me yet." She fell silent, and Vic had the distinct feeling she wanted him to say something.

"Okay." He pointed at the door. "I'm going to interview Holden Beck."

"Thanks. And Vic?"

Vic turned back to her.

"Get moving on this. The mayor called me, but I expected that. What I didn't expect was calls from two of my largest supporters. The ones who fund campaigns. Do you understand me? We need a result."

And there it is, thought Vic. Hana would be perfectly happy swinging that saber on the Gettysburg battlefield. Some family traits didn't change.

"We're on it."

"Good." She held his gaze for a moment and looked down at the papers on her desk.

Meekly, Vic let himself out of her office.

As he walked the hallway to the elevator, he wondered about the meeting. It felt like Hana had something in mind about the FBI's interest in him. Something that might help. She seemed to be sending that message. Yet he was sure she wouldn't help him if she knew how he really found Lettie. She was trusting him, even after he'd warned her not to.

He should be thankful for her support, there was no question about it. But his mind tossed out another possibility. She hadn't called him to her office just for an update on the case. That was why she wanted him alone. She'd wanted to gauge his concern about the FBI investigation, and he'd signaled there were things for the FBI to find. No wonder she'd mentioned her political backers. She was supporting him as much as she was planning how to sever ties if things went wrong.

That saber really was hanging in her office for a reason.

Chapter Thirty-Seven

When he reached his car, Vic texted Craig and asked him to chase the cell phone company again. They desperately needed the phone number that accessed the tracking app on Melanie Beck's phone. If the interview with Holden Beck went as expected, the app was their one and only lead. He started to put his phone away but stopped. The tracking app. There was something he was missing about it, but he couldn't identify what. He sat, trying to sort it out. Still struggling with it, he texted Liz and asked if she was on her way to Holden's offices.

Liz's return text was immediate. *'Already here.'*

He started the car and put it in gear. He'd worry about the tracking app later. As he drove, he thought about the questions to ask Holden. He'd spent the night before composing a list, but he knew there was a better way to get Holden talking. Ryan had suggested that Holden was repressing his real sexuality. People hiding things, Vic knew, were often desperate to confess. He needed to give Holden the opening to reveal his secret life, and if he did, he guessed Holden would take it.

Liz was sitting on a couch in the entry to Holden's investment firm, reading something on her phone. When she saw Vic, she asked the receptionist to let Holden Beck know they were ready to see him.

As they waited for an escort to Holden's office, Liz turned to him. "How'd it go with your friend Hana?"

"She wants us to solve this yesterday."

Liz straightened. "Look at that. The honeymoon is over."

"Yeah. Lucky us."

Holden's administrative assistant opened the double doors that led to the office. She glanced around the reception area. "Just you two this time? Craig didn't come?"

"Sorry to disappoint you." Liz's sarcasm was heavy enough to sink Styrofoam.

Holden's assistant blushed. "Follow me."

"What is it with girls in this town? Is Craig the only white guy with a job?" Liz muttered to him, as they followed the assistant through narrow hallways and aisles into the long room with the offices against each wall. Vic wasn't about to unpack all the insinuations in Liz's statement, so he set his face and didn't answer.

Holden was sitting in his usual seat at the conference table near the corner windows, a woman Vic judged to be in her late twenties seated at the same table. When Vic and Liz were announced, both Holden and the young woman stood.

Vic expected Holden to excuse the young woman, but instead, he gestured to her. "Detectives, meet my daughter, Samantha Beck. She just flew in this morning from the west coast."

The young woman stepped forward. "I'm very pleased to meet the detectives investigating my mother's case." Vic heard a falter in her voice as she spoke the last two words.

She looked at Liz. "Liz, right? We talked on the phone. About allowing you to go inside my mother's home?"

"I remember. And thank you for that." Liz smiled, and Vic actually thought the young woman might have charmed her.

Samantha turned to Vic, and he was suddenly uncomfortable. Her face was a younger version of her mother's, with the same widely spaced eyes and high forehead, the same honey blond hair. Samantha's hand was cool and strong.

"I'm sorry." Samantha smoothed her hair and stepped back. "I flew the red-eye in and came straight here from the airport. I must look a mess."

A hint of dark smudges under her eyes was the only concession to overnight travel. Her fitted blue jeans and light-yellow blouse had the same fresh-from-the-ironing-board look. Somehow her ponytail made her look active and lively.

"Not a problem." Vic felt the need to say something more. "There's a third member of our team as well, Craig Luntz. He's running down a lead at the moment."

"And is there any progress?"

Liz shifted position just slightly, deflecting the question to Vic. He guessed that Liz thought his meeting with Hana had prepared him to answer that question.

"There is some," Vic said carefully. "That was why we wanted to speak to your father again this morning."

Samantha glanced at her father. "Good. Then let's get on with it." She plopped back down in her chair.

Holden gave them a 'what can you do?' look and waved at the two empty chairs. He pulled out his own chair and stopped, aware that neither Vic nor Liz had moved.

Vic wasn't about to start a conversation about Holden's latent homosexuality with Samantha in the room. "I think," Vic said slowly to Samantha, "That we should have this conversation just with your father."

Samantha frowned. "Why? This is about my mother. I'll stay, thank you."

Holden jumped in, defending his daughter. "I agree. Sam can certainly listen to this."

Vic took a slow breath. "It's about the afternoon when your mother was attacked," Vic said slowly to Samantha. He turned and held Holden's gaze, willing him to understand. "And your schedule that afternoon. We need to confirm your whereabouts. We know you weren't near the North Side that afternoon, but we have some questions."

"Of course, I wasn't near the North Side. I told you before, I was here..." He stopped mid-sentence, staring at Liz. Vic followed Holden's gaze. He wasn't sure what Holden saw on Liz's face that made him stop talking, but when Vic turned back, he saw fear in Holden's eyes.

"Oh, of course." Holden's florid complexion reddened slightly. He turned to Samantha. "I know what they're talking about, dear. It has to do with a client. I think the police are being careful about client confidentiality." He looked at Liz and Vic. "And I do appreciate how thoughtful they are being." He turned to Samantha. "Sam, I'm sorry. Do you mind waiting for a few minutes in the conference room until this is out of the way?"

Samantha stared at him. "Yes, I mind."

"I realize you do. I'll make it up to you. And then we can finish catching up."

Vic was impressed at the smoothness of Holden's lie. To his own daughter, no less. It occurred to him that he might have underestimated Holden's skill at finding and holding clients.

Samantha rose with an air of teenage huffiness that Vic guessed she only employed with her father. She stopped at the door. "I'd still like to hear where you are in the investigation."

"We'll arrange to give you an update," Vic said quickly.

"In fact," added Liz, "The other detective on our team, Craig Luntz, might be the right person. I'll ask him to contact you later today. He can give you a full update."

Vic stifled a smile. Liz might be critical of the way young women acted around Craig, but she also knew when to deploy Craig where that might be useful. Liz was betting that if anyone could get Samantha on the side of the investigation, it was Craig. And he knew she was right.

Samantha turned to her father. "You make sure that happens, okay?"

"Absolutely, Sam." He gave her a twinkling smile Vic guessed was reserved for her only. "You can count on me."

With a last glance around the office, Samantha left. Holden licked his lips, closed the door behind her, and walked to the windows overlooking the rest of the office. He fumbled to close the blinds, a slight tremor in his hands.

Holden joined them at the table. "What's all this about?" Holden's tone was so timid Vic guessed he already knew.

Liz placed her phone in front of him, swiped through a couple of screens, and stopped at a video. She pressed play. The black and white footage rolled, clearly showing Holden driving his BMW out of a parking garage. She paused the video near the end and pointed to the time and date stamps. "This was on the day Melanie Beck was murdered, about twenty-five minutes before the attack. And yet, you clearly told us you were here in your office at that time. You lied to us. You went out, and we'd like to know where you went and what you actually did."

"I wasn't anywhere near the North Side." Holden's voice was low and rough.

"For us to believe that, we need to know what you did and where you were," Liz said carefully.

Holden's eyes turned wild. Suddenly he pushed back his chair and bent double, placing his face in his hands. His shoulders shook.

Vic glanced at Liz. She was watching Holden, her face passive. They waited.

It was almost a minute before Holden straightened and wiped his nose with the back of his hand. "I'm sorry." He took a deep breath, composed himself, and looked from Liz to Vic. "You already know, don't you?"

"We'd like to hear it from you," Vic said slowly. "All of it."

"All right. Okay." He avoided looking at them, focusing on the roofline of a building across the street. "Ryan told you, didn't he?"

Vic and Liz stayed quiet.

Holden didn't need an answer. "Of course, he would. He tortures me that way. Always acting like he doesn't care. As if he could get in his truck and drive away if the fancy struck him." Holden gave a sigh that verged on a sob, his eyes wide and tortured. "Yes. I met Ryan. In Oakland. There's a hotel there we use. It's out of the way."

"Do you have a receipt?" Liz asked softly.

Holden nodded. "In my emails. I have a separate email address just for him. That's it, okay?" He gave Liz a beseeching look. "I'm sorry I lied. I just don't want anyone to know about this."

As Vic suspected, Holden wanted to talk. "There's some things I don't understand," Vic said slowly.

Holden turned to him. He looked defeated. "Like what?"

Vic thought about how to frame his next question. The night before, when he made the list of things he needed to know, he'd thought his questions were worded correctly. Now, with Holden hunched in front of him, so obviously tortured by this truth about him being known, the questions seemed clunky and stilted. He tried to soften what he had to say next. "Maybe you could explain something to us. You attended the same party as Melanie the night before she died. We heard there was an argument between the two of you. You even said so yourself. You made it sound as if you were tired of attending those events with her. You even told us clearly that Ryan was sleeping with Melanie. He says he wasn't. Which is it?"

Holden closed his eyes and pressed his palms together. "It's complicated," he whispered.

Vic caught Liz's eye, but she didn't press either. Like him, she knew it was better to let Holden talk.

Holden took a wavering breath. "It goes back to our divorce. I've always struggled with this. My whole life." He waved his hand at himself. "Who I'm attracted to. Look, I got married, we had two wonderful children. But I just didn't find our married life very interesting. When Melanie asked for a divorce, I was almost glad. I went along with it. It was the easiest divorce ever. Our lawyers were disappointed, I'm sure." A trace of bitterness edged his words. "I don't know why, but I never asked myself why Melanie wanted the divorce. And truthfully, I think I didn't want to know."

Vic wondered if Holden found it a relief to tell someone what he struggled with every day.

Holden looked at them, and Vic saw confidence in his eyes. "It was only after we were divorced that I, you know, I went out with a guy. And learned about the city's gay bars. After the divorce, I felt like I could. And then, one day, a couple of months ago, I went to a fundraiser, and Melanie showed up with Ryan. I was attracted to him right away. In a different way than anyone else. I mean, it felt electric to be near him."

Holden fell quiet, his face flushed. After a moment, he asked, "Do you know what that's like? To think about a person all the time, to hate it when they show up somewhere with someone else? And I could read the signs. Ryan was open to me. He hadn't flipped for me, but he'd left a door ajar if

I wanted to try it. And it made no sense. He was younger than me. Good looking. Athletic. But I thought, what the hell. I asked him if he'd like to have dinner. He said maybe, and asked where we would go. I picked the glitziest place I could think of. I knew by then it was better if I kept my male dates public. If I saw someone I knew, they would think I was entertaining a client. That was easier to explain away than if someone saw me coming out of a gay bar. Ryan liked the restaurant I suggested, so we went."

He fell silent, staring at something in the middle distance.

"Excuse me," Vic said gently. "The argument with Melanie Beck? At the party a few nights ago?"

Holden blinked. "I have to explain this for you to understand the argument."

"Okay." Vic glanced at Liz, and she shrugged.

Holden hesitated a few seconds. "Anyway. Ryan and I met several times. I always picked expensive places. Fancy places. I was worried if I changed what I was doing, he would lose interest. And then he was late to a couple of dinners. He apologized and blamed his truck. Said it kept breaking down. He couldn't get it inspected because it needed repairs. He wasn't pushing hard, just laying it out there. And then he suggested we go away for a weekend. I was all in on the idea. Less stress about running into people I might know, that kind of thing. But when I agreed to go, he brought up the truck and said no, it wouldn't work. He needed to get his truck fixed first."

Holden took a half-sob of a breath. "You know where this is going. Even I knew where it was going, and I couldn't help myself. I bought him a truck. A gift."

Holden looked out of the window, slowly shaking his head. He resumed talking, still staring at nothing. "So I got my weekend away. And I knew, I knew exactly what he was doing. And I couldn't stop myself. I hated myself for it, but I couldn't stop."

He turned and looked at Vic. "And not long afterwards, Melanie asks me to this party. Fine, I've helped her with fundraising before. But halfway into the party she comes over, and she tells me she knows about Ryan. That she's glad for me. And she says that was why she divorced me. She suspected I was gay, and wanted me to be happy. That she knew I wouldn't be happy with her. And I kind of lost it."

Holden wiped his lips with the back of his hand, and Vic saw the tremor was back in his hands. "I just lost it. Somehow I didn't want her to know. But mainly I didn't want her to be *right*. I didn't want her to be that *kind*. So I lit into her. Accused her of sleeping with Ryan. Loud enough so everyone could hear. Loud enough to stop the quartet playing. And then I hit on one of the women in the quartet. The viola player. Just to make Mel think she was wrong. Just to prove to Mel she was full of shit."

He shook his head slowly. "And I knew I had to end it with Ryan. The day I snuck out, we got to the hotel, and I told Ryan we were finished."

Vic remembered Ryan's reaction during his interview. How easily Ryan gave up Holden. Now he understood Ryan's lack of loyalty.

"Of course, I couldn't hold to it. I let him talk me out of it." His longish hair, usually swept back, framed his doughy face. His voice turned hoarse. "But I guess he gave me up to you. He must have. So he beat me to it, kind of." A tear slid from his right eye, and he quickly wiped it away. "So that's me." He looked from Vic to Liz. "Thanks for asking my daughter to leave. I'm just not ready to tell Sam all this yet. I don't suppose there's a way to keep it quiet?"

"There's no reason for it to come up in a press conference," Vic said slowly. "We'll do our best. But we do have to document why we don't think you're a person of interest. That's about the best I can offer."

He nodded. "I guess that's about all I can hope for. Anything else?"

"Not for now," Vic said quickly. In truth, he couldn't sit at the table any longer, and from the look in Liz's eyes, she couldn't either. Holden was slouched in front of them, his shoulders rounded.

Vic stood, and Liz was almost as fast. They thanked Holden and left the office. Liz crossed to the conference room and spoke to Samantha, reminding her about Craig. They followed Holden's assistant to the entry and took the elevator to the ground floor. Went through the revolving door onto the sidewalk.

"I need a goddamned shower," Liz said as soon as they were outside. "Can he make up his mind about any one goddamn thing? Quit hiding and be who he is?"

"I think he's pretty good at lying." Vic looked both ways down the street. Barely anyone was on the sidewalk. "Did you see how smooth he was with his daughter? And think about how much he has to lie to cover himself every day. Even picking a fake fight with his ex-wife?"

"Is it lying, or not believing in yourself?" Liz's irritation started to get the better of her. "If you're gay, be gay. If someone is using you for money and you know it, punch 'em in the throat. Don't give them the damn money."

"There's that." Something Liz said shifted inside him. She was right. Lying was just the symptom. The disease was Holden not being honest with himself. The fight he picked with Melanie was about more than him not wanting her to be right, or kind. It was Holden refusing to be honest with himself about who he was. Aggressively. As if Holden's attack on Melanie would help him overlook his inability to be honest with himself. And that was a motivation. He knew that characteristic was important, somehow, he just didn't know how. What to connect it to.

Traffic whizzed by on the street next to them.

Liz took a breath. "We headed back?"

"Yeah." Vic was still deep inside himself. A second thought came to him, rising like a balloon. "Look, this leaves us only with that damn tracking app Craig found. Not much more."

"That's true."

Vic suddenly understood what he'd missed about the tracking app. "So do this. Get after a judge. I want the phone records on Ryan, Jessica, and that Kwan guy in Melanie's house. And Holden."

Liz frowned. "What are you thinking?"

"The tracking app. If we found it on one phone, maybe it's on others. And out of that group of people, who *doesn't* have it on their phone?"

A UPS truck ground by, leaving a smell of exhaust. Liz smiled. "That's a point." She frowned. "But how do we convince a judge if Ryan and Holden just cleared themselves?"

Vic studied her. "I just said. Holden lies like a fish. He can't even be honest with himself. We're just asking for the phone records of the people closest to Melanie. Ryan misled us about his alibi, and Holden flat lied. Jessica stayed with Melanie the night before she died. Kwan lives in the house, and we have weird activity going on at three in the morning. That's where my head is right now. And I don't think I'll decide for sure that Holden and Ryan alibied each other out for a few more days."

Liz smiled. "Good thinking. You can never be too sure. And I would never burden a judge with too many details."

They smiled at each other.

Liz raised her fist and pointed over her shoulder with her thumb. "I'm that way."

"Vic nodded in the other direction. "And I'm that way. See you back there."

Chapter Thirty-Eight

C hen Yun studied the parking lot from the edge of his hotel window for several minutes, memorizing each parked car. He hadn't slept well, hounded by the glimpses of the white pick-up truck he'd spotted in his rearview mirror and the latest terse email from his wife.

He and his wife knew their emails were collected and read and that discussion of their personal lives was impossible. But her last email carried her clearest message yet, made explicit by what she chose not to say. She provided utterly no update on their son's development, no photo, even his name didn't appear. Chen understood what she was really saying.

If you can't be bothered to come home and be part of your son's life, then what's the point in telling you anything about him?

Their separation had reached that point. He knew he couldn't blame her. She'd put up with his absences for years. Everyone accepted that sacrifices must be made for the Party, how the needs of the nation outweighed the needs of the individual. Yet the husbands of her friends somehow remained at home. They held jobs during the day and returned to their families at night. He cursed his decision to listen to his college professor and join the regional police. He'd liked the idea of investigating corruption, especially among businesses. He knew those crimes often went unpunished. It never occurred to him the Party might find a way to pervert a unit like his and use it for their own ends.

He knew better now. With each case he investigated, he'd come to understand how complex and clever people could be in pursuit of power and wealth. How ruthless. The simpler motivations of revenge or hatred rarely applied. And his skill at untangling those schemes had brought him all the way here.

Hiding at the side of a hotel window, peeking under a curtain.

He laughed roughly at the absurdity of it and let the curtain drop. Fine. If that white pick-up truck followed him, he would spot it. He left the room with a quick glance in both directions of the hallway. Moments later, he was inside his rental car, headed for the Heinz Loft Apartments.

His route was circuitous and tortured, the better to tease out a tail. He knew that if it was one of America's major government agencies, they would simply track his rental car. Not a perfect solution, because the car's location finder only updated at intervals, but it would be enough. Yet he didn't think they were involved. If they were, why the pick-up truck the day before? Why risk showing themselves?

When he reached the Loft Apartments, he was sure no one was following him.

He circled the lot and parked a few cars down from Yiptou Ng's dented and faded Honda Civic. He crossed to it, thinking about the difference between that car and the BMW driven by Baihu Song.

Yiptou reached over and unlocked the side door. Chen slid inside.

"I wondered if you would show up today," Yiptou said. His legs were splayed, and he wore sweatpants and a T-shirt, the same clothes he'd worn in his kitchen the day they met, although the oil and soy sauce stains were missing. The driver's seat was halfway back and low. Chen liked that. Yiptou would be hard to spot inside his car.

"Have you seen the woman at all?"

Yiptou shrugged. "It is the same. She leaves at about nine in the morning, carrying a violin case. I don't know when she returns. I'm gone by then."

"I have that covered. So she is gone for the day now?"

Yiptou turned to him, the dark mole on his forehead almost a third eye. "No. Today is different. She has not left yet."

Chen tried not to stare at the mole. He thought about why she might still be inside the apartment. He had checked the symphony schedule and knew there was a performance that evening, and wondered if the practice schedule changed the day of a performance.

He turned back to Yiptou. "Have you seen an elderly Chinese man about? Perhaps out for a walk?" Chen took out his phone and showed him a photo of Liling's father. "Or perhaps movement in the apartment window after she leaves?" Chen wasn't sure why he asked the questions. He had no reason to suspect that Liliang's father was hiding with his daughter. In fact, he doubted it. A man like that was used to spacious rooms and people to order about. It seemed unlikely he would be here.

Yiptou thought for a moment and shook his head. "No. But I can only see the main door from here. There are two others. One around the back and a fire escape exit. He could take either of those, and I would not see it."

Chen nodded. He knew Yiptou's background. His family members were well known to the local police. No one truly dangerous, but all of them born hustlers. A little smuggling here, some black market there, organized theft if chance provided for it. Of course Yiptou would check the building and note the exits. He'd been brought up to always know his escape routes.

A little different than the two college boys, he thought. Their idea of an escape route would be a chartered jet to Vancouver with a Canadian passport in their hip pocket.

"Thank you," Chen said slowly. "Let me know when she goes out today." He hesitated, trying to think if he'd missed anything. Nothing came to mind, so he opened the door and rose from the seat. He closed the car door gently, out of habit, and scanned the parking lot. Froze.

Near the entrance a white pick-up sat in a parking slot. A slot that was empty when he entered the lot and checked the cars. From his angle, he couldn't make out anyone in the cab.

He bent to the window. "Yiptou, have you seen anyone else watching the building?"

Yiptou, turned to him, obviously surprised. "No. I would have noticed."

Chen knew that was true. Yiptou's survival instincts were too strong. Chen nodded to him and decided to be direct. He crossed the parking lot to the truck. The cab was empty. He swung behind, took a photo of the license plate, and looked about. The area was deserted. Slowly, he returned to his car, distracted and worried. On one level, America was an ocean of white pick-up trucks. On another, it was a coincidence that hammered like a headache behind his eyes.

He slid into his car and left. He crossed the bridge into downtown Pittsburgh, the white truck a shrinking dot in his rearview mirror.

As he moved through traffic, a sense of things loosening wouldn't leave him. His instincts told him he needed to end this assignment. He needed to get home, the sooner the better. To see his son. Rediscover his wife.

He drove, his gaze constantly shuttling to his mirrors. He remembered the concert that night. Yes, he thought. I need to speed this up. I should go. See Liling play. Get a good look at her. Plan my approach.

End this assignment and return to Hunan.

Chapter Thirty-Nine

Craig rose from his desk as Vic and Liz walked into the office. He'd been working, watching for them out of the corner of his eye. As soon as they were close to their desks, he called, "I got the phone number, the one accessing the app on Mrs. Beck's phone?"

Vic nodded but took his time removing his sport coat. Liz carefully hung her leather jacket on its hanger.

Craig didn't understand why they were so placid at the news. It was as if they knew it was bad news.

"Okay," Vic said, plopping into his desk chair.

"I, um, emailed it to you both."

Vic stared at him, his brown eyes steady. "Here's my bet. It isn't a number we recognize."

Craig was relieved. Vic had already guessed the problem. "Right. I did search on it. Looks like a prepaid."

Liz scratched her cheek. "Now there's a surprise."

Vic smiled. "Craig, two things. Liz is going to talk to the judge and get us access to the phones belonging to Jessica, Kwan, Holden, and Ryan. We want to see if any of them have the tracker app on their phones."

Craig saw the logic. "Whoever else has it might be the one who placed it on Mrs. Beck's phone."

"Right, or they were being followed as well. And if someone doesn't have the app, chances are they aren't involved. We can discount them. Although I guess they could have deleted it from their phone. But it's very likely someone bought a prepaid phone to access the app. It would be kind of dumb to use their own phone for that."

"Although dumb criminals is how we keep our close rate high." Liz peered at her computer screen, typed something, and hit the return key. "Dumb is good." She sat back, taking them in.

"Right." Craig sat down. He was embarrassed. He should have anticipated a prepaid phone and concentrated on how to move the investigation forward despite that. If he'd done that, he might have thought to examine everyone's phones.

"Oh, and Craig?"

Craig turned to the sound of Vic's voice.

"The interview with Holden went as expected. He fessed up to being with Ryan at the time Melanie Beck was killed. But you know..." Vic's delivery slowed. "I'm not sure I'm satisfied they both have alibis. What do you think, Liz?"

"Yeah. I'm not sure either." Liz stretched her words into a drawl. With a slow, exaggerated movement, she snapped the fingers of her right hand. "Wait, what's the word cowboys use? Maybe they were in cahoots. They murdered Melanie together. That's it."

Vic smiled at Liz. "Exactly. I bet they did it together."

Craig thought they sounded like a bad comedy act. He also understood Vic and Liz were giving him a message. For some reason, they didn't want to officially discount Ryan and Holden from the investigation yet. He understood his role. "Good thinking. Can't be too sure."

"In case anyone asks," Vic said pointedly.

"Got it." Craig worked it out. If they cleared Ryan and Holden, they wouldn't get permission to see what apps were on their phones. "You can never be too sure."

"I say that all the time." Vic considered Craig, and his gaze deepened. "That phone number, the one used to check the app on Melanie's phone. You said you couldn't identify who owned it, right? Did you call the number?"

Craig shook his head. "Thought I should wait for you and Liz."

"Good. Don't call it yet. Not until I say. I want to see what's on the other phones before we do that."

"If the prepaid hasn't already been tossed," Liz said quietly.

"Assuming it hasn't been tossed," Vic agreed.

Liz turned to her computer screen, and Vic did the same. Craig turned to his, thinking through the conversation. Somehow, when he took this job, it never occurred to him how many variations and permutations there were to investigating a crime. He liked it. It took some real creativity to turn a dead end into a new corridor.

The rest of the morning was spent consolidating their evidence, and after lunch, with the request for the phone data approved by a judge and delivered to the phone companies, they met in the conference room.

By four o'clock, they had a plan of action around three items: any information discovered when reviewing the data on everyone's phones, what caused the night-time activity identified by the motion detectors in the Beck house, and reinterviewing all the possible witnesses, including the people Melanie Beck worked with at the Symphony. They spent almost an hour covering the questions they needed to ask in each interview.

By the end, Craig chose not to tell Vic and Liz that he was attending the symphony that night to watch Eileen play. Mainly he didn't want Liz to make fun of him, but the questions reserved for Eileen's second interview were short and repetitive, a repetition of the first interview. Craig didn't see how that rose to a level that might require him to disclose his plans with Eileen. And anyway, it wasn't a date. She had simply provided him with a ticket and promised a backstage tour afterwards. It really wasn't a date.

No matter how much he wanted it to be.

But first, he needed to update Samantha Beck. That was something Liz asked him to do before he left for the day. Why she seemed to find the task funny, he didn't know.

Chapter Forty

After meeting Yiptou Ng, Chen Yun parked downtown. Unwilling to pay for a parking garage, he wasted twenty minutes finding a parking meter. Another twenty minutes later, as lunchtime crowds surged from the office towers, he was back in his car with a ticket for that night's symphony in his pocket.

As he drove, he thought about Baihu Song, the son of the Politburo member. Since dismissing him from brunch, they hadn't talked. Chen had meant to call Song the next day, but somehow never got around to it. More accurately, Song still irritated him, which made it easier to neglect the call.

He needed to change that. The other student, Yulong Lin, had picked up the slack, but it was too much to expect Lin to spend more time covering for Song's arrogant and irritating behavior. At the next red light, he called Song, waiting as the phone switched to voice mail. Without preamble, Chen asked Song to call him at his earliest convenience.

As Chen drove, he checked repeatedly to see if he was being followed. Spotting nothing, his attention drifted, drawn to the city's topography. The road followed the valley curves of creeks and small rivers, rising sometimes to peaks and glimpses of the wooly-textured tree-covered hills and low mountains that stretched to the blue horizon. Forgetting about the traffic behind him, he marveled at the bright and distinct colors surrounding him. The deep blue of the sky, the swaying, rich green of the trees. The clouds as billowing and white as taffeta wedding dresses.

He parked outside his hotel, his mind returning to Hunan. He thought about the pale colors of his home city, the heat-faded green and dusty-tan earth of the parks. The pale gray of the polluted sky. He supposed there were trees in the city, but he couldn't think of a single one that drew his attention when he passed. He suddenly wanted to show his son this place, watch his face react to the distinct colors, to the surprises following each turn in the road.

"Detective Yun."

Chen spun around. Approaching him was Tanming, last seen at the airport in Singapore.

Tanming's presence was so unexpected Chen blinked and shaded his eyes from the sun, as if to dispel a mirage.

"Sir. I've been waiting for you."

Chen caught just the slightest undertone of reprimand as Tanming drew closer, and it put him on guard. "Tanming, this is unexpected." Chen glanced at the parked cars around them. Behind Tanming, a small, silver sedan was new to the lot. He should have spotted it.

Tanming stopped in front of him. "Commander Wang instructed me to come."

Chen heard it clearly this time. A note of authority in Tanming's voice, a forcefulness he hadn't heard before.

"And how is our good commander?" Chen asked, trying a lighter tone, as if unexpectedly meeting Tanming in a Pittsburgh parking lot was an everyday event.

"Perhaps," Tanming said blandly, "We should speak inside. Not here."

As they entered the hotel, Chen nodded to the desk clerk. In the elevator, he noted that Tanming carried a soft briefcase that looked weighed down by a laptop. But why was he here? More questions teemed in his mind. Was Tanming the one driving the white truck? Watching him? The elevator discharged them onto the third floor, and Chen led the way to his room.

Inside, Chen waved Tanming into the armchair by the window. He pointed at the coffeemaker. "If you want tea, help yourself." He wanted to reestablish command over his subordinate and wasn't about to serve him like an honored guest.

"Commander Wang asked me to come." Tanming repeated the sentence as if he was beating Chen with a stick.

"As you said. Did he explain why?" Chen wasn't about to ask why Wang hadn't emailed to say that Tanming was coming.

"Yes. Commander Wang asked me to come yesterday, or the day before? The time zones. I've lost track. But I left the same day as we talked. He said you might need additional resources."

Chen cocked his head, about to say he didn't, but realized it would be a futile argument to have with Tanming. Instead, he asked, "How did he think you could help?"

"He wishes this project to end sooner than we originally planned."

"When?"

Tanming hesitated, and Chen knew he didn't want to deliver this news. Tanming avoided Chen's gaze. "Within a few days."

Chen considered him. Normally, their projects stretched from six to eight weeks. Tanming knew that, and his hesitation to pass along the new deadline was understandable. But this new deadline suggested something else. Because the crimes most of their targets committed happened in past years, speed wasn't important. What mattered was the result, which meant finding the right approach to force a person to return to China. He wasn't close to identifying a weakness he could leverage against Liling Liang. And Chen was quite sure that Liling—who grew up outside China and worked at a prestigious job she loved—had no intention of returning to China.

Something had changed in the Liang case, something Commander Wang didn't want him to know about.

"I'm not sure that is possible," Chen said softly.

"I also expressed my surprise at the requirement to complete this project so quickly." Tanming finally met his gaze. "And there is something else."

This will be the nasty bit, thought Chen.

"When I arrived in Los Angeles last night, I found a voice message from Commander Wang. It told me to call him."

"I hope you did so immediately," Chen said, steeling himself.

"Of course. He asked me if you recruited Baihu Song to work for you. I told him I only knew about a Cantonese man who owns a Chinese restaurant here. He explained that apparently you did and that Baihu Song's father is a Politburo member. He said Song told his father that you are being insolent and arrogant toward him. That you viciously demeaned him in front of someone. As a result, Song's father has asked that your behavior be investigated and reviewed at the very highest levels of our force."

Tanming's gaze was cool and calculating, like someone examining a trapped animal.

Knowing that whatever he said next would become part of the investigation, Chen's first instinct was to stay quiet. But not answering was an admission of guilt. And whatever he said would be dutifully witnessed and repeated by Tanming.

"I fear there may be a misunderstanding," Chen said, finally, trying to sound unperturbed. Now Chen knew why Song hadn't returned his call. Song knew the crushing weight about to land on Chen's chest. Chen imagined Song laughing as he listened to Chen's voicemail, debating whether it would be more fun to call back to hear Chen's desperate apology and pleas to stop the investigation, or to ignore Chen's calls and let Chen spiral from desperate to frantic.

Fu shui nan shou, Chen thought. Spilt water can't be gathered up. It was done. The saying often described divorces, and given his relationship with his wife, it was painfully appropriate.

"Commander Wang wishes you to call him immediately," Tanming said.

"If Commander Wang wishes to hear from me immediately, then I will call him now."

Tanming gave the slightest of starts. "But it is the middle of the night in Wuhan."

"Immediately means immediately." Chen pointed at the doorway. "You may wait in the hall."

Chen saw annoyance flit across Tanming's face as he rose to let himself out. When the door closed, Chen tapped his finger on the face of his phone and watched it light up. He hesitated. Tanming had revealed not one, but three problems. The first was why Commander Wang didn't call him about

Tanming's arrival, or at least warn him Tanming was coming. Chen had filed his reports on schedule. Had something he reported caused Wang to send Tanming? The second was the investigation. Unless he won Song back to his side, his career was over. He would never survive the investigation. He didn't care if he lost his position, but what made him shudder was the impact on his family. He couldn't allow that shame to stain his wife, couldn't let his son grow up the scion of a disgraced man. And finally, there was the problem of Song himself. That slimy little weasel needed to be taught a lesson.

As did Tanming. Tanming was acting like a shark with the scent of blood. He was no longer the subservient underling.

Chen picked up his phone, stepped to the window, and dialed Commander Wang. It was the middle of the night in China, and sure enough, the call went to voice mail. Carefully, Chen left a message explaining that Tanming had just arrived and instructed him to call immediately, as he was now doing. He said he looked forward to discussing Baihu Song, and was shocked that Song had reported anything untoward. He would, of course, provide any and all information about their interactions. He ended by saying that he was now aware of the accelerated reclamation of Liling Liang, and would make plans to fulfill that goal. He stopped himself from asking why he wasn't warned of Tanming's arrival. He ended the call.

A new thought thrummed inside him. Possibly it was Tanming who purposely chose not to email or text him about his orders to visit America. Commander Wang might have told Tanming to come, expecting Tanming to forewarn Chen. Instead, Tanming had arrived unannounced, knowing that by doing so he brought the air of Commander Wang's displeasure.

Chen pocketed his phone. That gave him five or six hours before a return call, he thought. Perhaps a bit more, because he didn't plan to answer his phone during the symphony performance.

He took several calming breaths, staring across the road at the tree-swathed hills. They stretched into the distance against a sharp blue sky, like a series of green and foaming ocean waves frozen by geology and the turn of centuries.

Beautiful, he thought, surprising himself.

It was a type of thought he'd never had before. A kind of observation he'd never known might be inside him, or that he was capable of making. Given everything involved with Tanming's arrival, it was a wonder it would surface just now.

With a smile, he crossed to the door. He thought about Tanming on the other side of the door and hardened. Tanming had finally revealed himself. Chen knew he'd been right not to feel comfortable with Tanming, or to fully trust him.

Tanming was the best of what Party training produced. And the worst.

Chapter Forty-One

As Craig changed clothes to attend the symphony, he caught himself trying on at least his third pants and shirt combination. Oh no, he thought with a snicker, staring at his latest combination of gray slacks and white shirt. That just isn't the right message of suave urbanity and innocence. It will never do. He did a mock pirouette in front of the mirror and spoke in a high-pitched, effete voice, "Does this say maturity? Innocence?"

He laughed at himself, stripped off the clothes, and studied his phone-booth closet. He nixed the suburban uniform of tan chinos and a blue button-down shirt and grabbed the closest dark slacks and textured white shirt. That was good enough to match his gray sport coat, he thought. He knew he needed a better wardrobe, or at least one that was recently washed or dry-cleaned. But dressing well, he decided, just took too much time, thinking, and money.

He stopped at the bedroom door as his service weapon and handcuffs caught his eye. They lay on the bed, and he knew they should be under lock and key. He needed a lockable gun box; the sooner, the better. This was the first job that required him to carry a weapon, and he still hadn't adapted to it. He needed to. He carried his weapon into the kitchen and stashed it behind the cleaning fluids under his kitchen sink.

He reached the Symphony's Heinz Hall fifteen minutes early. He didn't want to take his seat immediately in case Eileen thought he looked desperate, so he wandered the narrow lobby. Scattered about were easels holding large blue placards with the words *In Memoria* across the top. Below the headline was a photograph of Melanie Beck and a biography. Craig took his time reading about Melanie's support of the symphony and her leadership guiding the symphony from near-bankruptcy to stronger financial footing.

Craig studied the careful wording. It must be tough, he decided, for organizations that depend on donations to survive. They can never say they are doing too well, or they might lose their most effective fundraising tactic.

He took his seat with five minutes to spare. Eileen's ticket was in the fourth-row center, placing him just above eye-level with the floor of the stage. She was already in her chair amid the understated cacophony of instrument checks and rustling sheet music. Craig tried to catch Eileen's eye, but she was focused on her violin. He wondered if these moments were like a warm-up for athletes, filled with personal routines and preperformance superstitions.

The stage fell quiet as if a switch was thrown. The lights dimmed, and the conductor walked briskly to center stage amid a swell of applause. He was followed by a reedy, white-haired man in a flapping navy-blue suit.

The conductor tapped his baton on the edge of his lectern to quiet the orchestra members and stepped aside. The stage darkened and a spotlight centered on the man in the blue suit. He stared at the audience, his full head of white hair almost a halo, his hooked nose shining in the light.

He introduced himself as the Symphony's vice president and in a deep voice, began to memorialize Melanie Beck, listing her activities for the Symphony.

Craig twice stole glances at Eileen as he spoke. She looked genuinely sad, her violin tucked against her stomach, her gaze inward. She didn't seem to be looking for him.

The man's tone shifted, and he told several anecdotes, including a genuinely funny one about Melanie's love of pickles and habit of dating and storing them in the Symphony's break room refrigerator. He finished on that warm note, the audience breaking into prolonged applause. Craig joined them and glanced at Jessica. Her viola on her lap, she stared at the audience, absent-mindedly clapping, as if she couldn't quite understand the outpouring of support.

It occurred to Craig that he didn't know why Jessica still lived at the Beck house. He remembered her saying she'd been in residence there for four months, and that seemed like a long time for a temporary stay. It felt like she was taking advantage of Melanie's kindness.

As the tall man left the stage, the conductor raised his arms, and Craig settled back into his seat. The music swelled. He didn't recognize the first piece, but knew from its combination of somberness and lilt that it was chosen for Melanie. It was a pity, he thought, that Melanie didn't know she was being honored this way. That she could no longer hear it.

Then again, he told himself, perhaps she could.

He watched Eileen as she played. She didn't close her eyes, even when the music turned sad, or filled with longing. But he thought he saw something in her gaze, in those moments, as if the emotions in the music drew Eileen closer to herself, were more truthful to her. Or perhaps, he considered, those are the feelings that scare her, they are the ones she can't bring herself to face. And then he stopped thinking and let the music carry him, through the intermission and the rest of the performance.

As the final applause died away and people rose for the exits, Craig glanced again in Eileen's direction. Finally, she met his eyes, a small smile on her face, and held up a single finger in a 'wait there' gesture. Craig rose and stood in place, allowing the people sitting to his right to maneuver past. He looked at the stage and saw Kwan stand and collect his sheet music. Jessica was doing the same thing. Craig wondered if they would drive home together.

He glanced at the stage, but Eileen was gone. He waited as the crowd thinned, until Eileen popped out from a door next to the stage, holding a violin case. She raised her other arm, quickly waving as if she was saying goodbye to him. Craig hesitated, decided she couldn't mean that, and headed toward her.

As he approached, she dropped her arm. "Sorry. I turned Chinese on you. That wave is how we tell someone to join us. I should have done this." With an exaggerated movement, she extended her arm and drew it back toward herself, in the familiar Western motion of waving someone over.

Craig found her arm movement comical and had trouble getting the grin off his face. "So much to learn. Great performance tonight. Especially that first piece."

"Everyone meant it. Everybody loved Melanie. It makes you want to put more into the piece."

"The audience sensed it. At least I did."

"Good." Her eyes flashed. "Tour time. Have you ever been backstage?"

"Nope. All I've done is help people on and off the stage."

"You need to widen your horizons. This way."

For the next ten minutes, Eileen led him about, showing him the dressing rooms, break room, and where the props and spare instruments were stored. Craig was surprised at the lack of space and the tightness of the hallways.

"Kind of takes all the glamour out of it," Eileen kidded him, as they negotiated yet another narrow aisle.

"Seems made for efficiency."

"That's a kind way to put it. All of the Halls are like this. Well, the one in London had rats in the basement the size of dogs. No one went down there." She looked up at him. "Or if they did, they didn't live to tell the tale."

"Pretty sure I lived in an apartment building like that right after college."

"The things youth suffer."

"But isn't there something true and good about being young and poor?"

They had stopped, jammed to one side of the narrow hallway so others could pass by. Craig felt her nearness as a warm, physical sensation.

Eileen smiled at him. "A little money and people get over it in a hurry."

Eileen drew him along the hallway. "There's often a get-together at a restaurant nearby after a concert, but I can't go tonight."

"Do you want to go somewhere else? Are you hungry?"

Eileen considered him. "I do, but not tonight. I'm sorry. Something came up."

Craig tried to recover himself. He realized he'd interpreted her invitation to the symphony and the backstage tour as a preamble.

"I really am sorry." Eileen touched his arm. "I have to get home. Maybe we could do something in a day or two?"

Craig saw just a trace of pleading in her eyes. He knew he had to agree, but he didn't want the evening to end. "Sure." He tried to make his voice sound light and confident. "Can I take you home? How did you get here tonight?"

"Oh. I took an Uber. But it's a nice night. I thought I would walk. I do sometimes. It helps me unwind after playing."

"Let me drive you." Craig was surprised at the concern that leaped into his throat. "You were worried someone was following you. You can't be out alone at night. Especially on that walk. It isn't a great neighborhood." He almost said it wasn't safe, which he didn't think it was, but didn't want to sound overprotective.

Eileen frowned, as if she hadn't considered the possibility that whoever was following her might be dangerous. He saw her come to a decision.

"Um, okay. Yes." She met his gaze. "If I remember, you already know where I live."

"Good. I'm in a garage just down the street."

"Then we should go." She hefted the violin case.

The sidewalks outside were already free of most symphony-goers, the car traffic thick and almost stalled as the patrons struggled toward the bottlenecks of the bridges. Craig was conscious of Eileen walking beside him and worried about adjusting his pace to a speed that matched her natural gait. He was pleased to find she was a quick walker, and they meshed naturally.

He was surprised at how happy that made him feel.

Chapter Forty-Two

C hen Yun flowed along the sidewalk away from Heinz Hall, Liling Liang, and the young American in his gray jacket twenty paces ahead of him. She held her violin case in her left hand, her right swinging just inches from the man's left hand. They were so close to touching, he thought.

He smiled to himself. Where there is an accomplished, good-looking young woman, there is always a young man nearby. But he wasn't quite sure what to make of their relationship. They seemed to be attracted to each other, but not yet lovers.

From his seat at the very rear of the Hall, enthralled by the music, he'd watched Liling bow with the other musicians at the end of the concert. He was still in shock at how he felt. Throughout the concert, as the music swelled and fell, gathered power, or tiptoed daintily, he hadn't been able to shake his feeling of awe. And Liling was at the center of it, her shoulders shifting and dipping as she played, her arm movements smooth, part of the music's creation.

Yet his mission was to end that. To drag her back to China, a place she hadn't visited since she was ten, and in effect hold her hostage until her father returned. End her career. Not long after the intermission, he knew he couldn't do it. He wouldn't do it.

After she bowed, he saw her gesture to someone in the audience. Interested, he waited until Liling appeared at the stage's side door and waved. Only then did he see the young man. He was good-looking and light on his feet as he moved toward her. Yet, when they met at the side door, their movements were restrained, lacking the carefree intimacy of lovers.

Then Liling drew the young man backstage, and he thought he'd lost them. Unsure what to do, he'd stepped outside. Only then did he realize that by standing opposite the Hall in the shadows of a parking garage, he could watch the building's front and side doors. He settled in to wait, his body still tingling from the music. Unsurprisingly, in those moments, Commander Wang returned his earlier call. Chen ignored it. After his decision not to force Liling's return to China, he needed time to formulate a plan. Hopefully, also one that blunted Song's accusations.

It was almost thirty minutes before Liling and the young man exited from the Hall's side doors and started along the sidewalk toward him. Chen guessed they were headed for a car, because they moved in the opposite direction of Liling's apartment.

He knew once they were mobile, he would lose them, but he had decided what to do, at least for that night. He would relieve Yulong Lin outside the loft apartments and wait until Liling returned home. That was important. He needed to know if she planned to spend the night with this *wai guo ren*, this foreigner, or if their relationship was something less involved. He needed to know if their relationship might be useful or a hindrance to recovering Liling's father.

Liling accompanied the young man inside a parking garage, and Chen peeled away, hurrying toward his own car. A few minutes later, headed toward Liling's apartment, he called Yulong Lin.

"It is Chen," he said simply when Lin answered. "How is the watch?"

"There is nothing happening," Lin answered. "She is playing in a concert tonight, so she isn't here, isn't that correct?"

"Yes, I attended and watched her play. She might be coming home soon, and I've decided to relieve you. You've taken on enough over the last two days."

"That would be helpful. I have work to do. Right now, the only thing I can see are lights in her apartment. They are still on, which is a surprise."

Chen thought about that. "What about last night?"

"She was home, so everything seemed normal."

"Good. Thanks. I'll relieve you in a few minutes."

"Yes. Bit I thought you planned to have Baihu Song replace me?"

Chen frowned. He didn't understand what Lin was saying. Song still hadn't responded to his earlier voicemail asking him to call.

"Why do you ask?"

"Because he's here. I saw him about fifteen minutes ago. He went into the apartment building."

Chen blinked, and his stomach tightened. What was Song doing? With a rush, he remembered Song's repeated requests to approach Liling.

Song couldn't be that stupid, he thought. But he knew it wasn't stupidity. It was arrogance. Song believed he could do Chen's job. Even when he had no idea how, what was at stake, and what was required to be successful.

Chen spun the steering wheel, turned off the bridge, and onto the road that ran to the Loft parking lots.

"I'm here," he said quickly. "You are relieved."

Chapter Forty-Three

"Tell me about your violin," Craig said, as he pulled out of the parking garage and steered in the direction of Eileen's apartment. He'd noticed that when she entered his Jeep, she carefully placed the violin case upright by her feet, holding the top.

"Of all the violins I've played, it's my favorite."

He glanced at her with a grin. "Stradivarius?"

"Don't even joke about that." She touched the case. "It is a Scott Cao. Made especially for me."

Craig wasn't sure what to say. He'd never heard of a violin maker with that name.

Eileen sensed his hesitation. "Their best ones are custom-made. Since you know about my father, you know that once he could afford it." She glanced at him with a small smile. "And I wasn't too proud to take it. Its sound is beautiful."

Craig noted the past tense reference to her father's wealth. He wanted to ask about that, but decided not to. He slowed at a yellow light and stopped.

Eileen noticed the traffic light as well. "You're a cautious driver. Or is that police training? Or..." She glanced around his ten-year-old, third-hand red Jeep with its torn upholstery. "Was that your car's top speed?"

Craig affected mock injury. "Don't. She'll hear you. In fact, this Jeep is a beast." He glanced at her and took a stab at the truth. "I was trying to make the journey take as long as possible."

From the corner of his eye, he saw her smile at the windshield. "What a complicated person you are, Craig Luntz. A philosopher, and yet cagey."

She turned her face to him. "Should I be scared?"

"Not of me."

"I believe that. I think I may need to be scared of myself."

They stared at one another, her statement between them, Craig absolutely lost on what to say. The nasal hoot of a car horn broke the moment. Craig turned and saw the light was green. He released the clutch and eased on the gas.

"I don't mind driving slowly with you, but perhaps not that slowly?"

"Fair enough," Craig managed to say, slightly embarrassed.

Despite his pokey pace, they reached Eileen's apartment building a few minutes later. Craig circled the lot and pulled up to the curb at the main entrance, unsure if he should get out and run around the Jeep to open her door.

Eileen solved the dilemma for him. "With this car, I feel like I must be very American. Rough and ready." She opened the door slightly so he knew she didn't expect him to open it for her. She fished her violin out of the foot well and placed it on her lap. "Thank you for the ride. Do you mind if I call you tomorrow? I'd like to make up for tonight."

"Please do."

She stretched toward him and planted a light kiss on his cheek. Straightened and smiled. "Thanks again for the ride."

"Glad to do it," called Craig as Eileen swung open the door. She climbed out, turned, and leaned through the open door. "Talk to you tomorrow." Her eyes flashed, and the door thumped shut. Craig watched her walk to the apartment building's front door, pivot and raise her violin case to him in a wave. She disappeared inside.

"Okay," Craig said to himself, slightly lightheaded. He worked the stick shift into first, made sure she was out of sight and rolled forward. It hadn't worked tonight, but tomorrow she would call him.

He was okay with that.

He was so wrapped up in himself he barely noticed the man walk past his Jeep in the direction of the front doors to the apartment building. It was only when he paused at the stop sign at the far edge of the parking lot that something shifted in his mind. He blinked and checked his rear-view mirror. Twenty yards away, a man crossed under the overhead door lights to the apartment entrance, stopped, and looked around. Craig tightened. Even at that distance, he saw it was a young man, Chinese, or at least East Asian. The man pushed through the doors into the apartment building lobby.

Craig stared, torn, his breathing shallow. The coincidence of it. Eileen's concern about being stalked by a Chinese man. And now, a single Asian man, following her into her apartment building. He hesitated a few more seconds, goosed his Jeep forward into the street and wrenched the wheel, turning one-hundred and eighty degrees. He bounced over the parking lot speed bumps a little too fast. He stopped on the yellow curb, grabbed a Sheriff's Office placard from under his driver's seat, tossed it on the dashboard, hopped out, and strode to the front doors of the apartment building. He stepped into the lobby.

He was just in time to see the elevator doors on the far side of the lobby slide closed. He bounced from one foot to the other. He knew he was probably overreacting. He tried to think of a way to justify what he was doing. Then again, it would take no time to visit Eileen's floor and check the door to her apartment. She didn't even need to know he was there.

The elevator doors opened, and a young man and woman stepped out, laughing. They crossed toward him, and Craig still hesitated. The elevator doors slid closed. Another thought came to him. Had Eileen come back from the concert to meet that man? Perhaps he was the reason she wanted to come home. Perhaps she didn't want Craig to know about this other man.

That just annoyed him. He decided to check her floor. Make sure everything was fine.

The couple brushed past him, and Craig ignored the quizzical look from the young man. He crossed to the elevators.

Chapter Forty-Four

Chen watched the red Jeep circle the parking lot and stop with the passenger door facing the front doors of the apartment building. A moment later, the dome light inside the Jeep lit up. Chen was too far away to identify who was inside, but something told him it was Liling. Several moments sluggishly passed until the Jeep rocked, and he guessed someone got out of the passenger side. The vehicle blocked his vision. He stared, and a few seconds later, a figure appeared at the doors of the apartment building, visible over the hood of the Jeep. He made out long black hair in the entrance lights, and then the person held up a violin case in a wave.

Liling. They'd come straight back from the symphony. Chen made a mental note of the red Jeep with its black soft top, watching it slowly drift away from the curb, heading toward 16th Street and the bridge.

A man walked past the Jeep from the direction of the corner of the apartment building. Chen studied him, and his heartbeat quickened. Song? He wasn't sure, he was too far away, but Lin said he'd been here earlier. The man stopped under the doorway lights and glanced about.

It was absolutely Song, and Chen knew in the same instant where he was headed. He'd told both students the number of Eileen's apartment so they could watch the window. He reached for the door handle and froze, watching the Jeep make a sharp turn in the street at the end of the parking lot and head for the apartment entrance. It careened over the speed bumps. Fifteen more seconds, and it stopped at the yellow curb outside the entrance doors. The dome light flickered as someone got out.

Chen didn't understand. Whoever was driving the Jeep couldn't possibly know Song. Could he? Was his operation betrayed?

The Jeep driver disappeared inside the apartment building. Chen weighed the possibilities. If Song approached Eileen, the mission was a failure. And with it, his career.

Chen launched himself from his car and strode toward the parking lot, watching a couple exit the building. When he finally reached the Jeep, he glanced at it and saw a placard identifying the driver as a member of the Allegheny County Police. Frustration rose inside him. Things kept getting worse. He stepped into the lobby.

It was empty.

Chapter Forty-Five

Craig repeatedly rammed his finger against the elevator button. Typical, came the thought, drifting through some part of his mind. Whenever you're in a hurry. He scouted the lobby for the stairs, but as he did, the elevator doors churned open. He stepped inside, jammed his finger on the fourth-floor button, and dropped his gaze to the door-closed button, momentarily confused by the arrow directions. He smacked the correct one several times, and the doors finally groaned closed.

The elevator rose slower than tree growth. Craig drew in shallow breaths. "You're just checking everything is okay," he told himself. Somehow he knew it wasn't.

When the doors finally ground open, Craig stepped into the hallway, staring in the direction of Eileen's apartment. Now that he was within sight of her front door, he started to feel silly. He took a few steps in the direction of her apartment, hesitated, and took a few more steps. "Just make sure the front door is closed," he told himself.

The shriek was high-pitched and cut off almost as soon as it started. Craig launched himself toward Eileen's apartment. The front door was closed. A man's hoarse shout was followed by a crash. Desperate, Craig turned the door handle and pushed, surprised the door opened. A small crowbar lay on the floor just inside the door. He glimpsed twisted and broken metal on the door knob's strike plate as he launched himself down the hallway into the living room. The man he'd seen outside was near the kitchen counter, kneeling among overturned bar stools, his left hand clutching Eileen's hair close to the scalp, cocking his right arm to throw a punch at an elderly, white-haired man in his sixties lying nearby. Eileen's torn blouse gaped open, her hands scrabbling at the arm that held her hair.

"Hey," roared Craig.

The young man stopped mid-punch and twisted to face him, eyes wide, the movement pulling Eileen along the floor and closer to him. Craig dropped behind the man, wrapped his left arm around the man's neck in a choke hold, and used his legs to stand. He was vaguely aware of the man feebly trying to get fingers between Craig's arm and neck and knew that meant he'd let go of Eileen's hair. He clamped harder, set his feet, twisted, and released his headlock as he slammed the man face down on the floor.

"Police," Craig shouted, straddling the prone man. He saw blood leak across the floor. He didn't care. He took a fistful of the man's hair, yanked up, and shoved down, driving the man's face into the floor. "Don't move," he shouted, aware of the force and control of his voice.

The man cried out, but it ended in a gurgle.

Craig caught the man's right wrist and pushed it up the man's back until he shrieked in pain. Straddling the man's back and still gripping the wrist, Craig looked around. Eileen was crawling past him toward the white-haired man.

"Ba," she called, "Ba."

Craig didn't need a translation. The elderly man's eyes were open, and he blinked. He looked surprised.

"Ba," Eileen said again, as she reached the man. She cupped his face in her hands.

Craig tucked the man's left arm under his knee and, with his free hand, worked his phone out of his slacks pocket. One-handed, he speed-dialed Vic.

The phone barely rang once before Vic answered.

"Vic, it's Craig. Need back-up. Eileen Liang's apartment. Someone attacked Eileen. I have him subdued."

"On my way. I'll call back up. Keep an open line."

Craig put his phone on speaker and placed it on the floor. He gave the man's wrist a jerk, pushing it closer to the man's head. The man bucked and squealed.

"Eileen." Craig looked at her. "Are you okay? What happened?"

Eileen stopped the conversation she was having with her father in Chinese. She looked at him, breathing hard, eyes angry, her blouse torn open.

"I don't know. There was a knock on the door, and when I asked who was there, the door just banged open. He grabbed me, ran me down the hall and, threw me on the couch, tore at my shirt. He...I yelled, and my father came out of the bedroom and tried to stop him. He pushed my father into the stools."

"Okay. Do you have a belt or a rope? I need to tie his arms. I don't have handcuffs with me."

"I can find something." Eileen spoke rapidly to her father in Chinese, rose, and disappeared down the hall. Craig shifted his grip on the man's wrist. His hand was getting tired and his knees ached.

"Let me go," the man on the floor said. "Now."

A shaft of rage passed through Craig. He pushed hard on the wrist, and the man shrieked. Craig got control of himself and eased the arm down a few degrees. The man gurgled, and his chest began to rhythmically heave. Dimly, Craig realized the man was crying. The realization filled him with delight. "You're screwed, buddy. Breaking and entering. Attempted rape. Assault. I won't let you go until you're in a cell."

"Perhaps we shouldn't be too hasty."

Craig snapped his head up. To his right stood a blocky middle-aged Chinese man. Craig hadn't heard him come in. "Who are you?" Craig liked the way his voice sounded. Smooth, unaffected by the surprise of the man in front of him. Commanding. He wasn't sure where the tone came from, but he liked it.

"My name is Chen Yun. Like you, I am also a police officer. From Hunan. In China. I have identification if you wish to see it."

Beside Craig, Eileen's father stirred and sat up. Craig saw him glance at this Chen Yun and his eyes narrow in alarm. Chen Yun saw it as well, and a hawkish look crossed Chen's square face.

"Step back. This is none of your business." Craig knew he was in a bad position. He couldn't control both of them. "More police are on their way. You shouldn't be in here. I need you to leave."

Chen took a step back but squatted so he and Craig were at eye level. He nodded toward the man Craig had pinned to the floor. "This man, I know him. In our country, his father is an important man. A very important man. His arrest will cause trouble. Arguments between our countries. Do you understand? This will happen at the highest levels. He is a Chinese national. I am a Chinese police officer. If you release him to me, I will see that justice is done."

"He's in our country; he answers to our justice system." Craig couldn't believe he was answering the man. But the man's English was so good, so smooth, and his tone so friendly, he felt like he was having lunch with an old friend and they were discussing the latest season of a favorite sports team.

"Ah," Chen said slowly. "But Chinese nationals are still under the law of China when they are overseas. It doesn't matter where they are in the world." Chen looked at Eileen's father and spoke Chinese.

Craig had the feeling he was repeating those two sentences in Chinese to Eileen's father, and something clicked in his head.

Chen turned back to Craig. "So you see, I can return him to China and make sure he faces justice there. We can avoid the difficulty that will surely come if you arrest him."

Craig nodded at the young man underneath him. "Who is this?"

"Song Baihu to us. You would say Baihu Song. The surname last."

"And what makes his father so important?"

"He is someone as important as one of your senators in Washington D.C. So you can understand the problem."

Beneath him, Song started a new round of sobbing, but it was muffled and personal, as if Song was starting to understand the depth of his problems. Craig made a silent wish that backup would arrive.

"Perhaps we have an understanding?" Chen asked gently.

Craig looked at him. "No. We don't. This asshole gets charged. That's how it works in our country."

Chen rose to his full height, and Craig tensed.

"I'm sorry to hear that." Chen shifted slightly on his feet, one foot back, and Craig went cold, preparing for an attack.

A volley of Chinese words came from behind Chen. Chen spun, a look of surprise on his face. In almost the same movement, he retreated two steps into the living room. Eileen edged out from the hallway, a field hockey stick cocked in her hands, ready to swing like a baseball bat. She shouted at the man in Chinese, the same haughty tone she'd used with Kwan. Suddenly the glass window was awash in red and blue light.

Back-up, thought Craig with relief.

Eileen said something more, and Chen slumped onto the couch. Eileen stayed just out of arm's reach, her face fierce, the field hockey stick still raised.

"Back-up is here," Craig said to Eileen. "Just another minute."

Eileen cocked her face toward her father, eyes still focused on Chen and launched into a rapid patter of Chinese. Almost immediately, her father rose from the floor. He stepped around Craig and disappeared into the hall.

"He needs to stay here," Craig said quickly.

"He has committed no crime," Eileen responded, staring squarely at Chen. "He is a victim." She looked sternly at Chen as she said the sentence. "He can leave if he wishes to. I will be the one pressing charges against this Song Baihu. And I will be the one who will decide if I wish to follow through on them."

Slowly, Chen nodded. And as Craig watched, a smile grew on Chen's face. He then huffed out a sound that sounded like a stifled laugh before putting his head back and giving himself to it, laughing hard. For a moment, he was almost overcome by it.

Eileen glanced at Craig, uncertainty and a question in her eyes. Craig retightened his hold on Song's wrist. His own hand ached. He shrugged at Eileen. He didn't understand Chen's reaction either. He swore under his breath. Why was backup taking so long?

A Chinese voice called from the direction of the hall, and Eileen responded. Craig knew Eileen's father was gone.

Only then did Craig notice it. Eileen was holding her field hockey stick left-handed.

Chapter Forty-Six

When Vic arrived at Eileen's apartment, the open door was guarded by two uniformed officers. Vic flashed his ID, listening to the voices and hum of activity inside the apartment. As he entered, he noticed the broken front door strike plate and a short crowbar nearby. He wondered at the force needed to do that to a metal door frame.

Sergeant Wroblewski stood at the entrance to the living room, his white hair stark in the dim light of the hall.

"Do you ever go home?" Vic called to him when he was halfway down the hall.

Wroblewski studied him. "Not being a Big Head, I work for a living."

For a moment, Vic thought he saw a glint of warmth in Wroblewski's eyes. "How's it looking?" Vic asked, dropping his voice.

Wroblewski nodded into the room, where a stocky middle-aged Chinese man sat on the couch in handcuffs. A young Chinese man sat on the floor, also handcuffed, the front of his shirt soaked in blood. His nose was bent, and the nostrils were packed with cotton. Every time the paramedic wiped at the congealed blood on the young man's chin, he winced. Craig and Eileen stood together in the opposite corner of the room. Eileen wore a bathrobe over her clothes. She and Craig were talking, heads bent to one another.

"Your boy, Craig," Wroblewski said in a low voice. "Between you and me, he's got his Dad's mustard. Stopped a rape, got the young guy down, controlled the room, although he needed help from the victim to keep that older Chinese guy out of the way. Not sure he was a threat, though. And there's something about the victim's Dad getting knocked down when he tried to stop the rape, but he did a runner."

"The father?" Vic frowned. He remembered Craig mentioning Eileen's father, and tried to recall the whole story. "Thanks. If you leave me a couple of uniforms, I can take it from here. We'll need transport. Do you have a woman officer for the victim?"

"On the way."

"Thanks." Vic studied Wroblewski. "Seriously. Get your dead ass home."

Wroblewski considered the offer. "Maybe I will. I was end-of-shift and ready to go home when the call came in. Heard it was Luntz, so I came here. Might be time to call it."

"You did that for Craig? What a sweet guy." Vic let his tone needle Wroblewski.

"I did it for his Dad. Craig hasn't earned it yet."

"Sounds like he's getting there, though." Vic smiled. "For a future Big Head."

Wroblewski straightened. "Takes all kinds." He turned toward Craig and Eileen. "Craig, your boss is here. I'm taking off."

"Thanks, Sergeant Wroblewski."

Wroblewski nodded to Eileen. "Ma'am."

"Thank you, Sergeant."

Vic heard a split second of hesitation before Eileen said Wroblewski's rank. She wasn't used to addressing people that way, Vic thought.

Wroblewski walked along the hall and spoke to the two uniformed officers at the door. He disappeared toward the elevators. Vic crossed to Craig and Eileen.

"How are you doing?" he asked Eileen. Her face was slightly flushed, her hair unkempt, and eyes bright. Vic thought she looked excited and alive. He'd never understood why women spent hours making themselves look pretty, when to him they looked best when they weren't thinking about how they looked.

"I'm fine." She touched Craig's arm. "Craig got here just in time."

"Yeah. Fortunate, that." Vic dropped his hand on Craig's shoulder. "Let's you and I talk." He glanced at Eileen. "Can you excuse us?"

Before she responded, Vic steered Craig into the hallway. He waved one of the uniformed officers into the living room to watch everyone and turned to Craig. "Now. About that. How *did* you get here just in time? I saw your Jeep outside the front doors."

Craig started to say something, reconsidered, and tried again. "Um, Eileen had a performance tonight. I was there, and I gave her a ride home afterwards. I'd just dropped her off."

"And then magically decided she was being attacked? How did that happen?"

"Okay, okay. Last night Eileen gave me a ticket to tonight's performance. When we were talking last night, she told me she had a stalker. A Chinese guy."

"You met her last night *and* tonight?" Vic wrapped his brain around his words. "You realize she's a witness in our investigation?"

"I thought about that. We interviewed her. She said she didn't see anything. I didn't see her as a witness."

Vic fought down rising anger. "Okay, understand me. I decide who is and who isn't a witness. And she said someone was following her. Did you ever think that might have to do with our case? That maybe she was targeted because we talked to her? She told us she didn't see anything. Other people don't know that. They might think she's cooperating with us and don't want that to happen. And oh yeah. One other thing. Maybe she lied to us."

Craig opened and closed his mouth. "I guess I didn't think about that."

"You *guess*?" Vic took a deep breath. "Craig. You don't date anyone within one hundred miles of a case. Do you understand?"

He nodded quickly, a flush rising up his neck.

"And why didn't you tell us she was being followed? Is there anything else you haven't told us?"

Craig looked down. "I just didn't connect it to our case. I thought it might be because she's in the symphony."

"She's a witness. The fact she didn't see anything is as important as anything she might have seen. Everything is connected until you are absolutely sure it isn't. Understand?"

Craig nodded. "And there is something else. I started to tell you yesterday when we were at Melanie's house, but Jessica and Kwan came home."

"Okay."

"Remember you sent me upstairs to check Melanie's bedroom and closet?"

"Yes."

"I noticed there was something sticky on the closet door that leads into Ryan's room. There was dust attached. It was on the bottom of the door."

"On the door or the frame?"

"Both."

Vic thought about that and saw a couple of possibilities. But this wasn't the right time to think it through. "We'll talk about that in the morning. With Liz." He noticed Craig was staring at the floor, a slight frown on his face.

"Craig."

Craig looked up. Gently, Vic said, "This is the time to come clean. Is there anything else at all?"

Craig hesitated, and Vic could tell there was something Craig didn't want talk about.

Finally, Craig met Vic's gaze. "Tonight, when that older guy came into the apartment, he told me to turn over custody of Eileen's attacker to him. Said he would take him back to China. I said no, and he didn't look happy, and I wasn't sure what was going to happen right then. But Eileen came out of her bedroom with her field hockey stick and got him to back off and sit on the couch."

"Okay."

"She was holding the stick left-handed."

Vic understood why Craig didn't want to tell him that fact. He thought about it. "That surprises me."

Craig looked at him in confusion.

Vic shrugged. "I looked her up on YouTube. Watched her play. She plays violin the regular way. Right-handed."

241

"Right. But all violinists do."

"Oh." Vic felt foolish. It was as if he'd asked if a baseball bat was for a right or left-handed player. He pushed the thought away and looked at Craig. He could see Craig wanted to ask why he'd looked up Eileen on YouTube. When he didn't ask, Vic decided to tell him. "I thought she was worth checking out. She has easy access to the trail where Melanie was walking, and we know Eileen was home. That's another reason you have to keep her in mind as a possible witness, or maybe something more." Vic leaned closer to Craig. "Which is why you don't date her."

Craig nodded solemnly, and Vic closed his eyes to concentrate. He opened them. "Okay. You met Eileen yesterday, and she told you she was being followed. She gave you a ticket to the Symphony for tonight. You went. You gave her a ride home from the concert. Now how does that get you inside her apartment and catching this guy?"

"After I dropped her off, I saw an Asian guy go inside the apartment building right after her. I thought that was weird, because she'd told me she was being stalked by an Asian guy about that age. So I turned the car around and came up here. I just wanted to check the door. I heard a scream and a crash. The door was messed up, so it wasn't locked. I came inside."

When he hesitated, Vic prompted him. "And?"

Craig walked him through the sequence of events. Vic took notes as Craig described each step. When Craig finished, Vic tapped his pen against the edge of his notebook.

"Well, good work on that part of it. Write it up when you come in tomorrow. Now go wait in the living room and tell Eileen I want to talk to her."

Craig nodded and slid away. Vic allowed himself a smile. Despite the glaring misstep of dating Eileen, Craig had done well. A lot of people would have ignored their instincts when they spotted the potential stalker. But then again, Craig obviously wanted to protect Eileen. The fact he liked her was obvious.

Eileen appeared in the hallway.

"How are you doing?" Vic said carefully.

"I think about as well as you can expect. If Craig hadn't arrived, it would have gone badly. For me and my father. So I'm half scared, half thankful."

Vic considered which question to ask next. He had several, all leading in different directions. "I guess my first question is whether you want to press charges."

"I do." Eileen's answer was so sure, and fast, Vic almost smiled. He liked her certainty.

"Then I'll have a female officer transport you to the hospital. I know he didn't actually go through with the attack, but you've got a red mark on your face, so I know he hit you. I want that documented along with any other bruises on your body. And we'll need the clothes you were wearing."

"Yes. And the man that attacked me?"

"We'll take him. We can charge him with assault. We need to take him to the hospital to treat his nose, but after that, he'll go to jail."

"Good."

Vic saw her satisfaction with that. He nodded at the man on the couch. "Have you ever met him before?"

She gave an exasperated shrug. "Not him, but his type."

"Tell me about it."

Eileen tugged at the edges of her robe, pulling it tight around her. "There is a police unit in China looking for my father. They monitor my emails and phone calls. They've visited me several times, just never in Pittsburgh. I'm sure that's why he is here."

"I don't think we can hold him," Vic said carefully. "He didn't interfere with Craig's arrest, not in any meaningful way. I guess we could charge him with trespassing, but he won't see jail for that."

"Let me handle that."

Vic studied her. "What do you mean?"

"I want to talk to him. Then I want him to walk out of here so he can talk to his Commander in China."

Vic fought down his surprise, "Why is that?"

Eileen considered him, and Vic knew she was making a decision about whether to trust him. Finally, she pointed in the direction of the young man sitting on the floor. "I think the two men may be working together. It was clear the man knew my attacker. If that's the case, I may be able to get the charges against my father dropped."

Vic had liked Eileen's certainty about charging the young man, but this was a different level of courage. "Where is your father? We'll need a witness statement from him. Plus he can press charges as well."

"Safe." Eileen looked at him evenly.

"I'll need a bit more than that."

"Let me talk to this man. If you do that, I will arrange for you to meet him, perhaps in the next day or two."

Vic had the distinct feeling he was being played, but ignored it. "Go ahead."

Eileen thanked him and crossed the living room. She stood in front of the man on the couch and launched into urgent Chinese. Vic thought the man didn't seem put out by her, just interested in what she had to say. Vic stepped out of the apartment, thinking, putting together what Craig and Eileen had told him. Through the open front door, he watched Chen sitting on the couch. He checked his notebook. The attacker's name was Baihu Song. Chen Yun was the name of the man on the couch. A fellow police officer. He wondered about that. He watched Eileen and the man trade statements until Eileen stepped away from him.

Vic returned to the living room. The paramedic was packing his belongings, preparing to transport Song to the hospital. Eileen and Craig stood together across from the couch. Vic waved the uniformed officer into the hall and stepped in front of Chen.

"Chen Yun, right?" he asked, reading from his notebook.

"That is correct."

Vic thought Chen's English was natural and unaccented. He studied the man's stocky build and square face. Black, short-cropped hair. Chen returned his gaze, and Vic saw intelligence and patience in his eyes. Vic knew Chen had already done the math and knew he would soon walk free.

Vic decided to see if he could get a reaction out of him. "Must be tough. Having Eileen's father right here and missing him like that."

"I just wanted a conversation with him. I will find him again."

"That'll be tough. Now that your partner there is going to jail." Vic jerked a thumb at Baihu Song.

Chen seemed to find this statement amusing.

"Have you got a better way to describe what this Song is to you? He shows up in the apartment, you show up right after him. You know him. You try to get him freed."

"I think," Chen said slowly. "You are not in possession of all the facts."

"Then tell me what all the facts might be."

Chen held up his wrists. "Are these necessary?"

"For now. Until we have nothing left to say."

"Then perhaps I have nothing left to say."

"Not a big problem. I can always get the facts from your friend Song over there. One of the first things I'll ask him is whether you two are working together. If perhaps you sent him in here to give Eileen a scare, so when you arrived, Eileen would be in a state of mind to tell you exactly where her father was located."

"That isn't what happened."

Chen's response was sharp, and Vic knew he'd touched some kind of nerve. He looked at Song, still sitting on the floor with his back to the wall, cotton sticking out of each nostril. He had the hangdog air of a child who'd received nothing for Christmas.

Vic turned back to Chen. "I don't know. Song looks pretty miserable. I feel like if I put the idea in his head that you asked him to attack Eileen, he'll grab it. That he'll tell everyone you made him do it."

Chen gave a sardonic smile and shook his head slowly. "He is, you can be sure, someone who will always blame others for his own mistakes."

Vic turned to the paramedic. "You about ready to get him out of here?"

"Whenever you are."

"Go ahead." Vic gestured to the uniformed officer to help, and he and the paramedic got their hands under Song's armpits and lifted him to his feet. Vic called out to the officer to keep Song under guard at the hospital until he arrived. The paramedic and officer led Song down the hall and out of the apartment. As they disappeared, a female officer arrived, and Vic introduced her to Eileen.

Vic turned back to Chen. "So this is your chance. He's gone. Before he blames you for what he did here, maybe you can put me in possession of all the facts." He waved at Eileen. "I guess Eileen has already given you a message for your commanders. That's one thing. But I think you need to be straight with me. Otherwise, your friend Song is going to blame you for all this."

Chen's mouth tightened, and he looked at the window. "He was not working for me when he entered this apartment. He did that on his own. But I will tell you the same thing I told your young detective. Baihu Song is the son of an important man in my country. You can save yourself a lot of trouble and embarrassment by handing him over to me." Chen settled his dark eyes on Vic. "And you would be doing me a favor, which I would not forget."

"I plan to press charges on him," Eileen said sharply from the other side of the room.

Vic gestured in Eileen's direction. "If she presses charges on Song, I'm duty-bound to follow up on that. And by the way. You owing me a favor doesn't do shit for me."

Chen smiled. "Then charge him. See what happens. But afterwards, let me take him back to China. I am sure his student visa will be revoked after this. I think this will work for all of us."

Vic stared at Chen. There was something else going on, Vic was sure of it, but he had no way to tease it out. But he liked Chen. There was a solidness about him Vic appreciated, and Chen wasn't intimidated at all. For someone a long way from home and working in a different language, that was impressive. Perhaps in a day or two, Chen might be willing to reveal the whole story, but Vic knew he couldn't force Chen's hand right now. He wondered if Chen was a flight risk. It seemed likely.

"When do you plan to return to China?" Vic asked Chen.

"Not for a few days yet."

Vic hesitated. He wanted a written statement, and the only way to be sure about getting it was to take it now. He sighed. It was going to be a late night.

His phone vibrated. Vic considered not answering, but checked the screen. It was the district attorney, Hana. He excused himself and walked down the hallway and outside of the apartment. He didn't know why Hana would be calling him now.

"Hana?"

"Vic. What's going on? I just got a call from my FBI liaison. He said you've detained a Chinese national?"

Vic frowned. Whatever Chen was involved in was already getting attention. Too quickly. "I've detained two. One for attempted rape, another who walked into the crime scene and suggested he should take possession of the prisoner."

Hana sighed. "You'd better give me the long version."

Vic did, explaining Craig's role in subduing Song but leaving out the fact Craig was on a date with Eileen. He knew that would come out, but he wanted to control the context when it did.

"You've been busy."

"Not me. Craig, mostly. I'm trying to sort it out."

"Okay. What are the names of the Chinese nationals?"

Vic checked his notebook and read her Baihu Song and Chen Yun's names.

"That one, the second one, Chen Yun." Hana said the name several times, testing out different pronunciations. "The FBI want him to walk." She chuckled to herself. "Well, they want us to release both of them, but if Eileen is going to press charges, there is no way this Song guy walks. If the press gets wind of us releasing someone who tried to rape one of the symphony's star players, I'll get eaten alive."

"I need a statement from Chen Yun."

"They want him free now. I'm okay with that. From the sound of it, there's not much we could charge him with anyway. Ask him to come in tomorrow to give a statement. If he doesn't, that changes things. And it'll give us a bit of leverage with the FBI."

Vic was relieved he didn't have to drag Chen back to the offices now and take an official statement. He pinched the bridge of his nose. "Okay, I can do that. Um, Hana? How the hell did the FBI know what's going on? That we have these guys handcuffed?"

"Apparently, that is above my pay grade, according to my liaison. As far as I'm concerned, he can shove it up his ass. I told him he needs to be in my office at eight tomorrow morning with a full brief. But for now, cut Chen loose. I'll call the FBI back and tell them we're holding this Baihu Song. If they squawk, I'll tell them to get a court-ordered release. But if they do that, I'll leak it to the press myself. Then it's on them."

Vic had a vision of the saber hanging in Hana's office. "Okay, I'm on it."

"Thanks, Vic. One thing, though. You said Craig was nearby and stopped this Baihu Song. How did that happen? Don't tell me it was coincidence he was near."

Vic tried to cover a sigh. Hana was too smart to miss something like that. "It wasn't. I already talked to him about it, and I will again. I can give you the full details tomorrow. Do you want me to stop by for the meeting with the FBI?"

"I wish you could, but they said it's classified. Only me. Sorry. I'll call afterwards."

"Okay."

Vic hung up and returned to the living room. Eileen and Craig had picked up the bar stools and were sitting at the kitchen counter. Chen was staring into space as if he was meditating.

Vic stepped in front of Chen and held up a handcuffs key. Chen raised his wrists. Vic unlocked the handcuffs and pocketed them, wondering who they belonged to. He handed Chen one of his cards. "We need a statement from you about what happened here. Come to that address tomorrow morning, and we'll take it. If you don't show we will put out a warrant for your arrest. Do you understand?"

"Perfectly."

Vic stepped back and waited as Chen rose. Chen looked as if he wanted to say something but thought better of it.

"I can just go?" Chen asked.

Vic gestured toward the apartment's front door, and Chen turned and left. Vic watched him go. He had a broad back and a powerful stride. Vic turned to Eileen and nodded to the female officer. "You should go. Do you have somewhere to stay tonight? That door won't lock."

"I'll find a hotel for tonight."

Vic saw Craig was about to say something and glared at him. Craig clamped his mouth shut. Vic gestured to the female officer, and she stepped toward Eileen.

"Wait." Eileen slid off the bar stool. She stood very straight and looked directly at Vic. "Now that my father has gone, my memory has returned."

Vic waited. Somehow he'd expected something like this.

"I do remember practicing by the window on the afternoon when Melanie Beck was killed. I do recall looking outside several times. I did see something you might find useful."

Vic struggled against the anger rising inside him. "You damn well should have remembered earlier."

Eileen's dark eyes were sharp. "Perhaps, but you must understand. My father's life is at stake. I couldn't call attention to myself, or him, and I assumed you would find a way to solve the case without me. But now that my father's no longer here, my memory has returned. That will have to be enough."

Vic glanced at Craig, who looked stricken, before turning back to Eileen. "Well, we're listening."

Chapter Forty-Seven

I t was almost midnight when Vic returned home. He took off his shoes at the front door and locked away his Glock before padding softly to the kitchen. He was exhausted. After leaving Eileen's apartment, he'd driven to the hospital and questioned Song. Now he wanted a shower.

Song had outright denied he attacked Eileen, calling her a liar as he pompously demanded to be released. He wouldn't stop rattling the bed restraints. Three times Song said his father was a member of China's Politburo and would personally end Vic's career. When Vic asked Song if he knew Chen Yun, Song denied it until Vic asked if Chen had ordered him into the apartment to scare Eileen. Hearing that, Song's eyes flared, and he claimed that was exactly the situation. He was only following Chen's orders. His voice suddenly pleading, he claimed he'd been set up. By the time they were finished, Vic liked Chen even more. Chen was exactly right when he said Song would never take responsibility for anything.

Vic drew water from the kitchen faucet into a glass and sipped.

"Late night."

He turned to find Anne standing in the kitchen doorway, a robe drawn around her. Her hair was tousled, as if she had just woken up.

"It is. And I need to be at work early. We finally got a break, but it's an odd way for it to happen."

"Can you tell me?"

"Turns out a non-witness actually is a witness. She saw something she hadn't told us about."

"Is it enough?"

Vic was struck again by the painstaking detail of what Eileen recounted. Of seeing Jessica Teel step between some shrubs that ran alongside the Riverside Trail. How Jessica's body listed as she walked, as if she was in pain or some kind of fugue state. The way moments later she bobbled a step, and, as she righted herself, pressed a hand to her lips the way people do when pressing back nausea. He trusted Eileen's memory. Years of scrutinizing every note and notation on musical scores would have honed her observation skills. Taught her to read the emotion expressed in tiny details. Trained her to automatically memorize all of it.

"I think she's very credible," he said slowly.

"Good. Then that's a start." Anne touched his arm. "And how's Craig? He's the one who called tonight, right?"

"That's a mixed bag. He stopped an attack on a young woman, but he screwed up because he shouldn't have been with the woman to begin with. She's the non-witness who is now a witness."

Anne crossed the kitchen and helped herself to his glass of water. "Tough call. Good he stopped the attack; bad he was there."

"Exactly. And somehow, the FBI is involved in all this." Vic silently chastised himself. He knew it was a mistake to mention the FBI. They were both too sensitive about the investigation into his time in North Dakota.

Anne's eyes sharpened. "In relation to you?"

"No. It isn't related to the murder, either. Somehow, almost right away, they knew we had two Chinese nationals in custody. They wanted us to release them. Hana agreed to release one of them, but we had nothing to hold him anyway. FBI is supposed to explain why tomorrow."

Anne leaned back against the counter. "Can you tell me about it?"

Vic sat heavily at the kitchen table. "Sure. You know the symphony violinist I told you about? Apparently, she told Craig some Asian guy was stalking her, and he didn't tell Liz and me. A red flag like that. Then she gave Craig a ticket to today's symphony performance." He glanced at the microwave clock. "Well, yesterday's performance. He met her afterwards and took her home. As Craig was leaving, he saw a Chinese guy enter the apartment building, remembered her mentioning the stalker, and went to check on her. Caught the guy attacking her."

"Maybe the FBI is watching her?"

"Possibly. But I think the FBI is focused on the violinist's father, who was hiding in her apartment. He's a fugitive from China. And there's a Chinese police detective in the mix, looking for the father. And I'm sure the guy we arrested is connected to the Chinese detective. I just don't know exactly how."

"Wow." Anne crossed her arms and closed her eyes. She swayed slightly against the counter, something Vic had seen her do thousands of times when she was thinking. She grew still and opened her eyes. "It almost sounds like the violinist was playing Craig. Keeping him close in case her information was really needed? I mean, if she had witnessed something and didn't want to say anything because she was protecting her father, she needed a way to stay close to the investigation."

"I hadn't thought of that," Vic said slowly. "But it makes sense." He met Anne's gaze. "I bet you're right."

"The question is whether you tell Craig."

"I'm ticked enough at him that I'll tell him out of spite. I know he likes her."

"You're a mean one, Mr. Grinch." She giggled. "Let's get you to bed."

"Good idea." Vic rose slowly, feeling the tiredness.

Anne took a step to follow him and stopped. "Wait. I have something for you. She opened the kitchen's junk drawer and took out an envelope. "After you left, I remembered we hadn't brought in the mail. I found this."

"Not a bill?"

"Nope." She held the white envelope out to him. "More interesting than that."

Vic took the envelope and turned it in his hands. It was addressed to him in block letters. No return address. The postmark was New Town, North Dakota.

Vic hesitated. It was too soon for a reply to his own letter.

He slid a finger under the flap and tore open the envelope. Inside was a handwritten letter and a photograph. Vic stared at the people in the picture.

It showed a smiling Asian woman with a plump child on her lap. A boy of about two. A hawk feather was attached to his black hair.

Anne shifted at his shoulder. "Wait." She put her hand over her mouth. "Is that who I think it is?"

"It is. I guess she and Jimmy had a baby."

"He's gorgeous."

Vic put the photo on the kitchen table and unfolded the letter.

Hey Mill Hunky Lenoski,

It's been a while. Thought you might like this. Meet Jimmy Fleetfoot Pronghorn. Two years old. You know his mother. All good here. Kelly Strongfeather says hello.

Funny thing. Had breakfast with Karl the other day. You remember him. He's still doing his state police thing. He told me some Feds called him. Wanted to know about that time you were out here. I said I barely remember it. He says he doesn't remember much either, except that your commander was an asshole. He told me to tell you all the crap related to this is out of your hometown. He knows the local Feds and they have no interest. So why did they call?

It's a mystery. I know that's your meat.

Hope Lettie is doing well. Kelly asks after her.

Stay true, my friend.

Jimmy Pronghorn

Vic reread the letter, trying to squeeze all the meaning out of it.

"I don't understand all that," Anne said slowly. She was standing beside Vic, having read the letter as he did.

Vic was no longer tired. "I told you about Jimmy. He's telling us he's a father. But mostly, he's passing along Karl's information."

"What's that?"

"That the FBI investigation didn't start in North Dakota. It started here. Remember I thought perhaps a relative of Lettie's father was looking for her?" Vic hesitated. He just didn't want to tell Anne more about Lettie's father. "But if that was true, the FBI investigation would be run out of the nearest office. For North Dakota, that's Bismarck. But Karl is saying the investigation is out of Pittsburgh. He wanted me to understand that."

"So that's good, isn't it?"

"Yes. Kind of. Well, it means a family relation of Lettie isn't behind the investigation. That reduces the chance we might lose her. But it doesn't help us understand why the investigation is underway. Basically, it discounts one possibility."

Anne sighed, her face tense. "Well, I suppose that's a start. We know more than we did yesterday."

Vic wasn't so sure it was a good thing. A distant relative of Lettie meant there was someone to talk to, to reach an agreement with. Now there was only the faceless bureaucracy of the FBI and naked laws, unadorned by the nuances of context and emotions. And sometimes, justice.

"That's how I'm looking at it," Anne said softly when he didn't reply. "And I'm going to bed. You should too." As she turned for the door, Vic could have sworn she brushed at a tear.

"I'll be up in a second." Vic felt disembodied. It was the odd combination of relief and fear the letter had given him.

"Suit yourself," Anne called over her shoulder.

Vic listened to her steps recede up the stairs. He turned to the stove. He reread the letter, turned on the gas burner, and took a pot out of the cupboard. Using kitchen tongs, he held the letter and envelope in the burner flames. When the paper caught fire, he turned on the oven fan, watching the smoke curl into the grate. As soon as the letter and envelope were enveloped in flames, he dropped them into the pot to finish burning.

He looked again at the photo and stepped in front of the refrigerator. He meant to use a magnet to attach the photo to the door, but caught himself. Apart from himself, Liz, and Anne, only Jimmy and Kelly Strongfeather knew the child's mother was alive. It had to stay that way. He retrieved the tongs and held the photo in the burner flame, watching the front blister and charr. Once it was burned, he dropped the remains into the pot and emptied the pot down the garbage disposal. Ran the faucet and the disposal.

As the range fan pulled the last acrid smoke from the kitchen, his tiredness returned. He turned off the oven fan and started the long climb to bed.

Anne, he knew, wasn't grasping the real truth behind the letter. Jimmy's letter told him the FBI investigation wasn't about helping a distant relative find Lettie. That could only mean the investigation was actually about the crimes committed while he visited North Dakota.

And that was much, much more dangerous. For him and Liz's partner, Levon Grace.

Chapter Forty-Eight

Chen Yun sat in his car, watching the front door of Eileen's apartment building. He'd watched a female officer shepherd Liling out of the building. They drove off together. He waited, wondering if there was a possibility Liling's father might appear. He doubted it, sure that he and Liling had preplanned somewhere for him to hide in case he needed to run.

Chen wanted time to think. If he went back to his hotel, he would have to recount what happened to Tanming. He also hadn't called Commander Wang back, and that couldn't wait.

For just a few moments, when he entered Liling's apartment and discovered the young detective had overcome Song, a solution to this mess was in sight. If Craig released Song to him, even the ungrateful Song would be thankful enough to drop the false charges and end the investigation requested by his Politburo father.

But he'd known almost immediately that Craig wasn't going to release Song. Chen understood why. The arrest made Craig look good to Liling, and Chen knew now that was all the young detective really cared about. He'd seen it in the way he treated Song.

And Liling. She was a bold one. Her solution was a barter. No charges against Song in exchange for none against her father. But she was being naïve. It would be easy for Chen's unit to secure Song's freedom and, six months later, reinstate modified charges against her father.

He slid out his phone. He needed to call Commander Wang. But he weighed the phone in his hand, his thoughts hovering around that last point.

256

He didn't think Liling was naive. She would expect the charges against her father would reappear. So why offer that particular trade?

The answer dawned on him. Most likely, Liling's father was trying to legally immigrate to the United States. Liling simply wanted time for America's immigration process to work. It would be riskier for China to recover the man if he carried a green card. Not impossible, but more problematic.

Chen immediately favored that scenario. It made sense to him. Another thought came to him. Perhaps there was a way to use Liling's offer to his advantage.

He took a breath, smiled, and dialed Commander Wang.

On the third ring, Wang's voice came through his phone, imperious and angry. "Detective Chen Yun. I asked you to call me immediately."

"I did," Chen said quietly. "As soon as Tanming told me to call you."

"In the middle of the night? You should have called me again first thing this morning, my time. I had to call you. And then you didn't call me back."

"Yes, I apologize for that, but I was trying to stop Baihu Song from being arrested and taken to jail. Unfortunately, I failed."

Wang's silence was louder than iron beams dropping like pick-up sticks onto a concrete floor. "What? He's been arrested?"

"Yes. For rape. He tried to rape Liling Liang. He was stopped just in time by a local police detective." Chen chastised himself. He'd wanted to slip the word 'rape' into those sentences at least three times. For effect.

"That is impossible."

Chen had never heard Wang deliver a sentence in that tone. He actually sounded scared.

"I'm afraid not. I tried to convince the arresting detective to release Song to me, but charges are being brought." Chen discovered he liked the thought of that. Song, in jail, anguished, scared, and desperate. Just the way Chen felt when he found out about Song's false charges and trumped-up investigation by Song's father. Chen knew his reaction was just cheap revenge, but for a moment, he reveled in it.

"You must do something," Wang shouted into the phone. "Get him released."

"He is already in jail." Chen doubted that, but Wang sounded scared, and Chen liked that as well. Chen knew he needed to stop thinking that way. He closed his eyes and played his Liling card. "I could, with your permission, of course, talk to Liling Liang. Perhaps I can convince her to drop the charges. I would guess she will want something in return, but perhaps I could see what that is."

"Yes. Of course. Do it immediately."

"I'm afraid I can't tonight. She was taken to the hospital. Apparently, that is standard procedure in rape cases. They want to gather evidence of the rape. To be sure they can win their rape case against Baihu Song."

Good. Three mentions of the word. Let that sink in, he thought.

Wang drew and released breaths in a ragged rhythm. Chen guessed Wang was trying to decide how to handle this situation in China. Who he needed to tell to protect himself. How not to anger anyone by doing it.

"Now, you wanted to talk to me about an investigation into my treatment of Song?" Chen thought he had just the right tone of breeziness to his words.

"Don't concern yourself with that right now. Your mission is to get the charges against Baihu Song dropped."

"Then that is what I will do. Oh, and Commander, I meant to ask, Tanming appeared at my hotel. I didn't know he was coming."

"What?" Wang sounded thrown by the change of topic.

"Tanming. I didn't know he was coming here."

"Oh. Yes. He asked me if he could make the trip. He said you made a good team in Singapore, that you executed against his plan there. I was impressed and gave him permission. He said he would let you know before he left."

"Ah. I must have missed his email. No matter. I will focus on Liling Liang. Convince her to drop the charges. That is my priority."

"Thank you, Chen." Wang's voice was distant again.

Chen didn't like to think of the questions surging in Wang's mind. Whether he could get away without telling anyone about Song, or if he must tell everyone to avoid being accused of withholding information. The questions were more mystifying than a Tao Te Ching passage. Chen wanted to remind Wang that he was due home with his family once this was resolved, but he knew that was pushing it. Right now, Wang was too shocked about Song to spot the nuances of what Chen was saying. But once Wang's initial dismay settled, he might detect calculation in Chen's words. It was best to end the call in the heat of the moment.

"Goodbye, sir. I will call you as soon as I have good news." Chen held up his phone and touched the hang-up button. He placed his phone on the passenger seat, started the car, and pulled out.

As he drove toward his hotel, he mused about Tanming. So that was the game Tanming was playing. Worming his way into Wang's confidence while looking for ways to push Chen off-balance. Arriving unannounced certainly was a ploy to make Chen think he was in trouble with Wang. A trick to distract him, perhaps force a mistake. And when Chen fell, Tanming would be right there to take his place.

Chen heard his grandmother's voice again. "Trust only this difference. Inside your head, outside your head. Inside this house, outside this house."

A new meaning to those familiar words came to him. He'd always thought they were specific to his English language skills, but now he glimpsed a broader directive. They were also a command to only trust his own beliefs and thoughts, no matter where he was, no matter the situation.

This is what the Party does to you, he thought. It teaches you to distrust others, not to make alliances. Because when each person is alone, each is easier to control. Bile rose into his mouth, and grimly, he swallowed it back down. Because now he knew something else. He was finished with this way of life with the Party. His grandmother was right. All that mattered was what was inside his house. Not outside. He didn't even need to make that choice.

He already had.

Chapter Forty-Nine

When Liz arrived the next morning, Vic gestured for her and Craig to drag their desk chairs into the aisle between their desks. They did, and in a lowered voice, Vic narrated the events of the night before to Liz, the attack on Eileen, the appearance of Chen, and finally, Eileen's revelation about who she saw from the window.

Vic finished and searched Liz's face for a reaction. She looked bemused.

"Jessica?" Liz turned to Craig. "Your girlfriend saw Jessica walking out from the trail? And held out on us?"

Craig's cheeks flushed. "I had no way to know that." His voice sounded small.

Liz studied him. "People damn lie to us. Nothing is more true."

Craig looked at the floor. "I get it."

Vic saw how crestfallen Craig looked. He didn't think Craig needed another reminder not to take witness statements at face value.

Vic turned to Liz. "The problem is what Jessica was doing between the moment Eileen saw her and when she ran into Craig and me outside Melanie's apartment. It's more than an hour, and that's a guess, because Eileen didn't check the time when she saw Jessica. A good defense lawyer could trip us on that. And something else. Jessica said she was shopping in the Strip District. Fine. Is there any route back from the Strip that includes walking along the trail?"

"No." Craig's eyes burned. "I thought of that and checked this morning. The only way to get from the Strip District to Melanie's apartment is over the 16th Street Bridge. The bridge goes over the trail, and there's no way down to it. To get on the trail, she would have to walk past the front door to the Heinz Lofts and double back to the trail. Jessica can't say she was on the trail as a shortcut home."

"If Jessica is in the frame," Liz said slowly, "There's something I want to check. When I researched her, I noticed she missed a semester of college. She graduated late. Let me call the school. It didn't seem important before, but maybe there's something there."

"After you've done that, I need you each to make another call." Vic looked from Liz to Craig. "Craig, you get after the phone company. I want that phone data for Kwan, Ryan, and Jessica. As soon as you can get it. We need to know if anyone else has the tracking app on their phone. Liz, you call Jessica, Kwan, and Ryan. I'm thinking we talk to all three together, maybe at the house today at lunchtime. We'll have them repeat their alibis for the time when Melanie was killed. I want to keep the pressure up, and maybe we can tease something else out. We still don't have answers to the stickiness on the closet door to Ryan's room and why the motion detectors in the house were set off at night. But most of all, I don't want to bring Jessica down here now and sweat her without seeing the phone data."

"But aren't you assuming that what Eileen told us is true?" Craig interjected.

Vic looked at him. "Craig, distrust witness statements, but don't automatically toss them out. First of all, Eileen's statement was detailed, and what she does for a living teaches her to interpret those details. Eileen also had good reason to keep quiet. Once we found out her Dad was staying with her, that reason went away. Also, I think she wanted to make sure we focused on Jessica. That's why she got close to you. She wanted to make sure we had Jessica in the frame. She knew that if we didn't, she would have to tell us."

Vic watched Craig blink and absorb his words. He remembered Anne's comment about Eileen using Craig, and watched Craig take the first whiff of that possibility. He clearly didn't like the smell.

"Okay, then." Liz scooted her chair back to her desk.

Vic's desk phone rang. He dug in his heels, pushed his chair back to his desk and answered.

"Vic? It's Hana."

"I was wondering when you might call."

"I had the FBI here this morning. At least I've got a better idea of what's going on."

"Anything you can tell me?"

"Not over the phone. But I have a request. You asked this Chen Yun character to come in and give a statement this morning, right?"

"I did."

"Good. Two things. If he hasn't showed up by noon, let me know. If he does come in, record the session. Send me a copy of the interview. There's some interested parties want to hear it. Don't ask."

"I'll let you know."

He hung up. He knew the interested party was the FBI and wondered why they wanted to hear Chen's statement. It annoyed him on two levels. He was now working for the organization that was investigating him, and he had no guidance on what to look for.

He looked at Liz, who put her phone on its cradle. "Called Ryan, and he got the others lined up. I guess Kwan and Jessica have to leave mid-afternoon because they play tonight. Jessica was complaining about it. But we meet at high noon."

"If we're lucky, it won't take long." Vic looked around the office. It was Saturday, and some of the detectives were out, giving the large room a forlorn air. His phone rang again.

"Front desk," said a voice when he answered. "We've got a guy down here, says you asked him to come in and give a statement. Chinese guy?"

"I'll come get him." Vic hung up and told Liz and Craig that Chen was downstairs. "We can talk to him in one of the interview rooms." He pointed a finger at Liz. "You and me. We need to record it."

"I'll keep chasing the data from the phone companies." Craig spoke so quickly it was obvious he was trying to redeem himself.

"I'll make sure the room is set up." Liz rose from her chair.

Vic found Chen Yun in the lobby, standing by the door with his back to the wall. He looked relaxed, his pants wrinkle-free, a sport coat over his open-neck and recently-ironed shirt. When they shook hands, it was an exchange of light pressure squeezes, like a couple of boxers circling each other.

Vic decided on an informal approach. "Call me Vic," he said. "We can skip the formalities."

Chen nodded, and Vic thought he saw a small gleam of appreciation in Chen's eyes.

Liz was waiting for them in the hall outside the interview rooms. She introduced herself and gestured to the open door. Chen and Liz were the same height, but Chen's square body gave him an obvious weight advantage. Liz led Chen into the interview room and they all sat, Vic and Liz on one side of the table, Chen on the other.

Chapter Fifty

Chen settled into his plastic chair and waited for the detectives to start asking questions. He was interested to see what approach they took and what they wanted from the meeting. He already knew what he wanted from it.

"You're a long way from home," Vic said, finally.

"I suppose I am." Chen glanced around the small room, noting the camera in the far corner, tucked against the ceiling.

"We're recording," Vic said.

Chen realized Vic had followed his sweep of the room. He watched Vic fold his hands on the table in front of him and tap his thumbs together.

Vic shrugged. "We just want to hear about last night. Perhaps you could just give us your side of the events? What you saw?"

Chen appreciated Vic's friendly approach, but he knew that starting with the events of the night before was almost silly. There were too many questions about why Chen was in Pittsburgh and why he was interested in Liling Liang. If Vic was recording the session, the answers to those questions were the real goal. Last night was the least interesting thing they could talk about. He decided to hint in that direction. "Where should I start?"

"Scratch that," Vic said slowly, and Chen knew Vic had understood him.

Chen watched Vic reconsider and cock his head, just slightly. "You're a police officer, right? Tell me about yourself. Where you're from and what force you work for."

That's more like it, Chen thought. "I'm from the city of Wuhan. Population ten million. So you understand, that is about two million people more than your New York, and not a large city for China. I belong to a unit attached to the provincial police. We handle special crimes. That is what brings me here."

"How is your English so good?" The Black detective named Liz shifted back in her chair, relaxing. Chen liked the way she accepted Vic's change in approach. They were a good team.

Chen picked the shortest version of his history. "I was taught from a very young age by my grandmother. She learned from American missionaries and translated for American soldiers during your Second World War."

"I didn't know there were many Americans posted to China then. I mean, I know we had pilots." Vic sounded genuinely intrigued.

Chen had run into this before. Americans were always ignorant of their country's rapacious colonialism, or willfully blind to it. He'd wondered several times what their children were taught in school. How to be happy? Clearly not the country's true history. Then again, he'd been fed a few lies during his own education. It was what governments did. He knew that, and it tired him. Despite it, he met Vic's gaze. "Your Navy had a large intelligence operation in China during that war. My grandmother translated for their commander. After the war, fifty thousand of your Marines were posted to northern China. Our Army pushed them out in 1949. So we are well acquainted with your armed forces." He purposely didn't mention how China fought America to a stalemate in Korea.

Chen waited. Vic stared at him. Not in a baleful or angry way, just thoughtfully.

"What made you join the police?"

The question surprised Chen, and from the look on Vic's face, he hadn't planned to ask it. It just came out.

Chen wondered if this was an interrogation technique he hadn't encountered. But Vic looked inquisitive, and Chen decided Vic just wanted to know. And perhaps he could use this opening to bring the conversation around to say what he needed to say.

"I was in my last year at university and unsure what to do. One of my professors mentioned a new government program aimed at what you call white-collar crimes. Corruption, that type of thing. They wanted college graduates, and offered quick promotion and command."

Chen hesitated. That was all true, but he sensed Vic wouldn't buy an explanation that was purely about ambition. He saw the lines in Vic's heavy-boned face. It was an honest face, he decided. Trustworthy.

"To me," Chen started slowly, organizing his words, "The worst crimes are committed by the rich and powerful. If workers dedicate their lives to a business that promises them money after they retire, and an executive steals those savings, to me that's worse than murdering someone. Both are cold-blooded crimes. One ends a life, but the other endangers the livelihoods of hundreds of elderly people and makes their entire working life a lie. I find that disgusting, and worse, the people who steal that money often escape. I thought this new program might be a place where I could help. After working in that unit for several years, I was moved to a related program called Operation Fox Hunt. That brought me here." He leaned forward. "And you?"

Chen wondered if Vic would understand this was a test. He'd been honest with Vic. Could Vic be honest back?

"Nothing that idealistic." Vic met Chen's gaze. "Pittsburgh in the late nineteen-eighties, it was dying. Factories going out of business, no jobs, all my friends leaving. I remember one night, I'd had a couple of beers and was standing on the street, looking at the stacks of a steel mill. I was thinking my father worked his whole life there. One hundred years that mill provided jobs for people, and one day they just closed the place. And I thought, if businesses are dying and everybody my age is leaving, who's going to take care of the people still here? I felt like it should be me. I don't know why."

"Your father worked at a steel mill?"

"He did. It killed him. Asbestos poisoning."

Chen felt something open inside himself, as if he'd found a missing brother. "My father also worked for a steel mill. In Wuhan. It killed him too. The backbreaking work."

"It's what happens when people don't have choices, I guess," Vic said slowly.

Chen held Vic's gaze. In the following silence, all he heard was the air in the ventilation system and the soft buzz of Fluorescent lights. Chen turned to Liz. "And you, why did you become a detective?"

Liz gave a wry laugh. "Look at me. That'll tell you. How people looking like me are treated in this country? I thought maybe I could change that. At least make sure everyone was treated the same when they got inside a place like this. Turns out in here is just the same as out there. I have to work twice as long as everyone else and toe the line harder." Her voice was bitter.

Chen saw Vic reach over and touch Liz's forearm.

She glanced at Vic, jaw set. "Yeah. I know. But I don't care if other people hear. Not anymore. Maybe it'll help them get it. If that's even possible."

Chen felt the tension in the air, how the anger behind Liz's words was palpable. It was breathtaking to hear her words out loud. It was a type of statement impossible to make in China.

But it was the forearm touch that stayed with him. It wasn't a 'stop what you are saying' tap, but a gentle show of support, perhaps a reminder that she shouldn't lose sight of why she joined the police, that she should stay true. Such a little, precious thing. The kind of genuine, human gesture he always looked for. In that moment, Chen knew he could trust Vic. Even Liz.

Vic turned to him, his face set. Chen had the feeling that Vic also knew they could now be honest with one another. Vic's words were slow and considered. "I think perhaps we've got to the place where you tell us why you're in America. It has to do with Eileen Liang, and, more to the point, her father. We know that much. But let's not kid each other. That raises a question. Are you here in an official capacity? And if so, why didn't you let local law enforcement know why you're here? Ask us to help?"

Chen spread his hands, palms out. "My plan was simply to talk to Ms. Liang. See if she might be willing to return to China and help us find her father."

"It's a pretty tall order for me to believe that Eileen would simply give up her career here and return to China, to help you arrest her *father*."

Chen smiled. "And yet just that type of thing has happened before."

Vic tapped his thumbs together again. "Not without leverage. Not without finding a way to make her do it. Forcing her."

"Correct," Chen said softly, seeing his opening. "That is the conclusion I came to myself. And while I was sent here to discover a way to make her return, I have decided I don't want to. That I will not work for a state that requires me to do that." He couldn't bring himself to say these words fully out loud. He knew that in China, those words were treason. He half expected Commander Wang to crash through the interview room door, raging at him.

Vic sat back, and Chen saw Vic was surprised to hear him admit he'd considered coercing Eileen into returning to China.

"Do you realize what you are saying?" Liz sounded as puzzled as Vic.

Now that the words were spoken, Chen felt as if a burden had been lifted. "I do. And I only have one request. I would still like to speak to Liling Liang. Eileen, as you call her. Just briefly. But you must know that I have accepted that I will return to China without her."

For a few seconds, Vic and Liz were silent, then Vic untangled his fingers on the tabletop and tapped his palm on the surface. "I doubt she'll want to talk to you."

Chen fought down a smile. "Ask her. I think you will find just the opposite. That she can't wait to hear what I have to say."

Chen sat back. Now he just had to wait for the chance to speak to Liling Liang. He knew the interview was just starting and there would be more questions. This Lenoski was too good. He would want to know about Song and Operation Fox Hunt. But he'd got across what he wanted to say on tape. Now he just had to wait to see if anyone reacted to it.

Chapter Fifty-One

Vic chose to ride to the Beck estate with Liz, knowing he could return to Pittsburgh with Craig.

"He is one interesting boy," Liz said quietly, her hands at ten and two on the steering wheel, eyes focused on the road.

"Chen? Yeah, complicated. I'll give you that."

"Are you really going to let him talk to Eileen?"

"If she wants to talk to him. And I think she will. Eileen spoke to him last night. I bet she asked him something. I think this is the second half of the conversation." Vic shifted in the passenger seat. "That's why he was confident she would want to talk to him. But that bothers me. If she's willing to meet, I think we do it in an interview room and require them to speak English, so we can hear what's going on."

"Chen did admit to hiring that Song kid to watch Eileen. He left himself open to an accessory before the fact charge. And that whole thing with coercing Eileen back to China? I didn't get that. He knew we were recording the conversation. He still incriminated himself."

Vic considered her point. "We can't make accessory before the fact stick. He didn't tell Song to attack Eileen, or even scare her. And if Song says he did, it's just Song trying to save his own butt. He's that kind of guy. To me, it felt like Chen was sending a message, but to someone different than us." He wondered if the FBI had listened to the digital file yet. He'd emailed it to Hana through the County's internal network after the interview.

Liz glanced at him. "Speaking of the FBI, you hear anything else about their interest in you?"

"A bit. It isn't a missing person case. I thought it might be someone in North Dakota looking for Lettie. Her grandmother on that side, or something. But it's out of the Pittsburgh office. Which makes it weird. And kind of worse."

"How'd you figure that out?"

Vic was silent for several seconds. "I just did."

Liz glanced at him, her gaze returning to the road. She didn't say anything more, but Vic didn't feel she was angry.

The gates to the Beck estate were already open, and Liz drove through and parked beside Craig's beat-up red Jeep. Craig got out from the Jeep's driver's side and slammed the door several times to make it close.

Vic climbed from the passenger side of Liz's small SUV and looked around. Despite everything roiling in his mind, he still felt the peacefulness of the place. The spreading, mature oaks overhead, the light breeze from the west, the high blue sky patterned with white clouds.

Liz crunched around the car on the pea gravel driveway. "You ready for this?"

Vic thought about that. He wasn't, not really. But then again, he never was. It was always a matter of diving in. "Let's give it a shot," he said, more to himself.

"I've got something that might help."

Vic looked at Craig, who was grinning. "Like what?"

Craig held out his phone, face toward Vic and Liz. "I got the cell company to move on our warrant for the cell phone data. Everyone's phones were where they said they were. But one person does have the tracking app on his phone."

Vic waited. He knew Craig felt this was a moment to redeem himself and didn't want to spoil it for him. He also wasn't about to tell Craig that he didn't have anything to make up. They'd all made stupid assumptions about witness statements when they started their careers.

"Ryan's," Craig said.

Vic felt the linkages falling into place, the stray facts they had picked up over the last week settling into a possible order. "The phone number that accessed the app on Melanie and Ryan's phone, it's the same?"

"Yep."

"What was the number?"

Craig swiped through several screens and read off the number of the prepaid. Vic thumbed it into his own cell.

"You thinking something?" Liz asked him.

Vic looked at her. "Well, we know the prepaid has the tracker app, and someone is using that prepaid to access Ryan and Melanie's locations." He stopped to give his mind time to digest that scenario. "Let's see what everyone has to say."

Almost on cue, the front door opened, and Samantha Beck appeared in the doorway. She wore a yellow sundress held up by spaghetti straps over bare shoulders. "Hi. I heard the cars." She glanced at the three of them, and her eyes settled on Craig. "You're Craig, right? The one who phoned me with the update?"

"I am."

Samantha left the front door open, crossed to Craig, and shook his hand. "Thank you for that. It was very helpful." She seemed slow to release his hand.

"No problem."

Beside Vic, Liz shifted her weight and whispered, "They only talked on the phone. You telling me his voice sounds good-looking as well?"

Samantha turned to Vic and Liz. "Hi. Good to see you again." The tone of her voice didn't match the words. Vic wondered if her father had admitted his confused sexuality to her, and she blamed them for it. That thought reminded him why Samantha recognized Craig. It was process of elimination. She'd met Liz and Vic in her father's office.

"Hi," Liz said, with overdone brightness. "You're staying here?"

Samantha frowned. "No. I couldn't do it. I stopped by to check on some things this morning, and Ryan told me you guys were on your way. I thought I'd stick around."

It crossed Vic's mind that Samantha had a nasty habit of showing up at the wrong times. "Well, let's see what everyone has to say."

Samantha fell in beside Craig, leading the way, talking in a low voice.

"Maybe use the dining room so everyone can sit down," Vic called and tapped Craig on the arm. When Craig turned, Vic drew him aside, leaving Samantha to hover a few steps ahead. He lowered his voice. "I want you to cover the dining room doorway to the front of the house. Don't make it obvious. But I want you on your feet, okay?"

"Yep."

With that, they followed Liz and Samantha into the house, passing cello and viola cases by the front door, as well as a large leather purse that Vic thought must belong to Jessica.

It took almost two minutes for Liz to round up Ryan, Jessica and Kwan, and convince Samantha that despite this being her house, she would have to wait in the study. Once everybody was seated and Craig was lounging in the doorway, Vic looked at everyone. Jessica tore her gaze away from her phone and placed it on the table in front of her.

"We just want to revisit where everyone was the day Melanie Beck was attacked." Vic turned to Kwan. "Let's start with you."

In his halting English, Kwan repeated that he had been at practice, then taken a car home.

"The only one at home?" Vic asked quietly.

Kwan looked startled. "Yes."

"So no one can confirm you were here. Did you make any calls or texts on your phone?"

"Yes. I texted my mother in Taiwan. I do that every day."

"Four or five in the afternoon here is what, four or five in the morning in Taiwan?" Liz asked lightly.

"Yes."

"Kind of early," Liz pressed.

Kwan blinked. "She leaves for work at five-thirty. I put a message on her phone every day for when she wakes up."

Vic let the silence spin out. Ryan was frowning and looking at Kwan, obviously not understanding where the questioning was going.

Vic decided they'd exhausted the questions for Kwan. "And you, Ryan?"

Ryan shrugged. "I already told you. You guys checked it out."

"Why don't you tell all of us?"

Ryan stared at him. "I don't get why it matters."

"I'll decide what matters," Vic said, noting the intensity of the way Jessica stared at Ryan.

Ryan blinked slowly and turned to Jessica. "Sorry Jess, I was saving this for the reunion, but I guess it can't wait." He turned back to Vic. "As you guys know. I went to batting practice, then met up with a friend. Went to a hotel."

Jessica shot out of her chair. "You have *another* girlfriend?"

"Oh, hell no." He smiled, clearly enjoying her reaction.

Jessica stared at him, eyes burning. Now it was Kwan's turn to look confused.

"Guy friend," Ryan said easily.

Jessica opened her mouth and closed it. Managed to utter a strangled, "What?"

"Guy friend," he said again, more confidently. He smiled widely at her, but his eyes were mocking.

Jessica's eyes darkened. "But you were sleeping with Melanie."

Kwan ducked his head at the vehemence of her voice.

"Why don't you sit down, Jessica," Vic said evenly.

Jessica glanced at him as if he was a pet who'd just made a mess on the rug. She turned her flushed face back to Ryan. "That's impossible," Jessica choked on the words. "You're lying. You were going into Melanie's room at night. Through the closet. And what we did at the last family reunion. In the barn. You aren't interested in *guys*."

Ryan smiled and spread his hands in a 'what can you do?' motion.

Liz cut in. "How do you know Ryan was using the closet door into Melanie's room?"

"I taped it." Jessica fell silent so quickly, it was like a stone dropping into an empty well. She plopped into her seat, unable to tear her gaze from Ryan.

"Okay," Vic said conversationally. "Just to clarify, you went into Melanie's closet and put a piece of tape at the bottom of the door to see if anyone was opening and closing the door."

Jessica didn't answer for a few moments. "Yes," she said finally. "A night or two before Melanie was attacked. I got rid of it afterwards. It wasn't broken, but that doesn't mean anything. He could have gone in some other time."

Vic glanced at Craig, who nodded. That explained both the sticky door frame and the triggered motion detector in Melanie's bedroom after she died.

Jessica turned from Ryan, her breathing shallow and rapid, eyes wild. "I also heard Ryan and Melanie downstairs. In the middle of the night."

Vic looked at Ryan, remembering the history of triggered motion detectors downstairs. "Is that right?"

Ryan shook his head. "Not me. I go to bed, that's it. I stay in bed." He shot a glance at Jessica. "I don't even open closet doors."

"I go downstairs at night."

Everyone turned to Kwan as if they were following the ball at a tennis match. Kwan dropped his head at the sudden attention. "I can't sleep at night, sometimes. I think about Taiwan a lot. I miss my home. I go downstairs. I practice the fingering on my cello without using the bow. Just so I am better. It makes me calm. And when I feel sleepy, I text my mother and go back to bed."

Silence settled in the room, distinguishing Jessica's raspy breaths.

"How about you, Jessica?" Vic said slowly. "Where were you when Melanie was killed?"

"I told you. I was in the Strip District. Shopping. I came back and found you in the apartment."

"You know," Vic said slowly, a memory returning to him. "Funny thing about that. When we ran into you at Melanie's apartment, you said the same thing. But you weren't carrying anything. No plastic shopping bags. Not even a purse."

Jessica raised her head and glared at him. "This is bullshit. I had cash and a credit card in my jeans pocket. And I didn't find anything I liked, so I didn't buy anything." She rose. "I'm done. This is stupid. Kwan and I have a performance tonight. We have to go." She pushed the chair back and looked at Kwan. "Kwan, let's go."

Vic rose as well. "We're not done."

"Too bad." Jessica gave him a long, angry look, grabbed her phone, and turned for the hall. Kwan stayed frozen in his chair. Vic followed Jessica as far as the doorway to the hall, Craig sidling into the hallway as well.

By the front door, Jessica grabbed her large leather handbag and swung the strap over her shoulder. She stuck her phone in her back pocket and bent over for her viola case. A phone in her handbag started to ring. Jessica froze.

Vic took a step closer to her. "You going to answer that?"

Jessica's face turned pale. "Not right now."

Vic held up his own phone. "Actually, that's me calling. I'd like to see that phone in your purse. Since your regular phone is in your back pocket."

Slowly, Jessica straightened up. She stared at him. "Sure." She slid her right hand into her purse just as the ringing stopped. Jessica yanked her hand from her purse and squirted brown liquid at Vic. Vic ducked and dodged, raising his forearm to protect his face. Pepper spray splashed off the wall where he was last standing and splattered the floor. Jessica grabbed for the front door, and a form shot past Vic and tackled Jessica from behind, slamming her against the door and spinning her to the ground. The cello and viola cases scattered.

Shaking pepper spray off the arm he'd used to protect himself, Vic watched Craig manhandle handcuffs onto Jessica's wrists, as she wailed and sobbed in a regular rhythm, over and over, "Ryan, you liar, you liar, you liar. It's all your fault."

From his phone, where he had dropped it on the floor, a generic voice instructed Vic to leave a message.

Vic picked it up, ended the call, and made his way to the kitchen, looking for a faucet to wipe down his arm.

Chapter Fifty-Two

It was two days before Chen received a call from Vic to say a meeting was arranged with Eileen Liang. Tanming wanted to attend, but Chen refused. He knew this was his only chance to put an end to Song's accusations against him, and he didn't want any interference. Before the meeting, he texted Commander Wang and told him that Liling's condition was that all charges against her father must be dropped. Wang agreed faster than a bullet train. Chen had no illusions about that. He knew the charges would be reinstated.

With the conditions set, the meeting finished in five minutes. Several hours later, Chen was standing outside the jail when Song was released. In his rental car, with Song slumped in the passenger seat, his legs splayed, and nose still taped, Chen explained that he had convinced Liling to drop the charges against him. Song barely lifted his head in recognition. Chen then called Commander Wang and gave him the good news that he was with Song. Song was free, and would soon be delivered back to his apartment. The charges against had been dropped.

Commander Wang was almost beside himself with excitement. When Chen dropped off Song, the young man somehow managed to mumble his thanks. Chen purposely hadn't brought up the investigation, but he suspected it would quietly disappear sometime in the next few days. If it didn't, he would have a more direct conversation with Song.

Afterwards, Chen drove to Yiptou's restaurant, thanked him for his help and promised to do what he could to shorten his uncle's sentence. He genuinely meant it. He bought a meal that he insisted on paying for, slipped a one-hundred-dollar bill into the tip jar beside the register, and drove back to his hotel.

It was dusk when he unlocked the door to his room. He and Tanming had agreed to update later that evening, and he had plenty of time to eat and watch a rerun of an American show he liked. It involved several young scientists and a blond woman, and he found it quite funny.

He closed the door behind him, surprised the curtains were drawn and a bedside lamp turned on. It was an unusual thing for the housekeeper to do. He walked down the hall and placed his dinner on the desk. He turned, and a tall man stepped out of the bathroom, between him and the hallway door.

Chen tensed. The man's hands were empty except for a cell phone, but Chen knew that didn't mean much.

"Hello, Chen Yun," the man said.

Chen stared at the man. He was easily six feet tall with a dark complexion, not exactly Black, but clearly not white, either. Chen spotted a military cast to his posture. Part of his left ear lobe was missing.

"And who would you be?" Chen asked, glad to hear his voice sounded level and confident. "Standing here in my room."

The man lifted his phone and texted a short message. Pocketed the phone. He met Chen's eyes. "Let's just call me White Pick-Up Truck."

Chen nodded. "I have seen you here and there."

The man smiled in approval. "That was the idea."

Chen steeled himself. He'd guessed the pick-up truck following him was a message, and suspected the phone call Vic received at Liling's apartment led to his release. Someone had known all along he was in Pittsburgh, and he knew now they had listened to his taped interview.

There was a soft knock on the door. White Pick-Up Truck reached back and turned the door handle without taking his eyes off Chen. A shorter, slight man with neat white hair and round tortoiseshell glasses slid into the room. He silently closed the door behind him before walking to Chen and extending his hand.

"Chen Yun. It is a pleasure to meet you. My name is Carter Quince. I was hoping we might talk for a few minutes."

Carter, Chen noted, was fussily dressed in a style Chen recognized but couldn't name. Blue Oxford button-down shirt. Striped silk tie. Blue blazer and gray slacks. Brown leather loafers. He remembered that way of dressing also represented a lifestyle, even as that life slipped away. Yet Carter clearly stayed true to it.

"I think you have already arranged that," Chen said carefully.

"Well, with your coworker just a few doors down, we thought we should be careful. I apologize if it upset you." Carter reached into his jacket pocket and produced a small black item, about the size of a shirt button. He held it out to Chen in the palm of his hand. "My own coworker," he nodded to the man by the door, "did a sweep of your room and found this. We certainly didn't place it here. It is clearly of Chinese design. It is voice-activated. Transmission of about twenty meters." He smiled, perhaps apologetically.

Chen fought down a flash of anger. Tanming had bugged his room. Somehow he wasn't surprised. He took the transmitter and placed it next to his take-out food. He gave Carter a quizzical look.

"It has developed a glitch and no longer broadcasts," Carter said smoothly.

Of course it has, thought Chen. He glanced at White Pick-Up Truck, who was placidly watching the proceedings, his deep brown eyes missing nothing.

"And what can I do for you?" Chen asked.

"I think this is more about what we might be able to do for you. Could we sit?"

Chen took the desk chair, and Carter perched on the edge of the bed. White Pick-Up Truck leaned against the door.

Carter picked a non-existent strand of lint from his pants with a pinching movement of his fingers. "I understand you are returning to China soon."

Chen shrugged. "Yes."

"And you have chosen not to, let's say, repatriate Liling Liang?"

Now Chen was sure that Carter, or whoever he might work for, had heard the interview tape. "I see no workable way to do it."

"It must be difficult for you. No success here. Two years away from your family. Not seeing your son that entire time? And that business in Texas.

The suicide. That was untidy."

Carter paused, but Chen stayed silent, again seeing Hu Zhao vault the patio rail into the Houston night, as smooth and sure as a gazelle, weightless for that split second before he just disappeared. Chen felt that same drop in his stomach and had to swallow it away. He waited.

"Singapore was better. Smooth. But Bingwen Zhu was older. It is a pity about his son."

Chen tightened. "What about his son?"

"He's resigned. It was in the Shanghai Morning Post today. Apparently, it was the shame of his father's corruption."

Chen couldn't help himself. He looked away, angry. He'd guessed correctly. Bingwen Zhu was never the target. It was always Bingwen's son. And Chen was the farrier. The one chosen to replace perfectly good horseshoes with ones better suited to how the horse trainer wished to guide the horse. In that moment, Chen knew he could never again support the Party. It was impossible.

Chen turned back to Carter and found the man studying him intently.

"It must be difficult for you, being part of these things," Carter said, a note of understanding in his voice.

Chen let the statement sit for a few moments, not trusting the tone of Carter's voice. "You said you might be able to do something for me."

Carter leaned toward him, just a little. "Well, perhaps more for your son. You see, us being friendly with a man like you, in a position like yours, we would feel the need to return any favors you might do for us. Perhaps, let us say—if the favors you did for us were enough—admission to a reputable American college for your son. A scholarship, of course. And if you have more children, the same for them."

Chen watched this Carter Quince. Here, he thought, is the difference in the way China and America do things. China is the stick, America, the carrot. America is a promise of better things, China a flat command telling you how to live your life. Is there a difference between the two, really? Both use your family. Both bend you into conformance with what their leaders want.

"What kind of favors?" he asked.

"We would leave that up to you. We are always interested in what the Party is thinking. Their direction. How they intend to translate their polices into action."

Despite his decision, Chen had a sour taste in his mouth. He wondered who this Carter Quince worked for. It was useless to ask, of course. The CIA? The FBI? He decided on the CIA. The FBI was a blunt instrument; they understood kicking down doors and arrests. The lifeblood of the CIA was information.

"I think," Chen said slowly, "that perhaps you have approached me at a bad time. You may not know, but I am under investigation. When I return to China without Liling, I will be in disgrace. Disfavor at best. In that position, I will be of little help."

Carter locked his hands under a crossed knee and rocked slightly on the bed. Stopped. "Your English is really very good. But let me ask you a question. Have you ever heard the English idiom 'turn the tables?'"

Chen searched his memory but couldn't come up with it. What popped into his mind was the word 'preppie.' Carter's style of dress.

"I can't say I have," Chen answered.

Carter smiled. "You, I am quite sure, understand the concept. In fact, you did it when you talked to Liling. She agreed to drop the charges against her attacker if your government dropped the charges against her father. In doing so, the son of a Politburo member went free. I believe that will help you survive any kind of investigation into your performance. Wouldn't you say?"

Chen saw Carter's cleverness, his way of untying and retying the same string into a knot that served a different purpose.

"I suspect it may," Chen said.

"There. You turned the tables. And perhaps you could do it again. In the way that getting the charges dropped against Song will likely end the investigation, perhaps there is a way to save the fiasco of returning to China without Liling. Perhaps she might return in a different way?"

"She would never return to China. And in truth, I won't force her. She should stay true to what she is doing here. If you have heard her play, you would understand that." Yet, as he said the words, something tickled in his mind. A tiny itch asking to be scratched.

Carter pursed his lips. "That is something of a problem."

Chen looked at the desk-top and saw the transmitter. And then he knew. The itch blossomed into a fully formed idea. He looked at Carter. "I like this idiom. Turning the tables."

Carter smiled. "Do you, now?"

Chen returned a small smile. "I would need some help."

"I would be happy to do whatever I can."

"Then consider this. Suppose, just suppose, I tell my superiors that despite our arrangement with Liling, I have convinced her to return to China. To discuss the charges against her father. As part of this, I ask my coworker, a young, overly dedicated, and ambitious man, to accompany her back. She arrives with him at the airport, ticket in hand. Flies with him to the city where she will catch a connection to Beijing. And then, poof, it all falls apart. She raises a cry. Claims she is being coerced. Kidnapped, perhaps. Your customs officials take this seriously and arrest the man accompanying her. I do not believe I would be blamed for my coworker's failure to complete such a simple job."

Carter gazed at Chen without seeing him, and Chen saw the gears working in Carter's mind.

Carter brushed away another piece of invisible lint, this time on his sleeve. "As Americans, we would take any attempt to forcefully repatriate her very seriously. Liling, after all, has a green card." He frowned, and his eyes cleared. "Would Liling go along with this? It's a risk for her."

Chen nodded. "I think she will agree. Consider it from her point of view. If China is caught in the act of kidnapping her, they won't try again. The diplomatic outrage and publicity would be too great. Also, Liling is very self-possessed. She is willing to take risks. I think she will consider this a worthwhile gamble if it means she will be left alone."

Carter nodded. "I can talk to her. Put it in those terms. See what she says."

Chen nudged the transmitter with his finger. "As I said, I like this idiom. Turn the tables."

Carter nodded once. "I thought you might. And you can turn the tables on anything. A cheating coworker. A disloyal superior. A country you no longer trust." He leaned forward. "However, I think you and I already understand this."

Without looking, Chen was aware that White Pick-Up Truck was no longer leaning against the door. A man like that, he knew, instinctively senses when action is near. And they had reached that point. This was the crux of it.

He remembered his grandmother's saying, "Inside this house, outside this house." And apparently, he thought to himself, I now have a new house.

Chapter Fifty-Three

Vic and Liz sat side by side in Hana's office. Liz was talking, explaining how Jessica used a prepaid phone to track Melanie and Ryan's movements. Vic was aware of the high blue sky outside the window, the white clouds scudding across the face of it. He noticed, for the first time, how the photograph of Hana's mustachioed great, great-grandfather faced the window. It wasn't a bad way to spend your afterlife, he reflected, watching the turn of the sky and seasons. He wondered what Jimmy Pronghorn would have to say about that. Jimmy would dredge up a line from some Greek poet, he was sure, then say it was a mystery. Laugh at himself. He missed Jimmy, he realized. He wanted to kid him about his new son.

"That must have been something, Vic. Theatrical."

Vic pulled himself together, unsure of the thread of conversation that led to Hana's comment.

"You dialing Jessica's prepaid as she went out the door," Liz supplied.

"Oh, yeah. I wasn't sure it would work. But she was leaving, and I needed a way to stop her without giving away we'd broken her alibi."

Hana smiled, then shook her head. "So let me get this straight. Jessica was in love with Ryan, even slept with him at a family reunion, and when she thought Ryan was sleeping with Melanie, her solution was to attack Melanie?"

"There's more to it than that." Liz glanced at Vic, and he nodded for her to keep going. "Jessica fell for Ryan at the family reunion and wanted him near. So she talked Melanie into hiring him. Ryan shows up and takes the

283

job, but he isn't interested in sleeping with Jessica anymore. Jessica thought it was because Ryan and Melanie were sleeping together, which to Jessica was insult to injury. And it turns out that Jessica went through this before. I'd noticed that Jessica missed a semester of college and graduated late. I talked to the school, and guess what, she was suspended for that semester. For beating up some girl she thought was trying to steal her boyfriend. She was already in the habit of going after the other woman when her boyfriend roamed, whether it was imaginary or otherwise."

"Seems extreme. And it turned out somewhere in all this Ryan decided he was gay."

Liz nodded. "Right."

Hana shook her head slowly. "And Jessica was stupid enough not to throw away her prepaid."

Liz gave a short laugh. "Seems to me the same moment people discover sex, they start being stupid."

Hana chuckled. "Given how guys talk to me in bars, that is an absolute truth."

"Ain't it, though." Liz smiled.

Vic glanced from one to the other. "Excuse me, guy here. If I could break up the sister bonding, I'd like to say that when I found out the tracking app was on Ryan's phone, I guessed Jessica probably kept the prepaid. She'd want to track him. Remember, she didn't find out Ryan was gay until we sat down together. That's why she ran out of there. She couldn't take it. Right then, she realized she'd killed Melanie for no reason."

Hana looked from Vic to Liz. "Maybe that explains why she confessed. There's a chance, I guess, that she actually felt bad about it. Good thing, because it was a hard case to make without the confession. We didn't even have the murder weapon."

"Yeah," Vic said. "Ryan finally figured out one of his baseball bats was missing. Jessica swiped it, and she tossed it in the river afterwards. There was no finding that."

Hana smiled. "Thanks, guys. Actually, Liz, sorry, but could I talk to Vic for a moment?"

Liz rose, said her goodbyes and indicated to Vic that she would wait outside.

After she left, Hana studied him for a moment. "Chen Yun. I watched the interview tape. Unusual technique you used on him. Asking why he got into policing. Am I missing something?"

"Not really. Asking why he became a cop kind of surprised me as well. I needed a way for us to be honest with each other, and that popped out."

"I guess he decided to trust you."

"Maybe. But I felt like he was talking to someone else on that tape. Like he was sending a message."

"No question about that. But he does trust you."

Vic stared at her. He wasn't sure where Hana was leading.

She was silent for a moment, the gaze from her brown eyes boring into him. "I've been asked for some inter-agency cooperation. Not the FBI. A different acronym. They asked if you could be available to talk to Chen Yun once in a while. Apparently, he made some kind of deal with them, but he said you're one of the very few he trusts to talk to. They might want you to meet with him once in a while. Apparently, it's a deal breaker if you say no."

Vic shrugged. "If it's just talking, sure. I like the guy."

"Because both of your fathers worked in steel mills? Having fathers in the same business is how guys bond?"

Vic thought about it. "I feel like it had more to do with what killed them."

Hana frowned for a moment, then gave a quick shake of her head. "Not sure I understand that. Okay, different topic. Have you seen the news the last few days?"

He understood what she was saying. "Yes. You settled the wrongful termination suit with John Lee."

"Exactly. It seemed the best thing to do. Even if it pisses me off because he was certainly the worst person I ever hired."

Vic saw she was serious. "But the story said you settled. I didn't understand that. I thought you said there was no case and it would be dismissed."

"I told you before, there is always another way to do things. Do you remember how the FBI jumped into that situation with Chen Yun and Eileen Liang?"

"Sure."

"When the Pittsburgh FBI director came over to explain it, I asked him why there was an investigation into you. Turns out the director didn't know what I was talking about. He went back to his offices and asked around."

Vic nodded slowly, again not understanding where Hana was going.

Hana sat back. "Turns out, a couple of the agents who used to work for John Lee at the FBI were looking into your time in North Dakota. Off the books. As a favor to you know who."

"John Lee?"

"Exactly."

Vic grasped at the ends of the strings, understanding. "Lee was still pissed at me for finding out he was the guy leaking stories to the news site? He blamed me for getting fired?"

"Couldn't have put it better myself. That, and if it turned out you were dirty, it gave him something else to use against me, because I hired you. So we sat down with John's lawyer and offered him a settlement. Half a million dollars. But John had to sign an NDA and agree not to bring any more suits against our office, or," here she made quote marks with her fingers, "to harass, investigate or libel me or any of our office's employees in any way."

Vic stared at her, stunned. It was like his last boxing match, that moment his opponent ducked away but landed a jab he'd never seen coming. The same jarred confusion, the vague awareness he was back-footed. Then his head cleared, and he understood what she was saying.

She had paid John Lee to leave her alone. To leave him alone.

"Thank you," was all Vic could eke out.

"There's always another way to solve a problem." She smiled at him. "Lee was out of line, Vic. Asking his buddies to do him a favor, hoping to find a way to hurt you. And me. If he comes after you again, he'll be in violation of his agreement, and we'll come down on him with both feet. This should be the end of it."

A shaft of warmth ran through Vic. He pictured Lettie at the kitchen table, utterly concentrating on drawing a picture. "Anne is going to be relieved. In a big way. I can't tell you how much pressure that takes off us."

"Not a problem. None of us need that kind of distraction."

"Thank you again."

Hana held up her hand. "One last thing. Keep in mind, we're both in the clear of Mr. Lee. But it was half a million *taxpayer* dollars, Vic. You provide good value to our taxpayers, that doesn't worry me, but you need to keep doing it. And me, now I get to protect this office a bit longer."

Vic nodded, his heart light, suddenly soaring with the clouds outside.

Hana gave him a dead level stare, and he swore the saber rattled in its scabbard. "Of course, given that amount of money, I promised myself not to take a raise for a couple of years. Just on the principle of the thing. And you should do the same. Because we're in this together."

Vic grinned at her. "Sounds exactly right to me." He rose, nodded his thanks again, and went to meet Liz.

Chapter Fifty-Four

Craig stood in his apartment, staring at the new gun case open on his bed. It was the size of a large encyclopedia. His Glock sat on the foam, and he had set the case's latch combination. To make it easy, he'd chosen the jersey number of his favorite Penguins player.

"Okay," he said to himself. He snapped the case shut, spun the combination dial, and looked around his bedroom, trying to decide where to keep it. He hadn't thought that part through. He knew his father always kept his service weapon locked in a case in the bedroom closet, so he decided to follow that lead.

A knock sounded on his front door. He looked at the case and hesitated. Did he need to remove the gun?

He shook his head. No one was knocking on his front door, planning to attack him. He walked through the living room and opened the door.

Eileen stood in the hall, her black hair in a loose bun on top of her head, wearing slacks and a blouse under a long, black, coat-like sweater. Craig shifted back in surprise.

"Hello," Eileen said. She was smiling in a way that said she liked how she'd surprised him.

Craig struggled against the emotions welling up inside him. The fact she'd used him, how she hadn't reached out to him in the week since she'd come into their offices to meet Chen Yun.

"Hi," he answered, knowing his tone was off-putting.

"I hope you don't mind me stopping over." She spoke softly, as if she was scared of how he might respond. "And you are probably wondering how I know where you live." She moved her arm, and a wheeled suitcase came into view. "I came straight from the airport."

"Okay." His emotions solidified, veering toward anger.

She shifted on her feet. "May I come in?"

He hesitated, keenly aware he wasn't holding up his end of the conversation. "Sure." He stepped back, immediately thinking that if he wanted to stay angry at her, letting her in was a mistake. As she manhandled the suitcase through the door, he added, "You shouldn't be here. You're a witness." Curiosity got the better of him. "How *did* you find out where I live?" The disjointedness of his statements sounded ridiculous even to his own ears.

Eileen worked the suitcase far enough inside to pull the door closed. She turned around, her gaze skimming the living room. Craig followed her eyes, glad the room didn't look too messy.

She turned to him. "The detective you work with, Liz Timmons? She called me. She said I should talk to you. That I owed you that. She was... somewhat angry about it. Very direct. And she gave me your address." She smiled, and her eyes warmed. "I like her, that detective."

Craig tried to process her words. Liz? Who always made fun of him when women his own age talked to him? He'd overheard her snide comments about him to Vic.

"And Liz told me that Jessica confessed." Eileen continued. "She said I didn't need to be worried about being a witness."

"Oh. Right." Craig knew he'd sounded dense. He already knew that fact. He tried to get hold of his emotions. "So, what do you want?"

She gave him a half smile. "I just flew to Chicago and back. I came straight here. Could I have something to drink?"

Craig turned and went into the kitchen, more to create space between them. His emotions had fully hardened and bifurcated into competing feelings of anger and attraction. The combination was confusing. He called to her and asked if she would like tea or water.

"Perhaps a glass of wine?" she tossed back.

Craig closed his eyes and tried to bring himself to bear. A quick deep breath and he turned to her. She was bending in front of his stereo, studying his vinyl record collection. The long sweater sat on top of the suitcase, her hair now loose down her back. Her arms were bare, and their movement—as she slid out albums to check band names—stuck in his throat. He turned back to the refrigerator and found the bottle of white he always kept in reserve, in case he was lucky enough to have company. He poured two glasses and carried them to her.

She took the glass he offered and smiled. "Oh, good, I always thought those stemmed glasses were silly."

"Me too." Craig focused on what she had said earlier. "Why a flight to Chicago and back?"

"Oh," she said easily and waved a hand. "I was thinking of returning to China, but when we got to Chicago, the man I was traveling with was arrested. So I came home."

Craig almost spat out the wine he'd just sipped. He swallowed hard. "What?"

She turned to him. "Tanming something or other. I didn't like him. He thought he was very clever. Very smug. Apparently, your security services didn't like him either."

Craig pushed away the shock of what she said. He didn't want anything to soften his anger. He felt he was owed that anger. "Why do I think this has something to do with your father?"

"Because you are a wise man, Craig Luntz. A philosopher."

"Then how is it I missed the fact you were using me?"

His anger made the statement rougher than he intended. But he needed to say it. To put it in front of her.

She froze for a moment, then carefully placed her wine glass next to the stereo turntable. She bent down and slid an album from his collection. Dylan. The Self Portrait album. She studied the front. "I listened to this so much when I first got to boarding school," she said gently. "I don't know what I would have done without it." She placed the album on the turntable cover, hesitated, and looked up at him. "Yes. To begin with, I wanted to make sure your investigation led to Jessica. I knew she was involved, obviously."

"And I was the easy target. The rookie. You were pretty sure you could tie me around your finger."

"It crossed my mind. Yes. But I learned almost immediately I was wrong. As I said to you, I underestimated you."

Craig stared into her eyes, and she didn't flinch. "You understand that isn't a compliment, right? Just the opposite?"

"Actually, I was being honest. I did underestimate you and regretted it right away. I asked you to the symphony because I wanted to start making it up to you. To get past that."

"But you were a witness. You knew something about the case, and you didn't tell us." He knew he sounded petulant.

For several seconds she didn't say anything. "And I came here today to ask you to forgive me. I know I was wrong. I was trying to keep my father secret while making sure you caught Melanie's killer. I went about it the wrong way." She touched him lightly on the chest. "I'm hoping that now, you and I can find a starting place."

Craig struggled to breathe. His anger started to leak away.

Softly, pressing her palm flat over his heart, her eyes searching his face, she said, "I desperately want to find a starting place with you."

Craig touched her cheek, the smoothness of her radiating through his fingertips and right inside him.

"When do you have to be home?" he asked, his voice somewhere between a whisper and a croak.

Her eyes warmed. "Does that really matter? I brought a change of clothes."

Chapter Fifty-Five

The first thing Vic told Anne when she arrived home from work was the news about the FBI. Lettie was running in and out of the kitchen as he recounted it, shrieking for no good reason that Vic could tell. Anne had her hand over her mouth for much of the last part of his explanation, fighting back tears. Then she hugged him, long and hard, and let out the tears.

After a dinner of hamburgers and salad, Anne insisted on getting Lettie ready for bed. Vic promised he would read to her. When they disappeared upstairs, he scrounged through the refrigerator and found a can of beer that had to be five months old. He didn't care. He cracked it open and stepped through the back door onto the steps to the back yard.

Vic had never understood how to care for a lawn and was reminded of that. The grass was littered with bare patches, scraggly areas that somehow held the light in the arriving darkness, like pale scars. He sipped his beer, the minutes and tension drifting away. He thought about Chen, wondered about him, what kind of arrangement Chen had made, and what it might mean. He liked the man; he knew that much. He would be glad to sit down with him again when the time was right.

As he finished his beer, he heard pattering feet from inside, and when he looked through the glass of the back door saw Lettie standing in the kitchen in her pajamas, looking first one way and then another, eyes bright, searching for him. Anne entered the kitchen, her hair mussed from giving Lettie her bath, sleeves rolled up, cheeks flushed. She was laughing as if Lettie had escaped from her.

Vic's breath left him, and he swayed, almost stumbled. He had to put his free hand against the door to steady himself. There, he thought, inside his house was everything that mattered. Why was he so often outside, he asked himself, when all that mattered was inside? He felt as if he had traveled a long way through a settling night, across continents, to arrive on his doorstep under wheeling stars to see his family inside, gathered about the hearth, laughing together and warm.

Safe.

Stay true to only that, he said to himself and opened the door to go inside.

Chapter Fifty-Six

Chen Yun held his son's hand and led him slowly among the white mass of narrow and upright gravestones. In the distance, his wife was bent over his grandmother's headstone, cleaning it with a damp cloth. He smiled at that. His wife taught elementary school and considered herself an independent woman, yet she still insisted on doing a few specific duties that were traditionally the duty of women. He wasn't entirely sure if she understood that quirk of her personality. When he'd returned to Wuhan, he was the one who suggested visiting the graves and cleaning them, fully intending to wash them himself. Yet when they arrived, she'd grabbed the bucket from him and shooed him away, asking for ten minutes.

As she always did.

It was as if, he mused, women don't trust men with the past. He thought about that, his eyes taking in his surroundings. The English language, too, was funny about the past. It only spoke of *the* past, or *a* past. As if there was only one. Yet here, surrounding him, were hundreds of pasts, all uniquely different. The English language spoke in the same way of the future. As if only a single one was allowed or imagined. Yet there were as many possible futures as there were people. As many futures as pasts.

His wife straightened and stretched the small of her back, her hand holding the rag. She waved to him with her other arm. He returned the gesture and raised his son onto his hip. He pointed his mother out to the boy and helped him fashion a wave in her direction.

He sauntered toward her, carrying his son. It wasn't just language that was the problem, he thought. In China, as in other countries, it was the Party that chose the single past they all learned and stayed true to. It was the same for that single vision of the future.

He stopped beside the newly clean headstone. He squatted, balancing his son on his thigh, and touched his grandmother's headstone. "Great grandmother," he said in English. He guided his son's hand to touch the stone. "Great Grandmother," Chen repeated.

The boy said the words, stumbling over them, and Chen slid him to the ground. Freed, the boy patted the stone, mouthing the English words. Chen sounded out the word to guide his son's pronunciation.

Watching, his wife squatted next to him, the sunlight bright on her shoulders. After a moment, she glanced at him. "I read that in Beijing, there is a school where much of the instruction is in English. After your transfer, perhaps we could send him there to learn English."

Chen nodded. When he returned to Wuhan, he discovered he was being transferred to an anti-corruption unit in Beijing, attached to the Premier's personal security service. That a new teaching position waited for his wife. All of it neatly arranged by Song's father and justified by his success in Operation Fox Hunt. It was a funny justification, he thought. Because success, he knew now, was best defined by how well something protected people in power.

He guessed Carter Quince would be very excited about that particular development.

"I would still like to teach him," Chen said. "But we can look at the school."

"Many of the students go to good colleges. They become diplomats."

Chen smiled at her. "We will consider it."

Yet all his instincts recoiled. Elite schools of that type were designed to perpetuate the Party. To transfer the Party's values to another generation. He would never expose his son to that.

They both rose, and his wife leaned against his arm. He smelled sandalwood in her hair and felt her warmth. Their son ran to a nearby headstone, touched it, and stumbled out the English words 'great grandmother.' He ran to another headstone, touched it, and said the same.

His wife laughed at their son's confusion. Chen smiled as well, but thought his son might be right. He gazed at the headstones. All those lost pasts, all those plundered futures. Every buried soul both the lesson and the teacher. In a way, they were all his grandmother, a reminder to keep that hard bright line between inside the house and outside. To stay true to that.

Whatever house you chose to live in.

A Note from the Author

I think that most readers are familiar with the fact that, traditionally, people's names in China are presented with the surname first, followed by a given name. In this book, purely for the convenience of English-speaking readers, I followed the western convention of presenting the Chinese characters' given name first, followed by their surname. I apologize if this causes any confusion, but my intent was simply to avoid encumbering English-speaking readers during the reading process.

Keen-eyed readers will also notice that I use two forms of romanization when writing Chinese personal and place names. China developed the pinyin system in 1958, and today that is the accepted romanization system for the Mandarin language in China and around the world. I used pinyin for most of the Chinese character and location names in this novel. However, for much of the 20th century (until about 1979), the Wade-Giles romanization system was commonly used in the west. Furthermore, Wade-Giles is still used today by western academics when writing about China's past. As a result, in the few places where I referred to figures and locations from China's history, I rendered those names using the Wade-Giles system. Western readers are used to seeing the names of historical figures rendered in Wade-Giles, and in the interest of avoiding confusion for western readers, I chose to use the system that would be more familiar to them.

One storyline of this novel is that Chen Yun, a Detective for China's National Police, arrives in America under the auspices of a program called Operation Fox Hunt. Operation Fox Hunt is a global program run for some years now by the Chinese government. It has been written about in depth in various media including The New York Times, ProPublica and the Economist. The FBI website maintains a page named The China Threat, and a search within that page reveals articles and legal action taken by the United States against Chinese nationals working for China's Operation Fox Hunt. However, I would like to be clear that my accounts of the fictional detective Chen Yun's activities in the United States for Operation Fox Hunt are completely fabricated. This is a work of fiction, and while I borrowed the name Operation Fox Hunt, nothing else about Chen Yun's exploits are real. Chen Yun's character, and his exploits, are simply figments of my own imagination and do not represent any actual personnel or activities of Operation Fox Hunt.

Acknowledgements

What constantly surprises me—and humbles me, if I am to be honest—is the willingness of people to donate their time to help bring a new book into the world. This novel is proof of their commitment and passion.

I'll start with my critique group members, Barb D'Souza, Howie Ehrlichman, Kaitlin Greco, Caren Knoyer, Janet McClintock, and Steve Sharpnack, who all read early chapters and helped me tighten and clarify the prose and storyline. A second critique group of established and very successful mystery writers—Jeff Boarts, Annette Dashofy and Mary Sutton (better known under the pen name Liz Milliron)—read the entire novel in serial form and helped me with various mistakes I made in naming, police procedure, plotting, and characterization. I'm a bit surprised they continue to put up with me. Fengmin Chien, a colleague and friend from my years working in marketing, reviewed the Chinese names for authenticity and believability, and made several canny improvements.

Once the manuscript was in draft form, it was read in its entirety by my wife, Sono, who is always my first reader, and who puts up with a lot more from me than my critique groups. I apologize for that. It was then read by Tom Morris, a long-time college friend who tends to be downright gleeful whenever he finds a typo in my published books. I wonder what Tom will do if he finds a typo now? Steven Hastings, another long-time friend, also read and commented on the entire manuscript. This marks the third time Steve has read one of my manuscripts, and he can feel confident I'll do the buying next time we meet. He's earned it. Steve's daughter, Lauren, who happens to be a professional violinist, was also a tremendous help during the planning of this book, providing me with a comprehensive overview of what it's like to be a symphony violinist, the training and commitment required, and an inside view on how musicians compete for jobs. Her insights and suggestions were invaluable.

At Level Best Books, both Verena Rose and Shawn Reilly Simmons edited the manuscript, and I am truly lucky for their continuing support, enthusiasm, and commitment to the series.

About the Author

Born in Newcastle upon Tyne, England, Peter W. J. Hayes lived in Paris and Taipei before settling in Pittsburgh, Pennsylvania. He worked as a journalist, advertising copywriter and marketing executive before turning to mystery and crime writing. He is the author of the Silver Falchion-nominated Vic Lenoski mysteries, and two of his many short stories have been finalists for the Derringer and Al Blanchard awards. He can be found at www.peterwjhayes.com

SOCIAL MEDIA HANDLES:
  Facebook: Peter W. J. Hayes
  Twitter: @PeterWJHayes
  Instagram: Peter W. J. Hayes

AUTHOR WEBSITE:
  www.peterwjhayes.com

Also by Peter W. J. Hayes

The Vic Lenoski Mystery Series:
The Things That Aren't There
The Things That Are Different
The Things That Last Forever
The Things That Secrets Cannot Hide
The Things That Stay True

Plus, approximately twenty short stories published in magazines such as in *Black Cat Mystery Magazine, Crimeucopia, Mystery Magazine*, and the Malice Domestic and Best New England Crime Stories anthologies.